LA TERCERA

✳ ✳ ✳

GINA APOSTOL

SOHO

This edition first published in 2023 by
Soho Press, Inc.
227 W 17th Street
New York, NY 10011

Library of Congress Cataloging-in-Publication Data
is available upon request.

ISBN 978-1-64129-390-7
eISBN 978-1-64129-391-4

Interior design by Janine Agro, Soho Press, Inc.

Printed in the United States of America

10 9 8 7 6 5 4 3 2 1

For my mother
Virginia

"Despedida kan Kirikay"
(Goodbye to Kirikay)

Lakat na la, lakat na la kun malakat ka.
Saho ko man, saho ko man bis' ka ngain.
Lakat na la, di ak' ha im' mababaraka,
Ngan di ha imo magbibiling.
    An budo ayaw pagdad-a,
An bahaw ngan luwag,
Layas na kun malayas ka,
Diri matangis an ak' kalag.
    Kapara na, kapara na ha ak' paniplat.
Pahirayo, di ak' ha im' mag-aawil,
Pakadto na, gikan na ngan lurop ha dagat,
Bis' bugkoton ka hin bukawil.
    Diri gad ha im' mahawid,
Paturon han paglakat—
Ibilin kalayo, tubig,
Di ak' ha im' maglalanat.

(Go, go, if that's what you want! / I don't care, don't care where. / Just go, go, I don't care! / I won't be looking for you!
    You can't bring the salted fish, / The leftover rice, the ladle. / Go, go if you must, / I won't be grieving about it, for sure.
    Get out, out of my sight. / Go away, I'm not going to miss you. / Leave now, leave, jump in the sea if you will. / If a conch gobbles you up, that's fine too.
    Well, I'm not stopping you, / Go on, get going, / Just leave the fire behind, the water, / I'm not chasing after you, never.)

—Eduardo Makabenta; trans. Merlie Alunan

Inday, inday, nakain ka
Han kasunog han munyika
Pito ka tuig an paglaga
An asô waray kita-a.

(Inday, inday where were you / When the doll burned / Flaming for seven years / No one saw the smoke.)

—Waray folk song

LA TERCERA

✳ ✳ ✳

PART ONE
LA PRIMERA

✳ ✳ ✳

Effects

Of the visible works left behind by Francisco "Paco" Delgado y Blumfeld and Jorge "Jote" Delgado y Blumfeld, what persists does not console. The long-dead brothers possessed the following effects:

1. a weird-looking guitar;
2. the rusted remains of chicken coops along the river Himanglos in Salogó;
3. a seawall, a.k.a. AWOL;
4. a digest of operatic libretti (in which a parasite has erased an etching of Lucia di Lammermoor and the ghost shape of a moth enshrouds the buried bride);
5. the name of a dog, Moret;
6. three volumes bound in leather, with a title in gold lettering, *William McKinley's World*, resting in a domed sepulcher;
7. a wooden box, 9 x 18 x 3, inlaid with capiz, and on its lid the initials *F.B.*;
8. the journals of a boy already at war but not yet in his teens, 1899-1901;
9. maps of the area called San Jose in Tacloban and of a gleam of land, now called Greenhills, in metropolitan Manila.

They were hidden in plain view around the Delgado family home, a forsaken place in the wilds of Leyte, and the question of which brother owned what was moot. We called them both *Lolo*—their identities interchangeable because it seemed they had none: their world was incomprehensible.

For a long time, I mixed the brothers up.

No one in the house touched their effects except the worms.

The Delgados are a fretful clan, prone to delusions of pathos rather than grandeur. We linger on the abstract, such as despair and pride. I speak of the Delgados I know—my mother's family—madmen and collaborators, so I'm told. By the time I had come across my mother's inheritance, the banality of objects in the material world inhabited by her grandfathers had lost, for my mother, even the sense of the ridiculous—she had ceased to see them.

Instead, the memory of La Tercera, a place she had never known, drove her mad.

I grew up under the shadow of La Tercera. It was a legacy not quite tangible but not improbable. And this ambiguity has led members of my family, through generations, to acts that have ended in a sense of loss that burdens too many in the place I am from.

Top of the World

The voicemail was from my uncle, Tio Nemorino, the honorable mayor as they called him years after his regime.

I'd been calling my mother the entire month. She had no use for Messenger. Skype was dead to her. She owned no computers. She was the last woman in that selfie-happy archipelago to have only a rotary phone.

All I had was her voice.

During the years I've lived in New York, I admit I never called her much. I hate the phone. I mislay it, I pretend I'm not home, I hate the need to call people. The rest of the family knows. They know they will expect no birthday greetings, they will hear nothing from me when my books come out, they will learn about my readings on Facebook, where all the Filipinos are. I'm on Facebook for my books. I have a phone for my mom.

Her voice was girlish, high-pitched, the voice of one, I thought, who believed too easily in illusion. My mom lived in the future, and the present was a dislocation. She had the trick of making you think it was your existence that gave her joy—partly because of her childish voice, her intakes of breath as she spoke to you, as if her diaphragm and lungs were not formed enough for her thrill.

"Inday!" she said when it was first detected, "I'm so healthy. I just had my tests!"

She always called me inday, sounding like she had so many children she had forgotten my name, though I'm her only daughter.

"But Mom, Tio Nemor said—"

"My heart is good, my cholesterol is great, my lungs are perrrrfect! All I have is cancer! Without cancer I'm on top of the world!"

And she began to hum that song from my childhood.

I could see her doing the cha-cha with the cord of the rotary phone, shaking her hips, dressed in satin and silk, lithe and unconquerable in her feline way, like the stray cats that perched on the unfinished cement wall in Mana Marga's dirty-kitchen, purring in the security of having so many lives.

When she was first told she should have surgery to take out her cancerous breast, she refused.

"How can you dance the tango if you have only one breast!"

I imagined her, Adina an guapa, pearled and perfumed, dancing the cha-cha to Karen Carpenter, in her high heels. I keep seeing her in her seventies bouffant—though in her last pictures, uploaded on Facebook by Putt-putt who never tags me but still I follow him, her hair has thinned. Her reflexive mode of existence was to go ballroom dancing. She wore high heels to water her orchids in the garden, and when I was a kid watching her use a brown eyebrow pencil to line her lips, she laughed as I stared—"Inday!" she said, humming as she did the weirdest things to her face, her deft fingers etching herself into shape—"does it look good, inday?" she asked.

"Yes," I'd say, and it was true.

I grew up with the daring invention of my mom's daily routines.

My mom wore her beauty in a way that was not a drag to others: we were just proud witnesses. Nothing marred her grace. People in Tacloban called her Adina an guapa, that was her nickname. Adina the beautiful. She emerged from her rituals looking somehow like

Gina Lollobrigida, who was famous in Tacloban because she once posed by our fantastical bridge.

Adina an guapa was a silk-and-organza spectacle from the time of that first dictator, the locus of my memory of my mom.

"Top of the World" was her brother Nemorino's campaign song, the one the band struck when Tio Nemorino ran for mayor in the seventies.

"You know that's not a good allusion, Mom," I said. "Karen Carpenter did not come to a good end."

She told me not to return home.

She told me what mattered was that I was an artist—how could I leave New York, she said, when I had my career, I was a hysterical novelist, as she called with pride my vocation, my work on events so forgotten neither victors nor losers give a damn.

"It's your dream, inday. You stay where you are. In Green Witch. To do your art."

"Greenwich Village, Mom."

"It says here on the postcard. Green Witch. Stay in Green Witch." So I did.

My mother's gift to me was that she believed in all of my dreams, including the stupid ones.

She kept up a perfect face no matter how ordinary or significant the moment, so that neither her illness nor her love sent me home.

It was Tio Nemorino's voice in my mailbox that told me she was gone.

The Court Case

It's no surprise that in a country that exists on the argument of conquest, laws about the possession of land are murky. On All Souls' Day, how many families, bourgeois or not, but mostly bourgeois, burn candles on the plots of the dead only to rant on and on about some long-lost, stolen piece of land?

The evidence of the existence of La Tercera is tenuous but not mythical.

Of my mom's lawsuit over her intestate Lolo Paco's lands, I remember the outlines like vague crisscross shades produced by the nighttime gauze of mosquito nets, that shadow-roof of my childhood—though all my life my mother kept italicizing the facts.

Lolo Paco had no will, he had no child, when he died who should inherit his properties but us—the children of his blood, of his only brother, Jorge Delgado y Blumfeld, my Papá's papá: your Lolo Jote!

I grew up with the incoherent details of Lolo Paco's life and times while I scraped out burnt rice at the bottom of the kaldero or slapped at bugs that got through the moskitero's gauze no matter how firmly my mom tucked me into bed. Minor acts or objects would set her off. Such as food. Once, the particular luster that day of her favorite—fresh hipon—the smelliest stuff on the table, I thought, though I was too polite and in awe of my mom's appetite to mention it—reminded her how much her Lolo Paco had loved the hipon of Leyte, which he called bagoong, and among the bundles that her father, Mister Honorable Mayor Francisco Delgado III, would take on his annual pilgrimage to her Lolo Paco at Greenhills were those jars of purple sheen, Salogó's hipon, wrapped in multiple layers of banig, so that if they spilled, the gusts of hipon would not ruin her father's clothes. Lolo Paco also loved danggit, dried squid, and all the most awful kinds of budo-bulad—basically, he had a taste for smelly things—and I see my grandfather, the Honorable Mayor, also the town's old music teacher, lugging the weight of his bounty from Salogó's dust to Tacloban's gangplanks to Manila's piers. I kept imagining, with a sense of my own humiliation, this proud man, my mom's Papá, arriving at his rich uncle the senator's doorstep—stooped, sweating, and reeking of pusit—to deliver his homage of fermented shrimp fry and salted fish, the province's bounty offered to Manila's gods.

Every year, when she had to pay the school bills to the Divine Word Missionary School for my dumb education, my mom mentioned how *she* could have gone to high school in Manila, you know—and not just college at Far Eastern University in Sampaloc! Anyway, she never graduated from FEU because she refused to wear sneakers during PE, but that's another story. If only her Papá had allowed her to live with childless Lolo Paco and his mean wife, Lola Chedeng, when he asked to take her—he wanted to adopt her when she was just a baby! Ah, instead, who got to be the child growing up at the senator's dinner table?

Oh, that cripple, that orphan—that Madam Charity Breton!

That poliomyelitic!

"Oh my goodness, inday, how could she call herself a Delgado—she could not even walk! Agi nga poliomyelitic! An American with no name, left behind by a GI, a ward of the orphanage, a no-name saved by the Gotas de Leche! Ay leche, that Gotas de Leche!"

And at that last word, that unholy *leche!*, my mom started laughing.

I can see my mom, lifting her head up from her usual occupations, pasting weeds on cloth canvasses or gluing baubles on homemade lampshades, her veined finger sticky with her pastes, raised to her lips.

"Oh, inday, do not say that word *leche*, it is bad!"

And then she crossed herself because she had said the word again.

Listening to the way her holiness mixed with her prejudice, a troubling jumble of ethics that as a child I could not pinpoint as a portion of my malady, only that I felt it, I felt my mind skip over my unease the way I always moved the fish's eye, prominent in my mom's beloved tinola, to make it look away from me.

"Ah, inday, what would my life have been, if not for that orphan who took all of Lolo Paco's lands, that greedy woman, your Auntie Charity Breton!"

"Well, Ma," I said, "if you had grown up at Lolo Paco's table, I think you would still be eating too much hipon and budo-bulad!"

It was the woman in the wheelchair, the cripple of Gotas de Leche, Auntie Charity Breton, who in my mom's telling of the famous court case won La Tercera. The wonders of Lolo Paco's money and the marvels of his generosity toward his poor relations in Salogó were equal parts torment and trophy for my mother. I once went with her to a musty government office in Manila—these were the times of her furious traveling, her flights from Tacloban, to become an "artist-businesswoman, an inventor!" She used to abandon us to the mercies of Mana Marga, her all-around servant and loyal clone, but at the time I was already in college, and she arrived at my dorm with her frames.

To my shame I called them that—her frames—canvases of stretched katsa or velvet on which she arranged wildflowers and vagrant grasses into intricate spirals of ineffable symmetry, using her own made-up paste to stick them into place (the glue, another invention, was called *Adina EVERLASTING!*™). She was disheveled but glamorous, wearing fuchsia high heels that almost matched her lipstick and eyeshade. On any other woman, that pink coordination would be fatal. Instead, my mom's boldness persuaded people her choices were correct. Even Salome, the malevolent night guard of Kamia Residence Hall, looked at the apparition of Adina an guapa, dressed in blue georgette, with the tact one offers movie stars or madwomen. Salome used to scare me with her dagger eyes if I arrived two minutes after curfew. But with her gun in her holster and pudgy in her tight uniform, Salome helped my mom carry her frames down to the basement, to Room B-12, where my two roommates, an accounting major from Dagupan whose name I've forgotten, and Aurora, an anorexic neat-freak Ilongga studying for the bar in between getting beaten up by her law-school boyfriend, were fortunately away. It was a few weeks before exams. Adina an guapa slept that night in my dorm. I did not. I was cramming Part II of *Don Quixote* for my finals in Medieval and Renaissance Lit, groggy from inertia and from resentment at my mom's sudden intrusion and from guilt that is the squire, the Sancho Panza, of my resentment.

I sat up on the edge of Aurora's empty, well-made bed, listening to my mom snore, wondering where she had been, when she had arrived in the city, what she had been doing away from home, away from my brother Adino who was still in school, a child in Tacloban.

She snored with a profound rattling, a heaving sound that made the cheap, metallic bed tremble, as if her entire body, her bones and her blood, her perfect heart and her healthy lungs, were unloading a misplaced weight, who knows who laid it, which in turn she was off-loading onto me, onto my bed, onto my dorm room at midnight, onto the haunted, postwar spaces of Kamia Residence Hall and my placid reading life with Sir Gawain and the Green Knight, with Proust, with the *Tale of Genji*, a life of books by which I had escaped Tacloban, though I now knew the sounds of my mother would never leave me, no matter how far I fled.

I woke up to my mother in my arms, her moist smell of armpit and Pond's Cold Cream, the uncomfortable fabric of humid, filmy georgette, a cloth I hate because it does not breathe, stuck to my sweating palms. My face was wet, as if I had been crying, but it was only the sensation from the hollow of my mother's neck, phantom tears from her clavicle soaking her dress, the cloth soaking up the sweat.

At the movement of my hand across her shoulder, she bolted straight up, and she said—"Is it Monday, inday, is it Monday?"

And it was on that Monday, a time in late February or early March (I measured time then by exams), that she took me to see her.

Auntie Charity Breton.

She needed me to help carry her frames. One was three feet by four, a gleaming glass object with what looked like gold filigree at its center, and I held it up on the four jeepney rides as if it were my doppelganger, the length of my seated body, held arm's length, tipped toward my knees. I could see my face in its dark, obscure mirror, veined by the grasses of my mother's gathering, with gold bunched at my chin like a stain or a puddle. How many hours had I spent in childhood watching my mother among weeds by the road, bent over and intent above wild grass, a high-heeled, hair-sprayed hunter-gatherer? From Diliman through Quezon Avenue, past Sampaloc where my mother did not go to high school, through the rotting, capiz-shelled homes of Malate toward Roxas Boulevard, I stared at the black canvas of my mother's labor. It never occurred to me then to call it what it was. Our destination, a low warren of buildings backing into Manila Bay, turned out to be an outpost of the Department of Foreign Affairs.

She gave the guard a name I recognized—it was my own.

Rosario.

What did I have to do with it?

The consul, as the guard called her, was in. We had to leave the frames with the guard, sharp objects were not allowed in the bureaucratic halls, plus, the guard said, they looked heavy, and I imagined the guard thinking, staring at our diesel-grimed selves and our burdens—how the hell did you carry those through the streets of Manila? In the government offices, my mother's beauty did not hold sway as it did in less malignant places. People looked chained to their desks, uniformed in funereal beige and wearing that candid smirk of official regard. We passed through the cracked marble that paved the path to the consular dens, I watched out for my mother in her flowing blue dress (now I know why she wore georgette, it does not wrinkle, and in the morning she never looks as if she had been stranded overnight, caught far away from her city, without shelter, and bamboozling her way into a security guard's pity and a daughter's pride, to snore the night away without redress in unconquerable clothes in a college dorm), I felt my own figure diminishing, sliding away from my concept of myself, twisting along on ancient floors without knowledge of my purpose through the dark cubicles of that Pasay office.

I was only a child, fearful and distressed about her mother.

How she carried herself, Adina an guapa, her bouffant hairdo and bright eyes. She had gone through her rituals even at Kamia, her steaming of her face in the morning, her scrubbing and scrubbing off of the dirt and the grime and the terror of the city I now called home, with an unfamiliar labakara that she found, maybe Aurora's, her application of Pond's Cold Cream, missing only her facial potage of pipino, sometimes pomelo, her dabbing of fuchsia lipstick and mauve eyeshadow, her slathering of her other translucent invented potion onto her feet, her calves, her knees—a lotion of her own she called *Adina PANTY-LESS STOCKINGS!™* I followed her upright and sturdy, but also somehow frail and frightening, figure in her pink high heels. I heard them clack, clack, clack before me on the grim marble floor of the Department of Foreign Affairs, with its thick Georgian porticoes and the immortal stains of its cold halls. My mother never deigned to look down when she walked, her head held high as if by looking down she would misrepresent herself, fail the image in her mind somehow, so I looked down for her to make sure that she did not fall into an ancient gap.

I have shielded myself with books against the ugly reality of my day-to-day, and I remember that moment in Pasay because it seemed as I walked through the dusty, American-era corridors behind my mother that that partition between my learning and my life, so painstakingly set up in my college days in Diliman, had all of a sudden broken down. I was supposed to be at school, exposing Don Quixote to his illusions in harsh, critical examinations. But I was back to being seven, dumped in a foreign country, which was in fact my own, and tasked to learn a strange tongue, which was in fact my primal one, and my only lifeline was my mom's self-image, her brave concept of herself in the face of her disasters. She knocked on a door, and then, without waiting, she opened it. I realized in that gesture, that sure twist of the handle, that my mother had done this before. She knew exactly where she was going, she acted with terrifying optimism, her belief in an outcome as if it had already happened.

I stood beside her, a wreck, malnourished, sweating, and sleep-deprived.

"Auntie Charity," my mom said.

I did not know if she was addressing me or the stranger within.

I was used to my confusion in my mother's presence, my sense that she was both protecting and careless, proud of my presence and also heedless of her action's effects. So I was not sure if she was introducing me to the phantom at the end of the room, or if she was warning it of our arrival.

Across from us at a massive desk, I saw it look up, the ghoul behind the name from my childhood.

So this was who she was.

A gray body in a wheelchair with insensible blue eyes.

I was surprised she was human.

It was the first and last time I saw her.

She looked up from some papers she was pretending to peruse. I had to adjust my lens to reconcile the poor lame ogre of the legendary court case with this ordinary sight of a basic bureaucratic official with powdered face and scalloped lace collars, on the edge of retirement probably much awaited by her subordinates. I looked for signs of her Delgado lands and millions, gold on her fingernails and her teeth. Instead, she had traces of what looked like Johnson's Baby Powder on her neck, though her bulbous pearls and giant diamond earrings gave off an obscenity that satisfied me. The mahogany trimmings, the ample dimensions of the dank rooms were clearly appropriate to her privilege: she was a woman used to underlings enacting commands at one glance of her foggy eyes. I imagine, with the spare kindness of my hindsight, that sure, maybe she had risen from the ranks with the normal Manila combination of pedigree and incompetence, pedantry and connections—nothing so out of the ordinary or sublime. Her large face, the bulk of her image, had the fat smoothness of the customarily overfed, not so rare in the heights of bureaucracy, and so the vulgar blankness of lifelong satiety in her features was only somewhat repulsive.

As recognition dawned upon her when her own lens adjusted to the blue and fuchsia figure of my mom, the consul's disorientation was slight.

"Yes?" she asked, with the look of one in the middle of matters of importance she was still deciphering.

"Auntie Charity, it is I."

It was at that moment that I noted the elegant calligraphy of the wooden nameplate that dominated the front half of her desk.

The Honorable Consul Rosario Breton-Delgado, Ll.B., J.D., Esq.

I realized the absurdity of it, one of the truths arising from my life as a daughter, that there was a past, an abyss between my mother's choices and mine, that I did not know.

Why had my mother named me after this stranger at the heart of her long, historical venom, her *durée* of hatred spanning decades before my time?

Rosario. Charo. Charito. Charity.

The mysteries of nicknaming, those aporetic declensions, that drove me nuts growing up.

I had always thought I had been named after some religious devotion I could not share.

The consul moved her wheelchair backwards from the desk. For a moment I thought she was retreating from our presence, and she had a button she could sound in her unlit room, an issue of alarm. I admired, from the slant of light in the window, the revelation through the day's sunlight of her antique wheelchair's ornate detailing, the carved grisaille of the capiz and the ancient art of enlaced wood-and-wicker that the inlaid capiz framed. The motes of the day gleamed through the graceful ventricles of the chair. She turned so swiftly, expertly on her moveable throne. I did not have the time to register my mother bent toward her lap, the consul's entire body was now before us, in front of her desk and the plaque of her name, a lump of a diplomat dressed in jusi and constructed of base metal and carved wood, and I see my mother now—so long afterward, so many years past that morning in Pasay—in a gesture that my memory cannot bear.

My mom, Adina an guapa, lowered herself before the consul. She took the fat wrist of the woman, the lady's gray flesh the same dirty color of the halls' long-tended marble, and she lifted the smooth, plump hand of Rosario "Charity" Breton-Delgado to her forehead.

It was a surprising act of affinity, of formal ancestral reverence, one of those marks of relation that used to move me when I was made to learn it as a child, when I returned to Salogó from America.

Adina an guapa replicated that childhood ritual—lineal hand to bowed forehead—upon that pale ogre, whose response for a transitory moment, I thought, was to stiffen her fingers and withhold, but in fact the woman allowed her hand to be uplifted, her saggy arms an appendage of my disgust as my mother spoke.

"It is I, Adina, your niece. Adina Delgado, daughter of the mayor, Francisco Delgado III, of Salogó. Son of Lolo Paco's brother—Lolo Jote. The Delgados of Leyte. Remember? I called you the other day. So I am here."

"The Delgados of Leyte?"

"Yes."

"You still remember me?"

"Yes."

"You remember what you did?"

"No."

"You called me a cripple, a woman with no name. Right here. In my office."

"That was not me. That was my aunt. I am Adina."

"You called me a demon, a foreign devil."

"It was my tita. Tia Pachang. Remember? Bonifacia Delgado, your cousin."

"You called me a usurper, an orphan with no rights, a no-name child of the Gotas de Leche."

"That was my cousin, the lawyer. Paquito. He is a US immigrant now, in Las Vegas."

"You called me *leche*," the woman growled. "*Leche!*"

It was a guttural anguish, the crippling sound, *leche*! I could hear buried in it a doubling of the decades, simultaneous degradations, a crisscross of curses in misremembered courtrooms, perhaps nearby, in the dim circuit of the Supreme Court buildings, here, in Manila's arena of officialdom, near UN Avenue, what my mom still called Isaac Peral, leading toward Dewey, now Roxas Boulevard—this damned sliver of reclaimed land, with its merry-go-round of naming, that one day must drown into the sea.

For an absurd moment, it seemed, this was what I was heir to, a historical polemic of dueling blood that resided in the body and the tongue.

"What do you want?" the lady said, as if catching herself, as if some absurdity in the situation also occurred to her, and her deep-seated, childish cry was also embarrassing, and not suited to her position, a large-bodied diplomat in the Department of Foreign Affairs.

"Why, I've come to introduce to you my daughter," my mother said.

I turned in fear to look at the high-pitched sound of my mom, her girlish tone of gladness. It was a gurgling pit in my stomach I was used to, when I heard this voice.

My sense of the world as a feint, the way my mom's voice constructed its own world, and my place in it was not fixed.

The blue-eyed woman glared at me.

My mother, smiling and shiny-eyed, stood beside the wheelchair, arms pointed at me, as if pulling me toward it, the chasm of her glad voice.

"Her name is Rosario. I gave her your name."

On that day I could see myself stripped of my solidity.

I was a pawn in my mother's games.

She had not come to Manila to visit me at Kamia. I was not mere bearer of goods on four jeepney rides. I was not named for this obese charlatan, this lame diplomat. I was a trick for this obscene ghost, my fake-tokayo aunt, this cunning woman with my name. But what was the trick for? For what was my mother's game? This woman locked in a wheelchair had lifelong experience in consular, diplomatic traps, she knew a con when it confronted her, she stared at me with my own disgust at my unwanted encounter with this cripple, yes, you're a cripple, I thought, *just a poliomyelitic!*, I hissed in my head at my namesake, this faux-Rosario. *Cripple*, I thought. *That is all you are.*

Leche, I heard in my brain, *leche nga yawa ka dida—ikaw nga gotas de leche!*

Laughter was trembling in my body, shame, hunger, and embarrassment. So many of my trips with my mother became a duel with her perceptions, which are part of me, inescapable.

"Come, inday, come to your Auntie Charity, I mean your Lola Charity, she is your great-aunt, the adopted—the ward of the—I mean the daughter of Lolo Paco, remember? The daughter of the senator, my Lolo Paco! Senator Francisco Delgado of the Commonwealth regime!"

"Oh hush," said the woman, brushing away that past, "the Commonwealth. We are a Republic now, Adina. And it is so long ago that we were together. Don't you see my diplomatic seal? Why talk about the past as if nothing has changed?"

Momentarily, my mom had a look of disorientation. She was not a person who remembered her past.

"Aren't you learning about it, the Commonwealth, in your history lessons, inday? You should learn about him in your history lessons! Lolo Paco—I mean Auntie Charity's—adopted—her father—he was a famous man, inday. An ambassador and a senator! Auntie Charity! My daughter is a student of the university, the University of Diliman!"

Just as I borrow my mother's prejudice, she borrows my pride. It had been a coup to gain admission, given my morose high school self, to enroll in the state university. By some miracle that did not escape me, I had gained my reprieve from Tacloban through no great achievement. All I did was take a test and pass. But the cliché of maternal pride in the Diliman daughter was something even I could not resist.

I saw the woman's eyes shift.

"The University of the Philippines?" the woman said, considering me from a different angle.

"Yes! She is an English student at the University of Diliman! She is studying to be a scholar, just like her Lolo Paco. Reading so many books, all the time all the time. Ever since she was a baby! Come, inday, bless! Bless your Auntie Charity—she's a Delgado, like you!"

The woman looked at me, her palms open, daring me to take them.

"That is a good school," the consul said.

My body is an automaton that does what disturbs it. I feel even now how my pride was demeaning, that bloating sense of my importance at the woman's words. I saw my mother smiling, beaming at my school's intellectual graces that in the future she will not condone. I saw in my mind's eye Adina an guapa's forlorn labor, tipped against the guard's desk in the vestibular limbo of this American construction, my mother's glass frames—her works of art—eliminated from this meeting with the consul though I finally understood they were the point—the reason for my mother's visit to this smug, alien relation. I saw my mother's ploy. It was pitiful. I was here to help sell her art to one more rich woman that she knew. I saw my mother's gambit, her instinct to toss whatever bait she had—in this case, the miserable past that bound them. I saw that the consul pitied her. I saw that the consul's motives for receiving us might be dim even to herself. I saw at my feet the ancient dirt of this marbled hall of the American era that would never come off, no matter how much the uniformed minions of the Department of Foreign Affairs cleaned it. I saw that this woman was surprised that Adina, some dismal relation from a far-off town in a wild place, Leyte, had a child who had even managed to get to college.

I felt dizzy, as if I were falling into something, a void. I stepped forward toward the wheelchair. I took the consul's hand. I steadied myself. I took her gross palm, I turned it to its obverse, its veined flatness with its heavy, pink, and pointed diamonds aimed toward my forehead, I knew how not to twist the wrist, in that filial way that is the first expertise of children, and I feel the ice of that memory still, of the consul's monstrous flesh on my forehead, her diamond's sharp glass, frozen in my brain, and the figure of my mother standing by, dissolving, like the gold dust in her unsold, banished frames.

Tangerine

I knew I was stuck in my fantasy, a fatality of a cursed clan, that the work I was doing in New York had urgency beyond my imagining. I kept working on my book on that roof deck overlooking the Hudson.

My suitcase was packed. I checked once again the one item I wanted if I left, I made sure it was within easy reach, ready to stash into my carry-on—the wooden box I kept up on the bookshelf, behind the sofa in the sala. The last of my mother's effects that I owned.

But I did not wish to return to bury her body.

I erased Tio Nemorino's voicemails and kept working, occasionally googling on my phone to check the prices of tickets, staring out at the expanse of the river toward Hoboken, and thinking again how strange to be reminded of that other river, the expanse to Carigara from Salogó—the expanse of the river Himanglos, a poor tributary trickling toward its more storied body, Leyte Gulf. I looked out toward the Hudson. There was no continuity or parity between Himanglos and the Hudson. Their one connection was the sensation of darkness sandwiched between shores. No matter which rivers I traversed, the Seine, or the Arno, or the Hudson, I keep seeing the same river, the river Himanglos of Salogó. It's that turn of fate, I thought, as I bent toward my novel, opening and closing my computer, starting and then stopping, looking at the screen then at water—when my mom returned to her hometown in the seventies, and my memory became condensed into that time of suspended expectation, when all I could count on was my mother's capacity to survive. Or maybe—nostalgia is a wedge, it keeps me from seeing more freely, even from loving enough. I stopped googling the flights, I forced myself to work.

My mother had never visited me in Manhattan. She had a passport, she could apply for a visa, she had a daughter. I never insisted. But I'd think about where I would bring her if she came to New York. What would she admire? Every time I see the Mondrians in the MoMA, I walk past quickly, though I had once stood to contemplate a picture, *Trafalgar Square*, its oranges and blues and yellows.

I stared with a twinge, a fleeting sensation.

She had once painted squares of color on our living room wall—bold, crazy, vibrant colors. Tangerine, gold, azure, each square carefully outlined in black. Then one day Adino, sweet Adino, riding along on his tricycle in the sala, accidentally elbowed her, and my mother lost it. I remember her shout, a desolate cry, as if she had woken up from the dream of her painting, and the smudge on the wall—I thought it was a slight touch, unnoticeable—seemed to have an inconsolable meaning to my mother. Mana Marga quickly took Adino away into the Haunted Room of Mr. Lee, as we called our playroom in our home at the time, on the mountainside of Housing. And I pretended to be supportive, going to her side, carefully stirring the paint thinner, taking in its harsh, metallic fume, arranging her paint brushes just so on her cotton cloths, as she wept, though I thought she was OA, overacting, and I wished she would stop. I didn't like OA, even in the movies.

So at the MoMA I always rush past the Mondrians.

But if she ever visited New York, I thought, I'd show her the brilliant paintings, especially *Composition in Red, Blue, and Yellow #2* and *Trafalgar Square*, to see in her face what might make her happy.

My mother never visited. What life kept her busy in Salogó and Tacloban, with Adino, sweet Adino, who in his teens had first flown off to his birthplace, Long Beach, to become a Certified Public Accountant, and then he returned to Leyte after his stint as a government auditor in the Bay Area. He came back to Salogó with early retirement and a penchant for grooming chickens. He came back hating Americans. In California, he believed white people were out to kill him. He spent his time now importing parliaments of fowl, happy in Himanglos. *Now he is all alone in the house in Salogó without your mother. You are now all Adino has,* Tio Nemorino's PM on Facebook told me.

I messaged back.

He also has the chickens, I said.

I used to imagine her with me in the different places I traveled to research my books. In Italy, I saw in its gruesome relics all the ways my mother would have felt at home: the preserved skull of Saint Catherine of Siena, encased in glass and clouded as if infernally breathing in the cathedral beyond the black-and-white checkerboard of the Tuscan piazza; the severed fingers of Mary-loving martyrs among the Byzantine mosaics of San Marco; the casual malice of the Venetian legend of touching the noses of the three Moors—*ay, moros!*, my mom would recognize, with her prejudice and faith in what she knew—carved into the walls of a building near the Jewish ghetto in Cannaregio; and above all, the outdoor altars to the pierced body, the Sacred Heart of Jesus, in too many ordinary, devout streets.

I thought briefly, when I was at a writing residency by Perugia, of looking for the patron saint of Salogó, Santa Rita de Cascia. A martyred widow in a black nun's habit whose forehead was touched by the bloody body of Christ. In the novena card my mom carried, rays of light shoot from the stigmata of Jesus straight to a hole on Santa Rita's forehead, a vision that worried me as a kid. The guidebooks said her uncorrupted body lay somewhere in Umbria. But I have a bad sense of geography.

In Padua involuntarily I made the sign of the cross at the sight of the statue of Saint Anthony in his medieval church. I came across it by accident, and I thought I should buy my mother a postcard—*I'm in his hometown—in San Antonio's Salogó!* Those endless novenas to Saint Jude and to Saint Anthony of Padua when I was a child—most acute during the time of the rebellion, when she was on the other side, of course, being a Delgado, sister of Tio Nemorino who had once sung "Top of the World" to their idol, in their damned world of Imeldifics, and I was the enemy, one of the demoniacs, as my mom called us, protesters of her president and his lady—those saints depressed me when I was growing up.

But still I entered the church, paid the three euros, and to be honest I have no memory of the place except for the thought as I wandered—how happy she would be in the actual church of her favorite, San Antonio de Padua, in his hometown.

I also knew there was something in my mother that defied the specifics of locality: her saints and all the objects of her mind were impervious to mere materiality, such as those medieval stones in an irrelevant city, Padua.

Other places mattered only in terms of Salogó.

Tio Nemorino began to call me hourly, not just texting, not just sending PMs on Facebook, asking me about my flights, my itinerary. He told me about legacy, obligation. He mentioned a deed of land. He repeated the word duty. He wished for my presence, my legal signature, he looked forward to my arrival. I left my phone in the apartment. I climbed the stairs to the roof deck. My mother would have liked this view, but contemplating the skyline would be boring. She snored in movie houses. She stopped reading books when she needed glasses. She owned *Gone With the Wind*. She thought her reading glasses disfigured her face. After a jeepney accident, in which once again she survived, against odds, she said what she loved was the instant facelift her surgery's scars had made. On weekends, she would drop us off on the beach, on her unbuilt land in San Jose, or in Candahug, Palo, near MacArthur Park, but she never stayed. She left us with the maids. She always had places to go. She had lived in America once, in California. She gave birth to me at Bethany Hospital, near Redemptorist Church on Real Street, then followed her husband, a townmate from Salogó, to Long Beach, then Wilmington, in Los Angeles.

The first time I returned home from the United States I was almost seven. I returned to Tacloban from Los Angeles with my mother, Adino, and the statue of the Sacred Heart. I followed my mom down the plane's suspiciously precarious jetway, she was cradling the just-born baby and the statue of Jesus like her twins, and I was clutching two fat five-centavo coins in my palms, proud of their weight.

My uncle Tio Nemorino had sent them to me from Cebu, or Tacloban, or Salogó. I jumbled up all the places. I was proud of the Filipino coins. American dimes and quarters were lightweight, I thought, compared to the copper five-centavo coins, with the figure of the smelter and his anvil and a smoking volcano in the distance. Tio Nemorino wrote me that the volcano was Mayon, the smelter was Panday Pira, your country is the Philippines. Later it turned out Tio Nemorino was no patriot, he kept asking about Los Angeles, especially the Lakers, whenever we visited him and his wife, Doctor

Tita Tita, in their fancy house in Cebu. He loved America. It's just that he liked to tell you the things he knew.

My mother, on the other hand, was a bigot. *Remember, inday*, she told me on my first day of school in America, *we invented adobo.* The Philippines is special. We are loved most of all by the Virgin Mary. Our mangoes are the best. No one else cooks rice in the right way, without measuring, with just the finger in the water. We are the only people in America who understand the mystery of the Sacred Heart of Jesus, carried on her lap all the way from Los Angeles to Honolulu to Manila to Tacloban. She said that Panday Pira, though he was a hero, should not be naked. He should put his clothes on, she could make him a shirt with piping on the collars, he would look good in it.

She was always revising her environment.

She had a book from Sears that she studied. She liked to touch the catalogs filled with squares of cloth in different colors—burnt sienna, rust, avocado, gold, azure.

Her favorite was tangerine.

She began painting the walls of the living room in Wilmington, California, in tangerine.

It was because of tangerine that my father slapped her when he returned home from cooking meat for sailors in Long Beach.

My mother screamed, she kicked, he held her by her feet, he dragged her to a wall. He pushed her against the wall, against the paint, so that her beautiful dark hair took on the orange of the walls and even her mouth had the color of swatches from her catalogs. This is my memory. I never witnessed it. I hid in my room whenever it happened. The first time, my mom said—*Go hide in your room, Rosario!* It was serious. She did not call me inday. She called me by my name. *Do not go out!* Her voice was my protector. My mother struggled against my father's body, his US Navy sailor's packed and muscled hide. My mother pushed him. She was wearing the dress with the daisy-printed collar. The collar was in the same pattern as her skirt. She was in the middle of sewing my miniature version, the way with pride I could look like her, if she had enough cloth left over.

I was afraid her daisy collar would get bloody, become tangerine. My mom grabbed at my dad's insignia, his petty officer shirt. My dad was beating her with both his palms as she hung on to him, swat! swat!, his sailor's arms creating a swish, what my gifted school teacher would call centrifugal forces, so that I heard it, I heard his bruteness in the air—and I heard my mom falling, against her faux-Tiffany lamps stationed between the centerpiece of our home's décor in Los Angeles: the Sacred Heart of Jesus and my mother's triad of saints—San Antonio, Santa Rita, and Saint Jude Thaddeus.

My dad also hated those lamps and those saints.

"You think you're so great, you think you can buy whatever you want, you're just a stupid bitch, a madwoman from Salogó!"

He called her madwoman, loka-loka, brain-damaged. He asked who took out her brains and stuffed them with catalogs. He asked who gave her money to take art classes in Burbank. Who was her loverboy—who?

At that my mother, caked in orange, lips and brow, laughed.

I think it was her laughter, glad, high-pitched, girlish, that made my father bash her one more time with his sausage-making, hamburger-grilling, fish-filleting fist.

He had a carnivorous odor, one more aspect of the bad luck of his Filipino job in America.

My lover is art, my mother shouted, laughing at my dad.

I hate my dad, but he was right. She sounded crazy.

Oh you, my mom said to my dad in Wilmington, California, you think you're so great, a US Navy petty, petty officer, but you know, you're just a petty, petty man.

She kept saying that, petty, petty, petty, and I'm not even sure if I heard her right. Maybe she meant pity. But I could hear her shrill voice, and my father's fury that spent itself swinging one more time, and my mom ducked, she ran around the house screaming, petty, petty, petty, or pity, pity, pity, and I, hiding obediently in my room, at the time I was their only child, I began screaming, too. Pity, pity, pity. Petty, petty, petty. I screamed and screamed and screamed. Now is the time, I thought: *Sacred Heart of Jesus and Santa Rita de Cascia, come on and do your job! Save my mother Adina from my father the sailor man!* I have no memory of what comes next.

I've never told anyone about these moments, not my friends nor my family. There is a vow of silence about tragedy growing up as Adina's child. Anyway, when we returned to Tacloban no one asked. On the plane home, it seemed as if my mother, in her dramatic black dress and dark sunglasses, were some movie star returned from a far-off location shooting, and we two, Adino and I, plus the statue of the Sacred Heart of Jesus, were the sparse souvenirs of her roaming. In the mess of disembarking, I lost one of the Panday Pira coins. I clutched its twin on the tarmac and howled.

"Sssh," my mom said as she and Tio Nemorino marched me to Tio Nemorino's jeep at the airport in Tacloban, "stop that bawling like a cat! We can get you another one. Your Tio Nemorino is going to be mayor! He has many coins! Do you think you're the only one with a broken heart?"

"Here," said Tio Nemorino, handing me his replacement coin. He was a man in dark sunglasses just purchased by my mom at LAX. He wore a hunting suit. He looked as if he were dressed to capture large animals to make a zoo. Many people at the time looked out of whack. The three boys in the car were practically deaf-mutes, sitting still in black suits and plastered haircuts, smelling of gasoline. They proudly named the hair grease when I asked, their voices in highlighter—*Brilliantina!*

Their mother, Tio Nemorino's wife, Doctor Tita Tita, the neuro, was waiting to hug me. She looked so uncommonly beautiful I thought she was a picture. She had a doll's high-cheeked rosy face and shiny lips. Ingrid Bergman, Ingrid Bergman. Ingrid was my favorite actress. My aunt had the cheekbones. She had jet-black hair teased up so that the tendrils made a halo, with flips of hair framing her on both sides, like apostrophes. When she laughed, her face carefree, she kind of looked also like Doris Day, a corny actress, but my aunt had golden brown skin. She was much improved. She laughed when

I told her she smelled like the Hanging Gardens of Babylon of King Nebuchadnezzar. Hah, said my mom (she was not a fan of in-laws)—that child of mine reads too much! My mom said—*stop showing off, Chicharita*. Sometimes she called me nicknames, which from her I liked. But my mom was also smiling. She was proud of my learning. That's in the Bible, Adina, corrected Tio Nemorino, it's in the First Readings, you don't read it, you hear it! Doctor Tita Tita said, it is just *Aliage*. And she took out the perfume bottle from her bag and let me hold it throughout the ride. I held the perfume, *Aliage*, and the substitute coin from Tio Nemorino, but it was not the right one. It had not traveled with me from Wilmington to Leyte to protect me from of all of the fears I had within my body, tied in a knot, as I boarded the airplane in Los Angeles.

I feared the fat cockroaches that scuttled about the airport as we landed. I feared the big bug eyes of the new land's dead flies, killed easily at the ticket counters with flat, plastic swatters shaped like cute animals, such as a kitten or a rabbit. I feared I would like everything in my mom's country, even the flies and the cockroaches and the swatters that killed them, and never want to go back to the scratched walls of Wilmington, California.

Above all, I feared the dead body of my mom's Papá.

It was for him that we had flown to Tacloban then rode Tio Nemorino's jeep to the scene of my mom's original memory. I don't know really if she had it: my neurosis, my doubling of rivers where every vision is Salogó. My mom disembarked in her black-chiffon robes—black looked good on her. Black defined her against the shimmery light. I was conscious of my role as the returning child of the dead man's daughter. Death gave me annoying significance. Children gathered the minute I stepped onto Salogó's dust. They pinched my arm to test my reaction, stared at my black dress that matched my mom's, followed me wherever I went in Salogó, except when I peed. I peed behind a creaky door covered in moss, into a hole straight into a river. Even toilets in Salogó were surprising, as if things were only about to be invented. I did not flinch when people pinched and hurt me, I believed it was a custom, I did not understand a word anyone said, except adobo and baboy, which I thought meant goodbye. Sure enough the dead body was out in the sala in Salogó for all to see, and the Honorable Mayor Francisco Delgado III with his cancerous corpse kept luring people to his lovingly pleated, blush-pink satin side—the oddly tender, feminine look of his winding sheet drew both the slippered folk and the fancy ones to weep for him.

On the day of the funeral, I thought my mom would never stop. She wept as they lifted his body, she wept as we began the procession behind the shiny musicians, the FrankenPresley Combo, the most fascinating humans at the affair, with their ruffled shirts and glossy vests. There was some question about the musicians' shiny outfits, they were dressed for a wedding, not a funeral, but it was a scandal no one allowed me to pursue. The walk was interminable, we seemed to be walking to the Sea of Galilee, but like Moses we were not going to get there, I mixed up the Old and the New Testaments in the heat and the exhaustion, my new black shoes were now as gray in Salogó's dust as my new white, ruffled socks, and still my mom kept weeping.

I kept my secret to myself.

My grandfather, my mom's Papá, the Honorable Mayor Francisco Delgado III, was finally lowered into his grave—an untidy denouement, by the way, that disappointed me. Only to descend into wild grass, after all the fuss. I watched as my mom, Adina an guapa, hung so close to her Papá's body, hugging his coffin until the end, that Tio Nemorino and his three boys had to hold on to her at his grave, as the men in the family should. I kept my secret to myself as I stood apart and heard my mother's weeping—there were many other reasons for her tears.

The Pig's Head

My mother never returned to America.

At first we stayed in the suddenly emptied rooms of her Papá's home, the riverine house in Salogó, after the mourners and the musicians, the debonair and shiny FrankenPresley Combo, and all the relatives absconded, one of them with a pig's head. I could not tell what the commotion was about, why there was furor in the kitchen over the loss of a pig's head when I could see there were still three pigs' heads to lament, each in a row in the kitchen. The muzzled guards of leftover grief. Baboy, baboy, baboy, baboy. I thought the women were saying farewell when in fact they were gossiping about a pig. I watched the communal making of the leftover funeral stew, the lechon paksiw, the bubbling of its vinegar. I watched the chopping of the snout and the ears, the inclusion of the gristle, the suddenly illuminating properties of cheek by jowl, which was kind of fatty, the textural function of the marrow, but especially the additive, the liver, and the simmering of the garlic and onions and peppercorn and bay leaves that summed up the most delicious portions of our sorrow.

I discovered that I loved lechon paksiw.

I could not get enough of it, and we had three pigs' heads' worth.

My mom was right. The Philippines was special. Every part of the animal's body is recycled to convey our unspeakable and limitless affection. And mangoes do not exist if they are not Filipino: I discovered every other mango in the world is incorrect. I ate so many mangoes my tongue got furry, I kept eating, I was hoarding the taste of mango against my future deprivation, back in Wilmington, California.

So much was lacking in the world that was not the Philippines. I had missed so much by living near Burbank. So much was unknown, suddenly revealed in Salogó: Mana Marga emerged as the hero. She told me the names and ingredients for everything, she told me about a song I liked, that is just an habanera, it is old, she said, she explained that that person was my great-aunt's first cousin by a lousy marriage, but her children's guapo looks made it okay, and that layabout was my mother's second cousin's unwanted third son, don't tell anyone! That one, with the look of copra, all beaten and burnt and smelling of tubâ, is your apoy—I am his apo—ha tuhod—Tay Guimoy! That lucky son of Apoy Bingo! He looks like a beggar, but his children are from estados!, and he's as rich as the Chinese Sian Co Lee! Do not be fooled!

What's apo ha tuhod?

Mana Marga laughed, and I knew I was a dunce.

Ah. How do you say? Grandchild-by-the-knee!

Also what is copra and tubâ, I wanted to ask, but I kept my idiocy to myself.

Estados, I gathered, meant being abroad. It took me a while to understand it meant a country—America.

She also explained the being of Tia Pachang.

Mana Marga spoke English with—how should I describe it— impatient care, as if she were in a hurry to get rid of the words that had taken her too much trouble to store, the dormant phrases stumbled on her tongue from lack of use, but they were always correct. Her English was in a vitrine, a relic both prized and dumb, her Waray was in the world, the unremarkable living thing that only I kept trying to grasp. Mana Marga was the active point between my mom's despair and the implacable figure of Tia Pachang—sister of the late Honorable Mayor Francisco III, matriarch of the Delgados of Leyte. In real life, Tia Pachang, Miss Bonifacia Delgado in her unimaginable girlhood, taught Spanish on F. Jhocson Street in Sampaloc, Manila, but among the Delgados of Salogó, a ring of power like a dead pope's odor of sanctity surrounded her desires, beyond the frail evidence of her stooped figure.

As mourning wreaths came in, with well-wishers' names curlicued on their ribbons, Tia Pachang simply mentioned those whose names were absent, and soon the missing good wishes arrived. The casket was overwhelmed with ribbons and flowers. Everyone did her bidding, though she never said much, and somehow I understood from Mana Marga's obedience to her that Tia Pachang was the force by which the funeral band played mournful habanera tunes instead of my mom's choice (Elvis, plus some Pilita Corrales), and that Tia Pachang's rules made sure pigs' heads were held to account, days of grief had a schedule, and her brother's funeral would be only properly spectacular.

My mom disrupted her Tia Pachang's order.

The day she appeared before the casket, all eyes gazed on the vision of Adina an guapa, travel-worn and wan in her filmy weeds like a widow, her tango-ready high-heeled shoes, her black Chantilly veil that framed her weeping figure, her gauzy lace over neck and shoulders in a mystical shroud as her body trembled, causing my own shuddering, at the sight of the coffin of her Papá. I held on to my mother, afraid of her falling, as if my slightness held any weight. Papá, Papá, Papá, Papá. There were so many words in there I did not decipher. Tio Nemorino finally took her away from her father's casket, and my mom turned to the crowd at the wake, a dazzling sight, a Hollywood foreigner, her mascara askew in a strangely cinematic way, like Sophia Loren in *Sunflower*, dressed in a black veil like a funeral bride, and she approached the little woman with the bun, who looked about as large as a wizened Tinker Bell, at the prime spot beside the casket.

My mom took the hand of her tiny Tia Pachang, also clad in black, and I noted later, when I saw the dead brother in his coffin, that he had that same pronounced shadow as she had above her upper lip, a prominent grayness around their thin mouths, so that in profile the siblings shared this pursed expressiveness in their lower faces.

Tia Pachang spoke no word, her thin lips tight, her gaze impassive, just looking up intently at my mother's face with her mucous-filled eyes, as Adina an guapa raised her aunt's hand to her forehead.

It was the first time I witnessed that antique gesture.

Then my mom looked at me.

Her eyes told me to step up.

She gave me the mottled hand of this woman I did not know, and I took it. With a solemnity that impressed mostly myself, I copied my mom, placing Tia Pachang's hand upon my brow, but twisting it, so I felt her palm on my face instead.

The old lady said, *ow*, and my mom laughed.

"Oh, inday, you will have to learn the correct way to do lamano so that you don't kill Tia Pachang!"

Then the old lady spoke, also in English, but with that rolling of the syllables that signified the choice was a strain, an effort weighed down by her real love, the dead one, Spanish.

"Only you, Adina, laugh in the *prrrresence* of the dead."

I could tell the hurt in my mom's eyes though I could not see them through her dark glasses.

"Marga, take Adina and her children to their rooms."

And so we were dismissed, in Tia Pachang's forked tongue, English, and my mother obediently followed that paragon, Mana Marga, to her old childhood rooms.

Mana Marga took us in hand, my mom, Adino, sweet Adino, and me. At first I thought Mana Marga was my mom's unmentioned sibling, maybe the spawn of a witch stepmother, as usual unexplained to me. My mother's mother, Mamá, was long dead, of leukemia, when my mom was only twelve. The way I heard people whisper *leukemia*, it was a curse, and if you said it too loud it would happen to you. So who knows if my mom had other step-siblings, like Cinderella, after her Mamá was dead? There were so many relations from all over the world for me to bless. This blessing of the hands of relations, *lamano!*, *lamano!*, began to lose its charm when it was clear as the days wore on that in Mana Marga's view I never had the option *not* to bless.

No one ever asked me to bless Mana Marga. It turns out she was a cousin, related to Mama Bia, from Capoocan, she had adored Adina an guapa since my mom was a child, she was the servant Nay Mimang's daughter, *on the Buñales side not Delgado!*, people said without explaining, so I accepted that such distinctions had meaning, and her worshipful protection of my mother from childhood on had persisted through Mana Marga's own marriage and childbirths. She was so attached to my mom I was surprised much later when I learned that she had three daughters, all older than me, with flourishing existences of their own.

Whenever Adina an guapa needed her, Mana Marga arrived, to

launder or to nurse her back to health or to manage the cooking of the lechon paksiw, wearing her eerie makeup, Mana Marga's fantastic semblance of my mom's aesthetics (the cosmetics, of course, were my mom's gifts), and she wore my mom's lip color and her eyeshadow in a way that, in my view, did not give comfort to others. Mana Marga looked like a scary and discolored toy. But she was in command. She treated me the way she treated Adina an guapa—as if I were hers to boss and to save.

In short, I was forever in her charge.

The trouble began with the rearranging of the funeral wreaths. My mom emerged in her sunglasses after I had sat there in the dark (Salogó had no light switches as far as I could tell), listening to her quietly sobbing. I did not know what to do, I thought everything in Salogó was thrilling and significant, I was like one of the animals getting off the Ark to an entirely recreated world, and my mother's sadness was a commentary on my lack of perspective. I held tight the ugly rat-body of Adino. He would come into his handsomeness only in the months that followed, he was so new he still looked wrinkled, and Mana Marga bustled about unpacking and making our beds.

When my mother came out of her rooms, she redesigned her Papá's bouquets.

It was the quiet time of siesta, the midday napping that struck me as a great habit of wise people. I opened up my notebook, scratching in my new words: *baboy, lamano, siesta, merienda*. Under merienda I listed an appendix—*binagol, bibingka, roscas, empanada*. All of the funeral sweets. My mom created a bower that led up to her father's open casket, displaying the flowers according to her critical eye, a reassembly of color and beauty. But when Tia Pachang woke up, Mana Marga quietly restored the old array. Adina an guapa had hidden the most prominent bouquet, the stiff, everlasting flowers from the First Lady herself behind the fresh blush roses of no-name cousins from Calingcaguing.

This new world of my mother's was so orderly I looked around me to think who among the women was the Second Lady, and the Third

Lady, and the Fourth? It's like that term *comfort room*—when finally we reached Papá's house in Salogó and someone asked me, *do you need the comfort room?*, I thought it was so civilized that every house in the Philippines had a room just for comfort, and even when it turned out it only meant toilet, I kept the word in my notebook—*comportroom*. In the kitchen, my mother was teaching the women how to pleat the paper napkins into origami petals, just so, a craft she learned in Burbank, California! It was a relief to hear her excited voice, still wobbly from travel and her secret sobbing, but Tia Pachang scattered all the serving women around her—*why waste time pleating napkins for the peasants of Santa Rin?*

In the scurrying of the ladies I could see Adina's shortcomings in Tia Pachang's eyes. Adina had no sense of priorities, grieving was a serious business not an experiment in design, and my dim sense that for Tia Pachang Adina an guapa had the stature of a child was disturbing, also thrilling. Every minute people shifted my view. My mother, left behind in the kitchen, taught me her petal trick with the napkins, she kept making her origami napkins with fierce focus, eyes behind dark glasses, she kept making them with complete indifference to Tia Pachang and to the world around her—even to me. She arranged her origami pieces along with mine. The gesture seemed like praise, and I felt warm. I considered our work with the napkins a kind of conspiracy. It made me happy.

We were the only family left in the house. The grandfather-by-the-knee Tay Guimoy with his face of copra and his brood, all nurses who arrived from abroad, estados!, had gone back to their beach place called barakasyunan, where Himanglos met the gulf—my mom kept saying, one day we will go, but we never did. The cousins from Manila were gone, Paquito the fiscal in Quezon City, the school teacher with cat whiskers on her face, the diplomat from Singapore, the congressman and his foul-mouthed wife, Mana Talia, alongside her genteel opposite, a glamorous woman who never perspired, Lola Sayong, and lastly the Provincial Board Member of District Two, called Tia Nunay, a woman with the helmet hair of a soldier and the red lips of a Dracula, who gave me a whole twenty-five-centavo coin to keep—*the money is small but da lab is as big as a carabao!* For years in my memory the solemnity of Tia Nunay's voice left me with no sense of her gift's meanness. Even Doctor Tita Tita had gone home with the Brilliantina boys, John-john, Putt-putt, and Mick-mick, who turned out to be not as mute as I thought—they just did not want the trouble of speaking to me in English. Once we figured we could ransack the place in our shared misunderstandings, we investigated for days the vast, rotting house in Salogó, with its ground floor made of dirt to make room for pigs and hungry chickens, and a seawall on which we roamed, like the Swiss Family Robinson, and a balcony that jutted out, beyond the seawall, right above the water, so Putt-putt, the daring one, kept trying to fall into the river just because he could. But now the boys were all back in their opulent home in Cebu. Only their father Tio Nemorino was left behind because he was candidate for mayor of Salogó though he liked to live elsewhere.

The last straw was the disappearance of the pig's head.

The culprit was Adina an guapa.

It turned out she gave it to the daughter-in-law of Tay Lucio, the carpenter, who had told us the story of her fisherman husband drowned in Panalaron Bay, during Typhoon Klaring, an unseasonal storm.

It was the last straw—the pig's head was the height of *caprrrricho*.

That was Tia Pachang's word.

I liked the sound of it, the hiss and the snarl of it.

Capricho.

I rolled the *R*s on my tongue. I added the word to my alphabetical list in the notebook I had bought from my favorite place in Wilmington, the stationery store next to Food Co in Los Angeles.

The guests were all gone, and Tia Pachang did not stop speaking.

Her skinny frame shook with fury, incandescent to me—her gray bun shot out flames, her hairpins glared in the sun. I was only about to turn seven, and my powers of veneration were pronounced.

Tia Pachang's rant was glorious—her words an edict, the catechism of this mysterious place. I felt like I was growing antennae, fuzzy apertures tuning static, alert to ways of categorizing, organizing the new world.

A lack of respect for the correct order! The pig's head goes to the next of kin, or to the eldest cousin, not to some unknown in-law of Tay Lucio the carpenter! *O Dios, perdona!* Pasaylua! The trouble that Adina starts, it never ends! Waray hangkag! *No hay límite!*

Tia Pachang went on and on about my mother. Adina an guapa's errors, her scandalous vanity, her melodramatic ego as if the world revolved only around her, Adina thought only about herself, and not her duties and obligations, as a daughter, as a Delgado! She was always that way, even as a girl. She never changed.

Tia Pachang's voice, so timid and retiring in company, speaking in her multiple tongues, which I gleaned in retrospect, had that growl, a rasping force, that gave me profound shame for being my mother's child. I was out on the balcony, sitting with my notebook, looking out at the river. Tia Pachang's rigor and righteousness were like lightning bolts, or the burning bush of Moses, I barely understood it, except through Biblical passages, it created an opening in a part of me I did not touch, a part that analyzed my mother, the sun stood still on the river, Tia Pachang's voice was an oracular steel box, and I wanted to shut it down even as I opened it, it dislodged me into an unstable clarity, shimmering in refracted light like the river in Salogó.

"Did America make her go mad again?" Tia Pachang cried. "Ah, *Dios mío.* That—*separada!*"

At that, I heard a shout that returned me to myself, it told me from that day on I would love him, I would love him until the day he died.

"Tia Pachang, basta!" Tio Nemorino shouted.

Tia Pachang stopped in the middle of her speech.

She swallowed it, her saliva, her face was puckered, her jaw was a beak.

It was a silence like a startled bird's, caught on a limb.

The women putting away the cooking pots and the condiments stood still.

My uncle, the only man of the house when we returned to the Philippines, lowered his voice, as if apologizing, trying to reason also with himself.

"Leave Adina alone. You know how much Papá loved her. She was the love of Papá's life. That's what he was to her, since the day she was born—his Adina—an guapa. And ever since that day—she was only nineteen—you don't remember, Tia Pachang. You weren't there, Tia Pachang—Adina misses her Papá. She did not get to see him before he died because that bastard wouldn't let her. Who cares about the pig's head but the pig?"

Tacloban

When we moved to Tacloban, first to the lush place called Housing, a tidy community of low bungalows veering past Anibong toward San Juanico Strait, and then later to the home with the politician's veranda, on Juan Luna Street, I have no memory of how my mom managed it. I have no idea how the house was leased, who bought the furniture, where we got the money, how I knew we were never going back to that bastard, my father, though the ending of our escape was not clear.

It was now a new month, and we were not flying to LAX.

We were in Salogó, and Tio Nemorino said I should be in school, which confused me because it was June and September was so far away, and my mom kept bringing me to election dances and trips to Calingcaguing and Santa Rin to shake the voters' hands. Loudspeakers introduced me. I was the child from estados, which made my alienness seem special, or like a warning to keep away from a rare disease, my discomfort kept giving me variable impressions. I held out my hand toward the people, wondering if I should put everyone's palms to my head, standing in a line in a matching terno outfit with Adina an guapa, in the sizzling heat of voters' applause. We wore tangerine. I looked like a pumpkin with wings. The band struck that tune of Karen Carpenter, "Top of the World," the loudspeaker asked me to dance, but I wouldn't, and my mom laughed. She took center stage.

She and Tio Nemorino were practiced, a well-known pair. From birth they had been singing for a public. My mom sang "Please Release Me," and to each other they sang "Love Me Tender." No one but I seemed to think the song was disgusting, since they were siblings, then at the end of the program Tio Nemorino bowed: people demanded that he sing his song.

Ave Mariiii-iiii-aaaa.

They chanted their command.

Kanta! Kanta, Nemorino, kanta!

"Ave Maria" was always the denouement, after "Júrame," "Bésame Mucho," and "Cuando Cuando Cuando," and I thought the reason people went to election events was to hear him sing "Ave Maria."

I sat there in those plazas listening to the tremolo that was Tio Nemor's mesmerizing line—

Graaaa-atia—ple-e-e-e-e—

His long, high vowels that kept us in suspense.

I sat still. I felt pride and worry. How long will he be able to hold it? I could see his diaphragm rising, his neck tendons stretching, while that gold oozed out of his chest—his voice.

It turns out Tio Nemor, with his voice's liquid timbre and his ability to hold his breath, was famous all around the province for having reached the regional finals of Tawag ng Tanghalan, the national singing competition. Sadly, when he did not win in Manila, he went to law school instead. I learned these matters by osmosis, in the way biography in a family is kind of not really told, just in the air like mayflies you sometimes mistakenly breathe in.

And it was when he sang that I saw Tio Nemor most clearly.

He lost his sense of who he was.

He forgot his pomaded hair and the stiff flare of his trousers, the proud rigor mortis of its cornstarched seams. He forgot his need for people to love him. He stood in his isputing, striped polyester shirt and shiny leather shoes, called takong, which I learned later was not great, a mark of river towns and olden times, but when he sang nothing bothered Tio Nemor. He never cleared his throat. His entry had no cues. The band, too, was nonexistent. Instead he listened to something inside him, a place we all wished to enter but to which only he had the key.

And in the moment of song, no one mistook his gift.

It was for us.

He had the vacant gaze of an old Greek bard that centuries on people would remember as blind.

Amid the vulgarity of the world—the bunting and the Nacionalista election posters and the Coca-Cola advertising donated to Congressional District Two—I was in the web of his unbreathing—

Ple–e–e–e–e–e–e–e—na!

I thought people elected Tio Nemorino mayor because of hypnotism.

Because of Schubert's "Ave Maria."

My mom, too, was in her element at the election dances for Tio Nemorino. On top of the world. She brought me to fittings at Young's Fashionne House on Zamora, where I watched a prodigy my age, a child laborer who was a genius, sew delicate sequins on beaded, fairy-tale gowns. She dug out her ternos from the time she was the teenage hostess for the old mayor, her Papá, and she came out from her mourning in her butterfly clothes.

I thought becoming mayor was a family heirloom.

Singing for votes was our professional duty.

I thought with dread of the time I'd grow up, and I'd have to dance the kuracha for money and sing "Bésame Mucho" for votes. I was convinced my future had only one fate. For now it was my mom and Tio Nemorino who were the stars, a shining couple leading the tango in an open, swept dirt-space in barrio Santa Rita (it doubled as a cockpit arena feathered with dark blood spots), my mom holding up her black serpentina skirt, her other hand in her brother's as they faced each other in the season's light drizzle and swayed and waved their palms, that graceful rotation of kuracha wrists, under the plastic banners with the Nacionalista Party logo and the still intact motto of their standard bearer, *Re-Elect Ferdinand!* I memorized the other names on those posters—*Almendras, Aytona, Enrile, Kalaw, Maceda*—plastered all around Salogó (I remember the names even now). There were chickens and goats and pigs and those orderly santan bushes and delicate gumamela flowers lining the farmers' tidy yards and the radiant blaze of bougainvillea that seemed to exist just to welcome me.

The hallway of the house in Salogó was no mess of my mom's paints but a tangle of sequins, gowns with butterfly sleeves, also called terno or mestiza, everything always had multiple names, and pumps with bullet heels. With the intensity of an artist, my mom became Tio Nemorino's election manager, as if her transference of skill, from painting to politics, possessed value in equal measure. My favorite image of this time is a glossy picture of my mother about to lead the dance in a gown of black tulle, I liked the femme-fatale profile, her look of a vampira in the ballroom—I liked her shocking look amid the pastel dancers. In the picture, she's in some barrio hall, in her well-sprayed bouffant, her terno in that uncommon black, and high heels, her foot in the air about to take her first step, the entrada, and she is looking at no one in particular, at an absent demonio, who knows if in her mind it was at him, the bastard, my father, though the picture tells me she had no worry but the dance, she glanced in a side-view pose like an actress, Ingrid Bergman, Ingrid Bergman, and then we'd ride home in the mud through Salogó's farmlands until the next election event.

How many times have I been at a party with my mother, overwhelmed by our family's public face—this need for voters to love you. I used to wake up at night after those election dances and crawl over to her bed, put my ear to her chest, and hear her tired breathing, to reassure myself she was still who she was, and not the vampira of TEIPCO.

In a dream, one of the few dreams in my life that I remember (I sleep like a log, I do not remember my dreams as if I have no underworld life, and I have no insomnia, unlike my mom), Adina an guapa was the world's last ghoul.

During the time of the elections, people kept reporting the presence of a vampire. Out there in the city—on the rooftop of Tacloban Electric and Ice Plant Company, every day at twelve noon.

The whistle for lunchtime boomed out from the ice plant, and from the flat roof of TEIPCO came the city's shrill, prolonged signal for siesta.

AAAOOOUUWHOOOOH!

The siren was a banshee shriek, telling the city—

Time to rest.

Lingkod. Higda.

During her lunchbreak a saleslady from Reina's Toy-Land saw the figure, a floating torso, wearing what looked like butterfly sleeves, rising above the rooftop of TEIPCO. The saleslady swore the woman glowed in indigo blue, brighter than the sky, a royal figure, but she could not tell if she wore a mestiza dress or had bat wings. The saleslady kept staring at the vampira on the rooftop of TEIPCO as the whistle of the ice plant lowered its boom, and the rest of the city scurried about, hailing tricycle drivers to take them home to feed their babies or join their kumares for a brief stint at the mah-jongg tables or go off to Magsaysay Boulevard to take a lunchtime stroll along the water and soothe their workday nerves. The vampira on the rooftop of TEIPCO was next reported by a waitress at Primrose Restaurant on Zamora Street who saw it at dusk, casually picking its teeth, and then by a medical agent who was leaving Farmacia Watts for a smoke and swore the vampira had the face of an angel but the gloomy style of a kontrabida star, a moody one like Rosa Rosal or Bella Flores, all alone on the rooftop of TEIPCO.

The gliding lady in midnight blue, with bat wings and a melancholy aura, became a common sight. Once even I saw it, when I was lost on Veteranos Street, in second grade and new to the city, looking for Adino, sweet Adino, and my mom during lunchtime, and I made the error of walking toward downtown, toward TEIPCO, and I looked up, and in the haze of noon I saw her, the vampira of TEIPCO, wailing along with the lunchtime whistle, her sequins shimmering in the high-noon glare, as I searched for my mother, whose figure I had lost on Veteranos Street.

In my dream, the universe consisted of only the three of us—me, my brother in my arms, and our mother Adina an guapa—running along the gates of my new grade school, Divine Word Missionary School on Veteranos.

The place in my dream also looked like the parking lot at Food Co, in Wilmington, Los Angeles.

Or maybe I had dreamt this not in Salogó but later when we moved to the city, in Tacloban.

In my dream, Adino and I were the world's last children running from our mother, the world's last vampire, who wanted our blood.

But we were running out of luck, and I looked back to see—

Adino in her clutches.

He was next.

The last baby alive.

I woke up.

I felt my mother's breathing on my back, humid but cold.

She was sitting on my bed, hovering over me and humming "Bésame Mucho," fanning me with a newspaper to keep the mosquitoes and the heat away as I slept.

I smelled Vicks VapoRub on my back.

She was obsessive about mosquito bites and flies and pests—she hated them on her children. She liked to massage me with Vicks VapoRub, or fix my pajama collar, or swat at a mosquito on my bedsheet, and so disturb my sleep to make me comfortable.

I woke up.

I could hear her restless heart, my mother's insomniac breathing.

I heard her humming her election songs.

And it made me happy to hear—Adina an guapa was human, she was alive, she was her usual nighttime self.

Annoying me with Vicks VapoRub.

I felt comforted. I went back to sleep.

After my days of spotlight in Salogó, it was a letdown to be deposited, anonymous and with no audience, in the tranquil mountainside of Housing in the city of Tacloban, and to sit in the back of the second-grade classroom, Section Atis, in Divine Word Missionary School. The other sections were Balimbing, Caimito, and Durian, a fruity, alphabetical infamy in descending order of the pupils' averages. I realize now I should have been in Section Durian because I had no previous year's average to show, and all the details I write down here keep telling me how I got ahead without much merit. My mom spent the morning braiding my hair. She parted my hair in two, in pigtails, then made five braids in each part. She looped the five braids so that I wore two bunches of plaited rings on my head. Like satellites. I felt like Saturn. She pinned roses, shorn of thorns, on my light-pink uniform's collar. I remember them as the roses from the funeral, but the timing was wrong.

They would all be rotting.

It was almost July.

I wore a corsage of roses on my collar on my first day of school (though the school year had long begun, it turns out, in June). I thought it was a Filipino rule, for children to wear roses on their new, starched uniform's collar on their first day of school, for mothers to spend hours braiding your hair but never explain why she made you miss a whole month of classes, for you to feel so loved by your mother you did not complain when your hair was parted too tightly, and you never questioned her sequence of events.

Mana Marga had covered my new notebooks in creamy wax paper, each flap invisibly taped, precision-cut in Mana Marga's mysteriously expert way, and my mom wrote my name and grade in her careful hand, her elongated *R*s and the cowlick curls of her convent-school, Catholic *O*s.

I watched as she sat writing out my name, her face intent, with that pleasure that told me—*Do Not Disturb*.

Rolling my new school bag, a huge black rectangle on wheels, with its two sets of silver closures so firm they gave me dread that I would look like an idiot in class when I would not be able to unlock my own bag, I waited with Mana Marga for Man' Ramon, an binulan, to take me to school in his jeep.

On the porch of our new home in Tacloban, in her flowered caftan, like an inset floral pendant among the bougainvillea, my mom carried Adino, sweet Adino, against her hip and kissed me goodbye on both cheeks and on my hairline and patted my corsage, and I received her blessing to continue my education at her convenience.

The posters all along the walls of my second-grade classroom each displayed a boy in neat polo pants and shorts sitting at a desk with a book. No one in the classroom wore a corsage. I was surrounded by living replicas of the poster boy in the pomaded hair and khaki shorts of my classmates, I sat way back in the last seat of the classroom, on a wooden chair that had an arm that was also a desk, I wore a brand-new all-pink uniform with starched pleats made of Indian-head cotton, a fat, stiff cloth, and not the softer, correct fine cloth, tetoron, so I was marked on the first day of school as a wretched child, I smelled of death's roses plus Mana Marga's gawgaw, I did not understand a word anyone said.

Tagalog was my first subject on my first day of school.

The teacher, Mrs. Majablanca, also wore a uniform, peach-colored in fuzzy fabric, a plump lady whose extravagant hair had a little flip at the side, in suspended animation, like Doctor Tita Tita's. She did not smell of *Aliage*. She had mosquito wounds on her face. At first I thought they were freckles. She called out the children's names. One boy was named William McKinley Maceda. Another was Ferdinand Enage Dumpit. There was a tiny kid in pigtails named Trinatrono Almendras.

I was in awe of their names.

Maceda. Ferdinand. Almendras.

They were the names on the election posters. To me all words were connected because too many things were new, and I was ignorant. Of course my teacher did not call out Delgado. That was not my name.

But when in the middle of the class she called me—I had no idea what was going on—she repeated my name, *Rosario!*, I jumped up.

Yes, that is I.

I stood up from my chair, stepping out to the side like a sergeant beside the long-armed chair, the way I saw my classmates did.

"Filipino, Rosario!" said Mrs. Majablanca. "Filipino!"

Clutching my desk, I tried to guess what she wanted.

Guessing was my mode of passage throughout all those days of my long arrival, when I had no idea if my place amid novelty was a permanent condition. Everyone was related. Anything had consequence. The smallest objects had enormous significance because I did not know their names. Labakara, lingkuran, lamesa. Tuta, terno, takong. I was always on the edge of decoding a message. Some were easy to figure out, like frigidaire, that was a refrigerator, and only one person in Salogó had one, Sian Co Lee, the town's usurer and owner of the sawmill who had a generator, and you could get ice in bulk from him for a party, or store your funeral desserts for a fee. Too many things had many names, like the word *chair*—lingkuran, silya, banco, butaka. Also *bed*—kama, higdaan, katre, katurugan. Items of rest had many names in the language of my mother. But verbs had only one. Lingkod. Higda. Pronouns had no gender. Hiya meant him or her, and no one cared if you mixed pronouns in English, the way my mom would call me a him and my brother a she and Mana Marga would correct her—but that useless rule is the fault of English, said my mom, and even Mana Marga agreed. Later when I had to learn Spanish, I traced the Waray words in it. Spanish had meaning only as repository of more elemental trace material, its apparition in Waray—*lava cara* = face towel, *la mesa* = table, *la cama* = bed, *el aparador* = cabinet, *el comedor* = dining cupboard. I saw the occult joke in the meaning of *la mano*—hand. But really, Spanish was for the outside things, the things you could make.

Warays kept their words for the inside, the things that made you up.

I grew up with my mom's way with words, the way she spoke

Tagalog with indifference and English with guesswork—for her English was only this wartime novelty, like chewing gum or tennis shoes, some foreign implement of insufficient relevance. Her Tagalog was tokenism, misrecognitions from her Waray. It's her Waray that was the mineral hoard, a cave of treasure that if I were smart I'd scrutinize carefully, look for its veins and source, in the manner of the pawnbroker Doña Tesoro de Oro, examining a carat.

But I never read those words in school.

I was twenty-seven when I found actual Waray words in a book.

Uzza. Dua. Tolo.

I didn't recognize them.

I was in the New York Public Library, reading the chronicle of Pigafetta.

When I read those words in the book, translated into English and listed by an Italian chronicler for a French audience about the trip of a Portuguese explorer for the queen of Spain, the spiral of universes that brought my mother's language back to me, in a foreign city, made me dizzy.

At the New York Public Library, I saw the list of my mother's words with weird Italian spelling (the chronicler's spelling was as improvised as my mom's English), in Pigafetta's book about his journey around the world with Magellan.

Uzza, dua, tolo.

One. Two. Three.

Also, *chirei* (kiray: eyebrow), *botchen* (butkon: arm), *paha* (paa: thigh), *licud* (back), *sico* (elbow), *tuhud* (knee), *camat* (kamot: hand), *dudlo* (tudlo: finger), *liogh* (li-og: throat), *utin* (penis).

Dilla (tongue).

In Pigafetta's chronicle of his journey around the world with words, the man's spelling needed work. My discovery was that what was most ancient about us, our Easter Island statuary, is our words.

Espejo: mirror.

Self: translated.

When we returned to the Philippines, I was conscious of not

knowing my mother's tongue though I was her daughter. I thought my ignorance was unjust. I wondered at first why I did not know the words in Waray when they were supposed to be my own. It seemed that for some reason on a tarmac I had dropped them, or someone had taken them from me. My ignorance did not make me feel guilty, it made me mad. I thought you were supposed to come into knowledge once you reached your mother's country, that everything would click into place like my mom's heels doing the tango, and when I grew up I would know how to dance that tango, exactly like my mom. Athena came from Zeus's brain, I sprouted from my mother's words. That was the rule. I believed in these things, that my origins were a gift from my mother, and all I had to do was receive them.

That it turned out not to be so made me work harder to figure out the words, to repress the reality of my alienation. I would be mute for hours, just listening to people's words, match them with their gestures, write them down in notebooks. I made columns and columns of words in those notebooks. As Mana Marga got everything ready for my first day of school, I smelled the declensions of her labor in the increasing sweetness of the coconut coal, that pungent waft of my childhood, the red, glowing steam of burnt coconut in Mana Marga's wake, and I memorized: plantsa = iron, uring = coal, gawgaw = cornstarch, palda = skirt, kunot = wrinkle: as she scolded me in mixed messages to the maids—*pastilan, ini nga bata, and don't you dare sit on that lingkuran without fixing the palda behind you so all my uring and my gawgaw do not go to waste! Pastilan, uday, it kalingkod hini nga bata, ura-ura man—! Pagbuotan—uday!*

Pagbuotan—be good! Buot meant both to be thoughtful and to be still.

I had no idea what pastilanuday meant.

Every word I collected was a mixed-up spell, but each was an object that granted me permanence.

But there was no clearing, no ember of meaning that I could decipher in my teacher's words.

Filipino, Rosario. Filipino!

I stared at Mrs. Majablanca's suspenseful, comma-shaped hair as she repeated her question.

I stood in the back of the room and looked around me, at my classmates. I recognized the boy who sewed sequins at Young's Fashionne House, the tailoring prodigy was named Elvis Oras, his arms were clasped before him, his mouth was puckered, his eyes looked sideways at me, darting, his chin up in the air. Everyone was sitting neat and quiet in their rows, staring at the posters on the wall. Then they'd glance back at me, twisting their mouths, and then stare at the posters, as if afraid to register my embarrassment.

Trinatrono Almendras, the girl in pigtails (but she did not have my Saturn rings), was raising her hand, glaring at me, and with her other hand, she kept waving at the wall, as if to tell me I was going to the guillotine while she knew all the answers.

And the teacher repeated, *Rosario, Filipino!*

Did Mrs. Majablanca not see I was wearing a corsage, that it was my first day of school, that no matter how much she repeated the words, I had just arrived from Wilmington, Los Angeles, in California, with none of their languages to comfort me, and no matter how many times she repeated her question, I would have no answer?

Her mouth bubbled a string of dark matter.

None of the lists in my notebook could save me, I felt nausea in my bones.

"I don't understand," I finally said.

Her voice was sharp, and her grin was evil.

"Who do you think you are with your corsage and braided hair, looking like a satellite of Saturn, coming to school only when you want like a prima donna, pretending you are a replica of Adina an guapa, when you're really just a Filipino child who does not know her own language? Come to the front of the room!"

I only guessed what she was saying because my body was warm, I felt tears coming on as I understood her last phrase—it was in English.

My body was weak, I felt the heat of my breathing, my starched, uniformed chest, my tight, painful braids, I seemed to be going past a hundred rows of unmoving stares, while I moved from the back to the front, but I kept my tears in because I was also my mother's child. *It is not my fault*, I thought, *that I do not know your words. I am the daughter of Adina an guapa. No one can conquer me.* I stood at the front of the room, underneath the posters of the multiplied boy at his desk with a book, posed in the slight variations of his studious comportment.

I faced my classmates, William McKinley Maceda, Trinatrono Almendras, Ferdinand Enage Dumpit.

I had never in my life been punished.

I had been in Gifted classes in Wilmington because I had learned to read too early, I missed kindergarten because I was special, we were taken to the Zoo and to science labs, and we skipped class to go to museums and advance our learning. The unlucky ones—the sad white kids of Wilmington whose mothers did not wash their clothes by hand in huge plastic bowls or have their own clever bathing tool, called the tabo, or pray novenas to the Blessed Virgin (my mom said *never touch the white kids, they are not Catholic!*), the neighborhood boys who snatched my braids and tried to run me over with their bikes—they had to stay behind in school adding up dumb apples in their boring Math books because they were not Gifted, like me.

I understood I was going to stand before the rest of the class like Jesus before the Pharisees until the lesson was over. Kids raised their hand to answer Mrs. Majablanca's question. One by one they answered, and as I watched my fearful classmates I realized that *every single answer* to Mrs. Majablanca's questions was written on the posters on the wall. Each kid stared at the wall above me. They were just mouthing the words on the posters. The posters, it turned out, told us the Ten Rules of Good Reading and Right Conduct, illustrated in solemn poses by the kid with the book and khaki shorts, in the kilometrical syllables of that language, Tagalog, that turned out was foreign to all of us in the classroom, not just me.

So Trinatrono Almendras told me during recess.

My classmates were not my enemies, they were united in their hatred of Tagalog class, which they called Pilipino, and they had only scorn for stuck-up Mrs. Majablanca, a snob who thought only people from Manila mattered, and they explained how they had been trying to help me by pointing with their mouths and chins to the posters.

Didn't I see them helping me—with their mouths?!

But I understood only Trinatrono Almendras.

She explained everything in her impressive, solemn English, which was as kilometrical as my shame. She herself was born in Manila, like her mother, as she kept repeating to anyone in hearing, but she had a command of language and of the world of second graders at Divine Word Missionary School that made us hold our tongues.

Trinatrono was smaller than all of us—a frizzy-haired child with Chinese eyes, called singkit, and the fact that she wore glasses only added to her aspect of a sage gnome.

She spoke with authority beyond our reach.

"It was outrageous for Wild Gamao to persecute you like that."

She used those fourth-grade words, *outrageous* and *persecute*. She spoke her verdict on Wild Gamao (*what's a wild gamao?!*) like a lawyer, and we stood around her in a circle as she revealed the meaning of the moment we had just experienced.

"You are ignorant, but she was unfair."

I nodded at the clarity of her summary, though when I saw William McKinley Maceda and Ferdinand Enage Dumpit and Lorelei Pastillas and Margot (pronounced with a *T*) Abella and Queen Sirikit Alonzo and Benito Lupak and Winston Querer and Elvis Oras nodding, too eager to pity me, I wished to raise my hand to disagree.

"We must report her to the principal, but they are all collaborators, you know. That is the problem. They collaborate, these teachers. So we need a good plan."

"What is collaborate?" said a girl, her jaw remaining open in awe before Trinatrono Almendras—a beautiful, fat-cheeked child standing apart from us, Divina May Kiring—yes, it is she, the famous Bahrain Doll, she was our childhood friend in Tacloban—but at the time she was nicknamed Sirit for her lackluster participation in recess games.

She never understood what was going on and so gave up, never joining.

That's why she was called Sirit, I learned—it meant, *that's it, I give up!*

But Trinatrono always calmly explained the rules, even to Sirit.

"Collaborate is to be an enemy of the good," said Trinatrono Almendras. "You know they will collaborate even though she takes our snacks at recess, you know that Majablanca, that Wild Gamao, took my bag of M&M's, it was a Christmas gift from my ninang in the States, I had saved it up for up to Three Kings!, they will not do a thing if we tell them how she punishes us for knowing the right answer to her wrong questions, like when she asked what is the capital of Portugal, whoever thought that was a good thing to know, and I said Lisbon, and she said wrong, the capital is Oporto! Remember how I showed her my dad's *World Book Encyclopedia*, and it told her the truth? What kind of a teacher punishes you for the right answer? She's a dictator, a tuta!"

Despite the frenzy of her facts, Trinatrono Almendras, in her glasses, always spoke with grave composure, like a Thumbelina-sized Mahatma Gandhi.

"But isn't tuta a puppy?" I asked.

It was one word I knew from wandering the seawall with my cousins in Salogó.

"Correct," said Trina. "But tuta is also puppet. You know, like puppet of imperialism. You're welcome. Now you know."

She pointed to a kid with a cowlick on his brow like my mom's Os.

"Benito," she said to the boy even smaller than Trinatrono, wearing comical long pants, "remember she likes your ice candy?"

What everyone knew about Benito, I learned, was that he sold ice candy during recess to help pay for his Catholic-school tuition, he never even changed his pants, he was a child in need, and kids bought his goods in solidarity and greed.

Benito nodded.

"She never pays."

"I know what to put in her ice candy," said Trinatrono.

With the prospect of Mrs. Majablanca's death by poisoning for the sin of asking me a question in Tagalog, I failed to sleep that night after my first day of school in Tacloban.

I have a restless organ of collaboration, I begin to feel sympathy for even villains once their doom is apparent, I used to spend anxious days as a child thinking of the agony of Judas Iscariot once he kissed Jesus and was on his way to hell. The whole night I imagined Mrs. Majablanca's tortured face, which was already full of mosquito scars, her nest of hair in a bind and mostly choking her sweaty neck after she ate Benito Lupak's entire ice candy only to find warts and lesions of leprous plague multiplying on her body because she was obsessive about Good Reading and Right Conduct.

During recess that day, after the Pledge of Allegiance and the National Anthem, after the entire school's Good-Morning calisthenics during the Flag Ceremony, after Religion then Tagalog, I sat at my desk, my arms clasped on its long arm, keeping my pee in, I was not looking forward to the images of carnage to be done in my name, as Benito offered ice candy in grape flavor to Mrs. Majablanca.

Mrs. Majablanca kept eating, slurping the purple juice, smiling at nothing in particular because we were all looking away then looking again, waiting for disaster.

"De puta nga yawa nga iya iroy, nga Benito ka, nga birat ka nga bata ka. Come here to the front!"

Grape flavor was spurting from her nose, she finally had the look of a wild gamao, a feathery flying duck with crazy hair, she kept shaking herself, her head, her lips, her ears, her hair, from the effects of the sili sunk deep in her ice candy, the hot chili pepper from the garden of Trina's well-read, crazy dad, the Widower Almendras. Mrs. Majablanca cursed and shrieked and spewed ice candy in front of us, the collaborators, while we sat at our desks in shock at our victory. This was how Trinatrono Almendras consolidated her power among second-graders at Divine Word Missionary School—she enacted justice in thrilling ways.

Teeny-tiny Benito, on the other hand, had to plead his innocence before Mrs. Majablanca and was going to be sent to the principal, who was actually my Tita Patchy, my mom's cousin, a woman I had no clue about but Trinatrono Almendras knew of our ties.

It was I who was to plead Benito's cause.

So Trinatrono Almendras declared.

My classmates crowded around me at recess.

They tore at the plastic of their ice candy, slobbering and excited, they kept saying only I could do it, the girl with the corsage and the many-ringed over-braided hair—I must put in a word with the principal, who was my aunt Tita Patchy.

I was flattered at my importance, but I could feel a warring buzz in my stomach, which felt like fear, and it contradicted my vanity, and I had no idea who Tita Patchy was.

Trinatrono Almendras told me it was my duty, and she gave me the words for teeny-tiny Benito's liberation: advocate, civil disobedience, tyranny. Narrate! She told me to advocate, that inserting the sili in the ice candy was just a form of civil disobedience against Mrs. Majablanca's tyranny. It was just like being Mahatma Gandhi! She told me to narrate my woes to the principal about Mrs. Majablanca and the posters of Good Reading and Right Conduct.

I thought my classmates were correct, it was not right that Benito was being punished when the sili came from Trinatrono's garden, but why was Trinatrono's part in our conspiracy not included in the story?

Trinatrono looked at me with scorn.

"Never reveal the Queen of Spades if you do not need to show it."

I soon learned the source of Trinatrono Almendras's mystical wisdoms, but my first encounters with them in their organic state are etched in my memory. Trinatrono dragged all of us to the principal's office, with the name embossed on the door: *Mrs. B. Empanada.* I noticed the principal had the name of a snack, a word I already knew. It was a savory, filled with ground beef and peas. We went in double file, the way Trinatrono said the student street marchers did in Manila, on television—teeny-tiny Benito, the sadly accused, up front with me, his advocate, and Trinatrono's disciples behind us in pairs,

William McKinley Maceda and Ferdinand Enage Dumpit, Margot (rhymes with igot) Abella and Queen Sirikit Alonzo, Elvis Oras and Lorelei Pastillas, and Winston Querer should have had a partner, except that Divina May Kiring, also called Sirit, lagged behind, not sure it was a game her beauty queen looks should join.

My aunt the principal, Tita Patchy, was a stern lady with black marks on her face that looked designed: a symmetrical triplet of moles, with hair. She had bloated cheeks that told me maybe she liked savories. She wore cat's-eye glasses. I was afraid of her smile—it was a Cheshire-cat smile, with her mole hairs like whiskers, and she would eat me if she could.

"Oh, Rosario, how are you?"

I got confused.

"Come, bless your Auntie Bonifacia. Remember?"

I stared at the thrifty constellation of the principal's moles.

She held out her hand and placed it right on my forehead, shortening the distance expected of respect, a generous innovation on lamano that I had not anticipated.

And I realized that I had met her before—at the funeral of my mom's Papá.

I remembered her cat whiskers, and I remembered the wreath with her name on it—*Mrs. B. Empanada and Family*—I remembered her name that was a funeral snack.

"What is it? Are your classmates bothering you?"

I looked behind me at my new world in Tacloban, my classmates in double file in khaki shorts and pink pleated skirts made of tetoron cotton almost identical to mine, except theirs was soft and mine was starched and stupid, holding hands with their fierce, brave partners in our second-grade indignation rally for justice.

I looked down at the tight pigtails of Trinatrono Almendras, a whole head shorter than me, who stared up firm, unmoving, with her dark, intent eyes on Tita Patchy.

Also, Trinatrono looked like she'd throttle me if I didn't say the right thing.

I looked beside me, at teeny-tiny Benito with his too-long pants and ashen face and a white film of dry mouth that established he had no mother to wipe him in the morning with a labakara.

The whole world of justice and crime and punishment was on my shoulders.

And it was only my second day of school in Tacloban.

I felt my tight Saturn braids—I had slept on my braids during the night, disturbed by my unremembered dreams.

I felt the painful stretch of hair across my bursting brain.

I broke down.

I began to cry.

I wailed with my hands on my tears. I pushed my fists into my eyes. The sound of my bawling surprised me, I had never heard it so loud before, and worse it was in public.

My ears hurt and my nose gave off a stream washing over my chin and embarrassing me.

I took the handkerchief of a classmate, scalloped in lace embroidery with his name, Elvis, in careful cursive, which I noticed even as I took it, thinking how I would ruin it, his nice, clean, cross-stitched name.

Throughout my time at Divine Word Missionary School, the tidy, hygienic ways of my classmates marked their honor and the prospect of my humiliation in their eyes.

"What's wrong? What is it?" asked the principal.

I howled.

And so it was Trinatrono Almendras who explained everything to my stern aunt, Tita Patchy.

In her adult English, looking like the Thumbelina-sized version of Mahatma Gandhi, she told the whole story of the posters, and the Tagalog question of Mrs. Majablanca, and she blew up the shameful moment of my spectacle in Tagalog class so that by the time her story was finished, the ice-candy crime of Benito Lupak was only a weird and inevitable sidelight to the tale of my ignorance.

Trinatrono Almendras had a way of combining oratory with hand gestures, her eyeballs bulging out and so focused on you it was impossible to imagine her story's gaps. I was weeping but impressed, Benito was absolved of his sins, and who knows what my stern aunt Tita Patchy said to the poisoned Mrs. Majablanca.

All we knew was that after Trinatrono spoke, we won, and we scattered to the playground by St. Paul's Creek to play bulangkoy until the sun went down.

In the days to follow, Trinatrono took me under her wing as if I were her disabled charge, a deaf-mute with no understanding of the world around me. I learned her real name was Trina, and Trono was her mother's name, but she held on to her middle name like her anchor, an attached limb, because her mother was dead. Trina Trono manipulated people for their own good, and I was comfortable being treated this way because it allowed me to take in my new world without too many distractions. I went to school, rolling my black rectangle of a bag full of waxed notebooks with my secret glossaries and alphabetical lists, and every day I trailed Trina Trono, squire to her knight-errant, I listened, I learned, I collected phrases and languages without quite knowing how I acquired them, I acted like a spy figuring out clues and decoding messages, and by the time my apprenticeship was done, the world of Tacloban was illuminated for me through my silence—its vicious gossip and banal lies, its hierarchical moods and superficial wounds, its mysterious prejudices and shallow hopes—Tacloban had become my norm, without my quite knowing it, never to be erased from me, imprinted as if by an anvil, by Panday Pira.

Until the time she left us for Manila, where her crazy father, the Widower Almendras, resumed his job as a radical professor after his legendary grief for his vanished bride, Trina's prematurely dead mom, I was Trina Trono's pet.

She protected me from malice, such as her defense of my corsage from Lorelei Pastillas's libel.

It was November (Tio Nemorino had just won his election for mayor with the victorious Nacionalista Party—*Re-Elect Ferdinand!*), and Lorelei made a joke about the outfit I wore on my first day of school.

Four of us, including Sirit, the living baby doll, were playing jack-stones, creating multiple triangles out of our outstretched legs on the concrete patch by St. Paul's Creek.

"You're just bitter," Trina said to Lorelei, watching Lorelei's jack-stone moves with her intent eyes, "because your mom manages the lukaret on Juan Luna Street, instead of making corsages for you."

"Oh," said beautiful Sirit, mouthing her distress.

Sirit hated conflict.

Lorelei's lip trembled but she did not speak as she made Around-the-Worlds and Onesies-Twosies.

I immediately felt pity for Lorelei though I only pretended to understand Trina's revelation. What were lukaret? I willed Lorelei to complete her final tricks so she could win the game—Ferris Wheel, Lollipop, Double Trouble—but sure enough Lorelei's weak spirit failed her.

She tripped on Falling Star.

Sirit, always the follower, collected the jacks to give them all to Trina, next to her.

"It's not your fault, though," Trina said, taking her turn, spreading out the stones and sweeping up one after another of the colored jacks, not skipping a beat, concentrating on the game—"that's just your mother's job, it's a good job, but you should not be mean to others just because your mom also takes care of the prostitutes, and not just you."

Sirit looked like she was going to cry for Lorelei.

Once again, Trina won.

Trina Trono always had a sore truth to tell. When later we met up, Lorelei, Trina, and I, reunited in college, and in the same freshman dorm, too, at Kalayaan, where Trina shed her last name, defined only by what she loved, her mother's memory, it was Trina Trono who took me to the lightning rallies against martial law, and then later the rebellion and its denouement—the ouster of the first dictator. Lorelei would have nothing to do with us. But at Diliman in our freshman year, I was obedient once again without question before Trina Trono's sense of right. Even now, if Trina called me, and she returned to her old certainties—instead of the scurrilous capitalism that is now her calling, agent of grave robbers and publisher of canards—I would follow Trina to the end of the barricades, past the barbed wire fences, to revolution, if she blew that horn.

Tacloban versus Salogó

My phone died, and I didn't charge it. I kept my computer on, and the FB notifications kept pinging, saying to me *inday, inday, inday,* so I shut off Messenger notifications. But still I got private messages on Twitter, on Instagram, I got likes on old posts about my novels. The private requests were in ghost sections of my online persona—the spaces of neither followers nor friends. I did not open them. I kept to my schedule for my book, climbing up to write on the roof deck, which had no electrical outlets, and I pretended that if I kept working on my laptop and lost memory, I would be okay. Every summer once school was done, my mother sent me and Adino off on the jeepney from Tacloban back to her family's old home in Salogó, the rotting home of the Delgados of Leyte.

Salogó marked my separation from my schoolmates.

It existed off the map.

My classmates laughed at the town's name. I dimly understood it was a symbol—of backwardness, Neanderthals, like creatures of the Cretaceous period from the *World Book Encyclopedia.* The red-shit place. My classmates called Salogó red-shit-red-shit because all the people did in Salogó, they said, was drink tubâ, the coconut wine.

Trina Trono, who overeducated herself with her father's books, said once—*hmph, don't mind them.* We were about to graduate from sixth grade, and she looked up from her book.

If Emma Bovary had been born in Tacloban, she declared, she would have strangled herself with an abaca fan the minute she came out of the womb! Hah! No need to wait for the slow death of growing up among the boring people of Tacloban!

Easy for her to say, I thought, she was leaving even before the graduation ceremony to help open up their home in Teacher's Village. Every day she talked about her house where she had once lived with her mother in Manila. One of its rooms held only books and an electric fan, she boasted—nothing else could fit, it has so many books!

I had no idea who Emma Bovary was, but I got the gist.

Whereas in Tacloban our best pleasure was Bruce Lee movies, plus the seasonal arrival of James Bond, especially when he was still Sean Connery, since Roger Moore was a pale shadow—at brand-new Kyrex Theater and Rovic Gold. Above all, for the maids in the kitchen who were my childhood heroes, the gift of the gods was Nora Aunor.

Who cared about that chubby elite, Vilma Santos, a white-skinned blot on Mana Marga's universe (though even Mana Marga admitted Vilma was a good swing dancer)? Who cared about elections, typhoon seasons, presidential proclamations, when the movies of Nora Aunor and Sean Connery appeared at Kyrex and Rovic Gold, and sometimes at Bonanza Theatre that only did second-run?

Mana Marga, who stayed on with us when we moved to Tacloban, my mom's faithful, made-up avatar in her kind of too-big, Daisy-Duck heels would hustle us after school to Orchestra. The upper level, Balcony, was for the lovers. Rats lived in Orchestra, gnawing at our shoes, but we just put up our feet and never moved.

For kids, the actions of the lovers on Balcony were more terrifying than the rats.

Once, Mana Marga and I were at the movies, sitting through *Lollipops and Roses at Burong Talangka* for the third time in one afternoon. Watching movies in Tacloban was a timeless habit, that is, you didn't care what time you came in. We entered when the movie was half over, then we stayed in for the next show and saw the whole movie through, and the third time Mana Marga was humming the words to "Close To You" even before Nora could begin (all the movies came late to Tacloban after we read about them in *Song-Hits*, and once they came Mana Marga at Kyrex stayed in her seat after the credits in order to imprint Nora's sweet dreams—boating in Central Park with the wrong blondie, Don Johnson, or losing her heart in Blue Hawaii to her true love Tirso—onto her own unbalanced, high-heeled frame, in Orchestra with the rats). But we never finished that third round of *Lollipops and Roses at Burong Talangka* because the siren from TEIPCO began screaming at the wrong hour, four o'clock, and the entire cinema burst onto the streets, and it turned out it was only that damned Marshall Lo, said Mana Marga—*ah buwisit*, said Mana Marga, *TEIPCO's siren was just practicing the curfew, and now we missed the movie.*

Ay kabuwisit hito nga Marshall Lo.

In the alternate truth, the movie was *Sleeping Beauty*, because my mom told Mana Marga if we were going to Kyrex we could watch only Disney, so when we went to see *Live and Let Die* or *Blue Hawaii*, Mana Marga told us to say we saw *Dumbo* or *Cinderella*. I ended up not getting those movies right, and anyway, the whale's teeth in *Pinocchio* were as scary as the scorpions in *Diamonds are Forever*. In truth Adina an guapa, making her art and lampshades, never looked like she cared. And so my other memory is watching *Sleeping Beauty* on the first day of curfew, a story about falling under an amnesiac spell, limbs and cooks and spinning wheels stopped in motion, a kingdom soon to be covered by a thicket of brambles. I always remember that movie as violent.

Being a Nora-lover was incurable, a malady bequeathed to me, so I have this involuntary weepy feeling whenever I see grainy snatches of class-conscious romances, with random musical episodes—the local color of those times. Mana Marga and Man' Leon, a tricycle driver, her crush, would kill us with their eyes if we moved from our seats in Orchestra and made them miss a single scene in the sagas of their beloveds—Nora Aunor and Sean Connery.

My other pleasure in Tacloban was the stories of the ghosts and the duwendes and the witches.

Mga aswang ngan mga panulay.

Our labanderas from San Jose had intimate knowledge of magical dwarves who lived in malunggay trees, and the costureras of Gomez Street, who measured me for my school uniforms and later costumes for playground demonstrations for the First Lady's future birthday visits, liked to gossip about the vampira of TEIPCO, half-bat, half-ballroom dancer howling up on the roof of the ice plant for no reason anyone could understand—it's just that in Tacloban there was a vampira up on the roof of TEIPCO, a lonely figure in a butterfly outfit.

We looked up at TEIPCO's siren waiting with the entire Nora-loving city now anxious to get tricycle rides back home that day after the fiasco with *Lollipops and Roses at Burong Talangka*. The cinema would not let us back in without paying again, and Mana Marga cursed once more. But when we got to Housing it was even worse. There was no TV. The maids, Candy and Delilah, were staring at gray slides on the television, signifying The End of the day's programming, though it was only five o'clock, and *Would You Believe* with Inday Badiday, the gossip show that had only one topic, the love team of Nora and Tirso, also known as Guy and Pip (it was a no-brainer, except to me, that everyone in showbiz had an alias, a secret name of affection, that everyone else knew), was supposed to be on. My mom was away, I think in Zamboanga, and we had the house to ourselves—me with the *World Book Encyclopedia*, and the maids to their shows—*Spin-a-Win* and *Dance Fever* with Deney Terrio, whom I thought was Filipino, so I was proud one day to learn in *Song-Hits* that he, a Filipino, had taught John Travolta how to dance. But nothing was on. The next day, Adino's Japanese cartoons did not appear, and he broke Delilah's bakya on the TV set trying to pop *Mazinger Z* out of the dead box. Just wait until ten o'clock, I said, when *Voltes V* does not come on, and there will be hell to pay in Housing. But I was only joking, and ten o'clock came and there was no *Voltes V*. I got concerned. Still, I had no time for his baby drama, and I went to the kitchen where the maids were whispering about Marshall—Marshall this Marshall that. He was like some Chinese gangster, Mr. Marshall Lo, come to collect tong in the gambling den in the Sunday kung fu movies, my favorite thing on the weekends. All day on Sunday we only had Chinese shows with women who could do flying kicks over balconies. I even liked the ads, for Caronia nail polish (*cocara so charming, manicura!*—*Confucius saaay*—*it's Ca-ro-ni-aaaa!*), with the Japanese-like Twiggy-looking people, the tandem models saying lines so garbled I'd stay glued to the kung fu intermissions trying to figure out the ad, whether it was really *Confucius say*—or *for lovely naaaail*—? But Sunday came with no kung fu, and worst of all, for everyone in the kitchen, there was no *Superstar!*, the singing and dancing extravaganza starring the diminutive, spectacular, and heartbreaking Nora Aunor.

My life was split between the world of the kitchen and the world of the sala—my mom's perfumed world of sequined matronas playing mah-jongg after praying the Novena to the Wounds of Our Lord, and the powerful universe of Mana Marga, whose business was to know the sins of all the praying matronas, my mom's bouffant-haired friends who smelled of mossy churches and *Chanel Number 5*.

That time of Marshall Lo was the time of the banishment of my favorite among my mom's praying matrons, potty-mouthed Mana Talia, who disappeared after her love, Congressman Quintana, rebelled, or revealed. Nothing made sense. Soon enough we would hear it all from Mrs. Conrada, she of the highest hair, the mayor-doma of the mah-jongg crowd who was soon to become Important Lady, wearing blue all the time and organizing events for her boss, whom she would call Madame. Madame this Madame that. Sometimes called Meldy, sometimes Madame. Madame was the partner of Marshall Lo—*Re-Elect Ferdinand!* Tacloban was not fit to hear the news from Manila now that the TV studios were shut down, and even the radio had been abducted, and the Con-Constitution was finally passed, with a sigh of relief from all the high-heeled mah-jongg players, and the bombers of Plaza Miranda were soon to be in prison, shot, or exiled. So we understood the loss of *Would You Believe*, and *Voltes V*, and the kung fu movies, and *Superstar!*—Marshall Lo took out all the TV studios for the good of the people of Tacloban, so we would not know the horrible news of the world from TV, just from gossip. Then one day, just like that, Adino did his ritual morning kicking of the box wearing Delilah's broken bakya, he turned the dial, and a man playing the cello on the street emerged. An American. An ugly, skinny boy with curly hair. He was part of a marching band, dragging a chair on the street so he could sit and play his cello with his moveable band. There was a voiceover by a woman with a crabby outlook, narrating the skinny boy's life. I sat rapt. Adino ran away, unimpressed with things that were not Japanese or robots. It was the story of a kid named Virgil, a sad boy of the slums who grew up to be a thief and a cello player. I watched this movie over and over, riveted. It was brilliant. It was all the TV would play in those first few weeks of martial law when the studios in Manila went black and the regime had yet to figure out what to do with the nation it had stolen and they played pirated movies from some art lover's stash. *Take the Money and Run.*

From my bedroom on Juan Luna Street, I could see the city, its layers of imbricating roofs that stacked middle-class ruin against shanty-town decay, and the concrete storm walls of Chinese and Filipino usurers and their pals, the gamblers and their goons, and the downtown grocery stores and mangrove-hacking lumber shops pressed against chicken coops and fish markets and glassware shops and jagged sidewalks that doubled as sewers where we kids played, during the monsoon season.

Trina visited past curfew hour—we spent our time indoors watching *Take the Money and Run,* and when that phenomenon was over we went through the encyclopedias again (she liked *H,* with the plastic overlays of the human body, I liked *M,* which had Greek mythology), then there were the suddenly appearing Grosset and Dunlap flipside books, during the season of rains. We made up games. Little-Women-Little-Women was always just a fight over who'd play Jo. For a while I pretended Beth was the best because Trina Trono always got her way. We spoke in the Tagalog of the Aztecs, following the lead of a hero from Mana Marga's joyful mysteries, her *Hiwaga* komiks: *Sene ke be? Enget ke ren! Eyew ke neng tenepe*—we drove the maids nuts: *Rosario, stop it already!*

But it was not our fault the Aztecs in the komiks had only one vowel, *e*. *Eng-eng-eng-eng*, we'd shriek. We were playing Virgil-Virgil, with Trina as Woody Allen the cello player and me as the chair, hopping along on Mana Marga's waxed cement floors, and in between we did the voiceovers—*On December first, Mrs. William Starkwell, the wife of a New Jersey handyman, gave birth to her only child*—when the catfish started swimming into the sala. Pretty soon both Trina and I were standing on the chairs, she on the blue ottoman that had finally arrived one day from estados, from Wilmington, Los Angeles, along with the wet-look miniskirts and the faux-Tiffany lamps and the linoleum TV trays streaked in gold-and-olive ombré and a washer and a dryer and a refrigerator, all in a bunch of boxes as tall as Mana Marga with the sender's name *U.S. Navy* stamped in large stencil, like the tardy closing credits of our life in the United States.

The house was flooded from the monsoon, almost reaching the pale-blue flesh of the ottoman from my mom's favorite place, Sears, and I watched the waves slosh upward, toward Trina's toes, and the whiskers of the catfish, wandering in from the garden's gutters and the floodlands of Leyte, looked like lost antennae, as if they were feeling without radar for a way out of the city, just like us.

Women in long skirts that they wrapped about their legs then tied at their waist in businesslike knots came out with their gihay after the storm, and that whish-whish-whish of street-cleaning gihay—stiff brooms made of the midribs of coconut fronds, bunched at the top by abaca twine and slashing at debris like so many tentacles commanded by the maids' strong arms—that fierce sound of women's gihay cleaning up the city in the monsoon season clarified my childhood in the time of Marshall Lo.

Charcoal smoke from caramel desserts steamed from the corner plywood stall on Juan Luna Street—Mana Belen's kamote cue and banana cue sizzling in their sugar glut, the bubbling kalamay like boiling suns. The burnt sugar smell of merienda comes over me sometimes though all I smell up on this roof deck is diesel fumes likely from a movie truck. My memory is so deprived that the least con-junctions move me. Duwende and communists and vampira and food vendors and gamblers and conquistadors and singing contestants and aswang and fashionistas hovered above Tacloban's geography, which was quite limited actually, in a strictly cartographic sense. When we moved to our last place, on Juan Luna Street, my world was bound on the northwest by the harbor downtown, against Panalaron Bay, with its hotels unfinished since some earthquake in 1908, or 1968, and the makeshift stalls of mat weavers, immortal artists of ephem-eral grass, who have been underselling their talents since the days we killed Magellan, and the sellers of binagol, domed coconut desserts wrapped in pandan, everyone's last-minute pasalubong before you ride the tragic boats, lining the way to the tourist hotels. Southeast of us, winding down Real, was the airport, with its view of goats and carabaos and still-life fishermen from the runway, at the Pacific edge of the water, running into the gulf.

Conquerors had been landing upon our city since the sixteenth century, but no one, least of all us, its people, could care less. We faced the Pacific with a shrug. The Typhoon Path—but what of that? Typhoons lashed, and we treated them like pests, locusts, or fire ants. They savaged but did not conquer us.

We sweep them out with gihay.

Lunop.

Lunop is our peril—but we sweep that, too, under the rug, into our inop—our dreams.

Damage is in our genes, a cancerous lump. But who bothers to trace the source? It is nothing for us to be thrown to the winds. Nature is our unpredictable friend, the one we tolerate but do not like. We let nature do to us what we would do to nature.

It destroys us in order to be free. We destroy it in order to live.

Patas la.

Stalemate.

We limit our grand passions to petty feuds.

What raised pride was an Enemy: the scent of the other, whether a Tagalog from Manila; or Mormons in stupid suits knocking on our doors looking like Electrolux vacuum salesmen and coming to convert us to their Disneyland religion when we had just come from stupefying Mass already with our too-devout Pope-loving mothers; or the Chinese because they owned all the shops; or some Spanish Jesuit washing up without rhyme or reason in 1603; or a balding national politician born somewhere else (much to his chagrin when he comes for our votes, and all we want to know is the family name of his mother); or a sorry classmate who vacations in a forlorn town, like Salogó.

To reach Salogó you left the whiff of sea and braved bumpy roads cracked and pocked like Martian dunes, traveling inland into the jaws of—coconuts. I felt Mana Marga's resignation, too, as she packed our bags for our summer days without Nora Aunor, Kyrex, and Sundays with *Superstar!* It always seemed like an ending though it was the beginning of vacation. She was leaving her afternoon tricycle drives with Man' Leon through Magsaysay Boulevard (she bribed me with komiks not to tell). We knew we would be gone for months, the summer haze of April through June, with only the deader days of Lent as our reprieve. As usual she packed the *Song-Hits* and the *Hiwaga* and *Aliwan* komiks, including the tales of Zuma and the indelible sidekick who for no good Aztec reason could speak that one vowel, messing up my learning of Tagalog. *Eng lengket neye. Beket ke genyen.* Rosario, stop! The Aztec jester could hold up his head sideways only, hence his broken vocal cords and singular sound, his language engendering endless zest, never redressed. Later I read of a writer doing something similar in French, but *Hiwaga*, you know, had done it in installments a long time ago. Mana Marga told me I could take only two books, books were heavy, and she herself chose *Imelda Romualdez Marcos: A Biography* by Kerima Polotan, so that I was cursed to read it over and over (actually it possessed me, being the only book I read that had descriptions of Tacloban in it), and I chose that damned gift from my father, *The Secret of Larkspur*

Lane. She stashed Johnson's Baby Powder, her multiple globules of magic potion, a.k.a. Tiger Balm, her never-cold bottles of Mirinda for Adino and Lem-O-Lime for my annoying guts, and the individual packets of SkyFlakes plus White Rabbit candy, which never kept me from vomiting and still she believed in its potency, and finally she wrapped her goods up in all the labakara that she could fit into the olive-green military duffel, still stained with my dad's name, bound for Salogó.

The feeling of attachment that oppresses me now begins with this unpaved sense of alienation. Coconuts and coconuts and bananas and coconuts in inescapable, inland green, a horizon of palms with no end. The heart of greenness. I hated that ride. I vomited even before I got onto the jeep. I hated the song Mana Marga sang, urging her soul to accept her fate. She sang with well-rehearsed expression, a Waraywaray Nora Aunor with the palms rushing by and her voice hoarse and eternal, patting my nauseous head with her lukewarm labakara as if clamminess would make it all better. Lubi lubi lubi enero pebrero marso abril mayo. The months went on forever. *An asô waray kitaa!* The dust roads left no room for sentiment about the lushness of the tropics. The rattling jeepneys were no help, supposed to be only *based* upon American jeeps lying about in postwar heaps, not *actually* from World War II, but it seemed to me the jeepneys to Salogó, with their ramshackle guise of military surplus, were this alarming bricolage of history thrown together in the mere hope of cohering.

Summer in Salogó

Here on the roof deck, in these over-airconditioned days of global warming, I could smell it, or so I imagine, the light and battery fading in New York as I tap at these keys, my recall racing against the dark and the dying of my machine—I smell this brief, symptomatic tinge, the hiss and stench of Petromax lamps that dominated our arrival in Salogó. I threw up again when I arrived, that summer when I found

the opera book and the musical instrument and the antique journals with the gold lettering on the spine. But I always threw up. I
arrived at Salogó's bend, on the first sign of a concrete road named
after my great-grandfather, Cong. J. B. Delgado Street. I got out with
that feeling of having been flung from the corrugated trembling
of that tin-can galley, tottering as I clambered onto the dust, smelling
as usual of vomit and Lem-O-Lime, Mana Marga's drink of choice
for nausea.

Salogó was lit at dusk by kerosene and candles.

Peeking out through the roof deck's steel rails, a northward glint,
that gray spire of Manhattan appears incongruous in the light.
Soon there will be the moon. Like a game board's token—the archi-
tectural spine was just another dark, jagged thing until its colors lit
up, transforming its sky, and you remembered what it was. The top
of the Empire State Building. An idle sight that still surprised me,
a distraction from where I was. The Empire State looked small and
inconsequential, not so much a legend but a wish. Salogó did not get
full-fledged electrical wiring until the century was just about done,
three presidents and a rebellion after the funeral of my mom's Papá.
The sound of old men pumping away at Petromax lamps—hiss hiss
hiss hooo-ooosss!—who seemed to have been slaving away from the
time of the chronicles of Padre Chirino in 1603 mixed with the sounds
of Angelus, so that Salogó's spell was always medieval—prayers and
oppressed farmers, plus the slow advent of science burping light into
shape.

We were condemned for months to the sole care of Mana Marga,
who marched us to the balcony that overlooked the river, with its
noncommittal view of Carigara, and the buckets and soap and
labakara were already positioned for our torture as Mana Marga
threatened us with the tabo over our heads, splashed us with water
from the pails, cleaned out our nostrils and ears and armpits of the
daylong journey's dust. The soap water drained through the balcony's slats, and when I opened my eyes I watched suds running
from our feet down toward the river. Then she made us eat rice and

tinapâ, plus her treat, banana cue, so that she could gossip into the night with the vendor, her aunt Nay Carmen, an ancient woman with the odd, though also kind of normal—everything fantastical was kind of normal in Salogó—look of a Disney witch. Then Mana Marga arranged the huge mosquito netting over our mats on the floor that spanned the sala's length, she had yet to prepare the grown-ups' rooms, which had the beds, I took it for granted the kama was not for kids, sleeping on mats was our adventure, and then she began snoring right beside us on the floor, under the phantasmal moskitero, as if the entire day were aimed toward this moment, when Mana Marga could sleep.

Every summer, I had no idea where my mother went.

The absolute darkness of the unelectrified town as I lay on the mat was bloated by my worry over her absence.

The black sky peeking out from the window was a mound of terror. Only the breeze playing with the moskitero gave me a sense that darkness had other dimensions. An entire midnight town lit only by moonlight and fugitive stars—that powerful whiff of doused paraffin and betrayal lulled me to sleep in Salogó, and soon not even moonlight pierced the capiz shades.

My mom's farewell figure that morning on the porch in Housing, a signal of our doom as she kissed us, smelling so early of Clairol hairspray and already dressed up in her silver-lined caftan (*where was she going without us?!*), was a moment I repressed. I avoided her lips. The jeepney trip moving away from Tacloban was only the measure of our abandonment. My vomit was the gastric residue of its effects.

But once Nay Carmen returned the next morning, this time with her basket of bibingka still steaming from the smoke of her old stone ovens, I forgot my mom.

The figure of the mother when she conditions us to our autonomy plants the seed for her destruction.

I was always busy in Salogó, making alphabet lists, reading novels about orphans, muttering the words of the sidekick of Zuma, *kenene be yen, eng behe nete!*, coveting Calumet cans and guava jelly jars in the kitchen and snatching them before they went into the trash. I made them into towns and families complete with middle names and nicknames, such as Bimboy and Chick-chick, who had feuds over pigs. *Eken eng bebey ne yen!* I followed the progress of the house's goats and baboy living in the underbelly of our home on dirt floors with the santan bushes and the gumamela, I followed the chickens' stations in life from boredom to death to tinola while I waited for the boys of Tio Nemor.

Tio Nemor's wife, the neuro, picture-perfect Doctor Tita Tita, my mom's perfumed in-law, liked to take her time sending off her kids to vacation with us in Salogó.

Adino, sweet Adino, was just a baby gurgling around the house with the yayas and labanderas, so he didn't count.

I was the only child walking about in that waxed and darkened house of prehistoric things—scarred planks, wounded tables, amputated rocking chairs. The huge portrait of Mister Cong. J. B. Delgado Street and his shy-looking wife, the small, ghostly Maria, also called Mama Bia, stared at me as I wandered, the pair looking as likely to have been human as the house's lace doilies and capiz windows. Dulled by time as the old décor, silenced and still, their eyes followed me as I walked the rooms.

I kept seeing them in the mirrors.

Sometimes, in the many mirrored doors of the cabinets, the man-sized aparador, I thought they could see me.

I examined all the needless objects of a neglected, intestate home—the grumpy gramophone that still worked, with the cry of a crank if I turned it, the broken bicycles in the yard, the waterlogged pictures of dead people with their cheeks and noses effaced, the sepia photos displayed on the many waxed, carved tables that also held, in neat, untouched piles, vinyl records with the logo of a dog winding up *His Master's Voice!*, plus a bound set of *Reader's Digest*s from 1966, and in the bedrooms lay stiff serpentina skirts, their mermaid tails folded to an antique crease and their backs dotted with the steel rust of *corchetes* in the time before zippers, empty Cortal aspirin bottles, toothpaste tins *for fighting caries!*, and on the balcony the intricately carved benches with messed up hemp that pricked your butt if you sat on them.

On the bookshelves in a near-empty bedroom, facing the water, were the Webster's Dictionary heavy as a baby and as awkward to hold and one more lot of *Reader's Digest*s.

In a bedroom drawer I unwrapped dirty but surprisingly crisp maps of numbered terrain, a few captioned Greenhills, two of Tacloban— one in San Jose, another in Reposo—stuck in a Manila folder along with documents in carbon-paper typescript with the name of my mom, Adina Delgado, in capitalized bold letters along with others from the funeral, some with the same names—Bonifacia Empanada, Bonifacia Delgado viuda de Maruya, my uncle Nemorino, and all the other names like an array of desserts. The document's heading said Court of Appeals, Republic of the Philippines. A legal case. *Delgado versus Delgado*. I put the Manila folder back in the heap. I was most fascinated by the maps of Leyte and the equatorial divisions of the world—in which the Antipodes were always us, contrary to my expectations, and strangely our archipelago was off-center, dangling, like a humpbacked creature, off of China.

The maps told me some error had been made. We were knocked from our perch where we should be, in the center of our world. Even now I feel that urge to reset them, to redesign my environment, like my mom.

I was looking for that doll, my mom's doll from Valencia, Spain, but instead I found the opera book in the glass confines of a rotting aparador, and I began reading about Donna Elvira and Don Giovanni, about mad Lucia and her soulful but stupid end, about the aimless travels of Tamino and his luckless phonemic twin Pamina in a fable of fantastic idiocy, *The Magic Flute*.

I have always hated Papageno.

I had no idea music was involved.

On the final page, I noted this epitaph in beautifully handwritten, flowing, and faded pen:

F. B. Delgado
Moret Street
Sampaloc
Manila
Philippines
Asia
Pacific Ocean
Earth
Universe

Waiting for my cousins, I reread the opera plots, bored out of my skull. *Foreigners*, I thought, simply observing, *were nuts.*

The people in F. B. Delgado's opera book lived in plots of truncated reason, and the acts of silly Spaniards and crazed Scots had this sharpened clarity in Salogó, that river town that blackened into immobility every five o'clock—where nothing ever happened.

Waray-waray.

Nothing-nothing.

That's all we did in Salogó.

Then the boys arrived with Doctor Tita Tita and Tio Nemor.

I spent the summer with Putt-putt on the verge of burning down the house again or falling to his death from the basketball court—though it turned out it was John-john who would break our hearts. I liked being the leader, because I was the oldest, and John-john was a follower because he was too beautiful to be bothered by details, and Putt-putt was always about to die, to no one's regret, including his. We played tumba-lata and holens and Going to Market, hunted frogs and salamanders with a sumpit made from the midrib of agoho trees or the slingshot that Tay Lucio carved from old wood and rubber tires. At high tide we dared Putt-putt to jump off the balcony into the river, playing his role as a doomed hero—*consummatum est!*—and sure enough he'd plop, diving straight down below us, always to raise up his hands as he hit the water, *V for Victory!*, grinning and swimming with polliwogs, Coke tansans, and shit.

When it was night and we had only the Petromax lamps and were all wet and tired from Mana Marga's vigorous ways with the scrub and tabo, the boys refused to play with my paper dolls or read a book, so I told the stories from opera, with the hiss of paraffin for song.

By the end of summer I was sick of us, our four-musketeering, our cousinhood bonds. I stopped laughing at John-john's jokes about wise-guy Juan Pusong and his Pusong pigs that he heard from the gang of smokers by Nay Carmen's open-air banana-cue stall. A man saw Juan Pusong lifting up his pig to eat from the guava trees. *Hoy, Juan, Juan, why are you lifting up your pig? You can save time by scattering the guavas on the ground. And Juan replies*, and John-john was already laughing so hard we could barely hear the punchline—*What's time to a pig?*

What's time to a pig?

We howled, repeated that phrase, which was in English—*what's time to a pig, what's time to a pig*—all around the AWOL.

The punchline of Salogó.

Even the ritual of bibingka got old, the way in Salogó the burnt tops of the rice cakes puckered so that they opened up, gorgeous like budding roses, tender and hot, sold out of a straw basket atop her head by a witch, Nay Carmen.

Nay Carmen smelled early in the morning of a weird combination of tobacco and pee and looked in no way like her opera counterpart— the gypsy with a sad end.

Nay Carmen looked like the gypsy's opposite: the Antipodes of Love.

When the cocks crowed, we heard her slippers like the hush-hush of humay, whisper of chaff on the street's dusty path. Her toothless jaw jutted out to meet her sharp, beaky nose, and she looked like a walking carpenter's vise, part object, part trauma. I'd watch her prog-ress up the vast staircase, her basket of bibingka balanced upon her head—a humid, unsteady crown she bore with the superior indiffer-ence of the expert. We were allowed only one each of Nay Carmen's bibingka, but I stole half of Mick-mick's, its crunchy burnt-rose crown, and I told Mick-mick that the soft, warm insides were the healthy

part, for babies, and every morning Mick-mick offered me his bibingka's crown. Mick-mick was already five but still learning to speak.
The maids called him *Mongo*, typical of their endearment, and they all
cuddled and petted five-year-old Mick-mick as if he were a baby like
Adino. They called John-john *Guapo*, for his obvious good looks, he
had rosy cheeks like an encanto, a Santo Niño, and they liked to groom
his hair carefully, like a dog's—his lush curly hair. And me they called
Libro, an insult, because to be a reader was just a kitchen word for lazy.
I trusted their verdict. Putt-putt they called *Disastro* because he was
always falling down staircases, plopping into the river, or breaking his
legs. That summer I named him *Sarastro*: he had nine lives and kept
surviving. As for my brother Adino, sweet Adino—he was just a baby,
too young to be called any names, but that, too, would change.

Maupaaaaay! said Nay Carmen.

Maupay! we replied.

It was always exciting to get up in the morning in Salogó, though
it was downhill from there.

I wondered why we never finished the phrase—maupay—nga
aga!—but that was the herald of the times.

Mornings were always good when Nay Carmen appeared with her
bibingka, made in an ancient stone orifice in the back of her smoky
home across the street, amid talahib and bamboo.

But that ritual got thin.

Putt-putt and I liked to feed Mick-mick the food we cooked in
the dirty-kitchen beneath the house, near the enormous mahogany
stairs, that underbelly of bamboo, molave, and mud where they
slaughtered the pigs—and the goats and the cows and the chickens—
a month into summer, during the May fiesta for Santa Rita de Cascia.
Throughout the weeks building up to fiesta, we hid in the tall, wide
space beneath the house, cool and open like a huge, air-conditioned
pigpen—and that earth-smell of dried mud and crushed gumamela
petals and guava leaves and arid animal blood follows me in out-of-
time places, all signs of river and wet earth and farmland leading me
back to my mom's old home.

Pordiiiiiin!

In my mind's eye, looking at the Hudson, I hear it, that wail of pig herders by the river.

But by the end of May I hated the river Himanglos.

We spent weeks by the AWOL feeding Mick-mick our roasted frogs, burnt lizards, bougainvillea paste, and beaten santol seeds mixed with mud and rocks—he ate everything. Mick-mick thrived, he was a genius. We held baby Adino up high in our pretend Santacruzan parades, our gurgling infant king Constantino, and we practiced our town's never-ending search for Jesus's Holy Cross during the entire month of May—all around Cong. J. B. Delgado Street—as if Adino, sweet Adino, *pooordiiiin!*, were the Holy Roman emperor of Salogó, and we were his retinue, or, in my mom's ternos, we dressed up, *Going to Market!*, we were Reina Elena, the queen, the power behind his throne.

In Salogó, we were trained to know there was always a woman behind the throne.

I got tired of swimming at barakasyunan, guava-stealing from Tay Igme, playing tumba lata with Carnation Evap cans against the AWOL, a.k.a. the seawall, though it was by the river and the salt air was in Tacloban. The AWOL was a monsoon barrier all along Salogó's riverbank, the length of our street. Our balcony jutted above it, extending to a spot above the water, giving Putt-Putt permission to fall. We had the freedom of the river, but the AWOL's protection. As Tio Nemor, coming back at twilight from his duties (now that he had stopped campaigning and was so important, being the mayor, he had leisure time), never forgot to tell us every goddamned summer—the AWOL was built during the time of our great-grandfather Lolo Jote, the mad doctor who thought of everything, especially disasters! Lolo Jote imagined floods and earthquakes and an apocalypse of shit. True, he was kind of aloof, *isnab!*, a deaf-mute genius, so the stories went, a man who spoke his wisdom only to his chickens, like a kapre, a multo, speaking his old-time weirdo language whenever his brother visited—my mom's favorite, her Lolo Paco.

Lolo Jote was a dreamer who designed sewers and drainage and seawalls. And that's what he did with the pork barrel, so Tio Nemor repeated, holding up his fingers like the Pope, declaring from his special chair, his huge creaking butaka above the river as the sun lowered into the slow spread of its gloam.

Lolo Jote built things to protect Salogó! He brought home the bacon! And look how the people of Salogó remember him!

"But they named a whole street after him," I said. "Isn't he Mister Cong? Mister Cong. J. B. Delgado Street?"

Putt-putt and Mick-mick laughed: "Ha ha ha! King Kong! Kangkong!"

John-john was already gone to sneak a smoke with his peers, the budding druggists and drunks of Salogó.

"Ha ha. Not King Kong. Cong means congressman!" said Tio Nemor. "He was a doctor. A zoologist and a congressman. Ah! But streets are only one way of remembering."

I was sick of Salogó because I was waiting for my mom.

I knew her return would be unexpected, she left no messages by jeepney or phone (Salogó had no phones), the day she returned would be the usual ordinary day of eating freshly boiled jackfruit seeds with the same critical commentary by Doctor Tita Tita and Tio Nemor—the couple were connoisseurs of fresh peanuts, perfect jackfruit, the correct sourness of green mangoes, and the sweetness of my favorite, lanzones. Another sign of being grown-up in Salogó was the ability to nurture a secret voracious critic in one's digestive tract. It made one increasingly picky in old age. I'd imagine the clack, clack, clack of heels on the broad narra stairs, and I would not believe it at first, I would pretend to be engrossed in the mealy old jackfruit seeds though I never understood Tita Tita's urgent command never ever to throw away a single seed that you found in that fruit's bland, sticky flesh—an liso, an liso, inday, ayaw iglabog an liso!—and I'd be confused because the liso, the seeds, in the instant you extracted them, already looked like spoiled trash.

And then I'd see her shoes and her tired ankles, and the translucent

potions of her own invention, *Adina PANTY-LESS STOCKINGS!™*
on her calves, her knees, the fragmented way her body emerged from
my memory, and still I'd look down, not trusting my wishes, picking
out the jackfruit liso from its stupid sticky langka flesh, and without
my expecting it, she'd kiss me on both cheeks, smelling of cucumber,
Pond's Cold Cream, and sweat, and her arrival knocked the slippery
liso into its proper place, irrelevance.

To be honest, I have no memory of how my mother returned to us
during those summers at her father's old house.

All I remember is that one day I'd be desolate, the next day my life
was good.

When we caught Mick-mick eating the lump of hemp rope
by the AWOL, Putt-putt took it from him and started screaming
toward the house—*mamá, mamá, mamá*—although his own mother,
Doctor Tita Tita, the neuro, had already left us for her clinical
refuge in Cebu.

And there was Adina an guapa, laughing and kissing away Mick-
mick's tears as if she had been present all along in our Santacruzan
adventures. Tio Nemorino followed behind, and at their heels was
Mana Marga smiling and acting like the genie who had engineered
our reunion. Mana Marga checked Mick-mick's cheeks and jaw, and
my mom laid her hands over the boy, as if her touch were all he needed.
My mom in her travels gained this talent called "laying over"—she
held her hands over the patient and cured him, on top of her other
occult profits. Laying over the hands was a gift from her journeys
with holy people, the *cursillistas* and Rosary Crusaders, all around
Visayas and Mindanao where people took inter-island boats seeking
divinity. And sure enough, with my mom's hands praying over him,
Mick-mick was fine, anyway he was like Super-Boy: he could chew
through a chicken coop fence and come up with only drool.

Then my mom kissed me, and I let her, acting like her presence
were only normal, and not what it always seemed—a resurrection.

No one else noticed the way the world changed when my mom
was around.

Including my mother.

Like she had just gone away to buy torta in Carigara.

Jote Versus Paco

Putt-putt showed her and Tio Nemorino and Mana Marga our find, the chicken coop wiring embedded in the AWOL.

"Bah. Lolo Jote's chickens."

"Bah-chickens, bah-chickens," said Mick-mick.

You never knew which trifles might be of interest among the grown-ups.

"All along here—where he put up the seawall—Lolo Jote designed a house for his chickens. The country was at war with the Japanese, and he was building houses for chickens. He was the embarrassment of his brother. Nemor, what did he call it?"

"*Laberinto de gallos,*" said her brother.

"Ah, yes. Galyos, inday, means chickens. In katsila."

"Roosters, Adina," Tio Nemor corrected. "*Gallos* are boys. *Gallinas* are hens."

"What's a laberinto?" I asked.

"A maze," said Tio Nemorino. "A puzzle."

"A mess," said my mom. "Lolo Paco was so concerned about his brother, Lolo Jote. You know, Lolo Paco was the younger brother, but it was the older one Lolo Jote who had no worries. No responsibility. *Que se joda. Que se joda.*"

"Kesehoda, kesehoda," said Mick-mick.

Que se joda, according to my mother, meant *I don't care!* In katsila.

"No, it doesn't," said Tio Nemor. "Stop saying that word."

"Why," I said to Tio Nemor.

I thought, *que se joda, que se joda.*

"If you ever grow up to study katsila, you will know! Not like your mom, who never studied!"

"Hah," declared Mana Marga, "if not for her PE teacher at the

FEU who would not let Adina pass if she did not wear tennis shoes to the gym, she would be a graduate now! Ba-ah, that PE teacher!"

And my mom smiled shyly at Mana Marga's recall, both of them walking in the mud in their heels, lockstep.

It was a legend in the family that my mom never got her diploma because she wore only high heels to the gym.

"Lolo Jote only did what he wanted," continued my mom. "Sitting around in his sando, making me comb the hair over his moles. His hair on his back made him itch, his back was full of moles shaped like a map, an architectpelago."

"Ay sus, Adina—archipelago!"

"Hah? It was an architectpelago—you know, like the moles on his back—they looked like a design! Imagine—an iya manghod, his younger brother Lolo Paco was a senator, a bureaucrat, an ambassador for the independence in Washington, DC! Always in the papers. While Lolo Jote sat around in his sando, interested only in chickens and the insects in the yard. He collected them. The beetles and the mantises. All the things with wings. He put them in jars. Then he studied them, for hours, staring at the bugs. Don't you remember, Nemor?"

"Hmph," grunted Tio Nemor. "He was a scientist, Adina."

"He was bug-eyed," said my mom. "Lolo Jote never visited his brother in Manila, he refused to leave Salogó. He preferred his chickens and his bugs. And his friends, the fishermen and the farmers—always with Apoy Bingo, the dad of your Tay Guimoy. They were always together, playing that chess, watching over their chickens. So Lolo Paco instead—he would come to visit his brother, right here, right up these steps he'd arrive, the senator. Oh my gulay, Lolo Paco had skinny feet, in silk socks and shiny takong. Don't you remember, Nemorino—Lolo Paco's legs were so skinny and white."

"He had chicken legs," said Tio Nemor.

"He had katsila legs," corrected my mom. "Papá told me he could get anything he wanted if he only asked his uncle, Lolo Paco. You know, inday, before he was senator Lolo Paco was a top-notch lawyer in Manila. Ah, his house in Greenhills. It was like a museum. Maps and canes and coats from Hong Kong. Hats from all over—San Francisco, Rome, even Texas. Lolo Paco handled all the important cases of the Commonwealth era! The independence missions! The war reparations! He was part of it all!"

I could hear her Papá's voice in my mother's words, an inherited, helpless pride seared in my mother's brain.

"Papá could get shoes from Singapore if he wanted, or the woolen americana suits with the matching funny hats, but all Papá ever asked for were musical instruments and toys for his dog Moret. Ha ha ha. Oh my Papá. How my Papá loved his dog Moret."

And my mom would have that catch in her voice, her voice of grieving.

"Hah!" I said, wishing to comfort her, "and when one Moret died, he bought another!"

That was family legend, too.

My mom laughed, and I was glad.

"Hah," said my mom, "we still have the picture—of Moret Number Three!"

Tio Nemor proclaimed, "Papá wanted to be a musician, a bandleader. If he could only be in the old Constabulary Band, with the famous black maestro, Lieutenant Loving, that would be a dream, but he was no soldier. What he really was good at was training German shepherds."

These old people were like a bunch of mongo-bean collages. The beans were always a mess and had no real place to go. Whenever she was tired, the art teacher Mrs. Cabaluna gave us jars of mongo beans to paste on a piece of paper and shape into a design. But glue and legumes don't go well together—and my art would have been more useful to eat.

But I held on to the mess of stories. I liked to hear my mother's voice.

"Yeah, even the priests of Divine Word—they called in Papá to train their German shepherds. Remember Father Heiar?" said my mom to Tio Nemor. "He was just a Dutch, but his dogs were German. Papá trained the German dogs of the Dutch."

"That was his talent," said Tio Nemor, "training German shepherds."

"Instead he became mayor," I said sadly.

"Hah. That is the curse," said Tio Nemor.

And my mom told us the story again of the doll her Lolo Paco had given her, from Valencia, Spain.

"It had the most beautiful dress, inday, and I kept it on a shelf. A long-sleeved red dress, satin vest, lace puff-sleeved blouse, and the most beautiful, rick-racked multi-colored ballroom skirt. It had a sash of red and yellow and an apron with gold embroidery. And her headdress, inday—she had the most beautiful hair. I kept her in a glass aparador. When Lolo Paco saw it, he said—you don't play with my gift? I said oh no, it's too beautiful. He said, *thatttt is a shame*. In English. You know his English was from abroad, not here. He said it like that. *Thatttt is a shame*. Papá always repeated that story to the guests—*thatttt is a shame*, he kept repeating Lolo Paco's words. Papá said to me, Adina, that is a lesson. But what is the lesson, I kept asking my Papá."

"Yeah, what's the lesson?" I asked.

"I treasured my doll from Valencia, Spain, I wanted only to look at it, I locked it in my aparador, its jet-black hair and red mantilla with a comb."

May peineta pa siya! May suklay pa man din!

The extra chorus sung during storytelling times.

The Waray-waray songs of Mana Marga.

She flitted back and forth amid the telling.

"And then?" I said, though I already knew the story.

"One day, I looked at her in the aparador, and everything on her head had come off—the beautiful hair, the comb, the mantilla. Something had eaten her up on the inside. I cried in Papá's arms for days."

"So what was the lesson?" I asked.

"You should have put the doll in plastic," said Mana Marga. "Then the mites will not eat her."

And Mana Marga waltzed away on her next aria.

Inday, inday, nakain ka han kasunog han munyika—
An asô waray kita-aaaaaa!

I listened to her high heels go, clack-clack, up over the AWOL.

I liked that song.

Inday, inday, where were you while the doll burned—
You missed even the smooooke!

I wrote the words down in my notebook, with my caption, *translated by Rosario.*

When Lolo Jote died, my mom said, his younger brother Lolo Paco stopped visiting, and it was her Papá who went every year, during the summer, to visit his uncle in Manila. He stayed for weeks, visited the sights, returned to his old haunts near San Juan de Letrán, where Lolo Paco had sent him for his proper education when he was a boy, and he came back with his spoils, e.g., the Edison Bell gramophone, his records with the logo of the dog winding up *His Master's Voice!*, and dresses and toys for Lolo Paco's favorite, the baby—Adina an guapa.

If it were not for Lolo Paco in Greenhills, who knows what would have happened to them, said my mom—to the family of Lolo Jote, who was a congressman who thought only of chickens, who left nothing but an unfinished labyrinth and his jars of dead bugs!

The sun was gleaming against the river in the gloss I favored, as we stood against the AWOL and that light of day that gave my mother's stories their glow.

"Yeah, Lolo Jote was nuts," I nodded. "He was a collaborator. With the Kempeitai, the Japanese. That's why he died."

"Who told you that?" said Tio Nemor.

"Mano Junior," said Mick-mick, who could never tell a lie.

"Our own nephew," said Tio Nemor. "Who needs traitors when you have family!"

"Well, there is another version of that story," said my mom.

"Rosario Francisca Nemesia Bonifacia Mariana, you have no idea of the story of your ancestors," said Tio Nemor, "though you, of all people, should know. Since your mom for no good reason named you for all of them!"

"Except for Jote," I said.

"And you like to read the history books, so you should know the story," said Tio Nemor.

"What?" I said. "Tell the story!"

"Tell-story, tell-story!" said Mick-mick.

"Who would you believe," said my mom, "that Junior Igmenegildo or an ignoramus? I would believe an ignoramus."

"An ignoramus is a know-nothing," said Tio Nemor.

"That is what I mean," said my mom.

"Lolo Jote only pretended to be mad during the war," Tio Nemor said. "Don't believe the people of Salogó. Everyone says he was crazy—but he was only pretending. So the Japanese would leave him alone. He was a bad-luck politician. Lolo Jote was a doctor. But it was his fate to become a congressman. To be congressman during war is a curse. You have to follow the enemy's orders. But to be doctor is even worse. You have to cure your enemies! So Lolo Jote—well, he pretended to go mad. He pretended so he did not have to treat the Japanese."

"Fairy tales and bull's eye!" said my mom.

"You mean bullshit, not bull's eye, Adina."

"I mean bull's eye. You know, like a target—you shoot, then bull's eye!"

"Adina, fifty years of American rule—and you still use English like it's just for effects, not meanings!"

"Well, who taught me?"

"Americans," he said.

"Hah! Correct! Marga, remember that teacher, Mrs. Edith Taffie, the parasite?"

"Ay, peste, the Thomasite!" laughed Mana Marga, who was already on the other side of the AWOL, her heels making holes beside the garden of pechay.

"Oh my God, Adina," said Tio Nemor. "Thomasite. Not parasite!

The American teachers were called *Thomasites*! After that boat they came on! Though Mrs. Edith was only a kind of leftover from their ship. Pasobra la adto hera, by that time. I think she came by airplane."

"Who cares—parasite!—Thomasite! Mrs. Edith used to hit my hand with a ruler if I mixed up the she for the him and the his for the hers! So many different words for nothing, I said, why is that bundat. She did not like my jokes. Di ba, Marga?"

But Mana Marga had gone ahead.

"What, guapa-patata?" Mana Marga sang from above.

"Margarita was the good student. Always the model for good reading and right conduct. She never got hit."

"Yes, I got Excellent marks for English Grammar and Vocabulary," said Mana Marga, looking down at us.

"While I got hit if I did not regulate my verbs," said my mom.

"Conjugate," said Mana Marga, from her perch above.

"Oooh, Margarita, always correcting. Just because she was always six grades ahead. Ah, basta. Mrs. Edith was a terror. She was a terrorite! And if it weren't for Lolo Paco—"

"Adina, basta," said Tio Nemor, "Lolo Jote is the hero. And he is a he is a he! That's just the way it is. He! Not her, not she! That is the pronoun. He is the hero. For you, *Dios mío*, it is always Lolo Paco, Lolo Paco, Lolo Paco. And listen to Margarita. It is not regulate. It is conjugate!"

"No. It is regulate. There is regulate verbs, and irregulate verbs!"

Tio Nemor raised his hands in surrender and started climbing over the AWOL, back toward the house.

Mana Marga on the balcony was giggling.

"I think the best was the catechetical instruction," she sang out.

"What? That is not an English word," my mom murmured to me, shaking her head as if we were in cahoots against Mana Marga. Her conspiratorial look warmed me. We were a team. "Catechetical? That is a foolish word."

"Yes, it is a word," trilled Mana Marga above us. "It is English!

We had catechetical instruction with Father Ganzewrinkelstein, the German."

"Haha. Ganze-wrinkel-skin! That German. Hmph. I take it back, Marga—it is not your fault! It is English that is foolish. The right word is *catechemical*—not *catechetical*."

I scrambled over the AWOL to run up the stairs to get it, the huge Webster's Dictionary on Lolo Jote's leaning bookshelves.

"No," shouted Mana Marga, in her calm and commanding way, the way she corrected my lyrics for "Blue Hawaii" even as she told me the hips of Elvis were a sin—"the correct English is *catechetical*."

And Mana Marga and my mom kept at it by the balcony, like a grammarian Romeo and Juliet.

"Aha," I said, "Mana Marga—you are the winner! It is *catechetical*—means—*relating to religious instruction to prepare for baptism or confirmation!*"

Mana Marga and her midnight-black bun proceeded to the kitchen, her high heels clicking in triumph.

"Catechemical, catechetical—who cares," shouted my mom, "*que se joda!* What's the point of learning the words if they sound crazy. They just mix up the mind!"

Up on the balcony Tio Nemor was mumbling.

"Adina, you think a man like Lolo Jote—you know what they say—"

"Lolo Jote was a bandit, a katipunero!"

My mother was now up the stairs.

You could tell she knew hers were fighting words.

She stood still at the doorway, waiting for his answer.

Her mouth was turned in that way she had, serious, but ready to laugh if you thought differently.

My mom had this capacity for multiple instincts at once.

Tio Nemor on the balcony glanced back at her.

His shadow, hands on his hips, gobbled up the disappearing shards of the river's light.

His voice was hurt, facing the dark.

Soon we'd have only the Petromax lamps.

"Adina. The katipuneros are not the bandits. They are the heroes. Get your history right. Do you think a katipunero, you know what people say about Lolo Jote—you think a rebelde—do you think he would collaborate with the Japanese?"

"Why not," said my mom. "If it will save his life."

And Tio Nemor gave her his last shot.

"You think, Adina, a rebelde from Balangiga would collaborate?"

And it was my mom's turn to stop and glare.

"What's Balangiga," I said, still carrying Webster's.

"Sssssh," said my mom, "Don't say that word."

"Why?"

"It's a bad-luck word," said my mom. "And put that book away. It is full of ants!"

Anyway, it did not have the word Balangiga.

"Hah!" said Mana Marga from the kitchen. "My aunt Carmen is from Balangiga—Carmen Catalogo Buñales! That was the name of her mother. Her mother, my lola, but only an in-law, she only married a Buñales—she was from Giporlos, barrio of Balangiga."

"Nay Carmen? Who makes bibingka?" I asked.

"No," said my mom. "Mana Carmen is from Capoocan, out by the barakasyunan."

"But your Nay Carmen's apoy, also named Carmen, she was from Samar," Mana Marga sang out. "Also where Guimoy's tatay is from. But yes, they all grew up in Capoocan, your Tay Guimoy and Nay Carmen—ha barakasyunan ha may Himanglos!"

"Ah yes, Tay Guimoy," said my mom—"he married a Cubilla, urupod of Mamá, that's right, but his cousin, Nay Mimang, Mana Carmen's mamá, yes, she married a Buñales, urupod of Mama Bia. That is how we are related, inday."

It was all Greek to me.

Sometimes, their genealogical debates could go on for hours, and I learned to prepare my patience and find other amusements for my gaze.

"Yes! But you see his father was Apoy Bingo," said Mana Marga. "So Tay Guimoy—he was also apo ha tuhod of the original Nay Carmen—from Giporlos!"

Grandchild-of-the-knee!

"Margarita," sang my mom, "pakadi na gad la pag-istorya. Stop shouting at us from the kitchen!"

But Tio Nemor on the balcony was sticking to his topic.

"And you know, Adina, your own favorite, your Lolo Paco—you know what Lolo Paco did when his brother died, in 1946?"

"Stop," said my mom.

It was my favorite time of day, this twilight in Salogó.

The river was gilded, framed, lit up at the sides, and the palm trees across the water, shading Carigara, joined with their shadows to catch the water's glow. There was a tug of light between river and trees, and I watched the divided glimmer, this slow surrender, an entangling of shades settling upon us all, the house, its acacias and its fruit trees and its palms, and all along the riverbank the light loitered, then it left.

Soon the entire river would be as concrete and impenetrable as the AWOL, the river and its gray stone buttress becoming one.

Tio Nemor settled into his preferred position, reclining on his butaka to stare at darkness wrestling with Carigara. I sat on the bench with the broken hemp, which aired my butt, and I listened. This was my primal spot, listening to their partial stories in the dark. Tio Nemor looked out across the river and began rocking, rocking, rocking, as if by rocking he could somehow rescue it, the body of his Lolo Jote floating on the river Himanglos.

"Lolo Paco, his brother, was already a commissioner of the War Damage Committee. So you know it happened after the war—in 1946. That Junior Igmenegildo likes to tell the story of how Lolo Paco arrived at the riverbank during the war, that he was right there when Lolo Paco found his brother's body by Tay Guimoy's landing. But the war was already over. The newspapers will explain how that is true. Lolo Paco was in charge of war reparations when his brother died. That is why he was in Leyte. So that is how we know the war was over. And Lolo Paco did a weird thing."

"What, Tio Nemor?" I asked. "What?"

"Whatchunemorwhat!" said Mick-mick.

"What a liar—that ignoramus, that Junior Igme," said my mom. "How could he remember—he was only two years old in 1946! That pigmy, that Igme."

"Pigmy! Igme! Igme! Pigmy!" Mick-mick said.

"Lolo Paco put his hand on his brother's bloody chest."

"No, he did not, Nemor—Lolo Paco did not. He was a senator. Like you said, the War Damage Chief!"

"He was a War Damage Commissioner," said Tio Nemor. "He was traveling around the islands in charge of war reparations. That's why he was in Leyte. To check out the damage after the war. They say—he smeared his brother's blood across his own face. Especially—"

"No!"

My mother put her hands over her ears.

"He rubbed the blood all over his scar, the townspeople say. The scar he got from the war—the war he fought before the country was even a country—Lolo Paco covered his own scar with his brother's blood."

"Nemorino! You think Lolo Paco is like the vampira up on TEIPCO, eating his brother's liver on top of the ice plant? And what for would he do that, acting like an aswang?"

"Well, you are the one who believes there is a vampira up on TEIPCO eating people's livers on top of the ice plant. Susmaria. You and Marga, especially Mana Talia, who should know better. Hesusmariosep! She is the wife of a congressman! Well, ex-congressman! Poor Congressman Quintana. Tsk, tsk, tsk. He is going to the Balkans. And all Mana Talia will do is—talk about vampira!"

"Ssssh," said my mom. "Mana Talia is coming, no matter what you want, Nemor. She is my friend. After all she is going through. How can I say no?"

My mind see-sawed with the topics.

No one even bothered to cue us, to warn—*sulibanco pa man!*

"Anyway, it's his fault," said my mom. "Why did he rebel?"

"Quintana did not rebel," said Tio Nemor. "He revealed—nothing! Waray! Waray may gin-reveal. Nothing was in the envelopes. Hehehe. Waray kuno. Haha. At least, that is what the newspapers say. Oh, you and your praying women. You are the bottom-feeders of tsismis. So superstitious! Believing in the vampira of TEIPCO. It's just the smoke rising from the ice fumes and the diesel whistle of the ice plant! Is that not *claro*, my God. Anyway, yes, you know how even Papá never spoke of it. He left the room whenever the topic came up."

"The topic of what?" I asked.

"Of war."

"Which war?"

"All of them!" said my mom. *"Inday—it is all one war!"*

"Oh my God, Adina. One is the revolutionary war, against the Americans! That was in 1899. Lolo Jote was a fighter in that war."

"Sssh, Nemor," said my mom, "don't say bad words."

Tio Nemor went on: "The other is the Second World War, against the Japanese. It is two wars!"

"Well, it is just what I think," said my mom. "It is just what I feel. It is all one war."

"So the Japanese killed Lolo Jote by the riverbank near the house of Tay Guimoy?" I said.

"No. He was not killed by the Japanese. Inday. Didn't your Tio Nemor just say?" my mother explained. "He was killed by the Americans, the gorillas."

"Ah," I said.

Tio Nemor in his rocking chair said shush, shush, shush, looking out at the river, as if even this late in time war spies could hear.

Tio Nemor put his hand to his lips.

He was whispering, wondering.

"They found Lolo Jote by the river. By the home of Tay Guimoy. You know Lolo Jote and Tay Guimoy's dad, Apoy Bingo, they went way back—way back to their days in Samar."

Apoy ha tuhod! Grandfather-of-the-knee!

"That is a good way to say it," approved my mom, patting me on the head. "Apoy ha tuhod! Lolo Jote is *your* apoy ha tuhod, inday—your grandfather-of-the-knee, ha ha!"

Mana Marga came in with her two cents.

"Yes," Mana Marga said, "your Lolo Jote and my Apoy Bingo, they were the best of friends. Kamagsangkay gud nera. Going fishing together, watching the insects—they loved the mananap, ay sus, Lolo Jote and Apoy Bingo would sit by the water ha may barakasyunan, watching the dragonflies and the moths and the worms, the caterpillars—but above all they loved taking care of their chickens. They were always together, like this."

And she put two fingers up, crossed and twined.

"That's because, after their days in Samar, their escape—the place of their rescue—was Salogó."

Tio Nemor was still whispering, so I whispered, too.

"Why were they in Samar?" I whispered.

My mom glared at me.

"Ssssh," she said. "Nemor, basta."

"But in 1946," continued Tio Nemor, ignoring me, "out there at his home by the barakasyunan, Tay Guimoy found him. His father's best friend. That's right, they were like this—twins. Tay Guimoy always said—he was glad Apoy Bingo was dead. He did not live to see Lolo Jote's body. How Lolo Jote loved that place—an barakasyunan ha may Himanglos. They say they could not at first imagine that it was he—his body on the beach—the body of Lolo Jote. But Tay Guimoy said—you could identify him just by his moles. On his back. They had the shape of islands. And by the scar on his cheek, of course—like the scar of his brother Paco, but on a different side—ha iya wala, diri ha to-o."

And I touched my cheek—my left and then my right.

Both sides of my grandfathers' scars.

My mom said, "I used to comb the hair on his back. He liked me to do it—to smooth the hair over his moles. Scattered on his back, an architectpelago!"

"Ay sus, Adina. Not even Lolo Paco, the senator from Manila, could save his brother Jote. It was just after the war, the country was a mess, and that is how they got him. Yes, Adina, you are right. For once. It was not the Japanese who killed him. The Japanese were gone. The Americans were the ones—the Americans and their friends, the guerrillas, killed Lolo Jote."

And for a moment, in the silence, one could hear a fly buzz.

The flies buzzing over the body of Lolo Jote—the flies he liked to watch, buzzing on the river.

"The gorillas were not the Americans?" said my mom.

"Oh my God, Adina. Guerrilla, Adina, not gorilla. One is a monkey, the other is a man!"

"Oh, yeah," said my mom. "I forget. Gorilla, guerrilla, gorilla, guerrilla."

My mom looked as confused as myself.

"What's the difference?" she said. "They sound alike."

"Adina. How can you communicate with your customers? When you cannot use words!"

"I excommunicate with my inventions, Nemorino—not my words."

Tio Nemor sighed. "Only the Pope excommunicates. While you, Adina, I swear, you do not communicate!"

"So it was the World War II guerrillas who fought against the Japanese—it was they who killed Lolo Jote," I said.

"It was the Americans," said Tio Nemor. "They finally got Lolo Jote, after the war."

"For talking to multo," said my mom, "for speaking in tongues, to ghosts, to insects and worms, for spending all that time making *laberintos de gallos*."

"*You arrre a bitttterrr soul, Jote,*" my uncle murmured to the air.

"What?" I said.

Tio Nemor said, "I remember Lolo Paco saying that once. A long time ago."

"Oh Lolo Jote!" said my mom. "When he was not treating the sick, he was just playing with his manok, his favorite roosters that even had names—as if we had no tomorrow. Or no war."

"All Delgados are crazy anyway," I repeated a mantra I heard all around the town of Salogó. "And Delgados are craziest about manok. Lolo Jote started it all. He built the best chicken coops in Leyte."

"Hah," said my mom, "Amo na! Yes, inday—people came to study his designs, but who knows for what, uwat!"

"See, Adina?" my uncle said, raising his ringed, manicured mayor's finger. "See what you get for bringing up the past? Your daughter's mind is full of *mentiras*. *Mentiras* of the past! It's your own lookout, Adina—if you don't watch out, one day your daughter will be good only for lies."

"I mean, inday, your Lolo Jote was not only a chicken lover. He was also an orinologist."

"Hah! Adina, he did not just design toilets," said her brother. "He was a certified gastroenterologist. One of the first medical students to enroll in the University of the Philippines at Padre Faura."

"Yes—a gastroentemologist. He cured people of systempsychosis."

"Systempsychosis?" said Tio Nemor.

Oooh, how do you spell that?

"You know—the worm disease of the people in Palo."

"Oh my God. You mean the schisto. Schistosomiasis! Susmaria."

"It's a system—in the stomach. But it eats up your brain. Psychosis!"

I spelled the word in my mind, so I would remember it.

"And then there is the kurikong that makes the elephantiasis! You know, when your feet become like an elephant's. He examined those patients, too, but he could never cure. It is a disease in the people of Palo, who are hopeless."

"Por bida, Adina. It's not just in Palo. But you know, in real life, it's true—"

And at this Tio Nemor took on that voice of wonder—"It's true that he liked them, the insects and the chickens, most of all. He liked animals, especially bugs. That's what Papá said. He kept saying his father wished he was a zoologist, or even just an entomologist, not an internist. You know how Papá said his father sometimes forgot he had children and instead liked to stare at pests flying around in his garden. He'd stop and stare for hours. And it was his mom, the Chinese trader, Mama Bia, who ran the home, managed the farmlands, sold the goods at the market. While his father, Lolo Jote, the doctor—he was obsessed with chickens. He never told a single story about it. Papá said—he never told a single story of his war."

"Which war?"

"His war." And my uncle's voice lowered, as if the revelation made him guilty. "The war against the Americans."

"Ssssssh!" said my mom. She put her fingers to her lips. "Don't say bad words, Nemor. Look what happened? A bad-luck congressman, killed by gorillas. Anyway, inday, he also studied toilets. Remember, he made the first flushing toilet of Salogó. We had the first flushing toilet. He used the river to his own advantage. Inday—Lolo Jote was not only a chickenologist. Oh no. He was also an architect!"

Lolo Jote should have fixed on only one occupation—his too many activities resulted in my inability to imagine him.

The Musical Instrument

My phone was ringing. The corniest one. "Close to You." I had a random shuffle of ring tones, and the fact that I included the song from *Lollipops and Roses* told me my mind was not working well. Tones from a cavalcade of Mana Marga's *Song-Hits*, signs of my weak will and the musical misery of growing up in that blasted decade. Embarrassing, but no one ever called me except spammers and my mom. I hurried to thumb the phone open, to shut out the song. A 212 number. For a moment, I thought—was it some lurking neighbor, waiting to mock me for my phone's musical taste, evidence of my absurdity? My vantage on the river, from this corner, was slight, a slither between roofs and water towers and windows giving scant cues of lives within. I hit Decline. I saw my phone was splotched with red notifications—even on moribund Skype. I should clean up my settings. I clicked the phone shut. I stumbled upon the oddly shaped musical instrument just as my cousins and I were about to return to school. By then I had finished retelling every single opera story from F. B. Delgado's book to my stupefied audience, my cousins, who found the wisdoms of *L'elisir d'amore* disgusting but fascinating. That the two lovers, Adina and Nemorino, were named after our parents made the tale doubly repulsive, but they lapped it up. Every day the boys clamored for another installment, and at first I obliged. The day I found my great-grandfathers' strange guitar—an gitara han apoy ha tuhod—I was hiding from the boys in the trashed aparador with twin doors, each with identical beveled mirrors, rusty gargoyles dulling their opaque sides.

I hid with a book.

As I said, I was looking for my mother's doll in the locked cabinets, the doll with the red mantilla, and I kept thinking I would find it intact, exactly as my mom described, the beautiful doll from Valencia, Spain. I already forgot the story's ending. The house was full of these humanoid cabinets, some shut in rusted glass, the silver peeling, some with mirrors. Every day we were followed around by full-length images of ourselves, orphans of summer, as our parents dashed off to their world of tango dancing and vote getting and other election manias, and then after Tio Nemor's victory, they still dashed off to their unknown devices and kept leaving us to our own. These towering cabinets around the house were stuffed with the dregs of someone's dismal biography—bullets and old guns, wrecked records, a waterlogged *National Geographic*, grim barong Tagalogs now as rigid as their grimy hangers, sleeveless jackets and jacketless books, lace handkerchiefs spotted with antique spit, a pile of woolen hats, one on top of the other, bitten by moths and gloom.

Finally I found the plastic limbs of the toy I thought must be the remains of my mom's doll from Valencia, Spain. But it was only one of mine, a scary robot of a Japanese doll. It was gross, with its jointed arms and legs, hinged like a crab's claws, the cheap metal pins showing. I had brought the doll from America, bought by my mother brand-new one Christmas after my father disappeared for a year, when he was based in Okinawa, and I prayed he would never return. In my memory, even the gifts his money bought have a hint of malice, this dread I felt that day he came back to Wilmington. The year without him, with only my mother and me, I was happy. My mom took a job, she became a teller in a bank, and once we wandered the aisles of Food Co, my eyes closed, and whatever my hand touched my mom bought for me. We made up the game. Grocery-Grocery. I went home with Oscar Mayer baloney, a green spatula wrapped in plastic netting, and a peach.

My memories of California are like this doll, fractured and unhinged, and then no matter how I try to recall that life whole, all I get is this dumb peach.

Beneath the Japanese doll, I found that old childhood treasure, a book.

Abraham Lincoln's World was clothbound in green, illustrated with a globe at its center. A span of time, 1809 and 1865, framed the gilt-edged globe. A log cabin with a huge axe drawn out of perspective ran through the log cabin's roof. I had no idea what the axe was doing there, bigger than the roof and as wide as the world, but I did not mind.

The book was beautiful.

It smelled of rain and old wood. The giant axe lay like a ribbon atop the log cabin, which was atop the stencil of the year 1809. A measure of time. As that summer ended, I read the book from cover to cover, then again and again. The book told the story of the world. Bolívar's Venezuela and France's Napoleon, Tecumseh of Tippecanoe and Charles Darwin of England, and most of all the childhood of little Alexandrina Victoria and the sad boy, Louis Napoleon, and the luckless baby, Dom Pedro of Brazil, all of the characters who grew up within the span of Abraham Lincoln's world, the golden, embossed age encircling the years 1809 to 1865.

Charles Darwin and baby Abraham were born on the exact same day, a great coincidence, and I read about young Charles collecting toads and shells and crabs in gentleman shorts while little Abe cried in a log cabin over his dead mother in Indiana. Little Queen Victoria was called Drina, a dutiful girl, inexplicably German, and Louis Napoleon's childhood was filled with tragedy, what with his uncle Napoleon having to visit his grandmamma Joséphine in secret or getting stuck in Russia's snows without friends or being exiled on sad islands, and to be honest I couldn't care less about Dom Pedro, he was a king who was a baby, so things were not looking up for Brazil.

I almost cracked the weird guitar into bits as I backed my butt into my mom's aparador to hide from my cousins, the opera fans.

All I wanted was to read *Abraham Lincoln's World*.

In peace.

I felt my butt hit something, and some wooden, hollow sound thudded against the aparador, and the loud snap signaled to the boys—*there she is!*

I tried to get myself out of my corner, I moved my butt then my butt twanged.

I don't know how I extricated myself from the instrument's strings, I got interested in the other object—the heavy, domed box that had fallen—and I was lucky my butt was not cut.

I discovered later that the fourteen-stringed octavina, sometimes called laud, is a nineteenth-century form of the medieval lute, a melodist in the classic Spanish rondalla.

The next week, I was enrolled in a stringed band, the rondalla, against my will.

Trina Trono was still the boss, but I had moved way up to the front of the class. Our grades from the year before were tacked on the door, and in the new year we were arranged, fifty kids in all, in the order of our posted values, beginning with number one on the far left in front. I don't know how it happened that I was up in front beside Trina, with Lorelei Pastillas to my right, and throughout the year Elvis Oras and Winston Querer and Lorelei kept exchanging seats. The mechanics of school were a mystery. All I can say is that everything was easy because everything except Tagalog and later Spanish and Latin was in English, the language of Los Angeles in California—so I had an advantage that was nothing to crow about. School was an inexplicable hive of abominable boredom with some illuminating, perforated vents that at some moments allowed me to breathe, such as when we read a whole short story by Edgar Allan Poe, and I thought I was alive, and I remember once a poem about an anvil by Amado V. Hernandez that I thought was about the smelter on the coin, Panday Pira, but who knows, I had stopped asking questions, everything was rote, a drag. I was promoted to the front and protected from despair by my indifference.

Introduced to the instrument, the octavina, by the rondalla bandleader Mr. Palitaw, a stunted man with long white hair and an all-white beard that made him look like the mad dwarf, like the nuno sa punso, a Rumpelstiltskin—I recognized it.

The awkward pear shape of the instrument.

It was a twin of that near-disaster my rump had squashed in my great-grandfather's aparador.

My other choice in Mr. Palitaw's rondalla class, a bandurria, looked like an obese ukulele, and I would have nothing to do with it.

So for four more years I played the octavina in playground demonstrations every time these old generals from foreign places arrived to honor themselves at our expense during the Battle of Leyte Gulf parades, every year on October 20, and then on July 2, the First Lady's birthday—these dates etched in my brain, that is, my primeval lizard brain that stores flight, fight, and anxiety, the neurons of my childhood's martial decade—and I sat in a cleaned-out dump truck every October 20, staring at whatever Douglas MacArthur had up his sleeve (ticks? centipedes? ladybugs?) in Palo, to serenade weepy old soldiers for no good reason that was explained to us, lively tunes for which, because we were mindless rather than passionate, my classmates and I kept picking up tempo and pitch, and by the end, we kid musikeros were speed-racing with our plectrums, notes shrieking like the west wind in October, as we sped through "The Entertainer" or "A Hot Time in the Old Town!," Mr. Palitaw's favorite tunes—a bunch of captive dwarves condemned to play ragtime faster and faster for Rumpelstiltskin, and none of us, as far as I could tell, was spinning the moment into gold.

The Domed Box

Mana Marga, that neat-freak, almost threw out my great-grandfather's papers, except that my mother, so they say, made her leave the notebooks alone, keep them in their place.

Let them disinterrogate without our help, she said.

Disintegrate! I can hear Tio Nemor exclaiming, but I was not around for that scene.

Now that I am looking back rather than making daily efforts to tune myself to my mom's moods, to sense from the rush of maids about the house whether Adina an guapa was here to stay or to go, not knowing if the restlessness that marked her presence would take her elsewhere, to Zamboanga or Cebu or Panay with her Rosary Crusade, on her artist-businesswoman trips—now that I look back, I imagine the house in Salogó wearied my mom.

She was the last of its children (meaning, the last of its women), and the yearly upkeep of its miserable decrepitude was her womanly chore.

Doctor Tita Tita, she of the high cheekbones and apostrophed waves of perfumed hair, was a fancy surgeon, a neuro, as they called her, an expert at cutting up people's spinal cords and scraping out brains. She was not too excited about home restoration. Anyway, she was only an in-law. Doctor Tita Tita had a modern place, all stone and concrete without nipa thatch or memory, out near Danao in Cebu, where she kept her sons on a short leash and Tio Nemor from doing his full-time job—as wedding-attending, beauty-queen-crowning, *Ave Maria*-singing, dashing municipal mayor of Salogó.

My mom's aunt in Sampaloc, the matriarch Tia Pachang, was too far away and irritable to be of use. My stern aunt Tita Patchy, the principal, though she was also named Bonifacia, tokayo of the matriarch, was only a second cousin. That layer of remove was fatal: she had right to nostalgia but no duty to maintenance.

Whenever my mom arrived in Salogó at summer's end, she already looked tired—agi, padiskansuha ako, inday!—duro an iya gin-agian!—agi, agi, agi, an iya kaagian—I scratched her painful puns on my palm—ha akon agi, I wrote, an iya gin-agian—though it was Mana Marga and her crew who bustled and cleaned and scrubbed. The maids scratched and waxed with their shaggy lampaso, feathery halves of coconut husks shedding miracle polish on the floors. The end of summer smelled of YCO Floor Wax. The maid on the lampaso was a dancer. One summer they were Candy and Delilah from Tacloban. Another summer, two modern girls held us in their thrall, Lheezah and Janice, accent on the first syllables, and the other name with *H*s I kept putting in the wrong place when she asked me to write her letters to her family, in Giporlos, Samar. We heard about their exploits at the beinte-singko dances with the boys of Alang-Alang and Tunga. Some boys came from as far as Catbalogan, some just from Capoocan. Lheezah fell in love with a boy, Chickchick, whose nickname I recycled in my games creating whole towns out of bottles and cans. Delilah's naked arch clutched the shaved coconut's bulb of a lampaso: her arch powered her dancing moves. The lampaso was another object of ingenuity, a sign of magic in the world of Salogó that impressed no one but me. Janice said I was an idiot. Candy laughed—the lampaso was just a husk. Sometimes we said, *let us do it, let us do it,* and the boys and I danced across the waxed floors with the lampaso, *twist and shout!*

We relished the job as long as it was our choice.

We were not good children. We never really helped.

After showing Candy how to do cross-stitches to repair tablecloth hems, or deciding with Tay Lucio where the nipa thatch on the eaves could be saved—Tay Lucio with his engraved, wrinkled face, cigarette on his lips, and melancholy gaze, as if already only remembering our home—my mother would sit, rocking upon the old mayor's butaka on the balcony looking onto Carigara, across the brown glaze of Himanglos.

She was the immobile center of the house's waxing and waning, and until the day she died she hung on to this property, the house of her grandfather, Lolo Jote, in Salogó, though at the end of summer this shamble was her cross.

Growing up, I thought there was a spirit of misspent time in the house—a clogged swamp beyond my mother's articulation—that sapped her. All the disparate Delgados, in Manila, in Las Vegas, in Qatar, in Baltimore, spoke of the house fondly at reunions, I think because they had escaped.

But every summer my mom smelled the actual river.

It's a fact long acknowledged. Even as a baby Adina an guapa looked like the heiress, an heredera, and her infant beauty sealed her fate. My mother was the favorite of her father, Mister Honorable Mayor Francisco Delgado III, and the pet of their great-uncle who after his brother died sent Nemorino and Adina off to college at the university he had founded, FEU. And for being spoiled rotten Adina an guapa was rewarded with this rotting home sinking into the river—while all the uglier Delgados got to fly away.

She tried to escape—once.

I smelled the same river in the spines of the journals I found in that ratty box. It was the size of a fat and overstuffed book, covered in gold and scratched vellum, with a lock but no key. Its curved lid was domed, like a miniature coffin. I could feel it was heavy. Stuffed and congested.

Of course, the boys found me, when that instrument the octavina clanged and started humming, and I stumbled out of the aparador, looking straight at my image in the hazy glass of the cabinet.

I saw in the mirror the reverse image of the domed box, balanced on my head like a basket of Nay Carmen's bibingka.

I glared at my cousins, Putt-putt especially, who if he touched the thing might turn it into smoke, given his luck.

I held out my hand to make the boys stand back, I bent over, cradling the swaying box, then I lowered my hoard onto the ground.

We all squatted before my find.

Discover-Discover was one of our favorite games, and our job in the summer was to make romance out of tansans and tin, out of nothing.

They held their breaths.

I paused with drama.

You have to let it air before you open up the past.

The box smelled of something moist and musty like a mix of clamshells, silt, and the odd, sweet ironing waft of burnt coals upon banana leaves, and something moved, it heaved a sigh the way beach sand does when a crab emerges, and a silver flash dashed across the leather and metallic lid, which was already gaping, half-ajar, and I was afraid something had already crumbled, eaten up from the inside like my mom's doll from Valencia, Spain.

"Yehey!" Mick-mick said as something else fell out from the aparador behind me. "Opera! More opera!"

Mick-mick went over, picked it up, and offered it to me.

Another box.

Look, he said, look.

On Mick-mick's box the initials *F. B.* were etched in white, but it was easy to see it was empty.

The lid with the initials was kind of agape.

I shrugged him off.

My hoard had metal, doublefacing locks that required two thumbs to open.

I moved my thumbs with opposing force—a centripetal motion!

The moment the latch caught, papers, folders, news clippings, and a bound book tumbled out, some from the domed top, which had these plaid, still-intact pockets.

The mess of papers, news clips, and dust, fell at our feet.

I raised my hands again, my hands swept about me to ward off the boys, and I bent over.

I picked up the bound book.

They are three different notebooks, but bound in one, separated by glazed sheets.

I laid my hands upon the beautiful whorls on a cover.

Gold stenciling, still intact, shaped its spine.

An entire newsprint page fell out.

It had ads in Spanish and the picture of a ship.

USAT *Liscum*, the caption said.

I opened up the book, to its first page.

William McKinley's World.

In letters so beautifully etched it looked like the slanted hand of the lapida maker, Agapito Padrax, carved on the grave of my mom's Papá.

We stared. It smelled. A slimy brown thing emerged from a vellum wrap.

A quiet, patient slug.

I could hear my mom saying—*systempsychosis!*

As carefully as I could, I put them all, the clippings, the folders, the notebooks, the bound triptych of a book, back into their faded coffin, their domed box.

I shuffled off the dust, the bugs.

I brought the opened box of papers out into the sala.

My mother shrieked.

"Oh my God, inday—you will give the maids asthma. Please—take that away. Let it rot somewhere else, not in front of human beings."

Mana Talia, the congressman's wife who was hiding in Salogó from the authorities in Manila, laughed at the sight of me carrying the antique box.

Despite her problems, Mana Talia's sense of humor was intact.

"Birat ka nga bata nga Rosario ka! Ay nga panulay. Why do you want to rebeal?"

Going to the Balkans

Mana Talia was sheltering in place with my mother in those days before she escaped with her love, her husband, the ex-ambassador, Congressman Quintana. The times were a mess. Mana Talia was going to the Balkans, a remote, disintegrating area that was just another name for punishment, not adventure, so implied Tio Nemor, whenever he mentioned Mana Talia and her love, Quintana—*tsk, tsk, tsk, they are going to the Balkans.*

I thought of the scattered life of Empress Joséphine, the boy Louis Napoleon's grandmamma, how all she had left were her kangaroos, swans, ostriches, emus, seals, llamas, and roses, all five hundred varieties of them, when it was time for her love to leave her, in her palace in Paris, the Malmaison, expelled as she was from Napoleon's life.

Mana Talia had to pack a lot of pantyhose.

But what could she do, said Mana Talia: she must follow her love.

I thought it was romantic.

The love of Mana Talia's life, Congressman Quintana, was a figure of whispering and tsismis in Tacloban after the excitement of the November elections. My uncle's party, the Nacionalistas, won three Senate seats! But the outcome was a scandal because there were eight seats in all. The rule was that one scandal must follow another, the next in line was the Constitutional Convention, and even I sat about marveling over the society the Con-Con delegates were going to be making while student protesters marched the country into hell, along with the communists and other demons of the nation.

It was like the time in *Abraham Lincoln's World* when the French people got all distressed about the new ideas of the uncle of the sad little boy, Louis Napoleon, who had to escape from his home with his mother, Princess Hortense, because the citizens of Paris wanted his uncle dead. Thankfully, little Louis Napoleon was saved by the emperor of Prussia, whom the boy kissed with gratitude in 1833, only to be imprisoned by the czar's son Wilhelm years later, when Louis Napoleon turned out to be Napoleon III—he of the eighteen *brumaires*!

The events in Manila were as thrilling as the Napoleonic wars. Tio Nemor's fellow Nacionalista, the president, *Re-Elect Ferdinand!*, was going to make a new world by decree, and we should kiss the emperor with gratitude for his revolution—*Democracy!* But the ex-ambassador

Congressman Quintana spoiled the fun when he "rebealed." He revealed the money in the envelopes given to him and nine fellow congressmen. He revealed receiving the money to vote the president's way in the Constitutional Convention. He revealed that the Constitutional Convention was a fraud, a straw document built by bribes. He revealed that he, Congressman Quintana, did not want the money, and the president was so surprised.

So was the rest of the nation.

For a moment, the Constitutional Convention was dangling from a thread held by Congressman Quintana and his decision to "rebeal."

All the best international journals, the *Reuters* from estados and the *Shimbun* from Japan and the *Straits Times* from Singapore, they were covering the story, boasted Mana Talia, and I relished the papers Mana Talia enumerated, like rosary beads—she told me how the world wanted to interview her love, Quintana.

But it's not his fault that he rebealed, she said.

He is not the one who gabe the enbelops!

He just receibed!

The little old lady in the stiff outfit, which spread like a generous *A* across her spindly legs, entered the house in Salogó with her hands on her hips, explaining the world coverage of the news to me, my mom, and Mana Marga, as if she were not involved.

At first, it did not occur to me that her life was at stake.

Mana Talia had the natural flair of a town crier, which Putt-putt and I admired. We loved Mana Talia. We high-fived whenever she said a bad word, like puta, or punyeta. We repeated her jokes so we could say her words—ay nga panulay! Pastilan, uday, nga peste nga yawa! Ay nga demontres!

Especially, we loved it when she said—*birat*.

Birat this, birat that.

Birat, birat, birat!

We had no idea what the word meant, but we knew it was the best word because it shocked the maids no matter how many times she said it, but it also made them giggle, laughing in the kitchen.

When my mom heard us one day in the garden, Putt-putt and me, calling out to a tuko we were scared of—birat ka nga birat—she took us both by the sleeve, she made us kneel by the Statue of the Sacred Heart, and she told us—never say that word!

But Mana Talia says it—we did not bother to explain.

We knew better.

We would never have guessed in our minds what it meant and gave its meaning words only when we grew up.

The old lady, Mana Talia, in her shiny church outfit and bouffant hair, her legs skinny in her Hanes stockings, was always grinning like a naughty child when she said it, with her hands on her hips, as if she knew she were being caught out in a prank—*cunt, oh you cunt you, cunt-cuntcunt!*

That is what it meant.

Birat, birat, birat.

Mana Talia was a marvel.

My mother threatened to make us pray Holy Marys with salt on our knees if we spoke Mana Talia's words.

But my mom listened with sympathetic nods to the sorrows of Mana Talia, our refugee in Salogó.

Mana Talia had arrived with one suitcase and a bag of hair chemicals.

Her love, Quintana, was nowhere in sight.

But why oh why did he rebel, I asked.

I carried the box to the corner where in her bass voice Mana Talia was relaying some new insult against her love, Quintana.

Mana Talia corrected me—He did not rebel, he rebealed!

Rebel! Rebeal! Rebel! Rebeal! said Mick-mick.

The problem with Quintana is that he is truth-telling, Mana Talia explained to Mick-mick, who had no idea what she was talking about, carrying his own bounty from the aparador.

Mick-mick carried his empty chest like a chalice, copying the way I carried the box of papers.

That is the fault of my love, said Mana Talia—Quintana speaks the truth, that is a mistake—I told him. It is only an uwat who tells the truth! Only a fool and an idiot. A tonto! Don't be a Jose Rizal, I told him—look what happened to Rizal! Shot in the Luneta in broad daylight with a bery bad haircut—what kind of a way to live is that?

We had to agree—dying was no way to live.

And in Tacloban, hair grooming always had something to do with it.

But what can I do, said Mana Talia—Quintana is my love.

At school in Tacloban throughout that year I had played the octavina, cut up a frog, and collected dicotyledon plants from the backyard while the Clairol Hi & Dri Hairspray gang came together to pray the Novena to the Wounds of Our Lord and contemplate the state of the nation.

Oh Jesus, pardon and mercy, through the merits of Thy wounds!

It was at first exciting then just normal how my mom's gang knew everyone's business, especially their president's. *Re-Elect Ferdinand!* Most of all, they knew the life of his wife. Madame this Madame that. On one hand, praying was prologue for mah-jongg. Three of the women—Mrs. Conrada Trinidad, Kringle May Kiring, the mom of Sirit, and my stern aunt Tita Patchy—went off to play mah-jongg after the novenas, at the home of Mrs. Conrada, who later would be chief of the Department of People's Facts, the new society's new agency of official tsismis.

Mrs. Conrada Trinidad was the boss of everyone. Her son was in section Durian, the last of the least, a dull boy with premature vileness, and she was the head of my mom's pack. You could tell because she had the highest hair, Mrs. Puff the Magic Dragon, Putt-putt called her, her hair so arranged that you could peek at aspects of her environment through the tendrils lofted by the energy and strength of her bold spirit, her bossy drive. It was clearly she whose opinions mattered in the post-novena gluttonous time, between the praying and the gambling—when the holy ladies sat around eating my mom's polvoron and Mana Marga's roscas and the binagol and the suman latik bought from the stalls near the pier. *The scalawags are in our midst!* Mrs. Conrada the Magic Dragon declared, in the way she also spoke the loudest during the responsorial psalm. *The Constitutional Convention is in danger! And so is the life of the Rose! Of Tacloban! Bedridden in Manila!*

And all the ladies crossed themselves—through the merits of Thy wounds!

Oh Madame, pardon and mercy!

I kept mixing up their gods.

Then Mrs. Conrada went on, but it was in a whisper.

I leaned in to hear.

Mana Talia must confess—where is her love hiding, the ex-ambassador, Congressman Quintana?

Why whisper?

Everyone was asking the same question in the kitchen.

The newspaper headlines affirmed Mrs. Conrada's facts—poor Madame, The Rose of Tacloban, was in the hospital, a miscarriage, so sad—due to the accusations of her cousin, Congressman Quintana.

Poor, poor Congressman Quintana, said Mana Marga, crossing herself in the kitchen, *he is just a truth-teller, a scalawag, going to the Balkans, tsk tsk tsk.*

Oh por Dios, that congressman will get it, said Mrs. Conrada Trinidad, biting into her roscas before going off to play mah-jongg—*tsk tsk tsk.*

She, too, crossed herself.

It was a dilemma—two Taclobanon on the opposite sides of the fray, the Rose of Tacloban versus Congressman Quintana—but everyone was on the same side—that is, on the side of anyone from Tacloban.

Mah-jongg was not my mom's game.

Proof was that she played mah-jongg during Lent. She taught it to me on a Good Friday once, before she sent us packing for Salogó, when Lent came too early and none of us had anything to do. I surmised mah-jongg was for the bored, when during Holy Week no one could leave home, even my mom, since the country was dead until

Jesus resurrected, and it was improper to go gallivanting around on the inter-island ferries, and all my mom could do was stay put sitting-pretty and repaint lampshades or retouch her frames. She couldn't even collect wildflowers and weeds. The jeepneys were resting. I was still in Catholic school and thought it was blasphemous to play mah-jongg on Good Friday, but she said, inday, people gambled the day Jesus died—you see in Siete Palabras, two men played dice! But they were sinners, I said. She shrugged and showed me her *kang*.

But she had only scorn for mah-jongg when she was not stuck at home and had other ways to rest her spirit.

My mom's Clairol Hi & Dri barkada was of a different order—older women who looked down upon the upstarts, e.g., Mrs. Conrada Trinidad and her trivial pack of bureaucrats and moneymakers. My mom's barkada was a set of wizened women in command of their spheres, e.g., beauty salons and dressmaking shops. Adina an guapa was their pet, like their baby mascot. Her joy at the old ladies' presence made them glad. I'd hang around with them—Mana Talia, Mrs. Young of Young's Fashionne House (aunt of my friend, the talented beader Elvis Oras), and the fabulous Lola Sayong, owner of Primrose Hotel and Restaurant and of whole blocks in the business district downtown up to the pier, from Avenida Veteranos (soon to be Imelda Avenue) to Zamora Street.

Lola Sayong's dewy face dripped with money—even her sweat had value, her moisture preserved and contained under her rouge. I wondered if I touched her rosy cheeks a fountain would spout: they were so smooth and plump and moisture-filled. But I was in awe of Lola Sayong not because she could wear twenty-two rings at once and her smooth wrist still looked languid, and upon even her bloodless pink pinkie finger fat blue diamonds hung.

I was in awe of Lola Sayong because she was never unkind.

She prayed with my mother and ate Adina an guapa's polvoron, or her one-of-a-kind doughnuts, or her special fried chicken.

Lola Sayong said she loved how my mom made everything from scratch, from her lampshades to her lotions to her snacks. Lola Sayong would open up the polvoron, the crunchy sugared flour wrapped in pleated, origami tissue, and say—*Ah, you see how everything Adina does is her own invention!* She liked the way my mom laughed as Adina an guapa showed off her new papier-maché lampshade, to be sold for Easter, shaped like the ears of a rabbit, but what does a rabbit have to do with Jesus Christ, so inventive—*Ah, you have the best laugh, Adina, you are happy like a child!*

I loved Lola Sayong because she loved my mom.

Mana Talia, on the other hand, had a sailor's mouth. That was her gift. She loved to shock the universe. She was just as rich as Lola Sayong, said Mana Marga, but her manners were no good. Mana Talia wore satiny gold-threaded suits, called jacquard, and thick pantyhose. She liked to show me the brand, Hanes, her favorite, she said—*see, hija,* she told me, baring her skinny, wrinkled, and bony thigh, *my pantyhose never slides! It's a miracle!* Mana Talia had the body of a grasshopper, one of nature's treasures (my mom kept boasting to her friends, very unimpressed specimens, as they saw me running around with a grasshopper jar, that I would be a biologist when I grew up, like her grandfather, *remember him,* she asked with doubt in her voice—*my grandfather Lolo Jote?*—and Lola Sayong would answer, patting her on the hand—siyempre, Adina, siyempre! An taga-Salogó nga congressman han district two, hi Doctor Jote!).

I liked to catch grasshoppers in the backyard—all angles and hairs and surprisingly soft sides.

But I had the sense that if I tried to catch Mana Talia, she would outwit me.

You could hear the gasps in the kitchen when Mana Talia showed me her fascinating body so that I could see her half-slip was made in France. She was a well-dressed lady who liked to explain the quality of her underwear. She announced herself at the house by not knocking on the door, and instead of saying—maupaaay nga aga—her twiggy, lacquered body came in, hands on her hips—nga birat nga demonio, pastilan, mga uday, have you started the novena without me!

Ay nga panulay!

Pastilan, uday!

Birat, birat, birat.

I would mouth her words, admiring.

Mana Talia until the end was full of prayer and buyayaw.

And she'd stand there in one of her many shimmery jacquard outfits, glaring at San Antonio de Padua and Santa Rita de Cascia as if all her trials were their fault.

That summer, Mana Talia, crossed by love, was at our home by the river, in Salogó, instead of praying with her hairspray gang in Tacloban. She sat out on the balcony on Lolo Jote's butaka, staring at Carigara.

Tio Nemor did not bother to dislodge her from his seat.

No one would tell me where her love Quintana had gone.

It did her no good when her husband the congressman "rebealed," she said—why did my love Quintana rebeal, nga yawa nga demontres, when all Quintana did was hurt Meldy, *hija*, you know all my love did was hurt Meldy, *hija*! His own cousin—a Taclobanon like him!

Nga birat nga pakasulay, but what can I do—he's my love.

Above all, there was this absent woman, Meldy Hija, whom they called The Rose, Madame, the star of their imaginations, these worshippers of the Novena to the Wounds of Our Lord.

In my great-grandfather's notebooks he did not mention himself by name. No mention of his bushy eyebrows, or the gray shadow about his pursed mouth (that thin-lined grimace, the almost-even line of his lips: a straight genetic line leading to my mom's Tia Pachang—her stern mouth—innocent in Mick-mick's face, angry in Putt-putt's, lovely in John-john's vanished glance—but just glum in his brother the old senator's, in the one picture we have of him).

No mention of the hairy moles that have bedeviled the Delgados, male and female, throughout the twentieth century, even Adino, sweet Adino, who has one babyish welt. The diary made no comment on the scar, a birthmark? a boyhood accident?—a swath across his left cheek that seems a shadow of a scimitar, an orange peel, or the dark side of a half moon, in the picture my mom has of Lolo Paco.

Baga hin luwag hin kaldero, ayaw pagdad-a.

Instead the diarist wrote dull descriptions of spiders, talked about an ant dragging fearful weapons around like an anxious baker.

Bagan panadero nga mabarak-on nagdadara-dara hin panakot.

At first I wondered why it ended with Tagalog—panakot—meaning: instrument of terror.

But the line came back to me one day—while I was watching Delilah pour *Silver Swan Number One, Silver Swan!* into a bowl of chicken.

The word meant ingredients: spices—panakot!

That is, panakot from Waray, *sakot*, meaning mix, not panakot from Tagalog, *takot*, meaning fear.

An tubak bagan panadero nga mabarak-on nagdadara-dara hin panakot.

The black ant like an anxious baker carrying his condiments around.

When I figured out the line, I felt proud.

The right word just clicked in place, and I had guessed a riddle I did not know had been posed, a problem-solving process secreted by the mess of words in my brain, and I tried to explain the miracle to the boys, but they were right—those pages taxed my efforts of translation for nothing.

All that thinking—just to read about bugs.

He described mice in the woodwork and mites in his clothes. One page named a boat, *Liscum*, a cavalry ship.

His schoolboy hand was beautiful, with its cowlick curls.

I preferred when he wrote in English, which I could easily read.

I tried to be patient, looked for traces of the doctor-congressman-orinologist-chickenologist-murder-victim-at-Tay-Guimoy's-barakasyunan in the handwriting of this stowaway on a ship.

But it was goddamned boring.

I went back to *Abraham Lincoln's World.*

We were playing Discover-Discover when she came up the steps. Her arrival was a surprise above all to the pigs. One of them had to be wrestled on short notice, stabbed, hogtied, singed, and roasted before his companions had time to squeal. Albeit, the chosen one also squealed like a pig. Singeing its hair was a harried occupation, rapid-fire torture with a blowtorch, clearly an improvisation, and blood dripped on the dried mud of the house's dirt space beneath us. We were sitting above the home of our enormous pigs, we had three at the time, all of them named *Pordiiiiin!*—we were waiting for snack time. It took too long and we went off exploring the ancient narra planks on the balcony to start our game, Discover-Discover.

We heard that familiar swine song: prolonged, high-pitched, inhuman.

We stopped playing for a while and peeked through the balcony's slats.

We could see the smooth stone of the AWOL, sloping toward the river. By peering sideways, straining our necks, we thought we could see Tay Lucio, jack of all trades and master of the universe, with his bold bolo slitting the pig.

That wail in June, when fiesta was over and school was almost at hand, the lonely screech of the dying pig in mid-afternoon, when in fact the hour called for merienda, with roscas and tsokolate, not lechon with vinegar, lemongrass, garlic, onion, and death, should have struck an odd note in my memory, but what I remember was the singing.

The singing at her entrance.

How had the musical band hired for funerals and fiestas, the FrankenPresley Combo, that shiny group with sideburns and growling voices, suddenly appeared?

Why do birds?

And then, what the hell—there was Tio Nemorino, back in his electioneering safari outfit and Ray-Ban glasses, instead of his usual karsonsilyos and rubber ismagol in the siesta hour, greeting the arrival.

He greeted her with his own election song, "Top of the World," which told me he was unrehearsed and she was not expected.

So much wonder in most everything.

Mano Oscar Aruta and Man' Bimboy Buñales, the great Franken-Presley twins, strummed their guitars with the fervor of tubâ drinkers who can smell roast pig in the air. We ran from the balcony and watched the mob from the entresuelo where we could see a platoon of men, dressed in blue, down by the guava and bougainvillea garden trampling the pechay, their Armalites almost hitting the hanging orchids, Putt-putt pointing out the thrilling sight, and we could see the maids right before us in their floral dusters and rubber slippers bustling about the dining room and taking the fancy plates from the komedor and flapping fiesta lace cloths onto their tardy places.

Fiesta had already passed, the twenty-second of May, feast of the town's patron saint, the nun with the miracle forehead, Santa Rita de Cascia, and I could see the dinuguan and lechon stains on the table-cloths that the plates barely covered. The purgatorial cleaning of the house in Salogó had yet to come. Tay Lucio's progeny, including his tragic in-law, the Widow Evangeline, pronounced Ebang-he-line, were hacking at silot, the milk of young coconuts spurting in the kitchen for the hostess's drinks, and I could smell the out-of-time spirit of fiesta, mostly ginger, vinegar, and garlic, amid the wrack of cymbals and drums. How the FrankenPresley Combo managed to get from the AWOL along the river and scurry up to the sala, I have no idea, but the snorting of the pigs in the dirt, right below our floor's wooden slats, the muted sounds of the gristly survivors, the extant ones, Pordin 1 and Pordin 2, had a melancholy flavor that added to the combo's soulful croon.

I first saw the woman's crown of hair, shaped for some reason in my memory like a black and burned bibingka—likely because it was Nay Carmen's rice cakes that usually trembled up that staircase in ordinary times.

The woman was tall—all hair and silk and sequins—a floating rem-nant of the Clairol Hi & Dri Hairspray barkada, except she towered above us here in riverine Salogó and not in the praying alcoves of the Novena to the Wounds of Our Lord miles away in seaside Tacloban. And how was it that it was not the FrankenPresley twins that were singing the song's refrain but the mayor himself, my Tio Nemorino, he of the high tenor voice made for the *Ave Maria*?

Schubert's hymn, the one for which he was elected, sung at funerals, weddings, baptisms, and beauty queen coronations in Salogó, was his voice's signature—not this tin-pan tune.

My uncle's voice had a tinge of honey unbotched by false modesty, which he did not possess. He sang with the confidence of his voice's smoothness, a longing from the diaphragm that seems to hang weight as it emerges, so that sound becomes solid, a thing.

But the flimsiness of this tune gave his voice no justice. There he was, Tio Nemorino, with the band seeming to rise from the river, a clanging serenade, swaying to the song's refrain—*It's the love. That I found! Ever since you've been. Around!*

I felt nausea. It was like getting stale old White Rabbit candy when you could have Nay Yaka's roscas. Or getting an animatronic Japanese doll with the metal joints showing when there was a magical object somewhere in your reach, if you could just discover it.

It was not in his range. It mocked his gifts. The moment was a travesty.

But I was a judgmental niece.

The arrival at the top of the stairs loved the song.

It was to her that my uncle sang.

I felt it, the vibration, the way people responded to her entrance and now her tremolo, her voice.

She joined in.

She knew the words.

Something in the wind had heard—whatever her name was.

And it was telling us that things were not the same.

The shock and the joy and the gasps at her presence, crooning the triumphal song.

She gestured with air kisses as she sang.

I wondered who this drama queen was, this giant Lucia di Lammermoor.

The person to ask was Mana Marga, but she was holding a rice pot in both hands, her mouth open, the way in the pictures of the Last Supper, there's always a servant staring stupidly—usually at Judas.

The singing woman was not arrayed as she would be in our future lives, when at the height of her power she glided about in the butterfly ternos, and soon her choice of fashion would rob even tradition of its solace. She wore glitter on the hems of her sleeves, glitter on her wide, sequined pants, called palazzo in the soon-to-come martial law magazines devoted only to her style, glitter on her shoes. She was a mountain of minerals. She was slim and tall, so tall I thought her hair would graze and topple the Statue of the Sacred Heart, placed awkwardly in an alcove facing the komedor as one entered the house. The portrait of Santa Rita fluttered at her passing. I made a move as if to steady the statue, she would knock over Jesus's exposed wound, the dramatic trauma of this statue that, if I thought of it, gave me my own private palm.

But she swayed and clapped her hands and evaded the Sacred Heart, she sang the song my uncle had begun.

Her voice could vibrate like no vampira of TEIPCO's could.

And everyone started clapping, mouthing her chorus.

All of creation clapping at her voice.

I cobbled up this scene later as I tried to understand its place in my childhood. So many caught up in its mess—John-john, Mana Talia, Tio Nemor, even Mick-mick—but as it rolled on to its denouement, the FrankenPresley Combo went on with the next song, probably John Denver. I sat there joining the incident to other scenes in my mind's book of harsh judgment, mostly from the Bible—my favorite in school at the time being *Bible Stories for Children* by Uncle Arthur Maxwell, a multi-volume set the school library owned though even as a child I could see it was not Catholic. It did not have enough Virgin Marys in it.

I thought it was religion that made me a hateful and judgmental child.

Once when my father suddenly arrived in Tacloban, and he brought me after all those years a pasalubong, a Nancy Drew book, he appeared in his well-shined shoes, flashy silken suit like Engelbert Humperdinck or Tom Jones, some polished crooner ready to sing "Delilah," or worse.

My mom loved Tom Jones, Elvis, so that as a teenager my job was to hate them. Suddenly there my father was, his scrubbed and lotioned face, his manicured hands and expensive cologne. His look of the homecoming scoundrel, the scalawag from estados, with his Chief Petty Officer glow. The revulsion I felt in me—I was only nine years old—was my secret: mute and unspeakable. *It's not unusual to see me cry, I wanna die.* I kept my feelings from my mom, who exclaimed when he arrived—*look, inday, see who's here!* As if she were expecting him, a true sight to give joy.

There he was, at the bougainvillea door in Housing and not by the scratched walls of Wilmington—my father. A spiffy man. His sheen frightened me. He came back as if the world were his oyster, and he was its pearl. He brought boxes of goods—Jergens lotion, Dial soaps, Prell shampoos—and everyone oohed and aahed in the unpacked sala as if the fragrant goods were magic, and not just bathroom products. Nothing was explained. He just arrived.

Every day I woke up praying to my mom's Saint Anthony and Santa Rita and above all to her Sacred Heart of Jesus—praying that it was not true, that in the morning he would be gone, back to Long Beach or Okinawa or wherever it was thoughtless men like him wandered, and then I'd see him across from me at breakfast eating a doughnut my mom had cooked from scratch, he wolfed the doughnut, his mouth chewed and smacked as if the doughnut were made just for him, which it was, and my hatred made me look away.

You would think I would have confessed my bad thoughts about my father to the priest, since I already had my catechetical instruction and was confirmed by then, with two more godparents than I needed (my stern aunt Tita Patchy and a woman named Mrs. Carrascoso, wife of the new manager of the Coca-Cola plant, a useless ninang who never appeared during Three Kings, the day of gift-giving).

I believed my mom when she told me I was religious because I was always reading illustrated stories from the Bible.

But I never thought of confessing my evil thoughts about my dad. Because I did not feel guilty.

I did not feel guilty about hating my father even though I was glad to see the Nancy Drew book he brought me. Every year when my mom made me write him Christmas letters, I asked him for a Nancy Drew book. Though I could see his present was not new, secondhand, with feathering on its spine, still I accepted it, read it over and over even months later, without guilt I took his gift, whose title I have misremembered though my memory of its cluelessness was the same, *The Password to Larkspur Lane*, while I prayed to the Sacred Heart of Jesus for him to disappear to a place no teenage detective could find.

I hated him.

I will say I hated my father not just because he could not even be bothered to choose a new book from a real bookstore in the United States of America. He probably got the Nancy Drew from the garage sale of our neighbors in Wilmington, a family whose name I remembered as Remorse (they were Irish, my mom said, so it was okay to say hello because they had a Catholic heritage), and my dad just grabbed the nearest thing, I thought I could smell on the book the pee-soaked pajamas of their kid my age, Christina Remorse, a bedwetter, I discovered, when I once stayed a few nights at their house waiting for Adino, sweet Adino, to be born out in the hospital where they had taken my mom—the naval hospital in Long Beach.

It was sad that my father was not a thoughtful man, but that is not why I hated him. I did not hate him for his fancy clothes, which had a melancholy air, in fact, I imagined him buying them, a brown boy in the fifties in America, what kind of terror was that, what kind of unrequited desire to be the man he could be in Los Angeles, coming from Salogó, and the image of him at a shop window, migrant hopes in his pockets, his reflection in estados, makes me pause, I did not hate his shiny, matte face, though its memory gives me a bad feeling that in my maldita judgment I refuse to place.

I hated him on behalf of my mother.

Because I could see in Tacloban that she could not.

She allowed him into our home though we were doing all right in our new place, with Mana Marga and the two girls, Candy and Lheezah, sometimes also Delilah and Janice, who helped with the laundry and the cooking and the caring for Adino while my mom made her frames or painted our walls any color she wanted, and Mana Talia and Lola Sayong and the Clairol Hi & Dri Hairspray gang came regularly to pray for everyone's souls.

It was a good life for me, a world of gossip and perfume and caring and women.

When one day he was gone, not even a goodbye, at least in my memory, which is selective, for a moment I thought it was wish fulfillment.

My father left, I believe my mom refused to go, and I was happy.

Only a few months ago, when my mother was dying, and someone thought maybe he should know, I was told that he said—*If you're asking me for money, I'm not giving any—she is not my wife.*

I have never felt guilty for hating my dad.

That's how I know it's not religion that makes me judgmental.

It's just that there are matters that anger does not corrode: it clarifies.

It's something in me, in my core, this hatred—my horror and judgment and inability to forgive some things, a dim cognition that I could not at the same time express.

In the game Discover-Discover we hid the game's treasure— usually one of our cheap, throwaway Easter toys, since Easter was really about the dead and so the soft-drink trinkets were weird, half-hearted, or maybe a plastic freebie from the Coca-Cola film trucks that came to the town plaza to show Charlton Heston in *The Ten Commandments* during the slow days of Lent. We'd hide then seek them in the cracks of the huge molave dining room table, or in the mahogany seams of the balcony, or in the ruts of the sliding capiz shell windows that must have been broken since 1944, when the house in Salogó was left to not one but two invaders, first Japanese when Douglas and his army abandoned us then American when Douglas and his army said they saved us.

The house's decay was perfect for the detective puzzling of Discover-Discover.

Cold, cold, I would yell, *cold,* as Mick-mick scurried away to search for whatever was the game's chosen loot.

He never remembered that the best hiding place was the house itself—its cracks and its rot.

Hot, hot, I yelled—and he stuck his hand experimentally into a fist-sized crack in the old molave table, right there amid the musical guests, which included random beauty queens, the current Miss Salogó as well as two still beautiful ones who were now expired, plus the usual people whose main talent was voting, all listening to Tio Nemor sing the wrong song, "Top of the World."

I expected the treasure to come out—a plush bunny with crossed eyes, so no one ever wanted it—but Mick-mick was unlucky.

His fist got stuck in the table's crack, a decaying hole.

Hot! Hot! I kept yelling.

Sssssh! Sssssh!

Mana Marga finally released her kaldero, put it on the table, and tried to pull Mick-mick away from the clapping guests.

I'm on the top of the world, I'm looking—

But his hand was stuck. She could not move him.

I could see the treasure was almost in his grasp, a fuzzy limb pushing under the table.

He kept wriggling his stuck fist, trying to get the prize.

He kept at it as the song ended, and the attention of the beauty queen and the ex-beauty queens and the musicians and the voters and the giant woman with the bibingka hair turned to him.

Everyone watched the progress of the deranged-eyed plush bunny from out of the withered crack of molave as Mick-mick, his one hand stuck, slowly drew the toy out from under the table leg with his other, free limb.

But Mick-mick's other fist would not budge from the top of the table.

Then in triumph he wrenched the bunny out with the other hand!

It was a feat.

I applauded.

The bunny's ears had brown spots from the rot in the molave wood, or were those fire ants crawling about its creepy eyes?

It was at that moment, with Mick-mick's one hand stuck in time and the plush bunny raised in the air by his other hand, that the guest of honor held out her glittering, jeweled arm toward Mick-mick.

"Oh what a cute boy! Bless!" she said.

Everyone called Mick-mick cute because of his flat pancake face—the way Mick-mick's wide eyes looked up at everyone with a blissed-out look of absolute indifference, which was not his actual affect, nor his defect.

It was just him: his face.

I looked at the tall, jeweled crone, one more among my mother's beautified gang from Tacloban.

Without looking at the lady, Mick-mick in triumph pulled his other, stuck arm, red-handed, from out of the crack in the table.

He did it so suddenly he almost toppled over Mana Marga, who was holding him, and he fell against the sequined lady.

I don't know what got over him—he was a genius, a Super-Boy, but also unpredictable.

Parasaway.

Ay nga pakasulay.

Both of his hands free, he took the outstretched palm of the glittering lady, and instead of blessing it—he bit it.

I laughed, Putt-putt and I screamed—*Hala! Punyeta!*

Ay demontres! Nga birat!

Putt-putt and I high-fived over our Mana Talia words.

Then Mick-mick ran the hell out of the room, repeating the words

Cuteboy! Bless! Cuteboy! Bless!, and the rest of us, happy at Mick-mick's triumph, ran after.

Mana Marga, as if on cue, rushed to the doorway, blocking us at the entresuelo, and for a moment we were stumped.

My mom knew better than to run off and capture Mick-mick, who had vanished, probably already hiding under the house with the surviving pigs.

My mom would have had to drag him from that dirt dungeon of our fragrant underground smelling of animal pee, smoke, guavas, and chickenshit.

But the blue-shirted goons of the glittering lady did not know that.

They stood at the doorway, where Mana Marga also kept them from going downstairs.

Please, she said—release him! Let her go.

Her pronouns were in disarray despite her years as the star pupil of Mrs. Edith Taffie.

The goons in blue ignored Mana Marga.

They pushed her aside and ran down the stairs.

Following the goons, we ducked under Mana Marga's armpits and dashed down to warn Mick-mick about the men in blue.

I could hear Mana Marga yelling—

No, no! Pssst! Pssst! Poison! Danger! The rodenticides and the toxins! They are coming to get you!

There we were, back in our haven on the dirt floor by the pigs, when two men in blue suits found us—John-john, Putt-putt, Mick-mick, Adino, and me—under the house with the smoke and the roasting lechon and the bantam roosters.

"Please—sorry for that, Meldy," my mom said, as one of the blue-suited men brought up howling little Mick-mick, with all of us now running back up to defend our cousin. I lagged behind carrying Adino in my arms. "It is the fault of his mother he is so wild—she is Cebuana, you know, from Danao, not from Tacloban."

So this was Meldy Hija.

Madame this Madame that.

The Rose, not the Thorn—Imelda Romualdez y Trinidad.

The name in her slanted script in a picture, memorialized in the coffee book table by Kerima Polotan that I was cursed to read over and over.

Madama in the Palace.

To be honest, it was only later that I put the two together.

And nowhere did I ever find, lurking amid the observers, the Second Lady or the Third or the Fourth.

All was only she.

She stood tall beside the ancient molave table and regally held out her bitten hand.

Mana Marga was hovering over the boy.

"Oh poor, poor Mongo," muttered Mana Marga.

Mana Marga spoke under her breath, and I, standing next to her, could hear—*He is just a mongoloid. No read no write—poor, poor Mongo.*

Meldy Hija bent down as one of her soldiers lifted Mick-mick up, and so each figure in the tableau—giant Meldy Hija, tiny soldier, rebel Mick-mick—adjusted their moves until Mick-mick hung in the air lofted toward her height.

A suspenseful scene.

I watched Mick-mick's floppy, dirty limbs dangling above me—a flailing plush toy.

"Bless," said my mom, gently nudging Mick-mick by his behind, "bless the hand! Agi, kay lamano gad, intoy. She is a Taclobanon!"

That was the woman's great distinction—the Rose of the Taclobanon.

Floating, suspended Mick-mick took the lady's hand to his forehead, and all I could think was—*Hot! Hot!*

Then a sudden lunge, and chaos came over the company of mooching musicians, post-election hangers-on, powdery matronas, and the beauty queens.

Of all people, golden-haired John-john, a.k.a. Guapo, the most pacific kid of us all, a dreamy boy whose aim in life was to smoke with the druggies and the pharmacists near Farmacia Watts, reached up and snatched his brother from the blue-suited goons.

From his suspended height bending toward the lady, Mick-mick came down to earth, and John-john ran off, his brother in his arms, down the stairs toward the AWOL, toward the banks of Himanglos.

At his second escape, no one bothered to capture Mick-mick, as if everyone knew the second feature of this double-bill of a trifling show would be a dud. Mick-mick's escape in the end drew shrugs, and the moochers and the matronas were about to return to their merienda of bibingka and their impatient expectation of out-of-season lechon, when a figure appeared at the entresuelo.

The rest of the goons had brought her up from the house's depths.

Please release her, Mana Marga had said.

She had used the correct pronoun.

In the goons' arms was their treasure.

During the game of Discover-Discover, we had not noticed her presence among us, amid the guava trees, the goats, and the chickens.

She must have been hiding out there by the AWOL, in her jacquard suit and Hanes pantyhose.

She had soldiers on both sides of her, and she did not smell of the waters of Our Lady of Lourdes—she smelled of animal pee, smoke, guavas, and chickenshit.

Her bouffant hair was messed up, dirty with santan leaves and bits of yellow petals from the kamia tree.

The goons of Meldy Hija presented Mana Talia, our refugee, out from her hiding place by the river Himanglos.

I could hear Mana Marga's sigh.

Mana Marga had tried to warn her by screaming—*Poison! Danger! The rodenticides and the toxins! They are coming to get you!*

But still—Mana Talia was before us, revealed.

"Birat nga leche nga demontres," grinned Mana Talia, standing tall as a dwarf, hands on her hips.

She looked up at the giant lady, her former student of music at Holy Infant Academy—Meldy Hija.

"Nga panulay! No need for this drama, Meldy. You know that my love, Quintana, loves you. He's from Leyte. Like you. But he's just a truth-teller. He means you no harm, not you in particular—you of all people, a Taclobanon like us! He is just a truth-teller. Who loves the nation. That is just who he is."

And then she sang.

Another election song.

It was enough to make one wish for one's own exile.

Please release me. Let him go.

I heard Tio Nemor going at John-john that night. He took his belt while the boy, bound to the abaca bench on the balcony, facing the river, lay staring up at his Papá, his lush curls flat that the maids liked to brush, his beautiful eyes wide open, refusing to cry, while his father's belt went at him.

Pak!

Pak!

Pak! Pak!

Pak!

Pak!

Pak! Pak!

A quadrupled set of whacks, then the effect multiplied by the maids' cries and his father's voice—not the singing voice of the *Ave Maria*, but a deep, uncontrolled, desperate sound, as my uncle's muscled arm beat up his son, not with rhythm, and so fast and hard that he twisted it, and the next day we learned Tio Nemor had broken his own wrist. That was how hard he hit John-john.

Our terrified pity.

His mom Doctor Tita Tita was not around, or Tio Nemor would have never seen the light.

It wasn't strange to me that it was only with John-john that Tio Nemor unleashed his fury. Throughout my childhood I understood it was only John-john who could release this charge in Tio Nemor, only John-john, his oldest child, had significance. I don't know why I took it that way—that I saw nothing strange in the double lives of these adults, my mom's family, the Delgados, the way that I loved them, though they were loving and scary, good and bad, giving and corrupt, and our role as children was to know such divided selves as one of the riddles of being alive.

Take that for humiliating me before Meldy, before the voters of Salogó!

We cowered in the bedroom next to the balcony, Putt-putt, Mick-mick, Adino, and I, peeking out at the scene, listening to the pak! pak! pakpak! of Tio Nemor's belt. We kept waiting for John-john to yell, to scream.

We did not hear a sound.

I think of that silence now, John-john's resistance.

The way he rebelled.

We did not hear him cry.

So many stories, inconsequential legends that we have repeated to ourselves, wrapped up in the house that right now, I know, we are destroying.

PART TWO
LA SEGUNDA

✷ ✷ ✷

Stowaway on a Boat

The boy arrives in Samar on one of those freights carrying mail, palay, and goats. Those tubs of death and wood that still ply the islands. My mom would send us on our last summer vacation, to visit our cousins in Cebu, where we'd play amid Romblon marble and American glass jalousies, and we'd say goodbye to her on Tacloban's pier from our ship, named like omens of disaster. M/V *Good Luck*. M/V *Sweet Hope*. That last look at my mother, waving at us—me, Mana Marga, and Adino—her bouffant hairdo and her muu-muu outfit with the faux-Pucci geometric shapes growing smaller and smaller in the distance: the sight of my mom on the pier would become the marker, for me, of that melancholy, vanishing point of summer—when I knew I had already wasted all my time but, staring at my mom's clothes of harlequin diamonds until she disappeared, still I hoped for the best.

The ship is the *Liscum*, an old Spanish cavalry boat used to transport horses from Manila to Zamboanga, renamed after some martyred US Marine when the Americans confiscated the boat from the Spanish after the Battle of Manila.

A faded news item, about the USAT *Liscum*, dated 1902, falls from the lined notebook.

In his careful schoolboy handwriting, the boy details a shipboard journey, mites and the antique cockling of the pages obscuring his witness. It seems no one mentioned to the boy that an old cavalry ship is like purgatory for humans, a place of crap and beasts, and the boy's vomit joins with horseshit, straw, and insect wings in puddles on the ship's planks. His vomit threads through dried animal pellets stuck like nails to the planks since 1521. (I'm glad to note his sense of irony.)

His spit tangles with the straw of his makeshift cot in the cargo hold.

Typical of a Delgado, his gastrointestinal system is weak.

He vomits on an American's shoes.

Before him, his splayed notebook lies on split rivets hosting horse-shit and grass.

The book smelled of earth.

I looked for traces of the future senator, or the entomological doctor, his brother, in this weak-stomached scribbler—the stowaway on a boat.

But the notebook disappointed me the way it did when I first opened it, when I was a child and I tried my hand at premature translation.

A mess of observations.

The stowaway talks about eating ants burrowed in the eyes of a pineapple and watching worms emerge from ears of corn. Vermin and insects, devouring things.

Mga yatot ngan insekto, sige hin kaon.

He sounds like Mick-mick, if Mick-mick could write.

True, there is a dissertation, a bit adolescent though the synesthesia has promise, on the smells and speeches of darkness.

Everything is in color—purple feelings of nausea, orange look of dread.

Paghihikasuka means ube.

An paghikaluya han lawas equals naranghita.

Not *naranja*—naranghita.

Sometimes it's in Spanish, sometimes Waray.

This lined notebook makes sense on the following levels.

One: he is likely eleven, because we know from history books that the year must be 1901, and the month is August. He has this childish reliance on the tactile, the witless clarity of his age.

Two: darkness seems to speak when you cannot see because your mind must imagine (I base this largely on my endless blackout nights in Salogó).

The diarist hears jungle noises, mentions owls. Leeches fascinate him, and his fascination, too, has color—a poxed blue: a purplish green.

An akon pamati pagsiplat ngada han limatik—may kolor hin muyâ nga baga hin napandok.

His gaze *feels* color: an akon *pamati* pagsiplat—

His colors are mixed, even diseased: muyâ nga baga hin napandok.

I had to consult a glossary to get that gloss: muyâ is "visible between purple and green," pandok is, as I suspected, smallpox.

I read through the words carefully—his aggregate of tongues.

Reptiles are a trip. He watches a slim, gray-green lizard up on a bulkhead, eating a cockroach. Then: a snake on a bulkhead swallows up a lizard, whose tiny limbs flail, an infant's tendril-like hands against both sides of the snake's mouth—hala!

An ipis ginkaon han butiki nga ginkaon han halas—hala!

The stages of life into a snake's guts.

The lizard's fascinating erasure is in slow motion.

An kawara han butiki, ha akon paniplat may kolor hin pakwan nga baga hilaw pa, o dila hin misay nga naghihiniyak.

Dashes of color suffuse this watching—a rose-glaze the color of watermelon not fully ripe, or a certain cat's tongue as it cries, veiling his careful sight as the lizard disappears.

It's odd because, the way I understand it, he's not actually describing the *color* of the lizard—he's describing the *color of its disappearance* in his mind: ha akon paniplat may kolor hin pakwan nga baga hilaw pa.

He's not quite certain of the right shade of the pale watermelon (nor am I).

He mixes up a sea voyage with descriptions of a jungle.

Sourceless vibrations in the forks of trees. Waray didto waray dinhi nga tingog tikang ha mga nagsasangang puno. *The snoring of someone on a shipboard cot—that he mistakes for the ravings of a toad.* Napapadla nga pakla. *The damaged beak of a dead bird.* An guba nga tusak hin patay nga tamsi. (But that anapestic tetrameter is, to my ear, a good touch.) *A swarm of forest tarantulas* "like moving mohair coat brushes, or a bunch of greenish-goldish touch-me-nots with a blush in the furred center."

That last was in English.

A beetle has the sheen of glass in the night lit up only by candles—and a comma splice.

Kandila la an lamrag, ha kasiruman an kagang may pagkasalamin.

Also—

An kaingin han kapaitan hit kapanitan han lanzones may asô nga baga bulaw—hala!

The kindling of the lanzones's bitter peels has a blond haze, hala!, the white fur of a santol fruit gains sacramental mystery on the page, ants colonize the thorax of a cicada, its molted form wafting in the wind before corpse—and conqueror—settle at sea.

Sweet ecphrasis on santol and ants.

A series of stations, ending in water.

Nangadto la—ha dagat!

Someone's hairy fist turns out to be a bat.

Ha ha, panic ng panic, yun pala paniki!

Paragraph-long descriptions on the difficulties of lying down upon rocks—slant rhymes in grass trenches.

Makuri gad udoy it talahib nga katre, it imo inop puno hin zacate!

And the usual random witticisms in two tongues, the pests of any Filipino gist—

A drunken shape!

Hubog na hubog.

Nag-aasô nga aso.

Dog barbecue!

That engineering imp of a bridge.

Ay, panulay nga panulay.

Agi nga agi.

Ow, that path.

(or is it, *wow, that script?*)

It's a long list.

Waray ako. I have nothing, I am not. A Waray.

And as I turn the pages, I can feel that unraveling coming on, rising up my chest.

Like those moments in Malacañang Palace, I have to keep making decisions, choose which useless detail must be deciphered.

An old, familiar ulcer.

This code-switching.

Waray and Tagalog, Spanish and English, gibberish and Latin.

Nothing, nothing, nothing.

In my wish for certainty, to understand, there's this wrench in me—acid reflux.

In one section, the diarist is always wishing to sleep.

To rest.

Dream.

Inop.

Lunop.

Tidal wave.

Lingkod. Higda.

He dreams of madmen in a cave. He strikes at ancients in a forest. Mga lurong ha lungib. Mga gurang ha kagurangan. He slurps gulaman, which he mislabels as thick sap forming on the barks of trees. The trees, in turn, rehash limonsito: but he uses the Tagalog word—kalamansi.

An aura of gold, slightly smelling of piss.

May anyong yaman, may pagkahamot hin yamang.

Yaman = wealth.

Yamang = pee.

Is it a Waray pun on the Tagalog, or a Tagalog pun on the Waray?

Too many of the pages are a chronicle of disjointed dreams.

Dream: marching straight into a ravine, he emerges on the other side of the pass with a missive in his hand.

Con un mensaje en la mano.

Dream: falling into some damned ravine, he dreams.

Dream: words on a wall. (It is only a recipe for kinilaw, involving malunggay.)

Dream: he is in a dream watching a jailer jailing him. His jailer eats bibingka.

Dream: walking toward a ravine, the protagonist of his dream pauses (he is not sure in this dream if he is the protagonist). He forgets what happens next.

Dream: a pile of roosters' feet.

Kadamo nga mga manok ugaring puro la tiil.

When he wakes up, sweating, his scream turns his throat dry, and it comforts him to know—

He is only dreaming.

Agi nga pag-ininop.

Sueño.

Panaginip.

Inop. Inop. Inop.

Lunop.

Tidal wave.

Agi agi agi!

Agi an agi han iya agi!

For a moment that trio was stunning: pain, path, and pen.

Agi, agi, agi!

Gestalt of unfinished events—why is he in a jungle with a letter in his hand then watching a dolphin leap in the distance, "look[ing] like a liquid splatter of diamonds"?

Every so often, the retreat into English.

Plus, you don't put malunggay in kinilaw: in Tacloban, it is in tinola.

Piecing the papers in chronological order takes a while.

Figuring out the Spanish from the Tagalog, the English from the Waray—

Should I consult a scholar?

So many names in the book. (Apart from the usual suspects, Emilio Aguinaldo, president of the Republic, Theodore Roosevelt, successor of the fallen McKinley, even Roosevelt's daughter, Señora Alice Longworth, has a cameo, touring the occupied country her father plotted to invade but never bothered to comprehend, et cetera, et cetera, et cetera.)

As I read through—

Hilario Sayo.

Arthur MacArthur.

Marcelo Badel.

The great future general Urbano Lacuna, *requiescat in pace!*

Ka Vicente Lukban.

Private William Grayson.

Macario Sakay—Mack the Sundang, Mack the Knife! (Mack the Barber. Mack the Beloved.)

Colonel "Fighting Fred!" Funston.

The righteous Ilocano Isabelo Abaya (but only implied by an incident with a hammock in Candon).

The valiant "brigands" of the Tinio Brigade.

And the servants of the house on Moret Street—

Mariano the mayordomo.

Ambrosio the cook.

Felicisima the labandera.

Tay Sequil, *El Cochero Exequiel!*

Will they all need footnotes?

Heaven forbid.

And last but not least, his main cast—

The two brothers and their father, Don Francisco The First.

The dead mother.

And in surprising, almost negligible minor cast: his grandmother Nemesia the Insomniac.

Above all—

A place untold yet central to the story—

This unknown town.

Giporlos.

I put the notebook down.

People don't really talk about Giporlos in my family, except Lheezah, a distant cousin—but on Mama Bia's side, so added Mana Marga—the maid of many *H*s who once asked me to write letters for her, to her family in Samar.

Staring at a page, I think of drawing-room reproductions of night-mare Magrittes.

I take the papers up again.

A lunatic sense of place throws me off—Manila, Malolos, Candon, Samar—and last but not least—

Salogó.

But I also feel—pleasure.

I keep reading.

I turn pages.

I cast off isolated objects from my reader's plate, pending compre-hension—e.g., a drawing of what looks like a drumstick, or a bayonet, whole pages in simple, childish Spanish even I can understand, novena prayers I know the responses to, a dormant figure on a mat, or is that a torture rack, a map all in blue, an extended description of an arrangement of chicken wire, disjoint song lyrics in different tongues, a host of incomprehensible words in an adolescent's theatrical hand, and too many Catholic cowlick *Os*.

The shapes of moths on long-lost words.

A blot that seeps deep, a well of gore, a calligraphic grave, inset in blank sheets.

Andro Leonardo

I kept getting messages from the unknown sender, not my follower or friend, on Instagram, Twitter, Facebook, and those out-of-date spaces still on my phone—Skype and Viber and WhatsApp. I deactivated Facebook, but the private messages kept coming. *Ireneo Funes RIP* was the first dirty trick she played on me. *#EmmaBovary #AbacaFan.* Question: *#SeneBeSele?* That made me laugh. Then—*Beth March, requiescat.* Jeez—she was going way back in time. She followed that up with—*#NoToProfessorBhaer!* And then a few hours later— *Prince Andrei Bolkonsky RIP.* Which she revised to *Andrei Androfski @Mila18.* Hah! She has the memory of an elephant, including the books we had long discarded. But when I saw *Andro Leonardo 1960-1987 #Butiki* I knew what she wanted me to know. That she was serious. She was in this for the kill and would not stop until I answered. But I held off. I turned off my phone. I took a breath. Of course, I turned my phone back on, and what the hell. She said— *Rudy Da Moody, Stayin' Alive! Ahahaha #StillAlive! #Hallo! #Ibid.*

That shit, that fucker. That woman of no scruples. The serial headings caught me. I fell into her trap. She knew my anger got the best of me. My judgmentalism, my juvenile self. I took her bait. She was not only my first publisher, she was also my first friend. Of course it was Trina Trono trailing me all over social media in private messages, in DMs, in the spaces of anonymous names. After college, she began her life as a researcher and had the knack of pursuit. I should have known. If there's one person who will get her way, no matter the slim dividends, the salt in the wounds—she'd be the one.

She changed when we got older. That was par for the course. Not only for everyone, but in a country that knows betrayal even as it rolls over, shows another side before it knows itself, has a knack for simultaneity and genius for incoherence, the capacity to live in calm with contradiction—our own kind of Buddhism, if you kindly think of it—the fact of reversal, a change of mind, is inevitable, sometimes a curse, often a consolation. We have been called *flips* and barely register the pun. It's not our job to resolve others' incomprehension of us: no one asked us to be conceivable, including us.

But there are ways that people remain the same, and even in their transformations you know their kernel because you knew them too early.

Your knowing is dangerous because they know the same about you.

She changed her name to her mom's when still in her teens, and for me that was touching. Her aptitude for sentiment was powerful but repressed. In college, she dragged me to the demonstrations and the marches, the midnight rallies to Mendiola and overnight teach-ins in La Union. I cannot blame her for my errors, my ideological limitations and my fantasist projections. That she can put me in my place, I have no doubt. That I have rejected her, I do not regret. I opened up her message, I read her piece.

So sorry to hear about Mana Adina I am going to funeral with Sirit the mayor's wife what??? Omg I still cannot get over the mayor Manny Trinidad ☹ you know Bling-Bling daughter of Sirit + Manny lives near you in NYC! will be glad to meet up deep sorrow over these circumstances when do you arrive in Tacloban. Condolence. @TrinaTrono1414

What the hell? Why is it that people who know better lose their minds online—their thumbs can't find caps. Filipinos like to text with no vowels. Everyone is a pragmatic semiotician. But more to the point—Bling-bling, daughter of Sirit and Manny? Is Trina Trono now in cahoots with the world of the Trinidads—the family of goons, the bagmen of the dictators that Sirit married into over the nation's dead bodies—the bodies of student activists, communists, labor strikers, protesting farmers in our crossed times of marching toward Mendiola?

It was Trina who dragged me from Don Quixote, man of La Mancha, and Sir Gawain, the Green Knight, to the speeches of Andro Leonardo. My introduction to that world was accidental, but I would not have spent those years any other way. Sure, Trina and I called him lizard—butiki—hallo!—ibid—but that was in self-defense, our guard against our crowd's worship. On campus, he was adored. He stood at this angle, taller than your average Maoist, wearing those leather Jesus sandals, and on him, we decided, it was not corny. Ironic, we thought, then just irrelevant. We forgave him a lot. He had bad hair—a side-parted mod cut from the wrong decade, or a cheap barber, with bangs on the side so stubborn it kept falling over his left eye. He looked Chinese, like a lot of Filipino rebels—the Chinese in the Filipino is the ignored font of our resistance. He was no fashion plate. He had the tendency to stand one leg forward, contrapposto, kind of bending, one arm on hip, the other extended as if about to take a cigarette. That's the pose of Andro Leonardo in my mind—an upright lizard, taking a puff, arm akimbo. Usually he held a megaphone. He never looked hurried. His words were urgent. He was tall, skinny, with a seeming curvature of the spine that his height mitigated. But when he spoke—and I always watched him from a crowd, I never got close, I see him even now from the distance of memory—he looked as if he were bending down toward you.

That day, I thought he was looking at me.

My skepticism is as pronounced as the part that venerates. But it was Andro Leonardo that kept me going to the marches after Trina Trono's invitations began to sound only opportunistic. True, she was a national-democrat nag, so I would call her myself, believing as I do in her faiths, but until she turned—into a capitalist running-dog, as her friends began to call her, and I empathized with her angst, her sense of the group's betrayal, the way they called her a fascist spy, a DPA, the most nasty thing, what a bad metaphor, a Deep-Penetration-Agent working for the military, they falsely accused her, and their betrayal of her was brutal—the way harsh jokes masked the group's split and killing judgments—I always believed in Trina. And until she turned—that trite lapse from commie to corporate hack—I remained on her side.

I have always believed in her first cause.

Our primum mobile.

In a violent state, that beacon, revolt, holds: and even now I believe in it, that cause.

The first time I saw Andro Leonardo, at AS Lobby, I was emerging from the Faculty Center walking toward PHAN. I must have been on my way to history class, PHI 101, because that would be the route of my passage. I'd walk down from Kalayaan to FC through AS Lobby to Palma Hall Annex. I was a freshman in an all-denim outfit sewn by my mom's paragtahi, not the costurera, Elvis Oras's aunt Mrs. Young, but Mana Coring, the one on Gomez Street who didn't make gowns. I was a provincial nerd in made-to-order, embroidered pants. I remember being self-conscious because no one looked like me.

I was proud of my look when I arrived at Diliman: Mana Marga and I had taken care to prepare this collegiate trousseau. But here in Manila people bought clothes in malls and called the library *libe*, not aklatan. I could sense that my way with English—which in high school allowed no extra currency, i.e., Tagalisms or lapses in Waray, or you got fined—caused suspicion among the worthy. People spoke in fragments, neither Tagalog nor English, as if sounding broken mattered. I thought they sounded like asses—donkeys in *Pinocchio*, unable to recognize their degenerating selves. My smugness was my shield. My classmates could not place me. I was absurd. Even my Tagalog failed me because no one ever said *ikinagagalak kong makilala*, or *ito ba ang tamang silid-aralan?* They smirked. Some laughed. But instead of acknowledging my strangeness, I thought everyone else was incorrect, too slow to figure me out. It's a quirk of my upbringing. *I am the child of Adina an guapa, no one can conquer me.* Or my oblivion is one more pathetic sign of an arrogance I cannot cure. I was passing through AS Lobby, with the different clubs and frats and sororities and barkadas grouped in this thrilling open-air space—this place of commingling, this sunlit agora, in which even if you walked alone, in your absurdly matching embroidered jean jacket and pants, it seemed there was something out there broadening your vision, though it was only a trick of tropical light. That day I noticed the biggest crowd was gathered before the AS mural, the one by the National Artist, Vicente Manansala, that I liked to examine as I passed—but white banners with red lettering obscured the cubist art. The crowd of students—sitting cross-legged, rapt, looking up at the awkward, skinny boy, who seemed to be leaning backward, one leg forward and bent, like the butiki version of Michelangelo's *David*—spanned four of the lobby's maroon colonnades. What emergency had happened? In the middle of them all was Andro Leonardo, carrying a megaphone and talking about Dante.

My memory is that he was quoting something in the *Inferno* that first time, about the horrors of neutrality in Limbo, or something, which had just come up in my exams, then he mentioned Gandalf, it turns out university radicals were partial to *Lord of the Rings*, then he exhorted the crowd to topple imperialism, bureaucrat-capitalism, and feudalism. The collage of allusions should be comic but it wasn't.

Instead, the fusing of these disparate matters was like a dream that in that moment you resolved. His gift was odd—a charismatic nerd with gnomic sayings, a jujitsu way with logic, in which without knowing it your sense of power was inverted. He had a slew of populist tricks. He spoke off the cuff. He brought up Joseph Conrad, then joked about Joseph Campbell, then recited a line of the Bhagavad-Gita, and of course he ended with John Lennon—whether before or after his death, on campus Lennon rhymed too easily with Lenin. People were moved. Nothing he said sounded absurd. Instead, soaking in Andro Leonardo's conviction, you believed justice could be done. The point is, I have never in my life met another whose speech—I don't remember him repeating a sequence, and once one segue, from Marx to Marcos to García Márquez, was perfect and perfectly nutty—I have yet to meet anyone whose speech seemed so improvised (who cares if it was not) yet galvanized others.

I was sixteen.

Of course, it is my ears that I affirm: his skill attracted a kid like me, the way he took apart my discomfort about the tossing of the knight in *Don Quixote*, quoting Cervantes then Marvel Comics to talk about injury and, weirdly, totalitarianism, upon which he digressed inexplicably to Zuma (oh he of *Hiwaga* komiks what the hell why not?), an upsetting unbalanced screed on colonialism (he tilted his head sideways, but not like the sidekick whose only vowel was *e*—*berekret-kepetelesme*, I heard in my head, *Rosario, stop it already!*), then in electrifying Tagalog he illuminated the means of action at our disposal so that his heavy-handed phrase gained its proper weight: *imperyalismo, ibagsak.*

But it wasn't just me.

Andro Leonardo had the entire crowd by Manansala's mural in the palm of his raised hand that held his activist schtick—his Camel cigarette. He must have been nineteen. I still remember that day I passed by AS Lobby and saw the leaning kid talking about *Inferno* and revolution. I remember his signature posture, as if he were about to take a step, a stroll, but instead he turned a phrase, and we were

with him. I stayed put. I did not go to class. I went with the crowd
to the AS Steps, where Andro Leonardo merged with a group who
unfurled more banners in red letters, and leading them toward the
street, now facing us all and holding Andro Leonardo's megaphone,
was my old elementary school friend, Trina Trono.

My college days were ordinary—street agitation in between
exams on English Romanticism. I remember a blockade com-
memorating the First Quarter Storm, how I jumped when an
economics professor whom everyone else recognized ignored
our flimsy barricade, piled-up desks and chairs and one disabled
jeepney. The woman professor looked so determined to kill us
as she crashed through our banners in her fancy car that I was
surprised when a fellow protester, instead of cursing the mother-
fucker, saluted and let her pass. His name was Jolliboy, treasurer
of an underground cell (not mine)—an econ major, of course. Jolliboy became a stockbroker in his afterlife, and maybe I should
have known. The professor, you may have guessed, was Paulita
Samson, whom a few years later I saw leading anti-dictator protests in Makati, and now she is back to being everyone's bourgeois
scold, but that is how the world turns. Time gives irony a lot of
leash. I lost my new shoes, bought at Cardam's at Ali Mall—a pair
of dumb espadrilles—in my first rally circling Quezon Memorial
Circle. I ran off to La Union for a teach-in near a dive shop (owned
by the family of a comrade in our half-assed self-educations, a
half-Japanese zoology major named Ogawa). Before leaving for La
Union, Chika Ogawa and I visited her sister, Michi, an employee
of the Commission on Audit, and told her—*We are not asking for
permission to go to our teach-in! But can you give us money for pamasahe?* We were righteous moochers, romantic idiots.

But I have no hesitation in saying—joining that cause was the
most correct thing I have done in my life.

So when a few years after, and I was already in America, trying to
finish a second novel and imagining an entirely new world opening
up to me in New York City—when I heard of the death of Andro

Leonardo, it was as if not just a door had closed, a life that I had abandoned. Something in my heart was rent. He was assassinated in broad daylight by goons whose bosses still no one knows for certain—the Philippine police? a political rival who was cousin of the new president? a military patsy who may not have known who the target was? I read the letter from Trina Trono, detailing the ambush, in my West Side apartment that held only books, many bought from years of scavenging and starving in Diliman, and a box of mementos I had stolen from my mother but never opened. He was only twenty-four. I found nowhere to mourn except a yoga studio by Union Square, a clear indictment of my life. I did not even know Andro Leonardo, personally. It was Trina who worked with him, an organizer of his crusades, she knew the details of his funeral, the reunions of his comrades, the weeping, drunken eulogies at his death anniversaries. It was just that he was part of a world of rectitude and meaning that escapes my words.

Her Inviolate Sense of Her Freedom

I never told my mother what I did in college, and she never asked. I was bound to my mother, but her inviolate sense of her freedom, or my inviolate sense of her freedom (they were both the same), gave me license also to be free. Her escapes away from us marked my childhood. When she returned to Tacloban from her flights, her mysterious fugues, she always brought me a gift, my pasalubong, like some act of contrition, but I imagine she felt no such thing. Her strength was her ardor. That is what I valued. Among the trinkets: a translucent bottle of holy water shaped in the blue-sashed figure of Our Lady of Lourdes, a velvet pair of high-heeled shoes, an emerald ring (my birth stone, she said, but it wasn't—my birth stone was opal, as she should have known since she gave birth to me—and still, happily I received it: I wore the emerald ring throughout the days of the rebellion, four days in February, until I lost it somewhere by

Camp Crame before we crashed its gates). One November, my mom
returned just in time to visit her Papá's grave for All Souls' Day—and
she brought a dog. Actually, two dogs, both mutts. One she insisted
was a purebred fox terrier—a sad brown dog that Adino named
Bruce Lee with optimism. The other she called a German shepherd.
She said he looked just like Moret, her Papá's old dog—that's why
she bought him, *purebred, inday!*, for four hundred pesos—*so expensive, inday, just for you and Adino!* I don't know why the dogs needed
to be pure. Anyone could see they were mongrels, and who knows
how she got them—maybe offered at discount, two for one, on the
boat she had just ridden from Davao or Danao, or maybe she had
found them abandoned on the pier. She had that knack—of picking
up strays, like Mrs. Carrascoso or Kringle May Kiring, the mother of
Sirit who had washed up in Tacloban from a province, my mom said,
that began with a *B*, with no connections that had any cachet, according to her hometown logic. But no one, not Tio Nemor nor Mana
Marga, contradicted my mother's whims on All Souls' Day, and we
took Bruce Lee and the German shepherd, the scraggly resurrected
Moret Number Four, with us to her Papá's grave.

At least she arrived for All Souls' Day. My greatest fear during
important events was that my mom would be absent. When I was in
grade school, and I was about to graduate valedictorian (Trina Trono,
who was always ahead of me, had left for Manila, so I got the honors),
I dreaded the moment I would be left up onstage, waiting for someone
to pin my medal when my name was called, and I would watch the
entire school pity me, the abandoned child of Adina an guapa.

But of course my mother arrived.

She was late.

She walked down the graduation carpet to the front of the crowd,
wearing her chartreuse gabardine skirt, a pristine, long-sleeved
button-down blouse, her white collar raised up around her pearls,
the way no one else in town did, like Audrey Hepburn in *Sabrina*,
and black stockings. No one wore black stockings in Tacloban. For
one thing, it's too hot.

From the stage I could see my mother, far off, sunlit, a green light by the gymnasium's entrance, and soon, I knew, I would see her face, framed by her favored huge dark glasses, her body dramatized by her neon-green look of the day, which contrasted against the red carpet. It took forever for my mom to get dressed, and her sense of time was impeccably disordered. She was centered on her own clock. But it did not matter what drama her entrance caused, or how the crowd stared—I was proud. She was beautiful.

Adina an guapa.

Most of all, I was relieved she had remembered me, my graduation.

So by the time I was ready, leaving my mother in Tacloban for college was not a wrench, not for my mother or for me. I was sixteen, too young to know I had no idea. She had a world I preferred not to see, the comings and goings of well-dressed women who prayed for nothing I wanted, business ventures that went downhill fast, companions in shady dealings I glossed over, church events, outings to Santo Niño sightings or bloody tears of the Virgin Mary all across the archipelago—her cursillo-designed *architectpelago!*—beauty pageant coronations with Tio Nemor, absences with no excuse slips, no explanations for me. About college, she told me to ask my dad for money. He had visited us in Tacloban that one time. I never saw him again. One day I saw my mom crying, staring at documents. Tikang ha estados, Mana Marga whispered. Adina an guapa wore her dark glasses in the house for months. I saw the divorce papers years later, during one more move. My mom kept them in a drawer, unsigned. She was Catholic. She did not believe in divorce. Once my mom called my dad when Adino had his appendix taken out. She wanted him to pay the hospital bill. He would not. I watched her on the phone talking to my dad as if they were husband and wife, as if she had never left him, refused to live with him. As if she had never seen the divorce papers. As if he had never beaten her, and she had never yelled, pity, pity, pity, pity. And at that moment I understood all of it—the performance of her phone call so she could get the money, the truth of the phone call because she believed that money was hers, and the horrible pathos in the phone call because she would never get that money.

And for each of those recognitions, my heart and my anger and my embarrassment were for her.

The hitch about my leaving for college was that my dad in America would not let me go. He said, and I quote, Tacloban is good enough. There's no need to spend extra money on Manila.

I cried.

It's the only school I want, I told my mom.

Inday, my mom said, with that same fierceness in her eyes she had when making origami napkins for the funeral of her Papá: *inday—you will go.*

That was that.

My mom had heard my desire.

I knew I would be going to Diliman.

I had no idea how my mom made money. On one of her many calling cards, there was simply her name and the word *Inventor*. She had the optimism of one standing on a cliff for whom the prospect of a fall does not occur. Her life was targeted—*fairy tales and bull's eye!*—toward the future. The present had no consequence, the past was made up. She was supposed to get child support from my father, whose idea of sustenance was an aspect of his vengeance. The lands of her grandfathers and the upkeep of her homes were vague encumbrances, traces of unexamined decline. So draped in the fantasy and mythology of Tacloban, her status was high but her funds were low, a mix of debt, illiquid assets, her sister-in-law's charity, and wantonness, the dregs of a family's pride. Invention was her survival.

She kept up with the ways she knew, maids, private schools, butterfly costumes, and my existence as her daughter who accepted her beliefs as my birthright is my lifetime's work of criticism-self-criticism. One of the most insistent words of my childhood was *prenda!* Prenda, prenda, prenda. Prenda this, prenda that. While I was cutting out magazines for my paper dolls, or finally reading Trina Trono's copy of *Madame Bovary*, which she left me before our graduation, or jotting down the names of extended families I grouped using Aji-No-Moto jars and Silver Swan soy sauce bottles, I heard my mom and her cohorts say *prenda this, prenda that,* and I did not bother with its meaning the way I never helped the maids or asked my mom why she wore dark sunglasses in the house after receiving the documents from America—tikang ha estados. Prenda means collateral, security, guarantee. It's a word in Waray that comes from the Spanish. I kept to my own made-up worlds.

I never thought about how hard it was for a single mother to bring up children in the last country in the world without divorce, where wives stayed with their lousy husbands because God willed it. *Separada.* I remember the word I had heard once, in Salogó, by the river. The rasp in Tia Pachang's voice. To divorce was a sin. But my mother, a *cursillista,* devout pilgrim to too many Catholic hauntings, had run away. She left my father, but she refused to become a divorced wife. Her situation in Tacloban was ambiguous and indecent, a matter of gossip that never occurred to me. Adina an guapa, who would not return to estados, kept up her masque of wifehood but stuck to her actual condition, that is—a woman who perceived what she wished and did what she desired.

At what cost, I did not bother to know.

Once she bought twenty-four live chickens from the market all at once. The gross smell of throttled chickens drowning in their blood, an intolerable, humid degradation, competed with the gross sight of the chickens floating in a giant, plastic bandehado as the maids plucked their feathers in the makeshift tub. Mrs. Carrascoso, the Coca-Cola manager's wife, had so loved my mom's fried chicken my mom began a catering business with her new friend. The city's Coca-Cola manager, who got transferred periodically, was always this transient from another place none of us cared about, Angeles, Ozamiz, or Misamis. Ours was a hermetic world where only our snobbery counted, and my mom pitied Mrs. Carrascoso, who was lonely because she was far from home, my mom said.

That's how Mrs. Carrascoso became my ninang at confirmation. A lady with the whitest skin and no eyebrows, just a swath of a pencil that made her look surprised—she had a barren face strenuously arrived at. The maids were always admiring her bleached skin. Her great catering triumph was for Gina Lollobrigida. No kidding. For weeks the commotion in the house centered on throttling twenty-four chicken necks for the arrival of Gina Lollobrigida. Not even just from estados—she was from abroad! Friend of Madame. When the actress arrived with Madame to take pictures of Madame's hometown, Tacloban, for a commissioned coffee table photography book, *The Philippines by Gina Lollobrigida!*, my mom's fried chicken would be in demand, said Mrs. Carrascoso. She had a friend on T. Claudio who was organizing events. All the VIPs from Manila, the ministers of tourism and the vice-governor of Human Settlements and Mrs. Conrada's Important Ladies and their minions, also in blue, would mingle with the hometown Clairol Hi & Dri gang—an entire barkada of women in turquoise caftans and sequined shoes would be eating fried chicken with Gina Lollobrigida. I ate up all the extras, fried chicken gizzards for lunch and merienda (I loved them, the batikolon, their crunchy top and dense insides that filled your mouth, and you had to concentrate when you ate batikolon because you might twist your jaw or spoil a tooth), and I gobbled up the other giblets, too—livers and necks strangled in onions and garlic. But the venture fizzled when Mrs. Carrascoso's friend canceled the order, Mrs. Conrada, now of Malacañang, never got in touch, Gina Lollobrigida came and went, barely impressed by San Juanico Bridge—what can one do, she was just an Italian, only spokening English—and my mom was left with the carcasses of twenty-four chickens with nowhere to go—their plucked skins a smooth wasteland like Mrs. Carrascoso's brow.

She quarreled with Mrs. Carrascoso.

They made up when Mrs. Carrascoso said she would sell my mom's papier-maché rabbit-ear-shaped lampshades to a shop in Davao, where Mrs. Carrascoso was from. She, my mother, and her new friend from Juan Luna Street, Kringle May Kiring, the beautiful young mother of

Sirit, went off to Davao, and that's how I received a translucent bottle of holy water in the shape of Our Lady of Lourdes. My mom sold two lampshades with the brand *Adina EVERLIGHTING!™* pasted on them. She spent more money on the boat ride than she got for the lampshades, and she quarreled with Mrs. Carrascoso.

Before we moved to the center of town, to Juan Luna Street, my mom had a stationery store on P. Gomez, leased in a hurry by her former classmate at Holy Infant Academy who went on the lam in the United States for trying to kill her husband's mistress, so I called her Mrs. Lam—at P. Gomez, my mom sold her artwork, quartets of painstaking canvases, each set called *The Four Seasons*, plus offhand creations, her greeting cards in rice paper with wild weeds pasted in delicate abstraction using her miracle glue, *Adina EVERLASTING!™*. We had to leave our place in Housing, with our beautiful door of bougainvillea. I didn't ask why. Prenda, prenda! For weeks, Adino and I slept on the floor of the greeting card store. We took baths at the home two blocks away, on Burgos, of Mana Marga's oldest daughter, it turned out, who kept her drinking water in a huge stone jar and whose bath water came from a Jetmatic pump. Mana Addie, the daughter, barely had water for her needs but she gave it to us, and as Mana Marga shampooed my hair in her daughter's outdoor bathroom, I felt guilty. But still I let Mana Marga shampoo my hair, guilt being the most useless sensation.

I did not understand we were homeless until I wrote this sentence.

In my mom's world, you could have no money, and a maid would still be washing your child's hair.

One night, I woke to my mother standing up, staring at the ceiling. I looked to see: a disfigured blob, a misshapen orb that looked subliminal, hanging from a beam. It was a wasp's nest—and below it was my mom's figure, swatting at the dark, as if her all-night vigil would save us from assault. Her rigid stance frightened me, and I closed my eyes, but a wasp came close to my face, and there was my mom, lunging at the pest. She lay her body across mine, a sweating heroic heave, and I could feel it. Her shaking. And I realized Adina an guapa, whom no one could conquer, was crying.

I did not want to see her cry.

I did not open my eyes. I kept pretending I was asleep. I did not hold out my arms to hug her. I lay still, my arms stiff beside me, feeling her wet misery upon my chest and the occult sense of a furry pest on my cheek.

I remembered an image in Los Angeles.

I have so few memories of Los Angeles—the parking lot at Food Co, a stationery store, a raincoat with a hood of fake fur, tying on roller skates, a wall of graffiti on my way to school—memories safely locked in a place my recall seals shut. I remembered waking up in this naval complex in Long Beach (before we moved to Wilmington). We must have just arrived in America: the angles of the rooms still had the sharpness of my lack of knowledge of them. I woke up to a light in the empty hallway, and I got up. By the door I watched my mom on her knees, cleaning the stairs of her home in this new country that was not hers—scrubbing and scrubbing the linoleum stairs as if her life depended on it, going down one step then another, in her bare feet, as if sleepwalking, but she had forgotten her heels. I remember the fear that clutched me. My mother wide-awake at midnight in America. She did not look up.

I felt like a witness to some awful secret.

I went back to bed.

When finally we moved to Juan Luna Street, the Sacred Heart statue took center stage in our new home's extra-large patio, a kind of covered veranda, our tall, mirrored hatstand diminished by the enormous space. A former Provincial Board Member, colleague of thrifty Tia Nunay—*da money is small but da lab is as big as a carabao!*—owned our house, and the patio could hold an entire barangay's political assembly. My mom filled it with orchids, and she arranged the portraits of her saints—San Antonio, Santa Rita, Saint Jude—against the mirrored hat rack, with the statue of the Sacred Heart standing guard, while she did her art.

It was there, in the borrowed home of an out-of-favor politician, that she did the work I most remember. A series of paintings that all had the same name: *The Four Seasons*. Of course the country had only two seasons: wet and dry. She would show me a bare, unpruned stalk on a canvas and say—*inday, that is Winter*. And then another had a few more leaves, a spare spattering of stems. *Inday, that is Spring*. And so on and so forth until a robust flowering of passionate intensity occupied the fourth canvas, as if a bloodstream of her own, made from plants, had sprung forth from my mother's hands. *Inday, that is Summer*. She created versions of *The Four Seasons* throughout her life. I would be riding on a jeepney with my mother, my shame in that moment would mingle with my love, and now in my memory my stubborn division of love and horror is unrelieved, and she'd say to the driver—*para, para*—and the driver would stop while she got down and plucked weeds from the ground. The driver and the passengers waited for Adina an guapa. The laboring world around her—drivers, maids, carpenters, shop clerks—was like this magical guard of honor attuned to her desiring. It agitated me, but I sat still, watching over her seat. She remained serene. Nobody was bothered. She was a woman with a look of command that was not worth fighting. Everyone stood by, lives at bay, waiting on Adina an guapa until she straightened up, gathered the weeds in her colorful scarf that she tucked into her leather handbag, and got back onto the jeep.

What I thought, at first, was that no one in Leyte was ever in a hurry.

I was confused by the way people treated my mom—as if she were both a boss and a baby.

I thought it was her beauty, the way it rearranged space in those public jeeps so that people shifted seats to make way for her entrance, her high heels and bright eyes and startlingly placed, geometric kerchief (sometimes at her waist, sometimes on a wrist), while bearing without apology or explanation those mortifying, freshly picked, earthen sheaves.

Tay Lucio would come all the way from Salogó to carpenter her frames, listen carefully to her directions on their measurements, and make sure he followed the minutest aspects of their construction.

She knew what she wanted. Canvases that were practically murals, to accommodate spirals of stalks and leaves and petals arranged in abstract constellations. I watched her work because it gave me pleasure. But I was absent to my mom when she worked. Her hand was sure, she had no nerves. She looked up as if I were a ghost. She had this considerate intensity, a beatific blank stare as she pasted a petal, gilded a stamen, and the leaves of grass became an extending web, an accretion of compounded mystery that had begun with a single weed, a dirty stalk whose potential for beauty only my mother could see.

In those moments, I was happy to be invisible. I was happy she was happy.

Nothing bothered my mother on that patio on Juan Luna Street— Adino, sweet Adino, kissed and cuddled as he wished, I nagged her for movie money she did not have, the mosquitoes came. The great anvil of her concentration hammered and shaped our home's peace. It was my favorite of my childhood places. She had a calm for which there were no words: she never talked about what it was like to do her work.

Actually, I never asked.

We just called them her frames.

Once, I came home, and the door was barred.

You cannot come in, inday! my mom said from inside the house.

I peeked.

She was up on a ladder, pouring different cans of paint down the door, watching the colors run.

When it was done, she asked me—what do you think, inday?

I saw the door's waterfall splatter of colors, dripping and braided with rainbow paint.

My mom sweating in her caftan, with a tangerine puddle on the floor.

I was very hungry. It was already dusk.

It's beautiful, I said.

She was always redesigning her environment.

It was there on that patio that as teenagers, on the verge of separation to our future colleges, Lorelei, Queen Sirikit, and pink-cheeked Sirit of the beauty queen looks would gather with me to talk about makeup or memorize the songs of Olivia Newton-John.

Without Trina Trono, I made do with the friendships I had.

Trina never had much use for beautiful, surprisingly stupid Sirit and insecure, rule-bound Lorelei. In the old days, Trina was the correct and righteous one. She was Anne Frank. At Saint Paul's Creek, we wrote in our journals about the sorrows of the world, and Trina got depressed, she had heartburn as she told us about the Nazis and the life of the Dutch girl Anne Frank. Her eyes watered at the memory of Amsterdam. We were in fourth grade. Sirit asked, tears in her eyes—Trina, are we Jewish? Trina's passion confused us. During the days of Marshall Lo, Trina and I fought over our one copy of *Little Women*—it was mine, from the set of Grosset and Dunlap's Companion Library, doubled-up books that, like a vinyl record, if you turned one upside down, you got a flipside. You turned over *Heidi* and got *Hans Brinker, or the Silver Skates*, you turned over *The Five Little Peppers* and got *Alice in Wonderland*. The books suddenly appeared one day on a brand-new shelf at Housing because my mom also loved itinerant vendors. (We also, briefly, had an Electrolux vacuum; the only well-dressed salesmen she turned away were the Mormons.) You bought the books on instalment plan, like the Electrolux vacuum, but I had no idea that was what you did.

Prenda, prenda!

They arrived, like Nay Carmen's bibingka, like magic. My mom had foresight, intuition about what I wanted, and Trina was so jealous of those books she acted as if *Little Women* were hers, picking it up whenever I put it down and reading so quickly she was finished with it, threatening to start the flipside, *Little Men*, before I was done. I felt authority over my friend because I owned the books she coveted. Trina would overstay until past curfew when of course she could not return home or the martial law stockade police would get her, and that's how she finished my set of Grosset and Dunlap's Companion Library of Classic Books. We spent that entire decade of martial law reading books on Grosset and Dunlap's installment plan and watching kung fu movies on TV and trying to figure out the words of—*Caroni-aaaaa!* One day the whole set disappeared, just as we had finished reading *Call of the Wild*, doubled with *Jungle Book*. Neither was impressive. I imagine the sad salesman taking them away from the shelves, the well-worn, over-thumbed books. Prenda, prenda. When we got older, we stole from our elders and traded—Trina gave me *Couples* by John Updike, and I gave her *Mila-18*. Tio Nemorino loved the Leon Uris books about heroic Jewish people in the Warsaw ghetto or making a nation in Palestine while Trina's dad was a man of no morals who had books like *Portnoy's Complaint* and *The Delta of Venus*—which at ten we devoured in our uncomprehending ways.

Lorelei, Queen Sirikit, and the beautiful Sirit were just hangers-on when Trina was around. They ate their ice candy in silence while Trina and I, in the days before she left for Manila, argued the merits of Prince Andrei of *War and Peace* versus Andrei Androfski of *Mila-18*. I liked *Mila-18* better because I actually understood it. Trina scoffed—that book is populist trash that commodifies Jewish pain. Or so I recall her words. She was a showoff. She liked to quote her dad though it was her mom that she missed. She fought with me in those last days in a way I understood she needed to break up over the small things, so it did not matter if she said goodbye. *Sybil*, the girl with sixteen personalities, had it better than Deborah, in *I Never Promised You a Rose Garden*, she argued, as if it mattered, after we found this psychiatric hash of smuggled goods, which my mom called boholano, at Sen Po Ek store, where Sirit's mom first displayed her nouveau business, the boholano shoes. We bought some new bakya and the books. They're both sad, I said. No, she said, Sybil is not sad—she makes things—you don't know anything about making things, she yelled, unlike your mom. I threw Chinese checkers at her, the entire board plus the marbles. Her dad gave us this book, called *Labyrinths*, and the only story we understood was about Funes the Memorious. We understood the boredom of crippled Ireneo Funes in the pampas beyond Buenos Aires. Any story about the provinces anywhere in the world was an emblem telling a story about our lives.

Still Lifes at Juan Luna

If I were to think about it, looking out at the horizon toward New Jersey, I'd say I've never read in full the chronicle of my place—the chronicle of the provinces where the capital was the point. It's no surprise I end up in this metropole of metropoles: the metropole of capitalism, glittering (in my view) for me. Who are my bugto, sorella, kapatid, semblable? There's the life of Emma Bovary, though not quite Jo in Concord-not-Boston, or of the women in Jane Austen who sneer-admired the new long-sleeved fashions from London. Of course, there's my supreme seventies frère, John Travolta in *Saturday Night Fever*, with his high-heeled takong, it occurs to me he's a version of Chickchick and the other beinte-singko dancers, with their hopeful glint of pomaded hair, favored by Candy, Lheezah, and Delilah. Above all, a bit too close for me when I first read it—the country of cows and goats and God in Edna O'Brien's *The Country Girls*. In one sense, that of metropole-desiring, probably nothing much separates me from, who knows, the world of Naples of Elena and Lila. And yet it is true I have never read in full the chronicle of my place. It's easier for me to imagine the west of Ireland or Naples. I still see myself in still lifes—in print, my home is yet to be automated with ease even in my imagination. I know what I lose. But what does the world lose with that void? Or—what knowledge do you not have, of what I have taken for granted? My life must be my own narrative convention. Since isn't it also that the desire of our world creates that metropole? When her dad, the Widower Almendras, finally shook off his long mourning and regained his wits, he took his daughter with him to his job teaching pre-Socratic aphorisms in Manila ("you cannot step into the same river twice—but you may as well wear bakya!" he once said during the rains), and left me with Queen Sirikit and Lorelei and fat-cheeked Sirit, who liked to compare manicures and replay their vinyl record of the theme song to *Superman.*

Sirit and Lorelei were my Juan Luna neighbors. Sirit and her mom, Kringle May— transplants from Butuan, or Bohol, no one cared, a family of improbably beautiful women, with alabaster skin and abundant, wavy hair, not like our bland straight cuts—lived close to the church, right by Plaza Rizal, in the old part of the city where one day Sirit met her doom, her husband. Lorelei lived next door to us, with her dad Man' Pete, a municipal employee who loved to take weekend showers outdoors with his pig, wearing only shorts and sando, and her mother, Mana Floria, who looked to me like an empress on a coin with her aquiline nose and square, sharp jaw.

A host of mysterious young women washed underwear and played mah-jongg by day at Lorelei's house then disappeared at night. To get to my house after school, I had to pass Mana Floria, then I saluted my piano teacher who rented the connecting apartment, the lonely Samarnon Miss Custodia Balasbas, with her legs like an elephant's, so we called her Elephant Katol, and then on to my mom on her orchid-filled patio, pasting banwa and talahib on her frames. Mana Floria liked to sit outside watching the neighborhood go by, a stately Roman bust on her child-size plastic stool decorated with stickers of big-eyed Japanese cartoon people. I liked Mana Floria because she blew cigarette smoke into the air like the *contra-vidas,* antagonist women with vile attitudes but perfect makeup, in the afternoon drama shows, and through her haze, she spoke to me like a grown-up. Mana Floria asked about my books and listened, one hand across her chest, the other elbow bent and cigarette in hand, her red-lipsticked mouth pursed with held-in smoke, as I described the problems of the Five Little Peppers, especially Phronsie Pepper, who was kidnapped by an organ grinder. She asked questions, like what's an organ grinder, and I told her, I have no idea. Together we figured out maybe it was a street musician, like Miguel, the epileptic who liked to sing "The Impossible Dream" outside Santo Niño church. His bad voice made him a lot of money.

Mana Floria, in real life, was the manager of a dormitory for impure women, so said Sirit, that prude. Just say it—prostitutes—said Trina, our voice of authority before she upped and left. Mga lukaret. Trina told me Sirit, though gentle in spirit, hence her dumbness, if she did not watch out, was going to become exactly like her mom, Kringle May Kiring, whose desire to move up in society was not least because of her unlucky name.

True, the languid ladies in chemises who came and went at Lorelei's house, drying their bras in public or meticulously plucking their armpit hair with tiny tweezers, their heads turned so that they looked like the swans in Hans Christian Andersen with their slender, straining necks bent over their underarms—they all fascinated me. Unlike Sirit, I had read *The Delta of Venus*, and I was proud when I discovered, from Trina, that I lived so near them when we moved— the prostitutes of Juan Luna Street.

Trina explained the joke of Sirit's unlucky name when Sirit was out of earshot and not joining our games at recess. Trina explained jokes like a teacher. First, *kiriring* meant—a telephone is ringing! The joke goes *Kiriring, kiriring!* And you answer: *Hallo, hallo? Who's there? Ibid.* Ha ha, Trina said. *Halô* is a kind of lizard. So is *ibid*. There was no joke on tuko or butiki, the other lizards. But *may kiriring* also means crazy: there's a ringing in your head. Kringle May Kiriring. Despite her name, Kringle May rose up first from selling boholano shoes house to house on the instalment plan, then lending money on the instalment plan, then taking away your land with cash. Prenda, prenda! By the time we were in high school, her daughter Sirit was walking to school with two maids, one carrying her bag, the other an umbrella, affectations that gossips appreciated. Her mom rose up with her look of a Madonna, a bosomy Santa Rita de Cascia. You didn't get mad at Kringle May for buying your land when your straits were dire because she looked like the white virgin in the scapulars sold by the Daughters of Saint Paul. The Kiring house on Juan Luna, by Santo Niño church, began to crawl beyond its origins. One day it even had a garage.

Life at Juan Luna, unlike at sleepy old Housing, was city

life—socialites and bar dancers, Manny the local druggie and *Chez Inez*, formerly Nestor, now the famous makeup artist come from pampering starlets in Manila who were named after soft drinks, Bombom the beauty queen who one day gave the city pride because she was on a national poster selling Magnolia ice cream, and street urchins and attorneys parading by. Even the beggars were upscale— my mom's favorite was Mrs. Kierulf. It was hard to tell how old she was—she could have been thirty-one or one hundred—a lady with deep-set eyes and a problem (appropriately old-fashioned—morphine), whose family once owned a building that spanned an entire block on Zamora Street, so my mom said, wide-eyed. But that was long ago. It became Bonanza Theatre, and now that's a ruin, too. My mom would make Mrs. Kierulf sit on the patio, and I was impressed by the lady's dress, she never changed from her tattered satin, her bedraggled puffed sleeves, she looked like a debased Snow White, or the Reina Elena of an eternal May parade, and they'd say words like *que se joda* and *verguenza*, the Spanishy things that were stuck like crud in my mom's Waray. Then my mom would give her a free cup of unboiled rice. Poor, poor Kierulf, my mom would cluck in distress when she was gone. We saw the faithful people in their fancy clothes on the way to Santo Niño church, we lived within earshot of the holy pealing of the *campanas*, our Sundays haloed in the privileged sound of the bells, we were the center of town. It was on the patio at Juan Luna Street that the Clairol Hi & Dri Hairspray ladies assembled in the time of the marches.

By that time Putt-putt was my town crier. I was on the streets in Manila. The ladies spent their days praying for their classmate from Holy Infant Academy where they had gone to high school in that time that's so old now—the twentieth century—their precious Madame who had made them legible on the nation's stage. Like them, she clutched at the history of her name, the fantasist totems of her birth, her story of ancestors and origins forcibly centered upon the nation, so that now all of us had to face Madame's childhood traumas and the dubious sources of her aggrieved pride. We kept getting dragged by her vengeful demons: a country stunted by the cuts that wounded and roused a trolling, ambient rage. In dire range of her pique, people just vanished. For instance, people forgot Mana Talia ever existed, ignoring my questions until I, too, forgot.

And no one remembered the time of the kidnapping of the famous golfer Tommy, when he was only across the beach from my mom's land at San Jose, on the island of Dio.

Mana Marga crossed herself, garbling the news: "It is said they have married in the Dominican Republic. Oh my, she did not marry Prince Charles!"

The president's daughter, against her mom's wishes, did not marry Prince Charles but instead eloped abroad with a divorced golfer. When they returned to Manila, the golfer disappeared. That was the time every Saturday I took my octavina to the house on Arellano Street of Miss Preciosa Margall, an ageless woman who looked like Tutankhamen's sister, devoted to the arts. Lorelei made me join Miss Preciosa's dance troupe so I could help carry Lorelei's unnecessary instrument of choice, the *bajo*, which was larger than her body mass. The country searched for the abducted husband while Miss Preciosa showed us that the wrist's movement in pandanggo sa ilaw was not sleight of hand—it was a miracle of nerve. Communist guerrillas were culprits! said the papers, but the golfer's family suspected the bride's parents. *Scándalo.* The Palace said their police were bound to find him—no worries. Mana Floria shook her head—*mmm-uhm, that golfer who is secretly married—he is dead.* Madame in the Palace prayed novenas but declared—*the Pope has authority even in the Dominican Republic!* All the women in the nation two-timed by their husbands were divided about the thought.

Miss Preciosa subjected us to strenuous exercises, bending my torso and arching my back to keep me in step with the dancers though I was only a musician. Anyone can improve, she said. *Practice, practice, practice!* That was Miss Preciosa's mantra. Her devotion to heritage was, in hindsight, a highlight. I imagine there are women like Miss Preciosa all around the islands—custodians of a skill and rigor past its prime so that its preservation has a cast of useless sanctity. Miss Preciosa's belief in her art was not ennobled by its function, which she did not resist—to entertain power. Sometimes I think her belief suffices; sometimes not. Her passion made my wrists hurt. Sirit was the star. We were only acolytes. Sirit was the Muslim princess of Singkil, the fan-and-parasol extravaganza of the Maranao people. She was the lead of the solemn Banga dance, bearing a suspenseful series of jars on her head, one then four then twelve in all, in that precarious parade honoring ancient ceramic vessels. Sirit had the knack of looking oblivious to her environment, perfect for folkloric dancing, thus she swears she never saw him, smoking a cigarette and staring vacantly at her dozen pots. Queen Sirikit and Margot were her kerchiefed maidens in matching checkered mountain costumes, also balancing some jugs, while I plied the plectrum and Lorelei plucked her *bajo*'s strings. So it was we, the musicians in the background, who saw him, and Lorelei missed a beat. Miss Preciosa glared. As always she sat in the shadows, a study in beige, impeccably dressed in her hemp-woven, Dior-like suit, watching intently as if her glance would will us to her goal, perfection. In the end, all we did was strum along.

Even now, if you asked, I could not tell you where this island Dio was. Before Miss Preciosa kindly dismissed me from her dance troupe (I had no focus, no prospect of graduating to balance even one jar), we were transported by boat half a dozen times from the beach at San Jose. Did my mom know they were using her land as a dock to get to Dio? From the strip where my mom used to leave us for weekend swims, we left for that lit-up island. From my mom's beach huts at San Jose, I never noticed it. At Dio, torches were ablaze leading us from the sandy landing as we carried our bungling *bajo* and bore our mounds of striped balintawak clothing, toward the enormous, glowing nipa mansion, ikat pillows strewn on the floor for guests, who gazed up at us, the dancers, and lolled in their beach outfits amid the haze of marijuana smoke. He was skinny but athletic, wearing a Hawaiian shirt and tennis shoes. His teeth were very white. He had the drawn look of a man sleeping too much. The nation was looking for him, the golfer, his face plastered on tabloids, but there he was in Dio, lying on the floor on antique tribal textiles much coveted by city people, and captive before Miss Preciosa's dancers. Occasionally he gazed toward the surf as if to see, in the distance, the diminishing returns of the Dominican Republic.

No one in Tacloban remembered the golfer Tommy, how he suddenly reappeared six weeks later by the same restaurant Las Conchas where he had been abducted, released from his captors, the rebels who demanded two million pesos in ransom, though from the start the commies said they had no idea who this Tommy was. The nation watched the golfer recite his message on TV for the president and his lady while the Minister of Defense sat beside him as he spoke: "I understand that your name has been maligned and your honor has been questioned. This I would want to rectify for the sake of the country and the Filipino people which you lead." But when I told my mom—*Do you know who we saw in Dio??* my mom said, *Ssssh, do not speak bad words.* Then she muttered, *Anyway, Preciosa said it was too dark. You cannot tell.*

Do you know they use your beachfront to dock their boat??

My mom shook her head and lied—I told them they could use it whenever they wished.

Marches

My mom and her friends prayed their novenas to Saint Jude Thaddeus and Saint Anthony of Padua—to keep their Meldy Hija safe from the demoniacs.

All throughout the months of the capital's street marches, my mom kept tabs on my activities by listening to the radio.

First she heard Putt-putt, stuck in Tacloban in his job as a deejay, an obligation he kept even after John-john died.

(Putt-putt reported for work within the week of his brother's funeral, a stoicism none of us could criticize. That event, John-john's death, is a wounding that I tuck here, in parentheses. I will not speak of how he died until a better time comes.)

Putt-putt came out on his radio show to denounce Sean Connery.

Throughout the time of martial law, we had only state television in Tacloban.

The marches in Manila were global spectacles, not that too many in Tacloban would know—the stations of that moment showed only James Bond.

Who cared about riots in Manila—if *007* was on every channel?

The maids watched *Diamonds are Forever*, *You Only Live Twice*, and *Live and Let Die*, all free, without having to suffer in Orchestra at Rovic Gold, amid the rats.

You Only Live Twice was on not twice but six times.

A crowd favorite.

Whenever Sean Connery, wearing fake eyebrows for his not so good disguise as an ordinary Japanese husband with a geisha girl for a wife, got in the tub with the lovely Kissy-Kissy Suzuki, the audience whooped. When Kissy-Kissy Suzuki fought with the ninjas on the side of James Bond (the movie was a classic of postwar bonding! East with West! Old Sean in yellowface and a robe doing transcontinental kickboxing!), she wearing only her sixties-style, beach-towel-fabric white bikini—the crowd cheered. No matter how many times they watched Sean and Kissy-Kissy, a debonair pair, judo-kick that German, the blond evil Hans, deep into the heart of a very fake volcano, the fans went, *Oh!*

Mana Marga began charging a peso a head every time her regulars, Juan Luna Street's drivers and labanderas, entered her overwaxed and hygienic sala to watch the shows.

Pretty soon, when they ran out of James Bond, Man' Leon hope-predicted this new TV programming would show the world's *real* greatest hero—Bruce Lee.

Everywhere in Tacloban the magic of Sean Connery cast a stupor on the fishermen's villages by the airport in Barangay San

Jose, on the government employees up on the hill at Provincial Hall, on the security guards at the elevated escarpment we used to call Cam' Bumpus (now a fancy hotel owned by the Trinidads), on the landlords and hoteliers of Zamora, and even on the mah-jongg players and sleepy-eyed girls at Mana Floria's boarding house next door to us, amid the still lifes on Juan Luna. (Putt-putt was sweet on one of the girls, Violetta, a sickly woman from Sagkahan, her illness, asthma, not quite operatic.) It was an orgy of Sean Connerys, an epidemic of Roger Moores. A Shangri-La of Kissy-Kissys. They even watched sad George Lazenby, in his only appearance as 007 in *On Her Majesty's Secret Service* (but he got to be the tragic one, who watched Mrs. James Bond, Diana Rigg, die in an explosion). Putt-putt told me how his girl Violetta and her comrades opened their doors to the neighborhood so that their suki tricycle drivers and the passing panaderos, the kids who sold French bread from Diorico's on their bicycles, could watch the serial miracles of Sean and Roger and sad George Lazenby on TV for free (sure, the women of Juan Luna Street hiked the prices for San Miguel beer—but that was also to be expected).

However, my mother was old style.

She didn't watch television.

She listened to the radio.

Sitting on the patio amid her orchids where she prayed to Santa Rita and San Antonio and Saint Jude Thaddeus, patron of missions impossible, my mom heard Putt-putt during his morning show, *Kanta! Bulig! Sayaw!*, on the new alternative station, DZDW, a mixed bag of news, charity announcements, and disco.

"Down with Sean Connery! Ibagsak nga yaik hi James Bond! Sean Connery is in league with the devil!" exclaimed Putt-putt in his role as Tacloban's neglected town crier.

He had found his calling in the usual manner.

Tita Patchy knew people at Divine Word College's radio station, and he got his first job through nepotism. But in the new dispensation, with Manila tumbling down, I admired my cousin and his suicidal tendencies, old bad-luck Disastro.

The trouble with Putt-putt's radical show was that no one was listening to the radio.

Everyone was watching James Bond.

"All of you—viewers—gago, tanga, uwat ngan padla! Watching movies made for sixth-grade brains! You are in bondage—to James Bond!"

He was proud of that line.

"Birat nga yawa," he concluded.

"Stop your dirty mouth, nga pututot ka dida, Putt-putt!"

My mom was his only caller. She had insider knowledge of his bodily defects and used it to her advantage.

"Hoy, Señor Jorge Mariano Delgado—Putt-putt! Nga putot ka dida! This is your tita, your ninang—your Tia Adina!"

Silence at the end of the line.

"Agi nga puro ka la buyayaw. Pastilan, intoy. Hala ka!"

No comment.

"Intoy! Putt-putt! Let me know. *Who* do you want to rule this land—if not The Rose? Of Tacloban? *A ver*! *Who?* The Thorn? Hala. It's your own lookout! You will stop this nonsense already! Just give me the news from the president, from Malacañang Palace, not your movie reviews!"

"It's a political statement, Tia Adina, not a movie review."

Putt-putt had recovered his tongue.

"I am denouncing the opium of Tacloban's masses," he said— "*James Bond!* The government is censoring the news—through the Hollywood drug!"

"Oh, huwow?" sneered my mom. "Opak-opakan ta lugod ikaw! I will opium-opium you! Hala. Just give me the news from Malacañang, not your opinions of Chinese action stars!"

"Sean Connery is Scottish, Tia Adina, not Chinese."

"Hah! Is he not a relative of the usurer of Salogó, Sian Co Lee?"

"That is not funny, Tia Adina."

"Ha ha to you, too!" said Adina an guapa. "Sian Kuno Lee! He is just an urupod of the usurer of Salogó!"

That February, my mother sat at home rocking in a butaka and being fanned by the maids who were trying to get rid of her nerves. Tio Nemor had already lost his job, and my family was scrambling to keep up pretenses. All over the archipelago petty functionaries found ways to despise the present yet disavow their past. Tio Nemor sent his remaining sons, Mick-mick and Putt-putt, from Cebu to Tacloban, the better to keep them under wraps, now that his future was in question, and lock them up with James Bond in my mom's home.

In his own home, his wife had turned mute, and the reek of mourning and silence unfurled from their marbled walls in Cebu.

But Putt-putt kept speaking out.

Not for nothing was he called Disastro.

One day, he returned to my mother's home on Juan Luna Street, his voting finger purpled with betrayal.

In Manila, I knew what I was doing to my mother.

We had just buried John-john.

Out by Doctor Tita Tita's opulent house near Danao.

I flew to Cebu for the burial, to a world that tasted of dust.

The call from Adino was jumbled. Adino had been left in the house in Tacloban, he was only twelve and still in school, and he was alone because my mom was in the hospital in Cebu, with John-john.

When I saw Doctor Tita Tita, on the day of John-john's funeral, I misrecognized her.

She of the high cheekbones and jet-black curls, Ingrid Bergman, Ingrid Bergman, smelling of *Aliage*—she had lost flesh around her mouth, her face was all bones.

She smelled of sweat, dried talcum, and tears.

Overnight, her hair turned white.

I thought she was the old woman who lived across from us in Salogó who once offered me noodles when her daughter died.

Pared to flesh, scraped to bone, like one of her patients with traumatic injury, except hers was the surgical incision of grief.

Her sunken eyes, darker than her dark sunglasses, looked out on a world she disbelieved.

John-john was buried January 14, two weeks before the street uprisings that engulfed Manila, and there was no avenue for our mourning. Even in his coffin, his lush brown curls looked golden, his face as smooth as a girl's, with that childish shock of hair—curly, unruly, sun-streaked sheaves of hair that jutted out of his brow. Wild, infantile. He had the look of a baby encanto, a sleep-deprived Santo Niño, snug in his unacceptable grave.

People know who his killers are, in Danao. They will always be in power and will never go to jail.

And still, Doctor Tita Tita, in her grief, two weeks after her son's death, at the height of the rebellion, called me up.

My group was off duty from occupying EDSA.

A disciplined affair, this street uprising.

The day millions began massing on Manila's main artery, refusing to leave the street, from Cubao to Makati, until the dictator stepped down, a campus resident from Narra, the next dorm over (I recognized Jolliboy, the econ major from an underground cell—not mine) organized us, English majors and music students and campus journalists and biologists, into a rotation to occupy the streets.

Residents at the dorms had our scheduled hours for taking over our section of Epifanio de los Santos Avenue, and we could not leave until the next group arrived.

Maoists are the best organizers.

The dorm's intercom surprised me with her professional name.

Doctor Teresita Delgado on the phone, paging, paging.

I rushed from my room in Kamia's basement to take the call, wondering what else had gone wrong for the family of Tio Nemor.

Doctor Tita Tita's voice had a syncopated beat, a gravelly scratchiness, her voice so weak the sound drew out my unwilling sorrow.

"You know, inday—Rosario—Chicharita—inday—I am calling—what are you doing to your mother?"

I could barely hear her from what I thought was static, the dorm's ancient, World War II wires, caught in the crucible of her voice.

"I just wanted to call you, inday. For your mother. She does not have the easiest life. Inday. Rosario. Chicharita. I ask you. For the sake of your mother. Go home. Fly back to Tacloban. I will send you money for pamasahe. Do not go on these—streets. Be safe. It's not worth it. No one wants—"

I understood.

No one wants another death.

I thought it was melodramatic.

A plea coming from the wrong side.

But I said, I understand.

Did she ask you to call me? I asked.

"No, of course not, inday. You know she would not. You know how your mother is. She hates it—you are doing the demoniac thing! But she defends. I know you won't believe me. She told Conrada and all the others—those tsismosas! those busybodies!—*my Chicharita has her own mind*, she says to them. They said—*ah, Adina, here we are praying, but you—you cannot even control your own child!* And your mom said—*That is because—I raised her to have her own mind, unlike your sons!* You know your mom."

I know, I said.

Nothing can conquer her.

"She won't back down. I know you won't believe me, inday. But she has always defended—against those women in Tacloban. No matter what she says."

I said, I know. I believe that, Tita Tita.

"It's her rule, you know—not to tell you what to do. She tells you what she thinks, of course. But you know, she leaves you to be free."

I know, I said.

"So I am calling," said my aunt, "for her."

I asked, And how are you?

I heard Doctor Tita Tita's voice reverberate on the phone at Kamia dorm, as if the static were now resolved. And I heard it, her pause, a strangled sob.

"I am all right. I also called to let you know."

I knew the news already.

"I'm leaving your uncle. I cannot stay here. I have all the papers. I got the tourist visa. I want to let you know. I am going to America."

Rudy Da Moody

I got the job from Trina Trono. We graduated, she from History and I from English, that March after the rebellion. Even Andro Leonardo, the most visible activist at school, went aboveground. He ran for office in Cavite—a gesture of trust in a new order, I thought. As if by wading in the muck one could change the sea. He didn't. Socialites were posing with commies against the backdrop of Army soldiers up on armored tanks waving upside down flags—we clapped for the military. Millionaire exiles from Boston took back radio stations confiscated by the dictator in 1972. Maoists came out of hiding and married their lawyers. Those were thrilling days when political prisoners, who had been only stenciled red names on our banners, came to celebratory parties looking disconcertingly ordinary, non-descript bald men in pressed khaki pants and takong shoes, smoking Camel cigarettes. A lady wore a necklace of balimbing to one party, so people ogled both the fruit and her breasts, signaling the next phase of revolution—tactless irony. Tortured detainees became evangelical Christians. Bourgeois poets, as usual, did what they do: they quoted Che. Ronald Reagan flew his friends, the dictator and his wife, to Hawaii, and Malacañang Palace was the trashed site of history.

Our job was to sort it out.

The collection of volunteers Trina gathered at the Palace right after its storming was harbinger of the missed chances we called change. A bunch of juvenile political scientists, earnest do-gooders, pseudo-anarchists, ambitious grad students, plus me, a trying-hard novelist. I had begun a novel about novels, a book about nothing, just objects of desire. I wrote in secret, between the marches. Recess from revolution.

I'd leave a rally, sit in a library, read *The Name of the Rose* or *The Literary Review*, and I'd scribble my secret book. Once, I read an essay, called "Teacher," by a writer I admired. I thought it was odd that such a writer taught. I took it as a cue. I took down his school's address. I paid Miss Noreen, the secretary at the department, to type my manuscript, I photocopied the pages of my secret book, I sent it to the writer in New York. Only Trina knew about my book, and she'd take the piles of paper from me and impatiently go through Miss Noreen's typescript, then she'd say nothing at all about the book. She would just demand to read the next chapters. It was like the time we were reading *Little Women*, except I was writing the story. I knew why she gave me the job at Malacañang Palace. I needed money to stay in Manila. She wanted me to finish my book.

Our boss was the formidable attorney Benigno Maria Espasol, the famous human rights lawyer and powerhouse in the new president's transitional Executive Secretary's office—Assistant Secretary to the Secretary of the President.

ASSP, for short.

Benigno Maria Espasol was a huge man, literally and figuratively. In the newspaper photos, it gave one a pang to see how, despite his well-chronicled, righteous life, he had this hollow, diseased look of corpulence, an obese, chalky figure in a too-tight barong. In the years of revolt, he had been legendary for sometimes riding a wheelchair with us to the protest marches, his bloated body pressed against the metal, his fat flesh folding downward around his chair like the melting sides of Salvador Dalí's symbol of time.

But our team's actual leader was the pockmarked nephew of ASSP's wife—Roderick Pakasulay Durano, Rudy Da Moody to us. His face looked like a crushed atis. He wore hunter-green Top-Siders and a series of pastel-colored pants, lemon or mustard or lime, inexplicably embroidered with ship anchors or seahorses. Later we learned it was his aunt who dressed him—a socialite from Cebu who gave him the threads of her son, his cousin, some wanderer abroad who refused to come home despite the family's change of fate, their return to power in heady times. Instead, Attorney Espasol's heir went around the world shedding outfits from *The Preppy Handbook*, and every day, the scion's sub Rudy Da Moody looked like a squashed fruit arriving from some never-ending cruise, dressed in borrowed drag, his face anointed with the leavings of the acne cream his aunt maybe also slathered on his face—cratered with the scars of smallpox? infantile mumps? arthritic psoriasis?

Some deformity haunted Rudy Da Moody, a sickness that had failed to kill him as a child.

Mister Rambo Tan.

So his uncle Attorney Benigno Maria Espasol called the pock-marked sailor boy Rudy Da Moody.

The insult told us that, after all, Rudy Da Moody was only an in-law.

At the time, Rudy Da Moody was in his thirties—finally graduated from San Beda Law School, with a sense of ignominy that gave his brashness its edge. Among the white-collar Jesuits of Katipunan Avenue and the M-L, Marxist-Leninists of Diliman, his pose of command was surly but uncertain—a goon with a chip on his shoulder along with the alligators on his pimped Lacostes.

We bumbling curators had vague orders to use our own good judgment about the army dossiers and lipsticked stationary pads and guest-book lists all around us in the deposed Lady's offices, the plebeian gloom beyond her mint-green Music Room, a space seared in me because Kerima Polotan had described it in "Madama in the Palace," in her beautifully written book legitimizing ugly people that I once read, over and over, during the doldrums of Salogó. It was as if I had seen these rooms before, ghosts of Polotan's compassionate, condoning prose stalking me as we rifled through Madame this Madame that's desks and drawers. Occult tunes rushed through my head. *Such a feeling's coming over me.* I held in my nausea. To do my job, I shut my mind. This simultaneous revulsion and attachment were my familiar haunting.

Rudy Da Moody with his wounded, acned face came around in his loafers and Ray-Ban sunglasses, once arriving with a gun at his hip, a plagiarized Glock, apparently a product of his hometown's factories, affecting this early in the revolution his future baby-gangster look, which did not go well with his beach-themed clothing.

He asked me, "What's up?" as if the answer were not his problem, but mine.

I was looking at a picture.

"I think that's my great-grandfather," I said to Rudy Da Moody.

I pointed to a figure in the photograph, a skinny man in a suit.

"Sure it is," said Rudy Da Moody, "and my grandma is the Mama Mary. It's from her I get my rosy cheeks."

And he sauntered off to do no good somewhere else.

At the Palace

At the Palace, I was surprised to see him—the picture of my mom's Lolo Paco.

I have speculated on the features of Lolo Paco's young face from the family's damaged sepia photograph (and one online encyclopedia). It turns out the history of the votes he cast and the bills he made is in the US congressional record of the Commonwealth era, a numbing form of biography.

The picture was taken on his return from one of the many failed missions for Philippine independence before 1946—one of those tedious OsRox missions to Washington, DC, that were the bane of my high school history classes.

The picture lies in the presidential records office at Malacañang Palace.

I saw him among a group of men in americanas—that woolen tripartite suit illogical though popular in the tropics—on a boat arriving from San Francisco harbor in 1931.

The caption was terse.

I did not recognize him—a hatless man with light eyes that looked blind in the Manila sun, the gray shadow around his thin mouth adding grim scale to his gaze—but I recognized his name on the

Palace plaque as I passed by the museum exhibit to get to my job at Maharlika Hall.

Senator Francisco Delgado y Blumfeld.

I have to admit I recognized the name on the plaque with surprise because by then I took my mom's stories with a grain of salt.

A whole childhood of hearing about Lolo Paco did not prepare me for his actual existence in a museum's glass.

It had become my habit to disown my mother's words.

The last time we fought was over the murder of a senator in broad daylight on an airport tarmac.

Personally, that senator was no hero to me—but the country was stunned, awoken.

We'd been marching for years, and only now were people shocked.

My mom visited and showed me how to play blackjack.

I saw her at Kamia, she laid the cards on the table, she told me how to win.

You just need to have the luck, inday—if you side with the good, you will have the luck, the grace of God on your side. So you should side with the good. Not the demoniacs.

At the palace, I looked more closely at the picture of Senator Francisco Delgado y Blumfeld to see if it was actually the man. A gray-tone photograph taken in the open air, enlarged to fill the double spread in a coffee-table book.

I looked at his eyes. I looked for his mark, the scar.

There it was.

A glister, like a slanting of the sun, cupping his cheek.

The shadow of a scimitar, an orange peel, the keloid color of a half moon.

Baga hin luwag hin kaldero, ayaw pagdad-a.

The letratos prominent in our sala in Salogó were eyes on our lives: the immense portrait of the house's ancestral couple Lolo Jote and Mama Bia whose eyes followed me in all the mirrors—Mama Bia in her cloudy pañuelo, Lolo Jote with his white curls streaming down his brow, his thin mouth and oddly cherubic, Santo Niño cheeks; the late dog-whisperer, rondalla musician, rocking-chair-enthusiast, and oldest child of Lolo Jote, Mister Honorable Mayor Francisco Delgado III, my mom's beloved Papá, sitting in his butaka, that mangled rocking chair, the river before him and his famous German shepherd, the first Moret, at his side; an 8 x 11 blow-up of charming Tio Nemor, trim and isputing in that polyester seventies way, in shining imitation of one of the great Neils of his generation—Sedaka or Diamond—as he shakes hands in 1974 with the dictator, his party's standard bearer, a boyish thug in a barong; Adina an guapa with her classmates in bouffant hairdos and butterfly gowns, at a reunion with their towering idol—the Rose of their Tacloban; and the 5 x 7 in a wooden frame, a studio photo in black-and-white proof, of the American-era politician, my mother's favorite, her Lolo Paco.

In the picture in our sala, he has a crescent shadow that marks his jaw, a half-moon scar.

The picture's top half is waterlogged by some wine glass or typhoon—so you almost miss his bushy eyebrows (another mark of the Delgados).

It is signed at the bottom in effaced script, and to be honest, I only assume the signature is his name.

There is no picture of the brothers together.

In the house in Salogó, there is no evidence that my mother's grandfather, the mad chickenologist Lolo Jote, was ever young.

His brother, an iya manghod, Lolo Paco died a year after I was born, and at the president's trashed and obscene home, Malacañang Palace, I was surprised to see him young and alive, sunburnt, sullen, and kind of skinny, practically swimming in his impractical suit.

That picture of Lolo Paco was part of an exhibit on the American history of the Philippines, set up in the months after the flight of Ferdinand Marcos in 1986. The president's liberated library was temporarily turned into a museum, and in an adjoining suite of rooms that needed cataloging, I was a volunteer, an amateur curator of abandoned effects.

My job was to look through piles of documents in cordoned-off offices at Maharlika Hall—a mahogany-and-capiz warren of desks and dens and hastily abandoned folders and files—to make sure no one swept history under a rug or stuffed it in a briefcase.

An anonymous citizens' brigade guarding history from its looters.

It was odd to be trooping about the spooky capiz and woodwork of Malacañang Palace, with our official badges and ruled pads like Poloniuses without a grudge, when for years we could not get past the barbed wires of Mendiola, the rutted road that leads to the palatial grounds of district San Miguel.

Blackjack

"Imelda must be so lonely because everyone hates her."

I found Adina an guapa at Kamia Residence Hall, sitting once again on the spot she liked, my roommate Aurora's bed.

She was playing blackjack by herself.

"Oh inday!"

She held up a pair of eights.

She stretched out her arms.

I went over to kiss her.

Her hair was coiffed, her eyebrows perfect, her pearls South Sea: awkwardly shaped thus true. Her heels on tidy Aurora's immaculate sheets were black from Manila's diesel.

"Meldy must be so lonely because everyone hates her."

She repeated this in her girlish voice, the one with the smile that tested your reaction.

"So I went to visit."

"Really?" I almost shouted.

In those days of conflict her way, which was to have several instincts at once, was the most unsettling thing about her.

Her speech reprimanded me, in her voice was a laugh.

She primed me for a joke though she was sincere.

Her head was turned to her face-up card, the queen of spades—*never reveal the Queen of Spades if you do not have to show it!*—but she looked sidelong at me, like that Vatican Sybil on the microfiche slides in my course in Western art, Humanities 11—her lowered eyes waiting for the burst of anger she knew would come.

"Really? You mean you went to Malacañang?"

I took my mother's bait.

"Oh my God. You're still on their side," I said.

It was a rhetorical point.

She would never leave their side, she and the praying mantises of Tacloban.

"Her henchmen, her goons killed the man in broad daylight, on a goddamned airport tarmac where everyone could see!" I said.

"No, they didn't," my mom said, calmly redistributing her cards on the bed. "Galman, the gunman, did it."

She spoke with no inflection, she lay down another hand. She tapped the card, as if deciding.

She dealt one more.

An ace of diamonds.

"That's why it's called an assassination, Ma—you pay a gunman to kill, like that sad fall guy, that Galman. How obvious can it be? That's why people are finally out on the streets—after two decades of extra-judicial murder and disappearances and the deaths of thousands. The assassination was so dumb even the damned matronas in Makati got mad."

"Aha!" my mother said.

She showed me her ten of hearts.

"Blackjack!" my mom crowed.

She laid down her cards.

"See, inday," she said, "this is what you call blackjack: ten, ten, one. Twenty-one. I won! And don't tell me it's not true—*I saw Galman do it!* He killed the senator. It was on the TV. *Pusila, pusila.* I heard him say it. *Pusila, pusila.*"

I stared at my mom, her eyes intent on her cards.

I did not bother to mention she won because she was the only one playing.

"Probably Cebuano," she muttered to the cards.

"Actually, Ma, he sounded like your cousin, the Junior Igme. He was more likely Waray."

"Hah—hala. Yes! Amo! Oh, that Galman."

She looked up at me, a truth suddenly revealed.

"Hala, inday! Yes! You are right. He is from that place of criminals and assassins, in Pasig Line. Siguro. Agi. Amo gud!"

She slammed a card face down on another.

"Taga-Pasig Line! Agi ito nga Galman. Hala. Kabuwisit hito nga tawo. Padla. *He's* the one, from Pasig Line, the crazy one who shot the senator, that Niño Bonito senador on the tarmac!"

"Ninoy Aquino, Ma."

"And they blame *her* for his crime! She must be so lonely in the Palace, people are saying so many bad things about her. So I went to visit!"

My mom started shuffling the cards again.

Her expertise troubled me.

She knew the rules of blackjack the way she knew the Novena to the Wounds of Our Lord. She shuffled with nimble fingers as she lay down the new hands. I could barely see her wrists move.

She had the elegance of a shark.

She doled out one more hand, to the dealer—herself.

"Really?" I said. "So you got into goddamned Malacañang Palace?"

"Sssh. Do not speak bad words. It is not goddamned. The Lord is with Meldy."

"You know that students can't get past the barbed wire at Mendiola, and you went visiting, just like that, at the Palace?"

"I thought she would like to hear someone speak. Who could speak to her in Waray. She must be so homesick. I knew she would remember me. The daughter of the mayor. She remembered how she came to see us in Salogó, in May 1964."

"She remembered the date?"

"No, I did. Oh it was so good we chatted. I reminded her that we sang a song."

"What song?"

"'Dahil sa Iyo.'"

"Oh my God," I said. "What the hell."

"What do you mean, inday—it's a love song. A kundiman!"

"Which she turned into authoritarian drivel! I mean, that song is just goddamned unbearable!"

"And look, inday—I have your tuition! I told you I would give it to you on time. I got the money for you."

That's when I saw a velvet bag by her side.

It was a purple pouch tied up in gold string.

Somehow my mother managed to scrounge money for my tuition—up to the time I graduated. I never worked for my education. My mother did. It would be late, it would come in scraps and dribbles, it would be piecemeal. But it was always paid.

On Aurora's white sheets, my mother was busy winning blackjack against herself in the posture of a child, one leg bent in a triangle, showing off a flagrant, dirty heel and safeguarding her cards, the other lolling off the bed, the strap of her high heels half off.

She bent over her knee, took a card, and tapped it. She gave herself another card. She turned over her dealer's hand—an ace.

I went and took the velvet pouch.

I untied the string and watched the cascade of coins fall on my bed.

My mom, across from me, was smiling. She saw the look on my face.

She started to laugh.

"See, inday! It's your tuition. Count it! Count it! You just have to pray, and good things will come. If you go with the good—instead of the demoniacs!"

It may have been because my feet were so tired, the heat and sweat from the streets laid a shroud over the body, a humid sheet, and I felt dizzy.

I fell on my bed, on the mountain of silver coins.

She gave me six hundred fifty-two pesos in all—in silver coins from the velvet pouch.

For a long time, growing up, I had stopped believing her reasons for arriving or going away, I did not believe that the Santo Niño she saw in Zamboanga had shed tears of blood, I did not believe that she healed people of asthma and lateral tendonitis with the laying over of the hands, I did not believe Halley's Comet passing over Manila symbolized God's sadness about People Power, or that her cousins owned Manila Hilton and bought a quartet of her frames for their lobby, or that her Meldy Hija had welcomed her at the Palace and given her the money for my tuition.

"She gave this to you at Malacañang?" I said, staring at the ceiling fan above my bed.

"Oh no, inday, of course not," my mom said. "Why would Meldy give me money? She was just happy to have me visit, to speak Waray with me! She was so happy to speak Waray. I earned that money! It's from my frames. My cousins at Manila Hilton bought a new set— four pieces! *The Four Seasons!* You should go see my work, inday—they put it in the lobby, by the grand piano, where my cousin Freddie the jazz pianist plays, under the chandeliers!"

Later, I did not ask her, when my hand felt for the pouch, why there was gold lettering on the velvet cloth. It said, *Manila Bay, The Floating Casino.* Off of old Intramuros, the walled city by the water.

Sitting on this roof deck, the dark about to descend upon Manhattan, I understand that this is how I had made my escape—through the secret life and desperate gestures of my mother by which she powered my desire, the way she let go of me so I could do as I wished, the way she knew, maybe even then, sitting on Aurora's borrowed bed, that I would be writing this story, betraying her memory— escaping what I did not wish to know and plotting to run away from the place that had produced both her and me.

Maybe it's true, as Trina Trono told me as we rummaged through the mess of Maharlika Hall, that my mother was not the enemy.

Trina was not trying to make me feel better. Trina did not have that capacity. Trina said—your mom is just one of a tribe, you know—semi-feudal, really—vestige of the landlord classes that feed petit-bourgeois dreams. Not even bothering to gain power for herself. A loyal peon. A Filipino of faith.

Like all of us—just petty bourgeois.

With vacillating desire, I added, having gone through the lessons.

Yup, said Trina. She's just vacillating petiburgis. The most traitorous of classes.

I wished to slap her, how she always had a smug truth to tell.

Look what I found, she said.

It was a high school report card from Holy Infant Academy, with that address familiar to us—El Reposo Street.

I expected to see next the picture of them in twin bouffants.

We saw multiple copies of report cards, glossy program invitations, July 2 birthday cards hailing from Apayao to Sulu.

We debated where they should go—the most trivial documents were a dilemma.

I looked through the pile of birthday cards, looking for one with pasted weeds and a calligraphic Catholic-school hand, her filigreed *R*, her cowlick *O*.

Tacloban is a Vampira

The lady was glaring at me with her hands on her hips—a tiny, twiggy figure in a stiff A-line skirt, spiky heels, and pantyhose.

The fall of a president does not interrupt the obligation to visit the dead.

On All Souls' Day, I saw this antic woman at the cemetery—I thought it was a ghost.

Her slightly unhinged assemblage of parts seemed to rattle in her suit of metallic brocade.

The apparition gave me, not a Marian feeling, not a sense of divinity, but an entirely earthly wash of longing.

In the mud of the graves in Salogó, my knees buckled.

My body was giving way, my limbs disjointed and surrendering to the fatigue of so many months in suspense, marching toward Mendiola, sleeping on rubble on the streets, and the writing of a novel that had cast me out of time.

I had yet to tell my mother—that I had received a packet from New York about my novel.

I thought I was hallucinating, my eyes weakened by premature nostalgia, a wash of memory, as if I had already left on a jet plane, missing my home, though my visa and my tests and the date for my departure were not set.

Rebel.

Rebeal.

She had completely disappeared from Tacloban after that day in Salogó—"Please Release Me," she sang. "Top of the World," Tio Nemor sang.

"Mana Talia!" I said.

"Ay nga panulay nga birat!" she said.

Even her words were the same—her potty mouth.

In this curious aftermath, after the rebellion, all the exiles were returning, even the ones that were dead.

"Oh my God. Mana Talia."

I held her veined wrist, I smelled her perfumed hair.

The material, bitter fumes of Clairol Hi & Dri assaulted me, an overpowering streak.

Even my mom had let go of her seventies bouffant. She now dyed her hair auburn, like Julia Roberts.

"Where have you been, Mana Talia? I'm so glad—it's so good to see you! Where did you go? I mean, where's your love, Quintana? I thought—you were going to the Balkans!"

"Nga leche nga Rosario ka! Padla ka la gihapon."

And she pinched my cheeks, a gesture of affection not typical of her old ways.

Her eyes were watery, looking up at me.

Hugging her, I thought I would break her osteoporotic bones.

It's true.

Mana Talia had resurrected.

After years spent in Tbilisi or Moldova, going to the Balkans.

She had spent the years touring the sacred grottoes of France, Italy, and Spain, especially pursuing the body parts of Santa Teresa de Ávila—the saint's right foot in Rome, her left eye in Madrid, one hand in Lisbon, and a finger in Paris.

It was all I could do to keep up with her treasure map of limbs.

She would show me Kodaks of all the rotting bones!

She talked nonstop, flitting through the graves.

I kept tight hold on her as we trod the gravestones, as if she might crumble, pulverize back into the ground—my grip on her shaking figure, her brokada frame.

"You mean you got Santa Teresa's middle finger, too, Mana Talia?" I asked.

And I raised my hand to make the gesture.

She pinched my wrist.

Ay nga birat ka la gihapon!

She cackled.

It was glorious to see her completely herself—her nasty humor intact.

Back at the house, she passed around the Kodak of the thumb of Saint Catherine of Siena.

She carried pictures and totems. She rummaged through her leather bag, etched with the word *Venezia*, and she took out a shot glass with a cheap drawing of Our Lady of Loreto.

"Here it is," she said, "I bought it at Our Lady's gift shop. In her church itself, in Loreto! For you."

I knew she did not buy it for me, but I took it.

She named all the Marian apparition sites—Fatima, Medjugorje, and especially her old favorite, Lourdes.

"Ay nga panulay, *hija*, I tell you it is true—if you sit in the waters of Lourdes, your panties do not get wet! It's a miracle!"

"Ah," said my mom, raising her hands, "it's a miracle—praise the Virgin!"

"But why would Our Lady of Lourdes be so concerned about your panties, Mana Talia?"

"Ay nga leche ka, *hija*, padla ka la gihapon!"

"Mana Talia," I said, "the miracle is that you're back with us. That you're alive."

Her wrinkled mouth trembled, so that a tooth showed through her smile, streaked with lipstick, as she touched my cheek.

"Hah, you are so sentimental, Rosario, ay nga birat ka nga bata ka!"

I reveled in her voice. I was, once more, a child.

Though a cunt of a child, as she said, that, too, was true.

But in Tacloban no one seemed to notice that her return was strange. It was only ordinary that a woman punished by their worshipped president for his own crime, of bribing Congress to change the Constitution to keep himself in power in what he called *Our Revolution: Democracy*, would be welcomed back home as if all the years of terror—I counted on my hand—*fifteen*—had never intervened.

There is an obduracy in Tacloban's affections that gives no hope for mankind but keeps ritual customs intact.

Mana Talia went to the Novenas to the Wounds of Our Lord and of San Pedro and San Antonio, eating puto and suman and showing off the fingers of her saints. It seems that instead of purgatory, Mana Talia and her love Quintana whiled away the intervening time, the time of Marshall Lo, testing the resilience of their underwear in holy settings. Their banished life was extended trips to tourist traps. I asked my mom—what happened, how had she survived? But my mom shrugged her shoulders, the reason for her was simple—Mana Talia's love Quintana was a cousin, a Taclobanon, related to Imelda.

That's why they did not kill him, she did not say.

My mom saw the world only through her province.

At the cemetery, I could not see Mana Talia separately from the spirit I remembered—a gnome of a woman who seemed always to be satirizing her time on earth. Even as a child, I thought she never believed a single smutty thing she said. When she had pleaded, *Please release me, let him go*, to her old music student that day when

Mick-mick bit the hand that ruled us, Mana Talia had challenged the assembly as if singing a cabaletta, an aria of airy repetition, with a response already known.

In my memory, she did not believe she would survive.

She was afraid.

But she had acted the opposite.

That is what I remembered.

I forgot that her love Quintana had grown up in Salogó, the son of a judge from Bulacan whose fate had landed him in this far-off province's civil courts. He was now buried near my mom's Papá. I watched my mom's fake German shepherd, Moret Number Four, poke at the newly swept and weeded territory of the dead. The other dog, Bruce Lee, had long disappeared before I went to college, eaten, who knows, by the vampira of TEIPCO.

This return home was the same as my first view of it, when I was seven—an untidy denouement: only to descend into wild grass, after such fuss.

Tacloban is a vampira. It does not change.

Acid Reflux

I kept getting acid reflux at that job in Malacañang Palace, long after the people had stormed it. It was not so much that I was betraying my mother—"how can you do that, inday, to a Taclobanon!"—as I sifted through the Palace's boxes, looking for incriminating evidence of the world my mother worshipped.

It was not just that our boss, the human rights lawyer Benigno Maria Espasol, gave us no guidelines, and his pockmarked minion, Rudy Da Moody, was a useless smiler with a paltik gun but no perceivable brain. Assistant Secretary to the Secretary, ASSP for short, Benigno Maria Espasol visited us in his blue-tinted barong and shiny Ferragamo shoes, the old activist wearing my uncle Tio Nemor's favorite cologne, Paco Rabanne. The secretary already smelled like the entrenched politician I hoped he would not become. Then he spoke, and I remembered the hoarse man in his wheelchair who had once held us marchers in thrall.

"Ah, democracy. Ever at work. Our president sends her gratitude to you all—for doing democracy's job!"

We were told to trash trivial domestic documents, grocery bills and to-do lists, and to keep only one copy each of the many, duplicated military files—so many versions of *Oplan Katatagan*. We were told to destroy photocopies and Post-its. But I thought even that blind receipt from Saks Fifth Avenue and the crumpled tissue with lipstick stains were suspect. History was a mass of everyday detail, and I thought we should disinterrogate, as my mom would say, even the dust.

I kept feeling this tightening in my belly, rising from my gut to my throat. Ateneo anthropology grads in white button-down shirts and U.P. political science students wearing trendy Ifugao backpacks and leather Jesus-sandals were rummaging through detritus amid the creepy, capiz-shelled shadows of Maharlika Hall—along with impostors like me. I was only a jobless English major, with a first draft of a novel that had nothing to do with the world I hoped would burn in its wake. I had a mind full of *mentiras*, as Tio Nemor used to say—*mentiras* of the past. Meticulously, I kept smoothing out each receipt and note pad and piece of stationery in those offices in the Palace. I made lists of what I found though no one told me to take such care. My stifled anxiety, from making choices I had no business doing, sorting out ephemera from fluff, society folders from military documents marked *For Your Eyes Only*, like dubious props in a James Bond movie, made me go back to my rooming house in Area 2—that unmarked place beyond the dorms where unmoored graduates go to nurse their sudden irrelevance—and every day I felt the ache of what turned out to be an ulcer, the tardy toxin of my angst: one more blasted souvenir from Marshall Lo.

Above all, I went through the guest books. Maharlika Hall had stacks of these books with people's signatures, hometown, province, date, and hour of entry and exit—lists of petitioners in the royal receiving line. I saw names of movie stars, mayors, famous business-women, regional councilors, balladeers apologizing for unnamed acts at gala events—along with the obscure supplicants who carefully wrote down their names in hopes of being seen by despots.

Lists and lists of names.

I was looking for her signature. Adina an guapa.

She must be so lonely because everyone hates her.

I kept looking for her name in the books.

My goal was dumb.

History was a mess, and all I wanted was to figure out my mom.

Everyone kept going into Malacañang to look at the stupid shoes, a sordid bounty of size 9s. And everywhere in the Palace were indel-ible proofs of the country's long misfortune. The picture gallery of the American years, 1898 to 1946, for instance, struck me as too brief an exhibition, given the length of its shadow on the times. I saw a picture, framed, of a youthful Ronald Reagan, governor of California, fox-trotting with the First Lady, Madama in the Palace, foreigners dancing in the room where I stood, amid the capiz of Maharlika Hall, with Ronald's wife Nancy, off-center, in the dictator's arms. Obscene tropes of imperial order, publicity stills in a hoard gathered up, who knows, by the minions of my mom's old friend, Mrs. Conrada Trin-idad, deposed regional director of the Ministry of People's Facts.

Important Lady in blue.

Vampira of TEIPCO.

And so when I came upon my mother's favorite, her great-uncle, in the photograph in that exhibit in Malacañang Palace, the pres-ence of Lolo Paco amid the nation's dishevelment told me that my mother's stories were not all delusions. Lolo Paco really was a senator, a bureaucrat, an ambassador for the independence, as my mother used to say.

But what exactly did he do in 1931?

The photo in the museum exhibit did not say.

Maybe, I thought, looking at the picture of skinny, gray-eyed Lolo

Paco with his thin face and fantastical scar, not everyone in my family is on the wrong side of the story.

On our last day, Assistant Secretary to the Secretary Espasol's minion, Rudy Da Moody, instructed us to take our boxes of material from Maharlika Hall to the incinerator on the Palace grounds.

And that's how we held a last sit-in at Malacañang Palace during the start of the new regime.

Trina Trono organized it and shook her finger at Rudy Da Moody. "This is damning," Trina said.

Despite her adult clothes, button-down polo shirt and khaki pants, she still looked like a Thumbelina-sized Mahatma Gandhi: her owl's-eye glasses and fierce face.

"It is criminal!" she told the acned lawyer—pink-shirted atis, Rudy Da Moody. "Every single piece of material in these boxes should be catalogued and filed, not burned and wasted without a historian's eye. Even the receipts for shoes and piles of lipsticked tissue and those love notes from dumb pop singers should be sorted out. History is in the details! We demand that you hire a Palace historian to deal with this—this junk!"

And as the pockfaced minion, Rudy Da Moody, Mister Rambo Tan, began explaining the wherefores and whereats of his decision in his high-pitched, rambling way, expletives marking his incoherence, gun bulging underneath his Lacoste, I thought of the rumors of this cheap-talking bungler, that he had killed a man before graduating from San Beda, using his family's paltik goods, and I kept staring at the unicorns on his peach-colored pants and hearing my mother in Salogó.

"Oh my God, inday—you will give the maids asthma. Please—take them away. Let them rot somewhere else, not in front of human beings."

Once, during the old days when you mailed letters to friends if you went abroad, I asked Trina Trono, teenage Maoist turned venture capitalist, cultural potentate, and my first publisher—

Whatever happened to our Maharlika Hall boxes, I wrote.

They went to an incinerator on the Palace grounds, she replied—where else?

On the roof deck, amid early-bird pigeons and the scurrilous leaps of these bright-eyed squirrels, I heard another ping.

A private message.

I didn't even have to check the sender.

So your Tio Nemor tells me your the one who has it your mother's inheritance your legacy, your great-grandfather's diaries! can't wait to see you I have an offer you can't refuse youll be so glad to hear!!!

The Future Consumed

A living silverfish darts out and tickles my palm.

A postscript pest.

Vermin are alive in history's tombs.

I preferred the southward view in the morning, drinking coffee amid sky foragers, some blasted pigeons, and where the hell do these attention-deficit hyperactive squirrels come from? To the east was the Empire State. Downward, westerly, if you imagined the line of water, was that statue, portending freedom. My sight's circumference on this roof deck is literally what my classmates used to call this alien world: the symbols of estados—cinematic vision of "abroad." The pages before me lay full of bugs—burdened drones escaped from hives. Trifles and minutiae. The diarist's focus is skewed. He stares at a lizard eating a cockroach, an event that takes two minutes, a lifetime for the roach.

Yes, I did.

I stole it.

That old domed wooden box I once found in Salogó, with its three volumes and news clippings and looseleaf bits of paper.

I left for New York—after the marches, the inauguration of a new president, and one more new Constitution—with one suitcase.

When I told my mom in Salogó, when we were at the grave of her

Papá, about my fellowship, that a writer in New York had picked me to be in his graduate workshop, and I had to return to Manila soon to prepare for the GRE test, get a medical exam, apply for the visa, for a moment, I saw a flicker in my mom's eyes.

As if something had knocked her off her world, worse than the president's flight.

An abstract, pained look before she reached out to hug me.

"Oh inday, you're so smart. That's so good. I always knew. Let me tell Tia Sayong and Mana Talia!"

She was stiff in my arms when I hugged her, but that might be because her high heels were wobbly on the cemetery grass, and she was trying to keep her balance.

I still don't know what this faltering was about—whether it was about her desire or mine.

And she said, before she showed me off—"Did you see? Mana Talia is back!"

I returned to Tacloban one more time.

My mother was moving houses again, this time to a cramped apartment on the corner of Gomez and Paterno. Tio Nemor now rented a house in Tacloban, up in the hills at Santa Elena. He had left Doctor Tita Tita's opulent home and clinic in Danao, sold to an unsuspecting dentist whose nightmares we won't know: he backed out from the deal— the dentist said he could not sleep in a haunted house. The house in Danao is moldering, a cavity. *"Great for fighting caries!"* But no one lives there. Tio Nemor was now an assistant to Tacloban's city fiscal. Though they were from different parties, he and the fiscal were fraternity brods, all was good. Doctor Tita Tita was in Baltimore, a neurosurgeon who emptied the bedpans of geriatric patients in retirement homes. A caregiver, she was called. She had abandoned her life without troubling to get any papers, she was still a tourist, hiding and hiding, I think, from memory. At Juan Luna Street, I found the old copy of *Labyrinths* that Trina and I had once shared, and that fat tome with the ax on the cover, *Abraham Lincoln's World*, now so dated, with its loathsome love of kings, and the domed wooden box.

Adina an guapa—who had arrived from California those years ago looking like Gina Lollobrigida, a seventies idol, no one could conquer her—came down the stairs in a faded duster and denim pale-blue bandanna. Denim was odd on my mother. She never wore jeans. The fabric on her head was out of place. Hino nagkawat ha iya? Who stole her? Someone had abducted my mom. It was early in the morning, and she was not prepared for her public. Her gaze had that wistful look of erasure without her painted eyebrows, and her morning whiff of cucumber and Pond's Cold Cream—her three *P*s: pipino, pomelo, Pond's—traced the house's humidity as she came down the stairs.

Something was off, a step, an awkward lunge.

My mother was limping.

She approached me, her right palm favoring her left elbow.

Her left arm was in a sling.

Her palm grazed the air below the bent limb as if her pose kept the arm from falling off.

"Oh inday!"

Her girlish voice.

She sounded as she used to, before our fights—as if it was my presence that gave her joy.

"What happened?" I said.

We hadn't spoken since the new president, the murdered senator's widow, had been installed, and my mom had called with her opinion.

"Oh, your president, that Cory, inday, she is so ugly, her nose is so flat, like a dried-up salukara sold in the shops of Borongan! How could you vote for her—so different from Meldy. Meldy is the Rose of Tacloban. And what is Cory?"

"The Thorn," I answered dutifully.

Pretty soon, I stopped taking her calls. I was getting ready to leave the country. For months in Manila, I was in a daze—a new country and a new life in tandem. My last months in the city I had nothing to talk about with my mother, I was sketching out my map of Manhattan in my head—where Malcolm X had told his autobiography to Alex Haley, where James Baldwin had once walked with Beauford Delaney, the lane e. e. cummings lived next to that neurasthenic hermit, Djuna Barnes, and the local pub where Jose Garcia Villa, the Pope of Greenwich Village, drank his holy water, Jack Daniels.

The future consumed me, the past was a mirage.

"Oh, this," Adina an guapa said, stooping as she approached me.

My mom looked down at her arm, as if she had already forgotten why she had lost full use of her body.

Mana Marga was glaring at me from the hallway, carrying bedding and a bunch of clothes—geometric muu-muus, a caftan, a pile of scarves.

I looked away from Mana Marga.

I had no idea what was going on.

I was determined not to feel guilty.

Mana Marga's usual rouge, her homage to my mom, or my mom's homage to her, made her look spotted, as if by rage.

She had been on a jeepney to Salogó to close up the house for the summer, my mom explained, her face lowered, not looking at me, and the jeepney had turned over.

Then her eyes looked sideways at me.

The way she had two instincts at once—to tell a joke and a tragedy.

"Praise the Virgin—we all survived—even the baboy on the roof! It lived, thanks be to God, to become lechon for fiesta!"

"That's not funny," I said.

"I did not tell you, inday, because you were busy with your exams."

"They're just the GREs. Those don't matter in writing programs. You should have told me."

"You needed to focus on your exams. I told them not to tell you."

"Those tests don't matter, Ma! Your life matters. You should have told me."

"Look, inday!" she said.

She pushed the faded bandanna aside so I could see the surgeon's stitches across her brow, razor straight, a tear through her smooth hairline that demarcated her brow from her dark hair.

A chill ran through me.

To see the fracture.

"See, inday," she said, grinning, readying me for her joke, "I got a free facelift! The surgery smoothed out my wrinkles. You just have to pray, inday, and good things will come. Thanks be to God!"

The accident broke her femur, her head went through a window, her crooked arm would never heal. Coming and going with my mom's possessions, Mana Marga kept giving me a look that killed.

It's not my fault, I wanted to tell Mana Marga.

Something in my soul was not right, her eyes said to me.

I had not gone home when my mom was stitched up, her head in bandages, her arm in a sling.

But how could I—I quarreled in my mind with Mana Marga—her catechetical gaze—*no one told me!*

How many months ago had this happened?

No one had bothered to call me in Manila.

Tio Nemor was busy with a new career in his new order.

Adino, sweet Adino, would soon be in Long Beach, reunited with the father neither of us knew.

Putt-putt, too, had left all of us—a journalist in Mindanao.

And now I, too, was leaving.

So attached I had been to my mother as a child, but when I grew up, I shed my concern like the cicada's body, its uncased, fragile, primeval form.

I don't know what I was expecting of my mother those last days in Tacloban. That she would begin weeping at the thought of my departure, that she would ask me all the questions she never did, such as, what are you writing about, inday, or where will you live, or how far is New York from Leyte?

What she asked was—are there any Catholics in Green Witch Village?

But I, too, asked no questions.

I wished for her blessing. I was resentful of her indifference. After she kissed me, when she got down from the stairs, she went straight to the patio to her unfinished canvases. Her old friend, Lola Sayong, needed artwork for her renovated Primrose Hotel. The country was opening up after the long pall of dictatorship, tourists, small businessmen, even cutting-trip joyriders from Luzon, going from Bicol into Samar, were coming through the city. Adina an guapa was busy. She had orders to fill. I was ashamed of my egotism, my desire to be seen by my mom in my last few days at home, while she was happy in her world, and she never told me that three months ago she had almost died.

She did not want to bother me.

But it was worse to realize—she did not believe it should matter to me.

I had my own life.

It took precedence.

That was her message.

My mother's intuitions about my desire were clairvoyant, painful, and absolute.

I had nothing to do in those last days at Juan Luna Street except watch my mother make her art and water the orchids and help Mana Marga pack her house.

I found the box in my mom's aparador, hidden among piles of *Readers' Digest*s, beneath the cranky gramophone that was now almost unrecognizable, its marvelous wood fractured by mites and time, the stiff velvet fuzzy and grimed, atop her mestiza outfits.

A record, with the puzzle of a dog winding *His Master's Voice!*, lay cracked in unrepentant shards.

"Wow," I told my mom, "I thought I had only imagined it. I've been wondering where this box of his papers went. It's been here all along. Remember when Mick-mick and I found it? What a crazy day! Mana Talia came out from hiding and was arrested by the martial law police."

"What are you talking about?"

"You know. When Mana Talia had to go to jail. When Meldy Hija and her thugs came down to Salogó to arrest her."

"No, they didn't. Mana Talia went to Europe. She has a daughter in London—she and the congressman went to live with her."

"But the guards went down to arrest Mana Talia—"

"Inday, you always distort. How can you become a writer if you know only lies?"

This had been my mother's point ever since the rebellion.

Mentiras—that's all I had.

Mentiras of the past!

"How can Mana Talia have been arrested?" my mom said with wide eyes. "She is the wife of Congressman Quintana."

"But don't you remember? The goons in blue uniforms found her with the pigs, on the dirt floor in Salogó, and she sang that drunkards' song of the FrankenPresley Combo. Please release me!"

And my mom just hummed.

I couldn't help it, I said the next line.

We sang, and my mom's voice had the Delgado tremolo that I couldn't match.

"Oh, inday," my mom said. "You always believe what you want to believe. Since you were a baby. You were always like that. You always had your own way. And my job was to let you go. Mana Talia went to Europe. She visited all the shrines of the Virgin Mary. She took all the Kodak pictures!"

"Yes, but before that, she was arrested, out there in Salogó! Remember Mick-mick? How he bit Meldy Hija's hand? And the goons—how they went down the stairs to get him, and instead they found Mana Talia? And John-john—"

"No!" said my mom. "No."

This time her voice warranted no contradiction.

"I do not remember," she said.

I stared at her, barricaded from me by her huge canvas of grass and flowers.

A squashed and gold-painted rose lay in the center of her design.

"Why should I remember such things?" she said.

I nodded.

Why should she remember?

"Malingkod ako anay, inday. Padiskansuha ako anay. Don't open that box—you will give yourself asthma."

Lingkod. Higda.

My mom's words of retreat.

I thought I could smell it—riverine mud, moist and musty like a mix of clamshells, silt, and the odd, sweet ironing waft of burnt-copra coals upon banana leaves. The flash of silver dashing across the leather and metallic lid. Something already crumbled, eaten up from the inside.

Folders, news clippings, three notebooks with glazed covers, tucked in the plaid, still-intact pockets of the box's lid.

I remembered how the moment I had opened it, pressed my thumbs against its double-facing locks, the items inside came apart with a kind of pained obsolescence when they hit my palm.

A faded rectangle, domed like a sepulcher.

I never asked my mother if I could take the box with me to America.

I just took it.

I've kept it under my bed—at grad school in New York. I've kept it in a closet, then behind the sofa in the various apartments I've lived in. It has been sitting on a bookshelf with my incomplete volumes of Blair and Robertson's *Philippine Islands*—a wormwood set that's full of gaps.

After Trina's messages, I lugged the box up here to the roof deck.

For years, I forgot I had it.

I never even opened it.

I keep it with me now. Just in case.

I read Trina's last message.

Can't wait to see you I have an offer you can't refuse youll be so glad to hear!!!

You never know who will come knocking at your door.

His Unmade World

The boy sits among his vanished brother's effects, staring at sketches of suns—suns atop pyramids, suns within suns, suns amid eyes. Pharaoh eyes, lion eyes, chimerical-goat-god, polyphemic eyes. And too many drawings of squares with compasses, masonic tools, the mark of a fetish. A note left behind in his brother's jesuitical hand.

Siempre el rebelde, nunca el amigo.

The little boy Paco sits in his brother's abandoned room.

The first the family hears of Jote after his flight from the house on Moret Street is the fall of Malolos, and Aguinaldo's troops throw wicker chairs and wives and sons and pots and pans and tabo and orinola and washing paddles into carromatas to retreat up north, chased by the men of Arthur MacArthur who burns a country in his wake—Batangas's sugar canes, Pampanga's rice fields, palms along the Ilocos coast, and leftover carabaos that have not yet died of rinderpest.

When the men of Arthur MacArthur capture Aguinaldo, the servants expect their young master home. They expect his mournful reappearance like all the others who return to surrender—barefoot squadrons in frayed rayadillo, burnt faces and gaunt cheeks, the Sons of the People, who laid their guns in single file at Bagumbayan, the Luneta, some with the sword peeking forlorn through their tunics, the glint of their loss, *tsk tsk tsk*, sayang, sayang, sayang, Tay Sequil, *El Cochero Exequiel!* reports, his toothpick flying at his last *tsk*.

But such is life, says the savvy kutsero, you fight, you lose.

Saba! Ayaw hin saba bayâ!

Mariano the mayordomo smacks that toothpicking Tagalog with the *Diario*, and he turns his back on Tay Sequil.

At first, Mariano the mayordomo does not see the ghost loitering among the flower bushes and the narra trees that shade the house's staircase, obscuring his view of the pigs.

Mariano is at the sala's window, above the mahogany stairs, pouring out overnight pee from his tin orinola onto the orchids, and then to the gumamela below.

His first act before facing his unmade world.

A figure, shaking his straw hat dry, leaps from the gumamela bushes, saying *leche leche leche*, but the culprit is innocent, only an orinola.

May anyong yaman, may pagkahamot hin yamang.

An aura of gold, slightly smelling of piss.

The ghost of a man stands beneath the narra trees, and another rain, a cascade of yellow blossoms, catches in the ghost's earlobe, his kamisa sleeves, and later when this skeleton enters the sala little Paco thinks that the man's golden aura is an illusion that Paco's body senses just because, for no good reason he can think of, he smells pee.

It is the old pretend-servant of Don Francisco the First, come back to haunt them.

Hilario Sayo, a.k.a. the valiant Hiloy.

The last time the boy saw Hilario Sayo was at Bagumbayan—in a crowd at the Luneta, when all he did was follow his nose.

But when he recognizes him, the apparition of Hilario Sayo gives the boy—emptiness.

A perceptual vacancy he feels but does not understand.

Blankness pushes against his breast.

(This is odd because the boy's scribblings denote sensory abundance, he tastes what another person touches, or what his father sighs is inside of him, a tickly, sprouting thing, color of smoke, or he colors smells and, weirdly, smells color.)

May anyong yaman, may pagkahamot hin yamang.

But his absent brother nga layaw is only what he is—lost.

The servants run from their posts to hear the news from the rebelde, Hilario Sayo, they remember him from the time of his hiding under their home when the fighting had not even begun, after the events long ago that December in Bagumbayan—

It's the valiant Hiloy.

Aquí está!

Aadi hiya!

But the valiant Hiloy does not move.

He stands in the sala, led up the steps by Mariano the mayordomo and bearing his moist straw hat slantwise across his chest.

Kuwento! Kuwento!

A feathery stirring rises in the boy at the sight.

An ivory tickling at his chest, like chick scratches.

But no story comes forth from the valiant Hiloy.

What has happened to you since we last saw you, Hiloy?

Hiloy opens his mouth.

In the gesture is a hint of—ice in the boy's heart.

The valiant Hiloy has lost it.

His tongue.

The servants are silent before the man.

As the rebelde breathes in and out, in and out, his mouth open— the dark space in the valiant Hiloy's mouth where the tongue should be—the returned-to-sender rebel emits a blast of ice about the boy's body.

It is he who feels what Hilario Sayo attempts.

Speech.

A lemon-tinged blast of cold, the way his finger, when it hovers about a block of ice, lifts off from its force.

He watches as, from his pocket, about his chest, Hilario Sayo, a.k.a. the valiant Hiloy, gives the widower, Don Francisco The First, a trinket.

A lace handkerchief.

The boy moves closer.

An alphabetical code.

A. B. y C.

Don Francisco the First stares at the handkerchief.

He takes it.

(But carefully—he tries not to smear—his tears—on the lace cloth.)

Paco goes back to eating his plate of mango, then a bayabas, then some grapes.

He swallows and bites and spits.

He eats.

The chewing keeps him focused.

(The ochre hues of his father's tears, the lime-pink cloud from the servants' breaths.)

He eats to concentrate—on food—

Food is the best distraction.

It comforts him.

Mariano the mayordomo gets it.

He looks at the cloth in the old man's palm.

He deciphers the sign offered by the valiant Hiloy.

"Señorito Jote is alive. In Samar."

Buhi hi señorito—ha Samar.

Mariano the mayordomo stares at the handkerchief's details, the insignia.

Giporlos.

That is the message.

So guesses Mariano the mayordomo.

Then just like that, before Mariano and Ambrosio and Tay Sequil can offer Hiloy his deserved baon, a bunch of langka seeds, roasted and warm, tied up carefully in abaca cloth—the rebelde disappears.

People just keep vanishing.

His last sight, before the war, of Hilario Sayo, the boy is in the middle of a crowd, searching for his father Don Francisco the First only with his nose. He doesn't know how he finds himself right next to his Papá, somewhere along the Malecon, on the watery edge of the Luneta, brought there only by smell and the hand of that man who turns out to be Jote's friend—Hilario Sayo, a.ka. the valiant Hiloy.

Later the man takes refuge under their home, on the dirt floor beneath the house on Moret Street in the open-air space where his abuelita Nemesia the Insomniac shelters her goats and pigs.

That boy Hiloy, Hilario Sayo in the newspapers (he becomes a person of interest in *Diario de Manila*, little Paco learns with thrill), takes on his tasks of war on Moret Street—drying out the beef tapa, collecting pig slop from the neighbors, salting the budo-bulad on the extra duyan—and lives by the outdoor hammock near the pigsty that's the coolest place after fiesta, when the sleeper's companions rooting in their mud are gone. And so the fugitive Hiloy becomes an actual servant, no kidding, not just acting, as Mariano the mayor-domo takes advantage of his sad, insurgent plight. But one day, Hiloy disappears—that's the way it is in the confusing months when the guardia civil are rounding people up, creating all kinds of trouble.

People keep vanishing.

Now little Paco thinks he has dreamed up this vision, this new version—of the valiant Hiloy—

So he writes in his notebook.

The katipunero who looks like a haunting of war, wilted hat and yellow aura, flecked with piss and gold—it had been five years since his last sight of Hiloy, the rebelde in league with his brother Jote, the baby encanto, his brother with his curls like the Santo Niño, an iya bulaw nga pelo nga baga hin may asô—and at this point, Paco has been through his third sacrament, Confession, to prepare for his fourth, Confirmation, coming soon, while the valiant Hiloy has gone through—what is it called—Extreme Unction—

And back.

Extremaunción.

But before Paco could ask—*what fruits could you pick in the revolution where did you cook rice why did my brother abandon*—the valiant Hiloy vanishes.

Again.

"Hah, Giporlos?" grunts Ambrosio the cook in the kitchen. "The bats will get señorito Jote first."

Mga paniki lang ang kanyang makakalasan.

The servants and the Tagalog, the driver Tay Sequil, have long lost their ability to speak to each other in their purest speech—each now mistakes the other's tongue for his own.

"And why is that?" says Tay Sequil. "Is he a monkey, an unggoy of the wild?"

"He will find in Samar only coconuts and drunkards! Mga lubi at parahubog. How can he save the country by going to Samar? Ano ba ang nandoon nga aadto," grunts Ambrosio the cook. "Por que bakit ha Samar kay ano, makakasalbar, ginoo."

"You should know, you coconut-head drunkard," says Tay Sequil— "You come from there!"

"Ah," mourns Ambrosio, "amo na—Marianing and I, we know what's coming to señorito Jote in Samar—damo nga karantahon ngan mga paragsayaw! Parasaway!"

Song and dance!

I cannot translate parasaway.

Imp? Disruptor? Mischief-maker? Panulay?

The men in the kitchen speak as if they have primeval knowledge—Samarnon men from Don Francisco's gallivanting days.

Galabanting in Samar

Don Francisco the First traveled with only a rattan case, his mother Nemesia's old tampipi trunk, and a companion, the young Sequil—*El Cochero Exequiel!*—those days of old when Don Francisco the First sowed his oats amid provincial farms, *galabanting* is the technical term—crisscrossing Luzon and the Visayas and settling in the abaca lands near Borongan, then Catbalogan—

Don Francisco finishes off his happy days by falling in love.

With the lovely daughter of Giporlos, Adina Blumfeld y Catalogo.

Of his Samarnon mother, little Paco has no memory.

After all, he had killed her.

That is how he says it—*la maté.*

"I killed her."

A terse phrase.

In her colorful katsa skirts and modest yet seductive blouses, Adina Blumfeld y Catalogo spends her days embroidering her alphabetical name on lacy handkerchiefs and linen pillows.

A. B. y C.

It's not clear whether the young Adina is training to be wife or servant, but she has skills—boiling salabat, shredding leaves off malunggay stems in single moves, spooling abaca hemp into fine thread.

The servants, especially Mariano the mayordomo, remember.

They're her cousins.

Kuwento, kuwento!

She has a small round face, smooth like a metal bead or the top of a pin.

A smile like sunshine.

She has sausage curls: coiling about her cheeks in the style of the foreign.

Style is her poor mother Carmen Catalogo's second rebellion.

Her brief biography—

Adina Blumfeld y Catalogo is the daughter of the weaver Carmen and a musical wanderer, the no-name bum from Leitmeritz (not Leyte), good-looking man from Bohemia (not Bohol). The singing rover, No-Name Blumfeld, is a musician in an inter-island travelling band who jumps ship in Samar in 1885, impregnates a local, and at an opportune moment when a passing pleasure ship comes by down San Juanico Strait, that good-for-nothing, that No-Name Blumfeld, rides that, too, arrivederci auf Wiedersehen hala buot ha nga tanan dida to his not-gypsy bride, and the last Samar hears of the musikero Blumfeld is the sound of his beautiful, Cebu-made guitar, strumming a tune from *Rigoletto* a few weeks after the cry of his epilogue in Giporlos.

The baby Adina.

A bad-luck child.

Who grows up to be a beauty.

There she is—spooling her thread in the big open barn with the abaca weavers of Giporlos, women in loose outfits and huge heads of hair, in that seemingly disheveled yet cultivated-wispy style of the times.

They stand in a row in the lit-up thatch amid hempen looms, making rough cloth.

The abaca rope, raw and thick, smells of earth and, strangely, cacao—which always smells of dirt anyhow.

Their woven treasures have uses for which every single lady has only indifference (their dreams have more lyrical shapes): carabao harnesses, coconut sacks, and above all—coiled, braided shipping rigs for the inter-island boats, fateful source of Adina's birth, and the archipelago's preferred mode of travel.

Don Francisco the First passes by on his mission to make hay while his money lasts, a man of moles and laughter.

His job is to be a colonist. His temperament is to be a bum.

(What's the difference? The diarist's pen, an iya agi, makes no answer.)

He wears leather suspenders over his sando, a Panama hat atop pomaded hair, a pair of heeled shoes absurd on the farms.

His smile is mocking and congenial, infectious.

He has scary, milk-gray eyes (cataract-filled in his old age).

He notices her first.

He sees her slim back, a supple column as her body in striped jusi, that pineapple fabric that cuts like glass—a shimmering razor of light—shakes with the movements of the ancient loom.

A postcard slips out of the journals—

The ladies at their looms, in doubled poses.

Like everyone else, he looks again when he passes, just to check if the sight is true.

So it is.

Adina Blumfeld y Catalogo, her figure fine as an unspooling string, her face round, fat cheeks, a beauty in weird sausage curls, sticks out from the rest of the weavers.

Is that her figure in the stereo card—in piña cloth like a stream of light?

It is the folly of her mother Carmen that her daughter goes about Giporlos like a plaster abnormality, an apparition in ugly Western hair, a cut-out woman from La Ilustración.

Adina thinks nothing of it.

She loves her mother without thinking.

She is a beloved child.

Her schoolmates forgive her strange looks.

A bad-luck baby.

Abandonada.

By No-Name Blumfeld.

One more ounce of pity does no child any harm.

She grows up with the girl weavers, in her sun-filled clothes and uncommon coif, playing patintero and sungka, peeling garlic for arroz caldo, jumping rope.

How do you catch a child like Adina?

In the usual local way—with hired guitar-strummers, a serenade of kundiman by her cogon window, then lumps of money in a paper bag.

At their wedding, townsfolk pin pesos onto their piña clothing while the couple wave their hands in delicate gestures, their wrists' kuracha grace.

The groom staggers during the dancing, drunk from his luck, the bride lets up her miraculous hair, tendrils stuck in a peineta, and the jusi mantilla, her mother Carmen's masterpiece, is the heirloom, the treasure over her glittering gown.

Don Francisco the First is a man of principle: he swears an oath to the once-stricken but not to be twice-bitten Catalogo clan.

He stays put in Samar.

No wandering lutist he.

A romantic but also reasonable lover.

He barely leaves his thatch home.

His one wish—to be with his bride.

To be honest, even in this story one can see the temperament, perhaps, of Tio Nemor, in this figure of his great-grandfather, Don Francisco the First. His easy will to be pleased, and its corollary: the tendency to accommodate, to placate others. A good skill for a mayor, and in Don Francisco's case the correct talent for a middleman, a trader overseeing his mother-in-law's lands.

A peaceable man with a gift for imagining that his desires are everyone else's good fortune, and it is for the benefit of others that they must conform to his hopes.

And so the Manileño (actually he was born in Bulacan) settles in with the Catalogo clan.

A hemp farmer, devout husband, and betel-nut-chewing lucky man.

In Samar he escapes the duty-bound gloom of his fellow insularists in Manila who sit around chomping on their cigars as they dream of Madrid from the Malecon.

Jote, full name *Jorge Mariano Carmen*, Adina's first child, is born in Giporlos, at the time a barrio of Balangiga, during a period of bliss, in the capiz-and-wooden house near her mother's abaca fields.

It is Adina Blumfeld y Catalogo's sweet time of kundiman, with her husband by her side and a boy at her breasts.

Who looks like a baby encanto, the Santo Niño.

Praise be to God!

The child's flaw: a bunch of pink and brown dots on his front and back.

But that is no wonder—the boy's father is full of them, too.

An archipelago of moles.

It is true—when the townspeople first see the baby Jote, they cross themselves in holy apostrophe, saying—

Santo Niño, bendisyoni kami!

The superstitious ones shade his fat-cheeked face with their supplicating arms.

A holy family in Giporlos.

It's when Adina Blumfeld y Catalogo dies giving birth to little Paco, full name *Francisco Nemesio Bonifacio*, that Don Francisco the First has a moment of nostalgia.

A desire to return.

To the broad molave planks of Moret Street, in Sampaloc, Manila, to his own mother, Abuelita Nemesia, the insomniac.

The grieving widower (he's in his thirties) uproots his stakes, returns home to the abuelita, Nemesia the Insomniac from the Pyrenees (or is it Fujian?), on Moret Street in Sampaloc, erases the traces of Samar's copra and abaca world, save for his two live baggages: ages six and zero; pier-side warehouses of sugar and hemp, abaca and molasses; and his passel of servants, efficient men forwarded to the bad-luck groom by the broken-hearted Catalogo clan of eastern Samar.

That his oldest son, Jote, turns out to be a savant with an actor's mnemonic talent at the old man's school (from which Don Francisco, to be honest, had flunked), first at San Juan de Letran, then at Ateneo Municipal, and on top of that there's his musical skill, an ability to play arias by ear, *al oído!*—the solitary legacy, so Mariano the mayordomo surmises, of the long-lost No-Name Blumfeld—albeit this boy's talent is of the high-pitched bandurria, and the boy's voice is comic, a feeble contralto—

The boy Jote, true, is somber, of few words, with a habit of silent observation—examining beetles on the kisame and mites on the duyan, tasting them, divesting them of wings, not at all shocked when they shoot poison at his curious nose, keeping the ugliest in perforated jars—and his shock of infantile hair never leaves him—*la cabeza cubierta de pelo!*—with the deep-set, shadowy eyes of his half-Semitic, half-Samarnon mother—Adina Blumfeld y Catalogo of the alphabetical initials, *A. B. y C.*—dead at age twenty-four.

Anyhow, the multi-talented boy is an unexpected comfort to the devout widower Don Francisco the First.

He can't bear to look at the other one, that wide-eyed mongo-bean Paco, with his big ears, thin mouth, weird sniffer of a Nose—nga iya Irong, an iya Nariz—and terrible, gluttonous hunger.

All the boy does is gobble, gobble, gobble.

Abetted by the cook Ambrosio, of course, but still.

One more ounce of pity does no child any harm.

Don Francisco the First, living so close to Calle Iris, has other, multiple comforts, of course, and at one point almost takes a wife, a needlepoint expert from the convent of Santa Clara—but really, why bother when a household of capable men, plus one woman, the slim labandera from San Roque, Mana Felicisima, font of joy of Tay Sequil, *El Cochero Exequiel!*, brings up his sons, plus there's a whole street, the lovely women of Calle Iris, to suit his needs?

His life living off his provincial goods is a comfortable oasis—until Jote vanishes. There's a sense that Don Francisco the First, with his undetected cancer and premature age, shuffles among his German customers and American sales clerks and Samarnon cooks and British agents, clutching at his fatal kidneys or liver, or whatever crushes out his guts as the yanqui gringos blast Manila's swamps and take over his city, as if he were gathering information about the war.

Like a secret agent.

My ears perk up.

In the diary I look for evidence of the widower Don Francisco the First as patriotic double-crosser, heroic trader selling foodstuffs and war implements to the enemy only to turn around and be amigo to heroes.

No dice.

Don Francisco the First, as far as evidence goes, is a war profiteer to the end.

The arrival on Moret Street of the second omen—the hemp agent, the British middleman from Samar, Brent Kipling, or Kipping, Esquire—flusters the household.

The boy hears the sound of the taho vendor but finds on the doorstep not only the custard man, ready with his favorite, his morning cup of pearls, syrup, and soy.

Tahoooooo!

He also sees the bearded white man, leaning on a cane.

Carrying a briefcase.

The wild man's shaggy beard and his eyes, so green and distracting, make Paco think of a mamaw, a disgusting bakulaw. Staring at the man, with the mirror in the vestibule between them, Paco sees his own milky eyes looking back at himself.

He shuts the door on the man, but the man calls him by name.

"Don Paco!" he says. "Do you not remember?"

He recognizes him by his accent. The man rounds out his vowels and cannot roll his *R*s.

His father's friends don't speak any language with competence.

"Señor Kipping! I mean Kipling!" Paco whispers.

Throughout the diary the boy never gets the name straight.

"*¿Que pasó a ti?*"

"Boy," says the corpse of a man, he looks like the castaway on the cover of *Robinson Crusoe por Daniel Defoe*, and the boy steps back— "I need to see your Papá."

Don Francisco the First, rocking in his butaka, does not stand up at the sight of the Englishman.

"What?" the widower barks.

"Ah, Don Francisco, my deep apologies. I have come—I have just—I have escaped—from the—americanos."

Señor Kipping, or Kipling's cane clatters in the sala as he settles upon a chair—the imported one, covered in silk.

The boy watches as the cane traces a path (an iya agi) on the floor.

Little Paco can feel the agent's warm behind, a bit sharp, but sinewy, the subtle crunch of his woolen pants' sweaty crust pressing onto the green softness of the silken chair's thin, easily torn cover. He waits for the fabric's sound, its incremental tear. Ouch! (an iya agi). Little Paco feels the pinch when the tired man sits down, but then, sighing, as thin butt meets cool green, and an almost invisible but faintly melon-colored geyser of dread pfffts out sideways from the man's bony frame, the silk squeaking like the brief opening *puc!* of a pakwan seed—

Little Paco relaxes.

Don Francisco's hemp trade in Basey! in Catbalogan! even in Giporlos! The yanqui gringos want the abaca lands! They are swarming over Samar!

As Señor Kipling, or Kipping, goes on, and on, and on, Don Francisco the First rocks even more furiously on the butaka, his feet pressed tight to the floor and his ancient butt upended so that little Paco thinks his father might break in two, killed by the physics of the rocking chair.

A battle of the butts! Skinny versus cushy! Pale versus gray!

Each creak of his father's furious butaka, back and forth, back and forth, is a crisscross of sensations in little Paco, a series of pink *W*s in weft, yellow *Y*s in warp, across both cheeks of the boy's behind, he feels it like a scribble, a penman's scratch, an agi han era agi, agi!, the feel of the native twine on his father's formidable behind reproducing a pattern of phantom sketches on the boy's own butt.

To filter out this competition—between Señor Kipping, or Kipling's violent Chinese silk and his father's gold husk of native twine—Paco concentrates on breakfast—

He's done with the fruit.

Now the taho.

Next the champorado.

They are greedy for your abaca, warns Brent Kipling, or Kipping, Esquire (who cares about that abaca?, munch-mutters little Paco, his tongue slurping up the tapioca—tell us about Jote!)—*they want your hemp for their shipyards and their sailing masts for their Navy! They wish—to rule the Pacific!*

With abaca? thinks Paco.

Colonizers! Invaders!, says the Englishman, his judgment obliterating his self-awareness.

Can you believe, reports the skeletal agent, the Americans accuse him, Brent Kipping, or Kipling, Esquire, of all people, an upright British commercial traveler, a man of principle from Leeds, of providing funds to the forces of the Terror of Samar, General Vicente Lukban—

That he, Brent Kipling, or Kipping, Esquire, is paying off the katipuneros with Don Francisco's abaca money, so the yanqui gringos say!

"And do you provide the funds?" barks Don Francisco the First.

The broker is silent.

Don Francisco sighs.

For a moment, the butaka is still.

Slurp slurp slurp slurp, goes little Paco over his taho.

"Don't worry. I know. It is the only way to do business. It is our lot. To give away to all, to the enemies and the friends, the occupiers and the rebels."

Enemigos y amigos.

The Englishman sighs.

"And you have no other news?" whispers Don Francisco.

"I have no other news," says Brent Kipping, or Kipling. "I am sorry, Don Francisco. I have no news of your son. I looked for your wife's family in Giporlos, I left your message, I have looked—there is one man who says—"

"No rumors! Just facts!"

"The rebels are everywhere. General Vicente Lukban, he has the guts. But the Americans—they have the guns. That is what they say. If your boy is in Samar—*señor*, I heard your own man tell me: Mister Pedro Duran, the abaca agent. He tells me the townspeople believe the child of the dead Adina is back, he's rising back to take his land. The Santo Niño, they call him. You know how they are. Full of superstitions. But in my view if the master Jote is in Samar—he needs to leave—it will not end we—"

Don Francisco is a towering barrel of a sorrowing man with fish breath, his biggest hairy mole clawing at his ear and mutant breast cancer creeping up his prematurely gray chest. He is a lover of opera, fresh danggit, spicy vinegar, the freaky bony juice of salted balut, and, only in secret (for in public he maintains his holy stature—his widower's grief), the putas and lukaret of Calle Iris.

But above all, he longs for Jote, his favorite.

Paco dares not look at his father.

His father's breath as the widower grunts and wheezes, not quite sobbing, just breathing, is a pit in Paco's stomach as he empties out the taho cup. Agi, agi, agi. His father's vinegar and danggit breath is a rolling pit of a santol in the boy's stomach—his father's breath a bit slurry like santol seed but less fleshy, and so, unsteady, it taps at his innards every few minutes or so, just so, just—so, just—so—

A silvery hush, a feather glance, in his eye.

Paco, a congenial but kind of passive kid, assaulted by sensations (the notebook is so open to the world, he feels even the emotions of silk and twine, the colors of farts, the touch of sighs, agi, agi, agi), finds that his father's grief adds to his sticky feeling as he listens: a sensation akin to the gooey slime of his feeling of loss, which he joins perhaps in misapprehension with his vanished maghurang, his brother, he never calls him kuya, he is not really Tagalog—he calls him akon bugto. My part. A part of his flesh. This abandonment that tastes of this runny custard in his mouth, dank and about to spoil—as he sits there, feeling guilty, licking the last bit of caramel off his spoon of taho.

"And do you have nothing else for me?" barks his Papá.

"No, sir, only—"

And Brent Kipling, Esquire, opens the briefcase. He takes out the folders he has carried from Giporlos to Catbalogan to Manila.

"This is from your wife's family, the Catalogos of Samar. They wish to have it in your safekeeping. Just in case. But that time is over, Don Francisco. Those days are gone. The Americans have imprisoned my agents—poor Teddy Hewes, he's on the boat, the *Liscum*, to the island of Talim where the gringos take the prisoners, and even the new one, my countryman from Yorkshire, the one who likes the drink—that careless Felipe—Philip—Felipe Larks—they have booted him out."

"The gringos are jailing all the anglos?"

"The gringos want the abaca lands. You will not get them back. I return to England. Good luck in your new country."

His clattering cane mimics the jangling of his fossilizing bones—crrracck crrracck crrracck on the mahogany floors.

Click click click.

His father's butaka goes back and forth back and forth.

Lick lick lick lick.

Paco furiously licks the caramel off his spoon of taho.

To Another Shore

He quarrels with the servants when they make him put it on—how can he, a brother of a Mason and a katipunero, he has been no idle reader of his brother's pamphlets, pretend to be a priest's acolyte?

It is the perfect disguise, it makes you look innocent.

No, it does not, it makes me look incompetent, like I forgot my pants!

A fool for the Lord, says Mariano the mayordomo, blessing him with the sign of the Cross.

Though Mariano is no priest and the boy is, as yet, no corpse.

Extremaunción.

It's a strange thing, he thinks, that there's a whole *código* and ritual for dying.

He wants no part of it.

He's a wisp of a kid, the coiled shape of a spindly, not-so-prized calf, cowering in the hold of the *Liscum* when the foreigners find him on the shore, almost drowned (so the soldiers of Company C of the US Ninth Infantry think).

At the last minute, the good men of Moret Street stow away no adult—*cochero, mayordomo,* or *cucinero*—on this sojourn to Samar.

What happened to the other stowaways, the kitchen musketeers, out to save señorito Jote, the notebook does not say.

The boy arrives wearing that cassock—like a shipwrecked altar boy, who forgot his pants.

He hides in the animal hold of the cavalry ship for eight straight days, a trial for anyone, but one can see that for a kid of his debility, his body's weird sensations before both natural and manmade things (i.e., his body's improper empathy toward both the life of roaches and their eaters the lizards, to ants and their catch the cicadas, to goats and cows and their pathos: their smelly, cramped space in the hold—bankâ ngan butiki ngan tubak ngan gangis ngan kanding ngan baka—ay kairo! ngan kabaho)—those days on the *Liscum* are a terror.

Ah—

So Lolo Paco *is* the stowaway on the boat.

I thought so, yes.

He's a fan of cloak-and-dagger—a faithful younger brother.

He's gobbled up the novels Jote has left in his wake, he gives the grasshoppers and beetles their feed of weeds and crumbs, he is alert to intrigue and anarcho-syndicalism, he's listened to too much opera, going off to the Teatro to watch his father's favorites, the bedroom plots planned by barbers and manservants and the silly court farces, and every man and his *cochero* in Manila it turns out has a summary of dumb scenarios ready to launch into action—

But still it discourages him when it turns out all the servants in the house are in on it—Ambrosio the cook and Tay Sequil, of course (though he acts so all-knowing, he is *not even the leader!*), but most surprising of all, Mariano the mayordomo—that pious man who runs Don Francisco the First's home.

Of all people, it's Mariano the mayordomo's words that send the boy to another shore.

And he has no clue, sitting there eating his breakfast of taho.

—*Hijo, Paquito! Nga iya irong!*

They're all in the kitchen—Mariano the mayordomo, Ambrosio the cook, Tay Sequil, *El Cochero Exequiel!*—when he hears his name and comes running.

The revelation of Mariano's criminality is a shock.

But worse is the boy's role, his extreme function.

Here's the grave man who takes him daily to Holy Communion, singing *Paternosterquiesincaelis* without skipping any syllables, lays down the rules for using the spittoons or the toothpicks in the palitera, shaped with genius like a pineapple (so he could easily stick back the used ones in the holes), or the orinola or the tabo—

And it is he, Mariano the mayordomo of all people—a criminal, a radical—

A Eugene Sue plotter!

A conspiracist!

A *filibustero*—

Just like that pathetic man, Hilario Sayo, a.k.a. the valiant Hiloy, and crazy-eyed Mack the Sundang, that smooth-chinned heavy breather underneath the house with the pigs on Moret Street during the time of the chaos in 1896, and the barber Juan and his cousin the baritone, Salustiano, who loves the habanera, and that lovely cripple, that harebrained hero, that crazy, vanished, beautiful son of the people—

The lost hero of Santa Mesa.

Shot by the Coward of Santol Street, Private William Grayson at Blockhouse Seven—

(But in the kanô papers Grayson is the hero.)

He—the double-crossing secret agent Son of the People—

Marcelo Badel y Zorilla.

Of all things, Mariano the strict mayordomo is one of *them*— felons and *filibusteros* who lurk under the house in 1896.

Ay nga panulay!

But the boy has no model for saying No.

Anyway, this honest servant has the last say in his father's house.

Apart from Don Francisco the First, of course.

His father has been lying on his bed for days, the path of his cancer wearing him down, not that he knows of it.

Urgent customers keep arriving at his bodega, the norte americanos of the new dispensation, Thomas Stearns Wesson the sugar trader and Mister Ernest Smith the rope buyer, but he will not get up.

The boy clips the news and keeps the articles in his book.

Mariano the mayordomo organizes. The boy obeys.

Amid the country's mess he has no time for disruption, parasaway, and Mariano does his duty.

What's his description of the war?

Ay nga panulay!

It's the tongue the boy knows beyond his Spanish.

It is his mother's.

It bubbles in his veins like kalamay.

His dead mother Adina Blumfeld y Catalogo is alive in the words of these men—Mariano the mayordomo, Ambrosio the cook, but not Tay Sequil, *El Excellent Cochero Exequiel* (in his American-era taxi ads)—he's just a Tagalog.

Obedience is the boy's sacrament.

The boy had once fed every bandit below the bodega as he was told—the carpenters and komedya actors and printer's aides, including the ex-mayor of Pandacan—offering them biko and arroz caldo and saging na saba.

So Mariano the mayordomo orders.

Below the molave floorboards on Moret Street, amid the powdery blossoms of the narra, the bloom of kalachuchi, and the waft of limonsito, Mariano the mayordomo sometimes descends to the pigsty himself to offer kamote, suman latik, and pancit bihon, just for starters.

Those greedy sons of the people—the pathetic barkada of his umangkon Jote.

And when they all leave for their next diversions—who knows where the panulay goes?—Mariano feels the relief of good hosts when finally the overstaying guests are not their business.

He never speaks of the fiends again.

They are aliens to his orderly world.

That boy Jote, says Mariano the mayordomo aloud, is a mess who keeps bringing home the crazies, the *demonio*, the disruptors, the imps of Manila, mga parasaway, ay nga panulay, he has a misplaced regard for street dogs and cripples!

But then—Jote, too, vanishes.

And every day since, Mariano the mayordomo wakes with dread, pours out his anxious pee upon the orchids, his first act in his unmade world.

No.

It's not his mourning for his boss Don Francisco, ailing on his katre at the disappearance of his boy, that moves Mariano the mayordomo.

No umbilical cord attaches him to Don Francisco the First.

After all, Don Francisco—is only an in-law.

Mariano's attachment is to the dead bride—the cousin, an iya patod, the dead Adina.

He thinks of the señorito Jote when the traveling fruit vendor arrives.

He presses the santol fruit with his fingernail, the vendor tolerates his half-moon print on the furry skin because Mariano is that kind of fastidious customer—he gets his way because he pays in full—and in passing Mariano remembers the boy Jote's sour, not sweet, tooth.

He recalls the look of the baby encanto, little Jote, in his embroidered, swaddling clothes out in the happy home in Giporlos—the baby's scrunched bawling face before his confused mother Adina, herself barely a woman, and it was Mariano the mayordomo, an iya urupod, who blows onto the baby's splotched belly and pastes the guava leaves for his weak stomach's balm.

Sheathed in his absurd cassock, the boy Paco has let himself be led by these teatro fanatics, Mariano the mayordomo and his confrères, to ship off in disguise to his non-consensual tryst with history—

First—he arrives among the Americans in Samar, then the sergeant Frank Breton bears him to safety as the island burns, and then—his landing in Leyte, though all he wishes is to be with the girl—the girl of the streams, yes she, Calista Catalogo of Giporlos, and instead he takes a test, for in such ingestion his talent lies—

Feeling in his body the innards and colors of words—

By his talents, a test, he ships off across the seas.

To become the ward of America.

He returns to these pleasant monsoon days on Moret Street, in 1908, this day of reading his brother's journals, while his friends wait for his signal—Lieutenant Bandholtz, Captain Henry T. Allen, and the boy's rescuer in Samar, Sergeant Frank Breton.

While Jote walks with his endless memory.

Toward the tranvia stop, to get to medical school at Padre Faura.

The History Iskolars

According to the Facebook group Salog Himanglos, Professor Iñigo Impikoño's claim to fame is that he *almost* graduated from the State University of Potsdam, New York. But according to commenter Igme1944, Professor Iñigo went nuts in the snow.

The place of my great-grandfathers in this history confused me.

My grandfathers-of-the-knee!

Apoy ha tuhod!

The authorship of the notebooks in the domed box was not only uncertain but obfuscating, as if written by fugitives either rebel then spy, with shifting time frames and cognitive abilities, presenting mixed impressions—

And not immutable facts.

In a lucid paper, Professor Iñigo suggests that Pedro Abayan, the mayor of Balangiga, in a polite letter in Spanish to General Jacob "Jakey" Smith, headquartered in Tacloban, had requested an American garrison for his town and its barrios, Lawaan, Guiuan, San Roque, Giporlos. But that two-faced Abayan, so says Professor Iñigo, also wrote to the revolutionary general in Samar—to Ka Vicente Lukban:

> *As a representative of this town I have the honor to inform you that, having conferred with the principals of this town about the policy to be pursued with the enemy in case they appear here, we have agreed to observe a deceptive policy with them doing whatever they may like, and when a favorable opportunity arises, the people will strategically rise up against them.*

This letter, in Spanish, captured by the Americans, lies in archives formerly in Washington, DC, now on UN Avenue in Manila, corner Marcelino Street, so noted Professor Iñigo.

"A clever kumplot," the war scholar Professor Iñigo replied to my private message, from his ABD perch somewhere in Tucson, AZ, a drier clime, where his Fulbright scholarship does not reach and his family of twelve American cousins feeds him broccoli and radishes with his sinigang, he adds, so many strange vegetables he barely recognizes the ginger soup (he is hiding and hiding from his dissertation committee with his loving, culinarily adaptive Fil-Am relatives, but someone needs to tell him to turn off his Google locations, *a.s.a.p.!*).

I consulted three historians via Googling, and all were candid, to my surprise. Adding to that, in a narrative lapse, or so it seemed to me, one of them turned out to be my old piano teacher in Tacloban, of all people, Miss Custodia Balasbas—how great it was to see her on Instagram, instead of Facebook, liking all the posts of @Demi-Mundo, the trans activist in Miami.

To go across the world with the sheaves of the story, and all along its scholar lived right next door on Juan Luna Street.

We called her Elephant Katol, and so I recall her—Miss Custodia, a caring woman—with useless shame over childish cruelty. Her legs were abnormally log-like. She lived in the extension of my classmate Lorelei's apartment. My mom respected her musical gifts. Adina an guapa herself knew piano only by *oído*—which I first heard as *widow*. *Oído, oído,* my mom would say in hotel lobbies when she took over the piano and people clapped: my mom would modestly explain after her surprising tunes that she learned only by ear. She's an overeducated woman, Miss Custodia Balasbas, my mom told me, with a lonely life—you know she's Samarnon. I did not know the connection between loneliness and being from Samar. But my mom made me take her piano lessons, and I'd spend an afternoon playing "Papa Haydn's Dead and Gone" while Miss Custodia sat there with her stout legs and stared sadly at my finger-placements. Her apartment—a room really—contained only books and paper, a typewriter, and her piano. Her lonely discipline, it turns out, has made her a celebrity among internet scholars focusing on the passion of church items stolen by Americans in long-ago wars. Even now I couldn't give a damn about those bells. I had no idea of her secret life as a patriotic historian, but I was an oblivious child, and when I found her paper on unnamed women of war its lyrical angst moved me. She was housebound now, tweeting to academic conferences around the world on discoveries about her hometown, Balangiga.

On YouTube, I found her and Father Vice-President Edgar Allan Pe and Professor Iñigo Impikoño sparring on a plaintive panel called *Genocide and Genealogy: Mess or Message?*

Her paper was a cryptic question: *Who will bell the cat?*

I messaged all of them.

You see, Professor Iñigo Impikoño explained to me, the katipunero chief, the Son of the People, General Vicente Lukban lured the Americans to Samar in order to kill them and steal their guns.

"It was a well-planned operation! A *complot* composition! The musical congregation that met Captain Waller disembarking from the cavalry ship *Liscum* was only a small slice of the one hundred seventy households of the town!"

Exclamation marks dot Professor Impikoño's messages, another sign of his nervous condition.

"Included among the rebelde were Pedro Abayan, the letter-writing mayor! Valeriano Abanador, his chess-playing chief of police! Father Donato Guimbaolibot, the tall and noble parish priest! Also Pedro Duran the abaca salesman and one Eugenio Daza. All in kumplot with the katipuneros spying on the Amerian garrison! No, I never heard of a vomiting stowaway on a boat. There is a servant boy named Francisco—yes. That is in the chronicles—the little boy helper of Captain Waller. He survived—listed on the boat with the Americans upon their rescue by Colonel Foote's company after the breakfast attack by the people! The boy migrated to America. Some reports say he married a woman from Havana and died in Santiago de Cuba. But what's he to us? It's the katipuneros of Ka Vicente Lukban who count, proof that revolutionary fervor was archipelagic, not only Tagalog—the Katipunan was a national conflagration spreading all across the islands!"

In his paper, events happen exactly as Professor Impikoño reports.

A Giuseppe Verdi version of uprising—a heroic operetta written in hindsight, with dashing cause-and-effect.

A top-down nationalist triumph, in which bungled intentions and slipshod chance are foretold, plotted from above.

A case History much prefers.

The dream of a snowbound brain, procrastinating on writing his dissertation in Tucson.

Another scholar, ex-monsignor Father Edgar Allan Pe, a Chinese notable of Tacloban and the defrocked Father Vice-President of Divine Word College, who forsook his vows and climbed down from his bureaucratic heights to be a humble student of colonial history (and marry his secretary), gives complete and unquestioning agency to the people.

They had no help at all from General Vicente Lukban, says the ex-monsignor, ex cathedra.

No, no, no.

The Thomas-Paine-quoting, freemason-oathtaking, French-enlightenment-loving, Alexandre-Dumas-reading, revolutionary Katipunan chronicled by the elites of Manila—those colonizing Tagalogs!—is a mirage in this revolt, says Father Edgar Allan Pe.

The attack in Balangiga on Americans in Samar is not a mere branch of radical plots to create a nation, a grand, prefabricated, planned action with a constitution and bill of rights, a nationalist conscription. No, no, no, says the good ex-monsignor—Balangiga is an organic, kind of fragile bud of raw passion, watered by the spit of a town's spontaneous rage.

A tale of local injury.

A drama from below, complete with cross-dressing, arnis matches, chess-playing, pretend coffins, rosary-wielding, a storefront brawl involving a lady and her cousins, a pair of twins, and a vile military lout—Trapp or Clapp or Wannebo—some dastardly kanô of fiendish designs. The storefront incident triggered shame, honor, uprising among the good townspeople—in sum, a great costume zarzuela of the masses, with the grievance of shared injustice and the heroism of populist rage.

"All it needs," he says, "is a marching band."

Uh, yeah—that, too.

But in her paper Miss Custodia Balasbas scoffs.

Erstwhile biographer of famed Geronima of Samar (in her still unpublished, semi-transnational, intermittently autobiographical monograph of the war), Miss Custodia spits scorn upon the scholars of Tacloban.

Conveniently, she says, they fail to acknowledge that Balangiga *is* the country's story.

To narrow it *either* to accidental rage *or* to unified conspiracy is to misread the war.

"Balangiga contains in its pivots, its confusions, its labyrinths the fullness and complexity of our revolutionary moment," says my expressive former piano teacher, andante con gusto.

She was quick to respond to my DM (on Insta, in order to follow her grandchild's exploits in Miami, she says—"the transgender Demi Mundo, have you heard of her in America?, I will send you a YouTube," and it was touching how proud she was, linking an awesome video of her apo, the activist Demi Mundo singing "Di Niyo Ba Naririnig?," the inevitable Tagalog version of the stirring song from the musical *Les Misérables*).

"It's a filarial story," wrote Miss Custodia (I noticed her metaphors were based mainly on Leyte's ecological conditions)—"a gross enlargement of vermin grief that fills our sacs of woe with the superfluity that marks trauma!"

She was eloquent, from a lifetime treading furiously in scholarship's unjust shoals.

"Balangiga is a worm, an infection, a leptospirosis, the endemic larval hardening of the lymphatic vessels that sits in us, birthing and breeding and bloating, stunting our music, naming our songs, and telling us who we are."

Our misfortune, Miss Custodia emphasizes, is that Balangiga is irreducible.

Site of triumph and doom, it spins binaries into infinity and makes her head ache.

Miss Custodia's own misfortune is that she has no time to finish her book, tentatively titled *The Elephant in the Room*, because she has to survive instead, teaching piano to tone-deaf children of Tacloban.

I apologized.

I am sorry, I said, for mutilating her favorite song "Greensleeves" long ago because I never practiced.

I hate "Greensleeves," she responded—it's the music for sloths and cretins!

I was sorry I interrupted.

"The city of Tacloban was a damned collaborator with Americans during the agony of the war, blind to the consequences of its historical indifference toward the people of Samar since 1901!"

Miss Custodia confessed how she has had to live with Tacloban's damaged self-absorption and pathetic concepts of its superiority (plus the butterfingers of its chubby toddlers who will never become Mozarts! or even crazy Van Cliburn! no matter how many grand pianos their parents keep stacking up in their beach resorts on Cancabato Bay because *no one practices!*) during her forty-two years of teaching "Papa Haydn's Dead and Gone" and "Für Elise" to the MacArthur-memorializing, Red-Beach-commemorating, Bongbong-voting, Trinidad-family-loving people of Tacloban.

I replied, ingratiatingly—well, I have always hated MacArthur—ever since I had to play the octavina before his statue every October 20 throughout elementary school!

My regrets added fuel to fire.

It was Miss Custodia's particular lament that for whatever

reason history cast her afloat, marooned from her past, in a city of idiocy and oblivion, so she details (but only on private messages via Instagram, as she does not want to alienate potential customers, who are all on Facebook). Whereas for Miss Custodia Balasbas, the past is an anguish that to this day she keeps like a stone in her limbs, a sour, livid flare, mostly about her calves and thighs, because the fact is, she also has elephantiasis, she confessed (and I was quiet about our malice as children)—that disease of parasitic filariasis in the lower extremities that blights the watery tropics.

And what she shared with me, this late in history, was her distended, magnificent spleen, her scorn for all those scholars, Professor Impikoño and Father Vice-President Edgar Allan Pe and Director Pinggoy Gomez, yes, he of the National Archives, scion no less of Padre Mariano Gomez, of Gom-Bur-Za fame—none of them will understand it!

Her intolerable, pinched, and plangent pain—

For none of them, after all, are from Balangiga.

"And Calista Catalogo, what do you know about her?"

"Who," she messaged. "I have never heard."

"She was a Catalogo," I replied

"Her last name starts with a *C*," Miss Custodia typed in quickly. "An iya apelyido taga-Giporlos."

"What do you mean," I said.

"You don't know? In 1849, the Clavería Decree?"

"Ah," I said, pretending.

"Every town in the Philippines was given a list of names, and families had to rename themselves from the list. The better to tax the populace! Punyeta those espanyol! Taking away everything, even our names. Balangiga was given *A* and *B* names. The *C* names—those are Giporlos."

"And the *D* names?"

"Ambot. Estrangheros, who knows. Seguro spy. Anyways, outsiders."

A Kumplot of Gold

It's the fault of Marcelo the bastard and that geriatric Urbano. (Yes, it is true, that old policeman in the crowd, that guardia civil, was the great future general Urbano Lacuna, *resquiescat in pace!*—but Jote will dwell only later on that.)

Women scream and men scuffle, and Urbano that geriatric, that guardia civil, arrests Jote at the Luneta and bears him away.

Marcelo the hunchback follows.

The three take a bend down Calle Real and walk away from Bagumbayan.

The men bewilder Jote. Urbano and Marcelo march him north toward Intramuros while the holiday crowd goes the opposite way. He finds the group, mostly men (though of the women, Jote also has memories), congregated in the alley near the ecclesiastical palace, corner Arsobispado, where the dusty angles of the school that he attends with Marcelo the bastard meets Nay Dayay the fritterer's stall at Calle Anda, that smoky corner by Ateneo Municipal.

There the group looks like a loitering queue of turon and maruya aficionados waiting for merienda, and Nay Dayay has all she can do, skewering one banana fritter after another, and wrapping the turon with one hand, then filling the banana leaf cones with the plantain and sweet potato bits scooped from the bubbling kaldero of her kalamay inferno.

Above all, after school, as he watches Nay Dayay at her steaming, pitch-black cauldron, so that the old lady's face seems to vanish, like a phantom, in the heat, Jote also likes to observe how the slab of kalamay, a molasses beast, melts in the boiling oil: a transubstanti-ation, the mutating, transmogrifying sight of boiling kalamay that shape-shifts from solid into liquid, so like one's mental processes— those bubbling sugar slabs from the southern islands that are among Don Francisco the First's most reliable goods.

In fact.

Unlike Jote, the rest of Manila has a sweet, not sour, tooth.

Thus Jote finds the heroes, so the nation calls them now that they're all dead, standing around eating the sticky, dripping turon and what people during the era of the next invaders call "banana cue."

Barbers and mechanics and printers and municipal clerks and fan sellers and government employees-cum-secret agents (e.g., happy-go-lucky Marcelo Badel, Jote's lame classmate, of all people, but that brave fact comes out only later), and, of course, the secret turncoat men of the guardia civil, those few, those anxious few, the Filipinos who choose to lead split lives—soldier for Spain, spy for the rebels—including the great future general of two wars—that geriatric Urbano, ancient and worn at the age of thirty-six—

The most noble and ever loyal General Urbano Lacuna—

Requiescat in pace!

A typical man of history, that Lacuna—i.e., forgotten.

But on that day Jote thinks: Jesus fuck—*o Dios ¡hay que joderse!*—I've been kidnapped by a gang of thieves.

He's a merchant's child whose father will look for him when the day's festivities are done. And, Jote thinks with admiration, it's a stroke of genius for the revolution to start kidnapping traders' sons, whose fathers have liquid assets, petty cash for fundraising, and to do it on the day the entire city of Manila is preoccupied with a much-awaited act—

The killing of a man for writing a novel.

These bandits—they're smart.

But Jote mourns—what have they done to his little brother Paco?

Where have the bandits taken Paco?

"I think we did it," says a slight man with a red nose that twitches above his well-oiled mustache.

Jote admires the thick petroleum sheen of the man's chocolate bigote, his graceful mustache curved on both ends like the *f*-sound-hole on a lute.

The man's nose is a botched red, like a tambis, a macopa, the kind that has fallen from the tree, squashed on the ground in the monsoon season.

The red-nosed, mustachioed man is addressing a linen-clad figure sucking on the tip of a sugary skewer.

The linen man's fingernails are lacquered, like the carameled bananas.

He wears a Panama hat over his slicked-back hair, and he leans on the ivory top of a walking stick as he tongues the dregs of his finished merienda.

A gleaming man of authority.

At ease.

"Who's he?" asks the man, flicking his manicured pinky nail and the tip of his tongue.

Elegantly, using his mouth as a demonstrative pronoun, he points his lips toward Jote.

Of all the men of Bagumbayan, Jote remembers him with the most piercing pain.

Mack the Sundang.

In real life Macario Sakay is a half-hearted barber and wannabe actor who loves to play the boss—the future King of the Tagalogs, wild-haired terror of the norte americanos, man of style for whom the foreigners will enact their Brigandage Law.

True, the last time Jote sees him, a few years into the new century, he's surprised to see Mack with hair down to his knees, his former pearly white teeth red-black with betel.

He has a wrathful look in his eyes though it's he who's asking Jote a favor.

And Jote understands—

How war diminishes.

Also—

It takes a toll on your hair.

For a former barber, Macario Sakay's hair, hanging down to his belly by 1905, is just—too modern—that last time Jote sees him, full of sorrow at the sight of his friend: a full ten years later, when the war is lost, and still Mack can't believe it, Macario Sakay never gives up our dream—he urges Jote to join his plot to kidnap—

The Lady Alice, La Señora Longworth!

¡Joderse!—that's the daughter of the president—of the norte-americanos!

Of course—why else would we want to kidnap the lady?

No.

Jote says.

Politely.

Once upon a time, Jote says to Mack, all I wished was to be an entomologist.

And now it is that time—1905!

And the papers note the tourist itinerary of Alice in Wonderland—in capitals and italics.

TO CROSS PACIFIC IN FLOATING PALACE — WILL HAVE HER OWN SUITE OF ROOMS ABOARD — LUXURIES OF TRAVEL WHICH SHE AND DISTINGUISHED ATTENDANTS WILL ENJOY — HER FATHER WILL PAY HER EXPENSES — WHAT SHE WILL SEE IN THE WONDERLANDS ACROSS THE PACIFIC — THE STOP AT HONOLULU TO BE WELL SPENT — RECEPTION IN JAPAN — WILL SHE MAKE SPEECH TO EMPRESS AS MR. GRANT HAD TO? — THROUGH THE INLAND SEA AT HONGKONG — TOUR OF PHILIPPINE WATERS IN A TRANSPORT — THE RETURN TRIP AND ACCOMMODATIONS — HOW EXPENSES OF OTHER TOURISTS WILL BE DIVIDED — REPRESENTATIVE LONGWORTH TO GO ALONG — TROPICAL ROMANCE ANTICIPATED.

© *1905 by John E. Watkins*

And thus Alice tours Wonderland—

Unmolested.

Still—the men of Theodore Roosevelt behead Macario Sakay in 1907.

Checking the news, Jote has dreams.

That look on the face of Mack the Sundang—a mix of scorn and rage although Jote sees how Mack stops himself, he does not take up his bolo to scar his scarred friend, and Jote thinks—

What would he give now to die at the hand of Macario Sakay—
What would he not give for death, that peace of mind?

Kamurayaw.

Peacetime.

His head hurts, it is dizzy, his gaze shifts, he follows the path of a luminous bottle-green fly, down Moret Street. His body moves into its wings.

The man with the red nose, next to the barber Macario, is the intrepid milkman of Sapang Palay, Enteng Leyva.

A health freak who likes to share unsolicited medical remedies.

Perhaps due to his too many physical failings.

With his good nutrition, Enteng Leyva lives long enough to be killed by the First Nebraska Volunteer Infantry in the second noble skirmish of the American war, at Santa Mesa.

Enteng points with his mouth toward General Urbano Lacuna.

"Ask Banong."

Everyone turns to look at the guardia civil, the man with the batuta who had fake-clubbed Jote to a feathery death.

Urbano Lacuna grunts and stares at Marcelo Badel.

"It's all good," says Marcelo, though even he looks embarrassed, as if at that moment he understands the error he has committed.

Bringing an estranghero into the secret society, a non-*ángulo* with no corresponding *triángulo*.

The secret society recruits in threes, but Jote, their decoy, is only one.

"He's my classmate from the Municipal! Jorge Delgado y Blumfeld, of Moret Street, Sampaloc, Manila! Jote, explain who you are and why you joined the revolution!"

Marcelo casts off his fake hump, the stuffed rags from his back, though he still stands with a limp.

His dumb disguise at Bagumbayan.

The actor who plays Marcelo Badel gives his shrug an exaggerated, overacting twist.

He plays Marcelo like a comic sidekick, an illegitimate clown in a Dumas tragedy—a minor character making the most of his cameo part.

It's always been hard for an actor to convey in his brief role why everyone felt consolation in the presence of Marcelo Badel, as if he knew your deepest secrets but was not going to tell.

And once again, on that makeshift stage of their fake Intramuros, somewhere in the jungles above Candon, Marcelo is as Jote knows him, a crippled boy of good cheer, Don Marcelo Badel y Zorilla, whose status as a bastard child among his classmates balances against his sunny temperament thus bullies leave him alone (plus, his father is a magistrate, the *oídor* with a rhyming name, Don Manuel Badel).

Jote glares at Marcelo's smiling face.

Marcelo gestures, pointing with his mouth, for Jote to speak.

As if he, Marcelo, like the rest of these men, understands something about Jote that Jote has yet to learn.

It was his chrysalis of action—that moment by Calle Anda in Intramuros.

Jote walks slowly, face to the morning sun, along Moret Street.

In Intramuros his body is digesting itself, releasing enzymes to dissolve its old slime, organizing its imaginal discs (discs for his hair, his thorax, his eyes), his imago of wings, his specular ooze that is also he, the gooey mold of himself, tucked inside his body, though only Marcelo Badel can tell.

And one day he will wriggle out from his pupal orb.

Is revolt a stage of molting, the miracle instar before wholeness happens?

Or is revolt the wholeness, the dazzling spread of his wings?

How does he, a pious lazy bum's son, get mixed up in this society, which includes carpenters, balut vendors, holy zacateros, and customs men with tenor voices?

Even now, at this distance in time, in 1908, as he walks toward the tranvia to his classes on Padre Faura, Jote sees their faces still, hiding in the pigsty beneath his father's house in the weeks following The Hero's execution at Bagumbayan—the Spanish celebration of a writer's death, and the scattering of rebelde that follows.

When all the running is over, their plot at the Luneta, their hope at Bagumbayan undone, he finds himself on a mat in the sala, listening to his friends—Macario, Enteng, Marcelo, Hiloy—snoring beneath his father's home on Moret Street.

The accidental barkada of Ambrosio the cook's pigs and chickens.

Cosme the fireman, a vain man, prematurely bald: Jote remembers Cosme for his poetic name, Taguyod, which means aid or support— the mama's boy Cosme, whose mother embroidered his handkerchiefs with his initials, *C.A.T.*, but Jote never knew what *A* meant, Cosme who escapes the Spaniards in 1896 only to be captured in Polo during the scorched-earth days of Arthur MacArthur, bequeathing to his erstwhile ex-friends, the americanos, the lace mystery of his name.

Jote remembers Cosme Taguyod's poetic name.

How about Alegre, Tomas Alegre, a grumpy man with the wrong epithet? Whereas that talkative bookworm Gimo, Guillermo Masangkay, is truly a friendly fellow who never returns the books he borrows. And it is sad to have never met that man of thought, Ladislao Diwa. Tales of his torture in future times return to haunt them all though it's his miracle escape from Fort Santiago that astounds midnight listeners at cramped talahib trenches from Laguna through Lingayen—how Diwa is the third *ángulo* in the storied Katipunan triangle that Diwa and Plata made with Ka Andres to start their society, ang katipunan ng bayan, a neologism with a cause, and before dawn at Fort Santiago that day the philosophical Diwa watches his prison cellmate old Oro, Oro Plata but no Mata, the silver-tongued Teodoro, dragged away to the firing squad, and the idealistic Diwa hears the muskets that flatten his soulmate Plata, and so he waits for the guardia civil. They will return to his cell to take him to lie by bullet-filled Teodoro, he thinks, but instead they give him his freedom in exchange for a guardia taken by his rebel cadres, a Spaniard named Pensar.

Poor Teodoro Plata. A man of gold.

Of the brothers Carreon—Francisco the customs man and Nicomedes the tram conductor—Jote remembers that one was a fine tenor, but he can't remember which.

Then there are the cousins, the tailor Salustiano and the other barber, Juan.

The revolution had too many barbers.

But no guns.

The funny thing was, Juan the barber was also a playwright, and he'd make his restless colleague, the wannabe actor, Mack the Sundang, enact short operettas in brief moments between battles, up there in Monte Dagot, Simminublan, and Monte Bimmuaya (while Jote has to learn Juan the barber's tunes, his renegade awit, on the bandurria, always the designated musikero because of his ability to play by ear, *al oído!*, a blasted talent, one of the songs being an annoyingly high-pitched aria for Juan's memorable one-act drama, "The Scarred Spy: A Moral Komedya").

With what fond yet surprisingly vague detail Jote remembers that time they were together, he and the two barbers, Juan and Mack, and all the others up north, singing songs of passion in Candon. Though his job, if he were honest, was no thrill in the quiet days in Ilocos— guarding the prisoners of war—the Spaniards of his father's race, and then the Americans hated by his father.

Odd to think how of those terrible days of northern flight, during the American phase of their war—their desperate escape—*¡demonyo nga yawa nga Funston ka!*—from that motley gang, the kapre "Fighting Fred!" Funston and those stunted traitors from Pampanga, the Macabebes—*ay demonyo nga mga pasaway*—as the noose of war tightens, and the norteamericanos burn the villages that shelter them, torch the markets that feed them—odd how Jote remembers—*most of all!*—

That he plays his bandurria in the forest.

Of war, he remembers music.

Tocando al oído.

Mack the Sundang, in his tonsorial former days, commands him to write the third act of Juan the barber's play, but that's to be expected: Jote is in thrall to charming men like Isabelo Abaya (his is the magic name in Candon) and Macario Sakay, that groomed savant, and Juan, the barber of Sariaya—not Seville.

It's why Jote leaves his father's home.

To be one with the crazies.

Ay nga panulay!

So the servants say—

—*Why are your friends the crazies?!*

Ay nga panulay—why are your friends the disruptors—the imps, ay mga demonyo, parasaway!

Jote remembers the artist, that short-tempered, youthful chef, Lagasca—Valentin? Venerando?

Anyway, the youthful Lagasca.

A former customs agent from Pateros who likes to cook—ducks, grasshoppers, mice—he can make a feast out of leeches. Sunken eyes, a peppery, splotched face, and the slender fingers of a weaver, the chef Lagasca makes banquets out of hunger. In the mountains he fashions Roast Beef a la Bayonet (from wild cattle that the picky cook hunts in the jungles of Bontoc) and of course, the President's favorite—Thunder Jelly! (miracle gulaman, a magic custard that shivers amid bullets and stays intact, even in the Battle of Badoc).

There is the lady in Vigan, he still remembers her marred face, a blurry veil of grieving: she of the bibingka baskets. She feeds everyone her bibingka, she feeds in secret even the pale, white prisoners of war, the captured men he guards in the clinic of Doctor Crisologo in his large, airy house in Vigan.

She's a weeping widow.

Her son is a prisoner of the norteamericanos.

He remembers the war mother's question—he ponders it—he watches—

She asks the white prisoners to whom she offers her sweets—

Will the enemy treat my son the same way I treat you?

He thinks of her cry at random times (staring at a star apple, snatching the kaimito above him in the shallow trench in Pozorubio, crawling through a kamote patch in Badoc).

Will the enemy treat my son the same way I treat you?

Jote has no mother to weep for him.

Jote waits in suspense for the reply of the captives in Vigan.

As for his childhood comrade from the Ateneo—Marcelo Badel y Zorilla, that patriotic clown—he was *i pagliacci* all by himself— how is Jote to know the way his end will come, three years later, on the first day of the war against the americanos, shot on the way to the whores of Calle Iris, at Pandacan, before Marcelo Badel can pursue his dream, i.e., to free his country plus become a pharmacist?

Would Jote have chosen differently then?

No.

He stops to look at a plot of earthworms, gathering their nerves on Moret Street.

And then there is a series of dead frogs, mga padla nga pakla, stomped on the way to the tranvia.

At Calle Anda, Marcelo, caught with a lie before the group, frantically signals at Jote—

Speak, man, speak!

Jote gathers his tongue.

"I came out this morning from my home on Moret Street on my father's kalesa for the hero Rizal," Jote says tentatively.

Viva!

All the men lift their banana fritter sticks in unison at the sound of the hero's name.

"I have grieved for years over the state of the islands, and I learned from the paskinadas at the Municipal and from the street corner posters the ways of revolt and the stories of the three rebel priests beheaded at the Luneta—Gomez! Burgos! Zamora!"

Viva!

All the men lift their banana fritter sticks again, at the sound of the famous names, passwords of their fight.

Jote's getting the hang of it.

He was only guessing, but he was getting it right.

All he needs to do is repeat words from rumors he has gathered in graffiti, plastered on school toilets and Intramuros's walls, and from the novel-reading boys, his elders, who hang around street corners, such as here on Calle Anda by the stall of Nay Dayay, queen of kalamay and saging na saba.

"Therefore, I have decided to become one of you—"

"The Sons of the People!" interrupts Marcelo, just in case he has no clue what the boring name of their organization is.

Viva!

And all the men finally release their banana fritter sticks to the air. A rain of slim arrows sticky with sugar falls at Nay Dayay's feet.

Nay Dayay picks up their garbage, tidy businesswoman that she is. Where is Nay Dayay now?

"But I see he is not initiated," a stick figure of a man declares.

The haunting figure has the gaunt face of a malnourished childhood—the man will never lose his hungry look, the way the hollows of his cheeks create a rhombus with his jaw, though at the moment like the rest of them he looks prosperous, in his festive clothes, his collared white suit and black-and-white takong, cooling off with a perfumed, intricately braided abaca fan.

The fact is, Apolonio Samson, though now a landowner, has raised himself up from the esteros and will remain a hardliner his whole life, a worrywart, ideologue, and annoying stickler for rules, whether in the thatched huts of revolution or the marble of American halls.

"What is that to you, Ka Polonio," another man, with cheeks just as gaunt, says with a smile.

Everyone in this crowd, Jote thinks, looks as if they're off to the Santa Ana races, malnourished but dressed to kill.

"We are all sons of the people," says the elegant man, nodding toward Apolonio Samson.

"Ah, Ka Andres—" Marcelo Badel turns to the elegant man for support.

But Ka Andres does not bother to look at Marcelo, waving him toward the man to his right.

At that, Marcelo turns to the man at Ka Andres's right, a.k.a. El Juez, in bowler hat and spats whose frame will always make him look too large, no matter if he were starving in Banaue or collecting rebel taxes from the people.

This obese impression comes from his body's curse: the lawyer has a short torso and barrel-boned hips.

A man of meat and muscle, shaped by Bicol's pili candy and genetics.

"Ah, Ka Vicente," Marcelo addresses the man, "we had no time to initiate my friend. I'm sorry. We needed a warm body, he volunteered."

Bullshit!, thinks Jote.

You guys beat me up at Bagumbayan with Urbano Lacuna's batuta and no warning—you bastards—

But Jote keeps silent.

Ka Vicente Lukban listens to Marcelo Badel with a poker face.

Stumpy and tubular Ka Vicente in real life is a justice of the peace from Albay whose virtue *is* his poker face—a stern glance that gives nothing up.

By the end of the war, the papers will call him the Terror of Samar (every man with a gun is Terror-this-Terror-that, the American headlines are not creative, Jote has to agree).

But to be honest, Ka Vicente has always been a furtive figure, something about his temperament, a man hard to befriend. Even when Jote comes to know him, out in the caves of Sohoton, Ka Vicente has this deadpan look, and when later he becomes an actually obese politician, electioneering being the glutton sport during Commonwealth times—even when they meet again, during what the English-language papers call *peacetime*—an kamurayaw—the inscrutable tact of Vicente Lukban does not cease to impress Jote.

To this day.

But that morning in Intramuros, Jote can tell Ka Vicente's is not the decisive voice, no matter his judicial guise.

Everyone is staring at thin-cheeked Ka Andres.

You can tell from the body language of the men milling around Nay Dayay's stall that despite their poses of merienda-hour leisure, licking their fingers or toying with fritter sticks, their eyes know exactly where the slight, well-dressed man in white linen is in the crowd, Ka Andres with his casual poise and spray of white kamia in a buttonhole (this is how Jote remembers him, and in truth he has yet to see an accurate portrayal of the Supremo, his uncanny self-possession, all in white linen—a wrinkle-free man of *la plancha*, Ka Andres) standing still in their center as if an invisible, taut string keeps him upright, or is it that all the men hold tight to that string—

They're not tethered: they're steadied by his will.

"In any case," says the great future general Urbano Lacuna—*requiescat in pace!*, "young Jote Delgado y Blumfeld has done his duty. He diverted the crowd at the plaza, I arrested him, I beat him up with my batuta, only pretending, you know, I tried not to hurt. And have mercy on us all, today's *acting performance!* will help to rescue the hero from the firing squad—we diverted attention to abduct the hero at the last minute and save him from execution, praise be the Katipunan!"

He says *acting performance* in English, with the melodrama of an amateur.

After all, he is, amid the whir of bats and invisible owls, technically on stage.

And the band of men—yes—the band—they begin to sing.

En campos de batalla, luchando con delirio / Otros te dan sus vidas sin dudas, sin pesar!

"Plus the plots of Alexandre Dumas!"

Says Marcelo Badel, breaking up the song.

He likes to play up his part—the comedy nerd of Calle Anda.

"Hmmmph," grunts Ka Vicente.

"The hero said no."

Ka Andres releases that sound, *no*, with a gulp, a sound caught in his throat.

It ends in a whisper.

Then Ka Andres scratches his throat, as if nothing were the matter. Silence in the crowd.

Jote can hear the gurgling of the kalamay in the pot, bubble, bubble, bubble, like the sound of things being drained, an improvised sound effect in the wings.

And the cicadas that are also their audience play a part in the silence.

"But the guardia civil—they are ready to die—the *fusileros*—the men with the pusil—in the firing squad up front who agree to withhold—pusila, pusila, they have it, the password—" begins Urbano.

"To withhold their fire—" continues one of the Carreons—the singing one, Jote thinks.

A baritone bleat.

They hear Urbano's voice catch.

"The hero says he does not want them to die for him," mutters Ka Andres. "The Spanish officers behind them will kill the *fusileros* anyway if they refuse to fire."

A tenor trill.

"But the *fusileros*, our countrymen, they have already signed their oaths to us in blood," says the red-nosed milkman, Ka Enteng, part of the chorus, undaunted.

"He does not want anyone to shed more blood—" says Ka Andres.

An anguished bass.

"And Ka Igue Resurreccion, the grass cutter, he's out there with his carromata and his bales of hay, ready to take him away—"

"He does not want to be smuggled out in the zacatero's cart! He does not want to endanger Miguel Resurreccion, his holy name, or his carromata. He says—he does not want to become—a fugitive from the law."

Bow.

A soloist's flourish.

A heave of sorrow rustles in the crowd.

"Coward!" says Marcelo Badel.

"Ah. He's just a quack doctor, after all, that agent of Bismarck."

"Figures," says Ka Vicente, though he wonders what he would do in such a moment—at the hour of his death to be promised rescue by a bunch of postal workers and zacateros in disguise.

Who wants to be caught, like a beast, with horsegrass in his mouth?

"He says his death shall set us free," ends Ka Andres.

"The hell it will," mutters the boy mechanic Hilario, a.k.a. Hiloy. "His death will hound us to our deaths."

Jote sighs as he walks down Moret Street.

He remembers the words of that makeshift zarzuela—their grief for the executed hero not really translatable in a one-act operetta, with its random half rhymes, and the Caviteños never know if they should clap for the fellow who plays Ka Andres (whom they assassinated after all) and the awkward use of allusions (so many are fans of the teatros, especially the Nacional and the Zorilla, and how Juan the barber-playwright would have loved the newsreel shows at the americanos' new place, Odeon, if only Juan had survived the Battle of Badoc against the same Americans). A sad moment in life and in art, as they flee the wrath of the americanos, the pincer plans of March and Hare and Kane and Abel, so many dumb names to forget, Kennon and Lawton and that stage name of a vaudeville hand, that bodabil villain, Arthur MacArthur—chasing them up to the hills of Bangued—where they practice their makeshift zarzuela.

Titled "The Abduction of the Hero."

Directed by the barber Juan, co-scripted by the barber Macario.

He, Jote, plays the part of Hilario Sayo, a.k.a. the valiant Hiloy.

He speaks Hiloy's words—the words of Hiloy after the debacle of Bagumbayan.

His death will hound us to our deaths.

He is haunted haunted haunted by words that turn into things, the transforming condition of his world, juvenescence of larva, the pupacy of moths, as he rounds the acacias, with its curled leaves, like larval spittoons, on his way to the tranvia stop for the medical school at Padre Faura.

The words of Hilario Sayo, a.k.a. Hiloy, that glum teenage mechanic from Muntinglupa, a depressing kid, in truth—for a while there, in the wild, Jote thinks the boy Hiloy will die of bangungot, terrorized not by war but by his bad indigestion—Hilario, a.k.a. the valiant Hiloy, Jote's comrade in arms, *los tres mosqueteros!*, their own *triángulo*, along with Marcelo Badel (who dies, also too young—not yet twenty in 1899), as he and Hiloy flee Manila toward Malolos, when their former friends the norteamericanos turn against them, though he does not expect them to turn so quickly, just weeks after Christmas and before the ink dries on the Treaty of Paris—and so Hiloy dies, at the hands of the mutants from Pampanga, the Macabebes, those dwarf men—Spain's stooges, America's amigos, the Devil's Tools.

There will always be people like them in times of war, Jote thinks as he walks along Moret Street, pitying everything he sees, the narra trees, the traitors, the acacias, the losers, the scalawags, the kalachuchi, the three gringo spies at the corner, Bandholtz, Allen, and Breton, the flame trees along Sampaloc, the ghosts, all of the men and the women and the hills and the farmlands and the doomed beloved country, caught in the noose of war.

He used to like the coños of *their* revolution—the men of We the People, their Sons of the People.

Too bad that William Jennings Bryan never wins.

It's just that—

Hilario's words after Bagumbayan return to Jote—or are those the words they make up in the play, he gets it all mixed up—the men in the group on that day in Calle Anda who scatter to the wind, their deed of rebellion—their botched rescue of the hero—a story unwritten by witnesses until now, here in the three notebooks that his brother Paco is reading (but how is Jote to know), packed in three neat bundles separated by whorled end papers.

La primera.

La segunda.

La tercera.

Each notebook has a straightforward, numbered title—the handwritten journey of the hunted brigand Jorge "Jote" Delgado y

Blumfeld, rebel first against Spain then against America—in this set
of notebooks that Paco is leafing through in their childhood home on
Moret Street.

Paco marvels at his brother's life.

His war against Spain in the part called *la primera*.

His battles up north in the part called *la segunda*, as Jote is pursued
by forces of MacArthur (*pére*, his *fils* was the other) beyond Santa
Mesa, San Juan Del Monte, Pandacan, fleeing all the way up, far
north to Cabugao then down to Bontoc, Jote crosses mountains in
Patapat and rides ferries on Lingayen, jumps ship toward Dagupan,
not quite revealing exactly how he gets to the Visayas (crisscrossing
eastward, hopping through Bicol, like their father Don Francisco the
First during his young wastrel times *galabanting!*), until Jote appears
in that long-lost town.

Giporlos.

The brothers' motherland.

The land of Adina Blumfeld y Catalogo, wife, mother, dead.

The endless coconut groves of Samar.

And Paco reads of his brother Jote's escape from the howling—
Paco waits, impatient for the romance—the philosopher Calista—she
of the brazen gaze by the stream (she has scornful eyes and a hard
heart)—he skips some pages skimming for the name—and then
Jote's irretrievable night of escape, sailing across the strait.

His Leyte landing.

Crawling their way through sapa and stream to fall upon the barakasyunan of Salogó—where Jote and Bingo his compadre nearly
drown, there where Himanglos meets the gulf—and they're saved by
chickens. They swim toward what they think is shore, but it is uneven
land and they wake a flock of sleeping chickens burrowed under
warmed sand—and the farmers of Salogó come out at the squawking
of their flock to see the lost men, and the fishermen of Salogó wade
in and drag the marooned swimmers to shore.

In Salogó, Jote rests.

Lingkod. Higda.

His odd change, his blessed time of kundiman, amid roosters, coconuts, and typhoons, the study of insects and wildlife in the wasteland called Leyte before the Americans catch up.

Here in Sampaloc.

On Moret Street in 1908.

With the aid of their sniffer, that talented Nose, the intelligent asset, Paco, a man with the talent of a kapre.

An Iya Nariz.

Nga iya irong.

True, Paco has a weird sense of his world's smells.

Once upon a time, they even had colors.

Out the window he gazes up from the notebooks and watches his good friends, the yanqui gringos, Captain Henry T. Allen, Lieutenant Harry Bandholtz, and Sergeant Frank Breton, observe Jote on his way to medical school at Padre Faura on that morning in June, 1908, during the early days of what in the islands people call *peacetime*—an kamurayaw—that other term for losing—when to his father's surprise his new friends, Señor Fenimore Browning the sugar trader and Mister Henry Wadsworth Colt the hemp merchant, have for no good reason come to stay.

A Translator is a Traitor

"Un tra[duc]tor = a tra[i]tor."
   Paz Tilanuday y Hua-Zhu

   Trans. Calista Catalogo, Giporlos, Samar

PART THREE
LA TERCERA

✳ ✳ ✳

On the Street

I saw her on my way from buying milk and fruit at D'Agostino's, and she accosted me at the corner of Bethune. I was used to these people on my street, models and others wearing nearby Maison Margiela for daily wear, and I avoid looking at them in general because I prefer not to give them their due. I pretend my resistance is a virtue—ignoring even those people of ambiguous ethnicity whom I think should be my allies, kind of francoafrican with mesoamerican inflections and that straight black hair I used to take for granted, this one dressed in antisexual armor usually designed by my favorite antisocial people, the Japanese. I was looking at the folds of her skirt, though, the way there is magic to certain kinds of pleating, a crossbias cut that challenges gravity.

Elvis Oras used to tell me, I have the heart of a costurera.

I hate the people who can afford those clothes, they are usually scum of the capitalist earth, but I love the art.

I did not hear her when she called out to me because there are also a few crazy people in the West Village that I ignore. My downstairs neighbor Begonia, for instance, a seventyish chapbook poet with dementia, whose husband, Günter, a retired mortician, used to greet me happily on the street, cuddling his neurotic dog, until it occurred to Begonia, for some reason, that I was out to steal her new poetic manuscripts, lurking to pounce on her from the roof deck. And now the pained look in her husband's eyes when he sees me going down the street, his demented Begonia at his side, makes me grieve for his sorry life. I made sure I never looked people in the eye, and I screened sounds from my earscape. I have a knack for alienation. It turns out it's not genetic. It's historical. I walked past the girl in the Yohji clothes.

She was facing me.

And then I heard that long-unheard name.

Only someone from my childhood would call me by that name, and so of course I did not believe I heard it as I turned on Bethune.

That's when she accosted me and repeated it—the nickname my mother called me.

I was dragging my Zuri bag of geometric African prints, a mark of righteous yet still annoying consumerism, bulging with tangerines and a seven-dollar gallon of milk. She tapped me on my Tracy-Anderson-online-toned arms as I swung my virtuous cloth shopping bag. I bring out these arch-bourgeois tropes of late-capitalist tendencies only to point out that, as a modern Filipino presenting an anticolonial history none of you want to hear about, I'm not into misery.

I work out, and I vent my frustrations by going to Sephora. The only nurses in my family are extremely rich people exploiting fellow workers by owning lousy retirement homes in Maryland. I live in the West Village because the old white people, though crabby, some nuts, are quiet; also, the walls in my prewar building are solid. The advertising says pin-drop-silence, and it is true. The silence allows me to write. I'm averse to misplaced notions of art as martyrdom. I like Karl Marx because I'm not into poverty—I believe in everyone's right to leisure and the eight-hour workday, and even better less than eight. And I understand that my choice of a comfortable life, without apology, condemns me in some people's eyes. That makes sense.

I did not immediately hate her when she repeated my name.

Chicharita.

I didn't even hate her when she appended—*Tia.*

Now calling me *Tia* is a provocation. For one thing, it's not only ageist. It's old-style. Now it's *Auntie this* or *Auntie that*. Or *Tita*. Or worse, *Ate* (the worst—for Warays, that's just a Tagalog affectation). And Manang, at least for me in Tacloban when I was a child, was for tinderas, the ones who gave my mother IOUs, for a can of sardines or a cone of tinapâ, if her clients had not yet paid. No one in my immediate family will call me *Tia*—I have no nieces or nephews that I know of. Adino, sweet Adino, back home in retreat after his years in the United States, is occupied with importing chickens. Society has castrated Mick-mick, more or less: our norms, no matter where you are on the spectrum, sound affectionate, but they're merciless. As for Putt-putt, he's rightwing, of course, in his middle age, becoming Praise-the-Lord as they call his spiritual turn in Tacloban, and who can blame him? He needs a crutch in evil times. We lost touch after my third novel though if I FaceTime him, despite what he thinks of me, I know he'll be glad.

That's just the way my family is—it's a struggle to have a family *and* proper judgment.

No, I did not immediately hate her when she said it.

Chicharita.

For a moment, I discredited the phantom syllables as fleeting melancholy schizophrenia. Certainly I have the right to my hallucinations. That, by the way, might be genetic, so I'm learning.

It occurred to me I heard my childish name, the one my mother used to call me, and I felt a moment of horror at my weakness, my imbecile grieving, and I kept going.

I don't believe in ghosts, not even the ones I wish to see.

Then she said—

Tia Chicharita. It's I! The daughter of Sirit!

That's when I hated her—when she told me who she was.

She spoke impeccable Waray.

She had grown up there, where I had grown up.

She was, as expected, gorgeous.

Grandchild of Kringle May—*may kiriring, kiriring!*—plus child of Sirit, the living baby doll. One of those untraceably mixed Filipino specimens that, to be honest, the eugenicists should have aimed for. Skin not caramel nor cream, nor burnt nor sienna, with the limber limbs of enviable animals who have no need for exercise, or even consciousness, of superior height and lissome heft because all the variables are on their side: wealth, health, the importable goods of all nations.

Her mother became a Bahrain Beauty, so Sirit was called in nasty columns when we were in college. Really, I felt for her. Manila's streets were raining yellow protest confetti when Sirit was in Bahrain, or Brunei, some petroleum nation with a fricative in its name, and her story was in the tabloids. These television starlets went to Brunei, so the papers said, to became odalisques of some Prince. Smacks of Orientalist smack to me, but that became the weird story of my childhood friend Sirit.

She left school to become a singer and dancer on a new variety show, *That's Entertainment*, before she left the country for her desert adventures.

I pointed her out to my friends, the activists, when we passed the TV room on the way to the marches and glanced at the lunchtime shows.

A girl from Tacloban, my classmate, my old neighbor.

We were once in a dance troupe together, I said, can you believe?

Karit, as we would say. Her fame surpassed even Bombom the model of our childhood on Juan Luna Street whose face sold ice cream.

The Maoists said her voice was no good, but her mestiza looks were unmistakably prime for the bourgeoisie.

She always had that quality as a child—the baffled look of a baby doll.

In school, her inability to take in information made you feel protective.

She told me a few stories of her life when my friends, my high school barkada of incongruent parts cobbled together by teenage boredom, left to me after Trina was gone, organized a trip, just for me, one summer in the teen years of this century.

Lorelei, Queen Sirikit, Sirit, and I. For a research trip for my fourth novel, a Fulbright grant during the last time I visited, we went to Samar, to Giporlos and Balangiga, in Sirit's outsize off-road car, a Montero or Pajero, some luxury monster. She drove it herself. We went from Manila to Samar. I never got to Tacloban, to Leyte. My mother was in the hospital in Manila, and we had only a day for the ride. I had to return. Also, Sirit's husband, Manny, was running for mayor, and I was in no hurry to meet him.

It was a jumbled-up time when my loyalties, as always, were tested.

I did not fail to disappoint.

Why have you stuck with him? I asked Sirit on the trip.

To be married to a Trinidad, of all Tacloban families, the unstable son of the dictators' bagwoman, Mrs. Conrada, she of the defunct Ministry of People's Facts—my mom's old friend from the Clairol Hi & Dri gang, whose son, so it was said, had once chased his girlfriend Sirit onto the street in a jealous, drug-fueled rage and cut off her long, black curls in public.

At the time, Putt-putt was still my town crier, writing me letters by hand, before the time of private messaging.

That's how I got my news.

It was also Putt-putt the people's journalist who told me the contemporary facts about my mom's friend—Mrs. Conrada Trinidad.

When you grow up in deranged times, so many people in hindsight lived double lives. At first, you imagine life's existential mystery, how we live in a garden of forking paths, making decisions without knowing our future ironic arcs. But really, under a dictatorship, we're just dupes. When the conjugal dictators fled, it's said their crony Mrs. Conrada held money, deposits into an account at the Bank of Philippine Islands in her own name, and rumors were out in full daylight after the exiled family's flight to Hawaii. Mrs. Conrada returned to Tacloban from Manila. She was flush with cash. Mrs. Conrada and her sons stayed put in the city, bloated with sudden rewards. Putt-putt said they were blowing it on elections, real estate, drug laundering, overwrought marriage celebrations.

Manny Trinidad, "the druggie," as he was known in our lives where everyone had their calling (the beggar, the epileptic, the Muslim, the tailor), was Sirit's old neighbor when she and her mother Kringle May lived in the old part of the city, by Plaza Rizal. Turns out it was true—he was the province's most famous drug vampira, so Putt-putt relayed. When we were kids he was one of those scary kanto boys, our age, whom we were told to avoid though as far as I could tell he was only a smoker who liked to watch us girls pass by, sitting with his gang along the unfinished walls on Burgos Street. But he grew up to become gross purveyor of the goods his mother, soon to be governor in the new dispensation, denounced.

So said Putt-putt.

On the way to Balangiga, I was not sure which of Putt-putt's headlines needed redacting before Sirit.

It's your fault, Sirit said to me calmly as she drove me to Samar: it was you who told me to go out with him.

I flinched.

I remembered that conversation we had before I left for grad school in New York.

I was hanging around Manila while I waited for my visa. Sirit called me up. It was out of the blue. The only classmate I spoke to was Trina and once Elvis Oras when he stopped over in Manila on the way to Hong Kong, where he bought Young's Fashionne House fabric for his rich Chinese clients, the glassware and construction magnates of Anibong. Sirit was lonely in Manila in the time of the reports of her escapades in Brunei, or Bahrain. We went to lunch. We laughed as we clinked glasses at the bayside hotel. She looked like the girl in the magazine pictorials in her *That's Entertainment* days— implausibly childlike, in floral linen clothes. In her teen idol universe, she was called, no surprise, The Doll—an munyika. Divina May, the Divine Doll, the tabloids called her.

She still had that clueless look that tested my empathy. We had sangrias. She remembered the day we demonstrated against the principal, my stern aunt Tita Patchy, and Sirit said she had no idea what was going on, but she marched with us, she was determined to be part of our game. That's not how I remembered it, I said, but anyway it was a long time ago, in second grade.

And look where we were now!

Drinking at a piano bar in the Hilton, in the heart of Manila with a view of the Bay, and the lights of the floating casinos in the distance.

She did not tell me about her life in Bahrain, but she looked sad, and I did not ask. I did not mention the stories in the gossip columns. I made a mistake.

I remembered my lame advice, dispensing it as if I were some free love advocate, Emma Goldman off to Russia—if you find pleasure in it, why not, I said, airily raising my glass. At least, it's someone you know. You don't have to marry him. Anyway, going out with him will pass the time, I said to Sirit.

Later, when I heard of her marriage, I felt guilty.

You mean, you remember what I said? I asked on the way to Samar.

Of course, Sirit said, I listened to you—you're the class valedictorian.

Oh my God. I forgot what Sirit also was when we were kids—she was an idiot.

That is true, I said to her, but I had no idea who you were talking about. I thought it was just some kid you knew from Tacloban! I did not know he was Manny Trinidad, your crazy neighbor by Santo Niño church!

I protested too much on that coastal trip to Samar.

I think I had a clue that day at the Hilton who she meant, her old Juan Luna neighbor, the boy who used to watch us from the corner on Burgos, follow her all the way home toward Justice, though he lived by Zamora, and he sent her roses and then later it seems Bottega Veneta purses that looked like they were constructed out of mats sold on Tacloban's pier, but actually they were made of Florentine leather. She was carrying one that day, on the open-air terrace with the grand piano in the corner where we had lunch—a deceptively elegant accessory, and I commended her on her taste. She said he had given it to her. She looked happy to hear my admiration, and I remember being happy that day for Sirit.

The fact is I am feeble-minded with people I know from childhood. It's a flaw. It's tough when you remember them as kids, bright-eyed, with dumb haircuts and bad decision-making skills. You wish for their lives to turn out well, just as you imagine they wish the same for you. Of course, you're also good for the gossip. And the life of Sirit was tabloid fodder. I mean, real tabloids, like *Taliba* and *People's Tonight!* Even that day at the Hilton, scooping up our last bits of ube sorbetes and Rocky Road ice cream (we were suckers for nostalgia and ordered what we would have when we used to skip our piano lessons with Elephant Katol—please forgive us, Miss Custodia!—to go downtown and spend our baon for the week at Magnolia House on Justice, corner Santo Niño), I could tell people were staring at our table because Divina May, the Bahrain Beauty—the Divine Doll—was in their midst.

Her face's startling symmetry, her shining skin, her jet-black curls. Even then, grown-up, she had that questioning look, the look that said *sirit!*, I give up, I don't get it, I'm not gonna play, when she did not quite understand what was going on, and so she lagged behind us, not quite sure about joining our games. Her look of dependence, of furrowed-up confusion, made you feel bad and make amends for being annoyed though of course that meant she'd never change.

Out in the foyer of that hotel by the Bay, while she waited for what must have been Manny Trinidad's chauffeur, we saw them.

They were positioned before you reached the bank of elevators—a quartet, a bouquet.

"Isn't that your mom's?" Sirit said with excitement.

I don't know how we had missed them coming into the hotel.

We crossed the lobby, passed the grand piano and the striped batik-style carpet and glass Murano chandeliers (the Hilton hoteliers gave one this confused impression of native and nouveau)—we walked, hypnotized, toward the huge canvases, four in all.

We stood before the closest one.

Dried roses and weeds and petals and leaves on a russet, almost-tangerine background.

"It's the *Four Seasons!*" Sirit said.

Yes, I said. How do you know?

"I loved your mom's paintings!" said Sirit—"remember how Mana

Adina would sit there for hours while we listened to your red record player, and she made her huge canvases? On that big patio, when you moved downtown and we became neighbors, on Juan Luna? Your mom would explain to me the names of each one—*Autumn, Winter, Spring*. They were never the same, she told me. She called them all the *Four Seasons*, but no set was ever the same, she said. Isn't that genius?"

I was staring at Sirit.

"But *Summer* was always the most beautiful," said Sirit. "That's what I thought. Is she still making them?"

You mean her frames? I asked.

"Is that what they're called—frames?" said Sirit. "I thought they were called art."

It still strikes a nerve.

Sirit's rebuke to me.

Though Sirit, as she always did, asked me as if it were a question, and I was the authority while she was the dunce.

Yes, I said to Sirit, she's still making them.

"I envied you, you know—that your mom was an artist. It was so cool, for one's mom to be an artist. And she was always so happy, doing her art. She always made me happy because she'd be glad to see us—remember how she'd greet me and Lorelei and Queenie?"

How?

"She'd start dancing—ballroom dancing. To the theme song from *Superman*. Remember?"

Really?

"Yes!" said Sirit who (despite what the Maoists said) did not have a bad voice. "Can you read my mind?"

No, I said, I can't. That's embarrassing—I don't remember that.

"She'd always sing that song when we arrived because she knew we were going to go to the record player and play it! It was our gang's theme song! By Maureen McGovern. Remember? We'd appear at your gate, and your mom would be on the patio, and she'd start singing before we even got in—*Can you read my mind?* She was just teasing, always the same song, she told us. She'd call us in. It made me happy, being with Mana Adina. She liked to dance the tango with me, you know. She liked me because I could do the tango, and we'd dance while she teased me with our barkada's theme song, singing and dancing all the while."

Yeah, I said, that's my mom.

"I always thought she was so glad to see me, but I think, really, Mana Adina wanted to just get back to her art. But she was always so nice to us. Even though we were interrupting her art."

It shames me that I never readily had Sirit's word for my mother's work.

Art.

All my life I had called them frames, as if they were a hobby and she were making crafts—and not her life's blood.

"And here they are," said Sirit—"The *Four Seasons*!—as your mom always said—she told me I'd see them at a fancy place someday. And here they are at the Manila Hilton! Wow!"

I know I buried that conversation in my brain, I left Sirit at the entrance to the Hilton, where her mystery boyfriend's chauffeur came to pick her up, and I thought maybe I should go back to the piano bar, to see if my mom's cousin Freddie was playing since I never did take my mom up on her suggestion—"You should go see my work, inday—they put it up in the lobby, by the grand piano, where my cousin Freddie the jazz pianist plays, under the chandeliers!"

Was this child a foot taller than me?

I felt dizzy, looking up at her in New York's glare.

Tia Chicharita! I was just coming from your building—I've been buzzing and buzzing! I'm Bling-bling. Bling-bling Trinidad! The daughter of Divina! Did Tia Trina tell you—

I looked up at her burnished chin, her foundation cream blended as if her skin were naked, naturally resplendent. As she bent down, I thought to hug me, I took in an overwhelming, florid aura, an expensive, maybe custom-made perfume, not countertop *Aliage*, and it was the most disconcerting feeling, to breathe in this profuse, godly scent coming from what seemed to be my old friend Sirit's long, jet-black curls.

But instead of hugging me, the girl was reaching for my hand.

She took my wrist to her forehead.

In downtown Manhattan, she did *la mano*.

It was OA. Overacting. A stinky performative gesture.

I took my hand back, rubbing it behind me.

What did she want?

If she was in the pay of Trina Trono, I did not want to know.

I just wanted to meet—my mom told me. I tried to call you on your phone. You know your VoiceMail is full. We're neighbors—I'm on Twelfth Street—I'm here for college—and I just wanted to say—

I nodded my head, I smiled.

Condolence, she said. *I was so sad to hear about your mom. Ninang Adina.*

She was your godmother?

Yes. My favorite one, said Bling-bling Trinidad.

Liar, I thought.

On Moret Street, in 1908, she watches him as he watches his brother Jote on his way to the tranvia to get to the medical school, on Padre Faura. She watches him bending toward papers, having glanced at the three men who loiter amid the flame trees, by the corner, as if casual, Lieutenant Bandholtz, Sergeant Frank Breton, and Captain Henry T. Allen. She carves scratches, notches in the mind.

Asociacion Feminista Filipina

I was staring at the painting Pinggoy Gomez, director of the National Archives, had in the background at home as I FaceTimed him. It was familiar to me, I was trying to place it, and as I fumbled with my question, I realized what it was. It was a Manansala, not quite the mural on the walls of AS Lobby at the university in Diliman, but a facsimile of the Master's cubist strokes—warm ochres and rubies and a recurring thread, a Piero della Francesca blue. As I stared, I realized it was no copy—the man had an actual Manansala in his home. The wall's paneling was that dark gleam of old homes proud of their ancestral luster, and I remembered that Pinggoy's patriarchal name was still on the map of everyone's hometown.

I had met him in New York at one of those events that bring together people who at no other time would have much to do with one another except for the fact that they're all archipelagic. It was an art exhibit at the consulate. The artist collaged passages from historical documents with filmed location shots from around the world—the most mysterious one being a two-minute reel of Andean llamas overlaid with a menu, a list, from the war diary of Aguinaldo's doctor, Simeon Villa, circa 1901. Pinggoy was a guest of honor, the artist's patron whose family heirloom, a Tagalog manuscript from 1903 about the dignity of labor in the author's own hand, was the crux of a six-minute film that was set, for some reason, in the Temple of Borobudur. Someone introduced me as a novelist working on a book on the early American period—that time at the turn of the century when suddenly under one more ruler the country switched tongues. I told him I had studied his grandfather's other work, an ephemeral piece subtitled *una novela Tagala*, published in Ghent in Spanish about Cavite, the author's home province, in the style of *costumbrismo*—not adding that his grandfather legislated both his masterpieces into obsolescence by promoting English as the national language by 1916.

I had written to him before our call. I wanted to know about a manuscript in the National Archives by a man named Canning Eyot, perhaps an Ilonggo, that tells the story of Clemencia, Mariquita, and Juanita, the Lopez sisters of Balayan, founding members of the Asociacion Feminista Filipina. The association first came together in the opening years of the American century, in 1905, I said. I wanted to know if he had ever heard of the feminist, Calista Catalogo.

He said, oh, just call me.

But it turns out mainly he wanted to talk about the Broadway play he had just seen on his last visit to America.

Then he went on and on about the pseudonymous man, this Canning Eyot, he kept laughing as he said his name, *do you know what it means in Ilonggo, Canning Eyot!, this fucker ha ha an obvious alias the Americans never caught!,* and he told stories about how he finagled the manuscript from its former owners, whom he knew, he said, from his time at Harvard—and he paused to let that sink in, though he had already told me that the last time we met, at the New York consulate, that he had gone to college at Harvard. I bided my time as, in answer to my question, the man then proceeded to tell the entire story of the Lopez sisters, adding to my research on Wikipedia, how Clemencia undertook a quixotic journey to the United States to see the new president, Theodore Roosevelt, who had just taken office after McKinley's assassination, you know, so it's really Roosevelt who prosecuted the nation's violent assimilation!—she left Manila for Hong Kong, first to consult with the exiled rebel junta, then she took that Atlantic trip, on the SS *Ivernia,* better named *Imbiyerna,* ha ha, after her useless undertaking!, *na-imbiyerna lang siya*—arriving from Liverpool to Boston, then riding the trains to DC with her Hong Kong friends, her fan club of anti-imperialists from New England who fawned on Clemencia, the determined Filipina. The goal was to gain the release of her brothers from Talim Island, the American prison for so-called bandits and insurrectos on Laguna de Bay.

But what did that broad expect, said Pinggoy Gomez—giving away in that moment that his peak intellectual times were the fifties—that she'd get an audience with Roosevelt simply by taking a train into Washington, DC? *Idiota.* Clemencia never got to the White House, he said. She became an organizer of women's rights when she returned home.

"Have you heard about this woman from Samar," I interrupted. "Does the name Calista Catalogo ring a bell?"

Even on FaceTime, mediated by technology and distance, Pinggoy Gomez's well-filled cheeks and tight jaw oozed his historical patrimony, seasoned by Botox. He was a jolly-looking, smooth-faced, digressing Filipino, whom I needed on my side.

He leaned into the screen, and his close-up nose had zero pores.

"Nah," he said. "Canning does not mention that feminist. Ay, that Eyot!"

His eyes crinkled, he was laughing at his joke before he told it.

"She's the one who went on that speaking tour, did she not, Calista—sponsored by that *lezzzbian*—what's her name—the only white woman at Apolinario Mabini's funeral—the Boston woman, Helen Wilson."

And the man said that word *lezzzbian* as if it were dessert in his mouth.

Death Tango

My mom wanted ballroom dancing when she died. A kuracha before her body left her childhood home, cha-cha and rhumba all along her funeral procession instead of the cries of the paid, ancient mourners, and tango at the graveyard when the last rites were done. An extreme function. According to her directions, I was to contact the DIs, the dancing instructors, on her list. I was to hire the musicians, the singers of "A media luz" and the strummers of "Oye como va."

Bling-bling Trinidad's role was to give me the Manila folder—the papers of my mother's wishes.

And spy on me—for sure.

But for what?

I did not ask her to go up to my apartment, or even to the roof deck, a more public, noncommittal venue. It was clear there was a protocol to this meeting—my part was to be hostess, welcoming the new one to the city, her part to be subservient, to show her respects to some fake termagant aunt, and one day in our future if all worked out she would be ready with a shroud for my funeral, plus an oration if she were asked, simply because we came from the same hometown, and now we were neighbors, too, catty-corner from Bethune.

I would let her know me over my dead body.

I accepted the papers, along with a crumpled Manila folder. I stuffed them in the Zuri bag with the oranges and the milk. I left her on the street. I could tell she wanted more, but I was not going to give it.

I'd be damned if I was going to give Trina Trono the pleasure.

My mother's reputation—*she is so eccentric!*—preceded her. Corroy Montejo, formerly known as Roy, Tacloban's giantess of choreography (literally, she was a giant, almost six feet tall, and her stature, along with her style, impressed all), would be ready with her choreography for the graveyard, Corroy emailed—Corroy had a sense of humor. Her current obsession was really flamenco dancing, but she'd do it for my mom, she said. A former philosophy student at Divine Word College, protégé of the intellectual defrocked priest, Father Vice-President Edgar Allan Pe, Corroy Montejo repeated her dictum to me, also tacked onto all her emails as her epigram—

Tango is Eros, tango is Thanatos, in tango do love and death meet!

Anyway, Corroy said, your mom was one of my favorites.

A passionate woman.

I ended up Venmo-ing the money for the wailing mourners, too, since tradition does not hurt. Plus, I gave money for a rondalla of Salogó ex-cons ready to strum old songs. This, too, was in the instructions. Rehabbing the criminals of Salogó had become one of my mother's pet causes. I guess her political outrage weakened in her last years. A popular occupation of Salogó people who migrate to Manila is to become hired killers, she used to say—it's their talent, my mom explained, at that time in revulsion: a mafia of guns for hire from Salogó out by Pasig Line—*pusila! pusila!*—gun-toting Galmans whose favorite hobby, apart from killing, is videoke. But she had a change of heart, and she gave me the number of a not quite anticarceral rondalla band.

Then my mom's cousin, that Junior Igmenegildo of all people, a disorganized swindler but also a tattletale, told on me to Tio Nemor.

That Junior was in Nevada but still a louse.

My uncle got wind of the plans.

I took his call.

He was sitting in the bedroom I recognized, the one with the alcove of saints and the Petromax stains that reminded me how long darkness used to fall upon Salogó. In the middle of the conversation, he moved to the balcony to get better reception.

For all its modernity, FaceTime can be incredibly analeptic—it brings you to the past in disturbing ways.

Tio Nemor told me to call everything off.

"Tango in the sementeryo? Who ever heard of ballroom dancing at the graveyard?"

"It's what she wanted. She wrote it down. She left me a letter."

"What will the people think of us? No! It's like when she came back from America—bah—no, inday, there will be no tango."

"But what about her letter to me?"

"You know, ever since she was nineteen, we let Adina do everything she wanted. Now that she's dead—"

"What happened when she was nineteen?"

"Bah! Water under the bridge!"

"People have mah-jongg at wakes," I said, "why not ballroom dancing?"

"No. Basta. We are not dancing the tango at her grave."

"But she wrote me."

"We will have playing cards and mah-jongg, plus five lechon because even the consul from Manila, the woman from Greenhills, Auntie Charity Breton, will come—everyone in Salogó will come if only to stare at the people from Manila—and we will have a funeral procession with the singing mourners, and a mass. Amo la. The End. Waray rhumba, waray chacha, waray rondalla. My God. Adina! Sus ginoo! She always had a bad sense of obligation. It was always whatever she wanted. Well, maybe the rondalla, they can play "Ave Maria," if they want."

And he said, as if in warning—"Sige. Makanta ako."

And so in the end we would hear, if I went home for the funeral, Tio Nemor's beautiful voice, a bit too high for a man, but just low enough to make one weep at right moments, when in the "Ave Maria" of Schubert the tremolo of *gra-a-a-atia ple-e-ena* unraveled in that line that used to keep me in suspense as a child, and no matter how often I heard it, I would sense my own heart stopping, cradled in my uncle's voice, that interminable wait for release, until my uncle breathed and spoke the next line—*Dominus tecuuummm*—the way death-in-life, a strange quality of music, restores the body even as it reminds us—

That the body will go.

So it would be that instead of the funeral tango, I would listen to a rondalla murder the *Ave Maria* of Schubert, a song not meant to be sawed at by that obese ukulele, the bandurria.

I signed off from the call, I put down the phone, I reached for the box I had carried with me up to the balcony after my encounter with Bling-bling Trinidad.

Someone was out to get it.

I kept the box within my frame of vision.

It is odd to be back on Moret Street, on this cul-de-sac in Sampaloc, amid the smell of citrus and kalachuchi. It is the season of the rain of yellow flowers from old trees—blossoms of random beauty with no memory but this perfume in their wake. And the sweet kamia flowers falling, falling, falling as he passes: the size of his thumb, with gingered hearts.

The horse that December, trotting toward Paseo de Azcárraga: and he's late, late, late for everything. He's hungry and unbathed in his childish Sunday suit (a barong over sando, linen pants), beside his father and baby brother, that champorado gobbler, that food sniffer Paco, and there are too many pedestrians as they turn toward the Bay, and the driver Tay Sequil, *El Excellent Cochero Exequiel!* (in his American-era ads) has to trot back home alone with the carriage.

Looking at the crowds, Don Francisco the First orders Tay Sequil to turn the kalesa.

Back toward Moret Street.

Jote remembers looking up at his father. He believes that is why the old man changes his mind, and so the gruff trader—his father loves him best of all—clambers off the kalesa.

To be one with the hordes of his city.

Why shouldn't his father love him?

He never bothers to ask.

So first Paco, then Jote climb down into the arms of Tay Sequil, who sends each boy off to walk to the field of Bagumbayan with Tay Sequil's betel-nut blessing—that is, the humid horse smell of his kutsero sweat and his sour, lime-and-areca saliva.

"God save the Philippines," exclaims Tay Sequil—savant of Jote's childhood who taught him rope tying, dominoes, and the art of cockpit gambling. *Artes de vergüenza!* his father grumbles—huego ng mga walanghiya hmph hmph hmph!—but Tay Sequil puts his finger to his lips, laughing at the boss, spitting out betel for good measure.

He is Don Francisco the First's oldest servant—companion in his young, wastrel days when he went *galabanting!*—joyriding in Samar.

Before he leaves them to walk toward Bagumbayan, Tay Sequil spits onto the street, his habitual gesture, and Jote recalls the red spume from the old servant that almost hits him but falls instead on the path.

Like a glob of blood.

It's a sight Jote remembers in his days in the trenches of Malabon, in the rice fields of Baler, in the grasslands of Tanauan—every time he sees squirts of red during the war against the Americans, vermilion spray upon talahib and dirt and hillocks, ruby ground burying his companions (Hilario Sayo, slain in Badoc, Valentin Lagasca, captured with Abaya in Candon, Igue Resurreccion, fallen in Malolos)—he'll think of that betel-nut blessing from Tay Sequil.

The dark red blobs of Tay Sequil's betel-nut spray fall right next to Jote's takong. On the day his brother holds in his hands the evidence for Jote's arrest (but how is Jote to know?), Jote remembers how he used to sit with Tay Sequil and the other spitting servants in the driveway of the house on Moret Street, surrounded by the men's spreading, thoughtful spit, the wet betel-nut flowering that looked like scattered gumamela petals and smelled of guts.

Where are Mariano and Ambrosio and Tay Sequil, *El Excellent Cochero Exequiel!*, now?

First-Class Ticket

The minute I took my uncle Tio Nemor's call, I knew I had decided.

I was going home.

It was not that seeing the patch of river beyond my uncle on the balcony was startling on FaceTime, my delayed recognition of a town that into my adulthood had neither electricity nor phones.

In the new century Salogó went straight from the Middle Ages into postmodernity—with not just voices but video on a phone, more mediations than I've cared to know.

Or that I felt a bit lost when for a moment I thought I saw my mom's gaze on her brother's face. Tio Nemor had the gray, cataract-thickened eyes of his father, my mom's Papá, and his father before him, the unknown Jote. He was angry, he was unshaven, he was in a sando, undressed, he was always the boss, he was disappointed in me.

My mom's eyes were dark brown—clear and bright and glad.

The last I saw her, at the hospital in Makati that first and only time I returned from New York, she looked like the matriarch of Makati Medical Center, coiffed in her recalcitrant, seventies way, silk-pajamaed (royal purple, one of my Christmas presents), a fawning male nurse admiring her freshly lavendered nails (she was allowed to have her own manicurist, her cousin Mana Nemesia, come and make her over at the hospital) when I first entered her haven. I was the interloper, the stranger, the foreign daughter whom she introduced to everyone with her usual gladness like Browning's last duchess.

A hysterical novelist from New York!, she introduced me to her nurses.

But I was just a visitor, going home on a writing grant, incidentally at her side.

Was it my mom's handwriting in her letter to me, her Last Will and Testimonies, as she called it, making up her own private English until the end, though all her letter had were the names of acceptable DIs—Barcelona-trained Corroy Montejo, chic Demi Mundo, and Kandarapa Khan, whom my mom must not have known also raps on the side, according to his Twitter bio—and the list of music she preferred—tango tunes, Pilita Corrales, the Carpenters, and Elvis?

Among the papers she sent me, along with her Testimonies, was a fuzzy, faded Manila envelope. She must have kept this envelope with her in her many moves, a miracle of cathexis. Court documents. *Delgado v. Delgado*. She sent me, from her deathbed, her long-held papers on her family's case against Charity Breton. I had seen these papers before—maps of surveyed lands, the list of court petitioners, which I recognized. Bonifacia and Bonifacia. Nemesia and Nemesio. I tried to decipher my mother's point, her voice from the dead, as I stared at the papers. They were not even complete. I read the Appeals Court Judge's entire argument on the fallacy of my mother's case, beginning with his refutations of the initial court hearing.

It turns out the trial in the Court of First Instance had been in my mother's favor.

The initial hearing declared Charity Breton was an orphan without legal standing, and therefore not the heiress of all the lands.

I could hear, in the voice of my mom, or was it the voice of her Tia Pachang—

She's just a poliomyelitic! Leche, that Gotas de Leche!

But six years later, in the Appeals Court, my mom and her family, all the Bonifacias and the Nemesias and the Franciscos of Leyte, lost to Rosario "Charity" Breton Delgado, who produced evidence of her adoption and of her father's Will.

But for me the key document in my mom's posthumous envelope was the page in her Lolo Paco's hand.

At this point, I recognized it.

A crisp script, a beautiful pen.

At the top of the page is the phrase—"... of my late older brother."

Hanging, aleatory, and I looked for the conditions that linked the document back to his brother Jote.

His English is ironic, even this moment long past his grave.

His final comment: "I surely hope that my beloved wife will make up inequalities from her share of our modest estate."

Dated *New York City, NY, USA, 6 April AD 1959.*

I know from his biography in the US House of Representatives, history.house.gov, that at the time he was ambassador to the United Nations. It was the year before Khrushchev pounded a shoe on the table after a speech from the Philippine delegation.

Which might sound heroic but, as usual, when I checked out the incident, the Philippines was just a pontificating stooge for America in the Cold War. I was thrilled to hear his actual voice in the UN multimedia archive, then I was sad when I heard what he said.

The page from my mother's papers was signed—*Francisco B. Delgado.*

With a final note: "This consists of three folios marked A, B, and C."

The note is initialed in his florid hand: *FBD.*

My mother's remnant page from her Lolo Paco's folio seems to be both a letter and a contract. But to whom and what for? The extant leaf has an intriguing gap. As the final page of a document, the third in a set of three "marked A, B and C," the page is carefully initialed, signed. It presupposes a codicil about his brother Jote's family. But annoyingly, the page included in my mom's envelope does not have the codicil, just its implied existence in the folios before.

An irritating lapse on my mom's part.

That she saved everything but the most important section.

Instead, in full, she sent me the surveyor's maps of Greenhills, included in the trial documents—the lands that went to Charity Breton—and a separate map, of beachland in San Jose, where she let random people dock their boats, that area you can see as you fly above the city, before you land.

Plus, an original deed of title to that land in San Jose.

What was my mom saying to me?

Even when I bought my ticket, I knew I was not well.

I paid for First Class.

It was on sale, but still, the amount was beyond my sense of right.

I was not even clear what my privileges were, arriving at JFK with the fathers pushing carts with thirteen balikbayan boxes and the family of nine all in the same teal shirts, the words Rebosura Family Reunion circling the drawing of a globe on their backs, the province of Bohol on a bulls-eye target in the center of their world. *Fairy tales and bulls-eye!* My world seemed to be turning upside down, or I was out of sync, because my flight was at two a.m., and I calculated that makes sense because that is afternoon in Manila, as if by deciding to fly home I had nullified the temporal facts of my existence in New York, and I had meaning only in terms of my childhood home.

It was an ungodly hour, but JFK was still a mob.

I felt like an impostor in line at First Class, and I thought, would my mother be proud of me or not—for enacting my whim, to hell with reason—spoiling and petting myself in honor of her, and I choked back something, I think shame, as I responded to the lady, the ticket seller at First Class.

She was asking to weigh my luggage.

"I only have carry-on," I said.

"You are flying all the way to the Philippines, ma'am?"

"Yes."

"You have two pieces allowance, thirty-two kilograms each. You're not using?"

"No. I have only this."

I showed her my straw hat and my bag and my suitcase.

She brightened.

She took my suitcase and weighed it.

"We can put this suitcase in for you, ma'am."

"No, I'll carry it."

"Ah, ma'am, you are very disciplined. Traveling so light!"

I could not tell from her tone whether that was an accusation, but when the baggage man said to the lady, ah, walang bagahe? sayang, sixty-four kilos!, I knew something in me was wanting, not even my carry-on suitcase was worth its weight, and I must have this perceptual vacancy, bringing nothing home.

I saw them again, the teal-colored family, and I followed the entire reuniting Rebosura clan with their identical water bottles and shuffling, new New Balance shoes as we walked against the flow of security check for the overnight Philippine Airlines non-stop flight to Manila.

It seemed we would never get to the end of the security check line, my new barkada, the homegoing Rebosura gang and I. I walked with my ticket open in my palm, checking it for my gate, and an attendant told me, glancing at the ticket—your line is over there.

I looked way back to the start of security check.

First Class had its own sweet section, a subset of aloof, minimally suited people that I had seen, barely five people in line, right by the TSA gate, and I trudged back through the miles of people and cargo that I had already witnessed, reluctantly leaving the Rebosura Family, with their squeaky, jaunty steps that were now familiar to me, and I could even understand their language, it was Cebuano, Doctor Tita Tita's language, a hallucinatory Waray that had the wrong adverbs and prepositions but familiar nouns. I left them to their oblivion of me, and I looped back through the troops of trolleys, a suspicious Filipino wearing a too-large, optimistic hat with only a handbag and a carry-on suitcase, an ingrate relative with no cardboard box emporium of Hershey's chocolate and Jergens lotion to signify reunion.

I did not let go of my suitcase, I heard my heels clack-clacking on the parquet, I clutched my handbag and my hat as I entered the clubby airline lounge I had never noticed before. PAL shared it with

Alitalia. I placed my hat in a booth but rolled my suitcase and took my handbag with me. The pancit and the siopao were Chinese Filipino but the drinks were Italian. The best of all Marco Polo worlds. I proceeded to drink from every single half-filled aperitivo bottle I found on the trays. The Disaronno, the Campari, the Martini & Rossi. I washed it all down with the Pellegrino at my booth, then I had the Absolut and the Bacardi. Along with lumpia and pancit. By the time my plane was called, my face was flush like a gambler at Manila's floating casinos, except I kept on my straw hat, its black enormous brim flapping as if Alona Beach, the bull's-eye of the Rebosura family's reunion, were already in my sight, and who knows if I was rolling my handbag or slinging my suitcase, and I could not tell if the pleasurable sensation I had on the plane came from my single occupancy of a double compartment that relaxed into a full-length bed or the alcoholic welcome, this time sparkling, that they once again offered me as I collapsed onto my seat, noodle grease and pork bits gurgling up my gut, my chest, my throat.

They offered mixed drinks for dinner, and I ordered a Manhattan, but they had none, so I settled for a mango margarita, then I had another. I felt ill but also warm and fuzzy and comforted. *Comfort room*. I remembered as a child, when I had first arrived, and someone said, do you need the comfort room, and I thought that was the most civilized thing, Filipinos are so civilized, to have a comfort room in the house, and all these years I have carried that thought with me, though comfort turned out to be a toilet, not an indulgence but a need.

And in the First Class toilet I vomited out all the lumpia and pork siopao and the Disaronno and the Bacardi, and I was soothed.

In First Class, I was spoiled and cosseted and wakened and fed by men and women of excellent skin and stunning teeth who looked so happy at my grateful regard. One woman, named Girlie, from Leyte—Pastrana—a few towns away from mine, took down the names of my novels. She called me Ma'am Rosario Francisca Nemesia, only some of my names, since not all of them fit on my flight card, and she slipped in a platter of lechon, not paksiw, though it was not on this flight's menu card. My stomach was empty. It was ravenous. I asked her if they also had danggit. Budo-bulad and tsokolate? She laughed, oh, ma'am, you are homesick! We have fried bangus, she said. How deliberate was this illusion that I had constructed for myself, my barrier against arrival in a whoozy, first-class cocoon? Who was I fooling with these luxury accoutrements, the hat rack for my elephantine Jacquemus, the arena before me for stretching my feet, with space in a plush void for the wooden box, its sepulchral dome that shaped my handbag and my grief? I lay there dreaming in the security blanket money thinks it can buy, *Hot! Hot!* then *Cold! Cold!*, the blanket slipping and sliding and scratching and erasing. Mostly, I was drunk.

Of That Cold December

Of that cold December, Jote remembers—

Words are the devil.

It's all Marcelo the bastard's fault.

Or is it the scheme of Urbano, that geriatric?

Jote circles the narra trees in the vast garden of their house on Moret Street. It is the season of the narra's yellow flowers, and the smell of kalamansi—limonsito, the servants squirt it on everything, even the budo-bulad and the arroz caldo—and the kamia falling on his hammock and upon his palm: gingered petals the size of his thumb.

The birds are singing, maya, maya, maya.

He sits up in the hammock amid the narra trees and the flowers with ginger hearts.

He thinks, *tomorrow?*

But he cannot figure out the words.

Are they saying maya, or vaya?

Mamaya means later—tomorrow and tomorrow and tomorrow.

Vaya, at that time in his world, means go.

Or are they saying baya: leave it alone?

He's grown up translating his world, servants' tongue into sala's mouth, Waray and Tagalog into glimmering, correct spelling in Spanish onto the schoolbook page: a kind of magic, or witchcraft, he thinks, as words transform from one meaning to another and yet sound the same, mimicking the mind's process, the way the world shape-shifts as he observes it, his brother into a moth, the armored beetle, kagang, into a leaf, pahina.

And later everywhere he goes during the war, there are many other shapes and sounds. But always, in his ancestral Waray—in Sampaloc, in Samar, in Salogó—

—bayâ is a warning.

You better or else!

This is normal.

Slightest shifts in consonants produce inconsonant worlds.

Vowels, ditto.

He thinks nothing of it.

The way he sees his father, Don Francisco the First, the mournful widower, as smelly Dried Fish and cigar-smoker merchant, language codifies his double vision, or maybe triple, quintuple, and his grandmother Nemesia the Insomniac is a cow and a Terror plus a Manunulay and a ghost, and his brother Paco, The Nose, is a pest and a pet.

Only his mother Adina is one thing: dead.

He's late that morning in December because he's mixed up the date. Late for the breakfast of champorado—his little brother Paco, that glutton, gobbles up his chocolate portion and then his two thirds of a green mango (the wasteful kid never bothers with the third part, the seed) and his santol fruit, when cracked open it looks like a priest's pate with a bald spot, on its separate plate of salt— Jote does not have a sweet tooth but a sour one, he is late for his morning bath with the copper tabo and the silver orinola in the middle of the kasilyas—tabo, *dipper*, orinola, *chamber pot*, kasilyas, *the outhouse amid the mosses.*

He's late for the kalesa ride toward the Luneta, the half-moon park by the Bay with the golden sunset. He loves going to the Bay, with its shrimp smell on rocks and streaks of eternity on its gray, metallic sheen, and its sense of an inner life always about to break, a stirring on its waves' slow surface, and all along the Malecon, as he gazes at the Bay, young Jote feels a spirit about to appear—ghosts of Manila galleons, the fluttering arm of a creature, half-woman, half-dolphin, about to rise out of waves—but nothing ever comes of it.

But pieces of shit and water lilies.

The bright flames of gumamela and the sweet passing of kala-chuchi and the tang of kalamansi, that dream-like citrus affair, give him nostalgia he has no right to feel.

He's only thirteen.

Jote is tall and slouched, a gangly figure in linen shirts. Later he bears that scar that curves about his mouth, like a scimitar or a ladle, a thin dipper, an orange peel: a glister in the sun. He has a face as smooth as a girl's and the shock of hair of a child, *la cabeza cubierta de pelo!*, barely smoothed by Brilliantina—curly, unruly, sun-streaked sheaves of hair that jut out of his brow. Wild, infantile. He has the look of a baby encanto, a sleep-deprived Santo Niño—but he has no thoughts about that, too.

He barely looks in a mirror.

At Calle Nueva, before they can walk toward the Malecon, the perfumed flutter of women's fans stalls the brothers' passage as the family waits amid the Bagumbayan crowd.

—Puta!

When Jote looks down, it turns out the wet, rustling movement about his pants is only the sticky, chocolatey hand of that glutton, that Paco.

Praise be, it is not his body stirring in his pants!

Why is that baby even allowed out on this day? He should be at home practicing his alphabet, the way he likes to pretend he's literate, bending over Jote's schoolbook sheets that the boy Paco keeps wasting.

The boy's head is turned toward his brother in the crowd's crush, holding tight not to his notebook but to the crease by Jote's crotch.

His face is round, like a bead or the top of a pin.

Paco will bear that identical scar, shaped like a scimitar or a ladle, an orange peel or the dark side of a half moon, but not now.

Baga hin luwag, ayaw pagdad-a.

—Puta! Paco, what is it? What are you doing? Take your hands off me. You're disgusting.

—Papá has disappeared.

The ladies have moved on, and a hunchbacked, sad-faced midget holding up an umbrella and wearing his shirt untucked from his trousers, a kamisa, not a linen suit, blocks Jote's view.

Sure enough, Don Francisco the First has vanished.

Nowhere to be seen though many look like him—lumbering, mole-specked, unsmiling men of ambiguous race, in three-piece suits and Panama hats.

Jote looks down at him, an manghod, and puts his finger to his lips.

It's a familiar gesture.

Don't move, Paco, until I tell you!

That's what it means.

It's their game.

Paco grins.

—Close your eyes, Jote commands.

Obedient, Paco, still looking up toward his big brother, squeezes his eyelids shut.

Paco likes this game. He's good at it.

—Now, Mr. Nose—says Jote—can you smell him?

The boy smiles as he wiggles his nose up at Jote and twists his neck about.

Paco is famous in the house as the sniffer—

Nga iya Nariz.

With his eyes closed in that game, *An-iya-Irong!*, Paco can detect the chance of pork humba for dinner from the umber smell of molasses and peanuts in the basket just come in from market, and Ambrosio the cook asks the blindfolded boy to nose the queseo, that is, tell Binyang the traveling milkmaid—lechera ka!—that her carabao cheese is old old old—even a baby can tell with his eyes closed!

Looking down at the boy's blind face turning about to ferret their father's smell of vinegar, cigar smoke, and danggit, Jote pities the runt.

An manghod.

This baby, his brother.

Que un loco, nga iya irong.

But he also marvels at Paco—

How can you tell just by your nose, with your eyes shut and all?

And the boy looks pleased but puzzled at his brother's question.

By the colors of their smells, of course!

The answer is obvious, thinks Paco—the scent of garlic is a white dot, bluish as it vanishes, and the smell of good queseo is a blushing rose, like a cow's teat, or the shadow of his own just-bathed heel: lined and pink.

Hah, Jote says, not understanding this baby talk—

You cannot tell smells because of colors in your mind! That's a madman's way!

Ay loco!

Que locura!

Agi loko-loko!

Smells are either bitter or sweet, sharp or nada, says Jote.

And still he pats the kid on the head, that infant duwende, that pest, that Paco.

Jote pities him—his motherless brother.

Though it's the kid's fault that their mother is dead.

As he stares at Paco's closed eyes, Jote in revulsion, but no surprise, sees the boy turn briefly into a garden creature—a green-gray bug, a locust or cicada—a flash of a thorax and a hairy flutter of a leg, a blur of a wing briefly obscuring the little boy's expression as the huge bug face settles away from Jote to contemplate a patch of grass toward which to fly.

Then little Paco's puckered face blurs into its own self again.

His round face, like a bead or the top of a pin.

These alarming visual mutations are so common for Jote that in the next minute, all he can think is—

Boy, you make me sad.

Nga iya irong—

It's Paco's closed, trusting eyes that give Jote that rush of tenderness before the world changes.

As it should.

It isn't the kid's fault that Paco, only six, is already a loser, with his dumb innocence and freakish smell and his hunger—always eating up the leftover fruit, eating everything about the fish in the escabeche (except the eye: that was for Abuelita Nemesia—which is the cue that she might be Fujianese), happy not to waste any aspect of a meal, burnt rice or runny torta—and still the kid looks famished and mortal, skinny as a gecko in a drought, his spine visible down his back.

Paco's closed, trusting eyes are the last things Jote remembers before he witnesses—why does Jote look up, how does it happen?

Does he witness or does he wish?

At the simultaneous commotion, simultaneity being the mark of his unmade world, Jote cannot remember exactly how it happens that the speedy kutsero, too well dressed to be Tay Sequil, takes his brother's hand—his game-playing, eyes-closed-shut, sniffing-for-father runt of a greedy baby brother—and ambles along with small trusting Paco, whose eyes are still closed amid the crowd.

—Hhhhooooy!

Psssst! Psssst! Pssst!

Jote yells at the pair, but the previous angry hunchback blocks his path, his umbrella adding to the distraction, and the guardia civil (Urbano Lacuna! *requiescat in pace*) has turned—both men lose their focus—when they hear shouts again—

And again—somewhere else.

The simultaneity of the sounds scatters the attention of both citizens and police.

Ambling down Moret Street, Jote remembers—

Words are the devil.

Maya, maya, maya, he hears the birds say.

Vaya, vaya, vaya, says the hunchbacked man.

Does the man say *later* or do the birds say *go*?

Or does the man say—*baya*?

That is another sound, Tagalog.

It means—*leave it alone.*

Though in the servants' Waray—bayâ is a warning.

You better do it or else!

Words doubling up on him, garbling his brain, images transform. It's a curse. A head of a horse, chest of a human, clutching him at his throat with its hooves, magically switching not just shapes but sounds.

This soundshifting is a problem in such an oral country.

And if he could, he'd much rather sit up, slap his cheeks to see if he's wide awake, and consider—does the man mumble *later*, or does he say *walk on*, or does he mean *leave it alone?*

But he never has time to think about these things, to think about why words have several possibilities but his actions only a single effect.

Jote stalls in Bagumbayan.

On his long walk toward the tranvia down Moret.

He pauses—right there on the corner toward the tranvia stops, by the flame trees of his father's home, on Moret Street in Sampaloc— he remembers that day in December.

1896 in Bagumbayan.

He wants to go after his brother, nga iya nariz, that mad nose of a Paco—to protect him. But he cannot.

He stands still, bound in a spell before the hunchbacked dwarf.

The thing is, that moment of recognition, as he glares at the dwarf, pisses him off.

Is it—of all people—what the hell—Marcelo Badel?!

The hunchback, is that him, Jote glares—that comedy nerd—that bodabil misfit—the hunchback points his vaudeville umbrella at Jote, then the other man, the guardia civil, lunges.

—What are you doing? Leave me alone!—Jote says to the guardia civil.

Urbano Lacuna, *requiescat in pace!*

And so Jote gets the brunt of it—the fake-torturing batuta of Urbano Lacuna.

Requiescat in pace!

Pak! Pak!

Pak-Pak!

On his calf, neck, back, and elbow, rapid thrusts on all sides of his body, Jote expects the worst.

But each smack on his flesh falls with a soft swish, the sword raised high but the blade descending in delicate—

Tap.

Tap.

Tap.

Tap.

While elsewhere—*pandemonio.*

Rumbles and women's screams and the mix of perfume and saliva and sulfur sour the air in Bagumbayan.

While about his body he feels tender lashes and feathery swishes, and he closes his eyes to imminent violence, and he wonders at the duality of things.

Expecting brutality Jote feels gentleness.

Amid shouts, he hears a whisper.

"Vaya."

"Baya."

"Maya."

But in Marcelo's voice, so close to his ear, he encodes—

"Laya," whispers Marcelo Badel.

His fate: to mishear.

And on Moret Street, in 1908, he remembers his redemption, how he becomes a Son of the People, kidnapped by Urbano Lacuna—*requiescat in pace*—to meet with Ka Andres and Ka Vicente at Calle Anda, corner Arsobispado. Where is Urbano now? And that payaso, his friend, his bosom friend, Marcelo Badel, who acted out the part of Don Quasimodo of Notre Dame, for good reason, it turns out, and Jote will bring them, assholes and azkal, asong kalye of Calle Anda, into the dirt space of the house on Moret Street, when they scatter to the wind, the war not of their making—especially that boy, Marcelo Badel y Zorilla, his comrade from the Ateneo with dreams of his kalayaan.

Marcelo Badel's faulty appearance adds pathos to his scary radical pronouncements. He occurs, like the sweet kamia trace of a falling star, in Paco's mind.

He Stabilizes the World

Little Paco, a skinny kid with gray eyes (he has a gaze future voters will deem troubling and others will call troubled: his milk-gray iris), is keen friends with the cook Ambrosio, who serves him all the extra liempo and champorado and saging na saba and chorizo that cloud Paco's memory of that time with a sense of plenitude distinctly Filipino—he remembers war with his stomach, which makes everything else irrelevant.

Stabilizing the world in the way he knows.

His sensations are neither mystery nor oddity.

At least for him.

Of course, for him, his ways are the norm—I get it. Why would he not think everyone comes into the world with mixed-up senses, smells that have santol colors, a pee-ish blur, and that telekinesis of his feelings, the way that liquid touch from your father's sighs travels to your tummy: your wet burps smell of your Papá's tinapâ.

Plus—your misapprehensions of your brother's world.

His body, after all, is all he knows.

His mixed-up senses explain why there is always war.

How can humans operate in peace amid this maddening responsorial bounty—when everything in the world is a part of the body?

He trains himself to focus, to find a center—eating with his eyes closed, the way Mariano the mayordomo has taught him to focus in prayer.

Prayer, the pose of focused consciousness, is another anchor.

He begins each day's sensory possibilities by stuffing himself, closing his eyes, concentrating on breakfast, narrowing his body's scope.

He is saying amen, but in fact he is concentrating on flicking his tongue against a guava seed.

To stabilize.

So he explains on the pages.

Para mantener la solidez.

He is overacting when he eats, say the servants, watching the greedy boy slurping and swallowing and taste-testing with his eyes closed—but Ambrosio the cook forgives him.

He's a bad-luck baby.

One more ounce of pity does no kid any harm.

Here, boy—pakadi, kaon! Usa pa nga kaldo hin arroz caldo!

The older boy, the golden one, who looks like an encanto even as he goes off to Ateneo Municipal, the house's Santo Niño, a grown boy past *confirmación*—the boy Jote upsets the servants, who cross themselves—

At the house's descent into heresy.

Fires from mysterious street riots consume Manila—pomegranate fuses in the air—and servants listen to Tay Sequil—*El Cochero Exequiel!*—his stories of coño doom and radical prophecy.

Plots of rebellion.

Catechemical instruction.

At dinner parties in the walled enclave the embattled Spaniards of Intramuros cleave to their power, now tenuous as the dried grease on their hair.

Tay Sequil cackles.

Ay the kilabot among the katsila!

Their sense of impending destruction as they munch on their

churros at their fin de siècle—Manila is suddenly a treasure, a once tiresome jewel now about to be stolen from their clutches, and the old complaints of the city's natural calamities and its disastrous drain on the mother country's resources are replaced by this unfamiliar nostalgia. Their existential vacuum, a humid brew wafting from their coffee cups, dogs them especially at dusk and makes Manila Bay's sunset more surreal than usual and their diabetes more pronounced.

Tay Sequil stalks about, hands at his back, pantomiming katsilas' gripes as they stride along the Malecon.

Tay Sequil rounds up his tales.

Corpses rotting on the streets, dragged from the huts of Tondo, dumped on the garbage heaps of Sapang Palay, lying like bad dreams in the killing fields of Caloocan.

Paco listens, eating his igot.

Chomp, chomp, chomp, lick, lick, spit out the seed, splat!

His brother Jote's tirades are not original, copying the anticlerical rants of corner louts by Ateneo Municipal. Little Paco listens to Jote go on and on at dinner, before their over-indulgent Papá, whose only response is to reach out for one more finger-dip of hipon, the bagoong from Giporlos—at home the katsila has the proper appetite of the Samarnon. While little Paco, when dinner is done and the fruits are out, lays open on his lap the illustrated periodicals purloined from his brother's room and munches on green mangoes and guavas and igot, that smooth, dark fruit he caresses in his palm before he crunches, a crisp lump of flesh.

(Later in his old age he will discover his mortal tumor, and in private he will press it, a comforting sensation from his childhood, an igot, sitting in his breast, above the heart, where he also notes its harbinger—his single, fly-shaped mole.)

One day, Paco will grow up to be just like Jote, a student radical who protests first before thinking, so Mariano the mayordomo complains in the kitchen about the older boy—but in the meantime little Paco waits for the vendor of taho.

The dim memory of custard in the morning, announced by a

howl of wakefulness—*tahooooooooo*—the symphony of street vowels—*baluuuuut, lecheeeee, tahooooooo*—each with its own signature shade—are marks of the boy's ever-loyal Manila, daliri-colored, beige tint that pinkens—ribbon of melancholy from Sarastro's temple, some intermittently chico-hued, some the teardrop drip of *uvas*, magic flute, lavender-ish, rising out of dark—

The opera song of joy and sago!

The songs of the street emit the following rainbow in Paco's messed-up brain—

Greenish pallor in the sound *lecheeeee!*

And for *baluuuuut* and for *tahooooo*—translucent colors of a blue-gray weft-stain in the air.

The cool hues of the street's arias round out for Paco his time of war.

Like me, breakfast is Lolo Paco's favorite meal.

He does remember the time his brother comes home after school when the norteamericanos are already swarming the Luneta.

Paco is concerned about his merienda, some turon or caramel kamote, his daily snack at three o'clock.

Jote is whistling as he pulls off his pants.

—What's that song? little Paco asks.

—Nothing, says Jote.

And he keeps whistling his tune.

Paco is happy to see Jote happy.

—Sing it, says Paco.

—*Hot time! Old town!*

—Hah! That is English!

—*Hot town! Old time!*

—That is the language of the enemy.

—Marcelo taught it to me. His mom sings it at the bodabil!

—What does it mean?

—It's the americanos' national anthem. We whistle it when we pass by the sentries.

—What for?

—Ay gago! So they let us go out after curfew. To Calle Iris!

—Ha? What's at Calle Iris?

—Ay tanga! You are too young. It is the sweetest street in Sampaloc! We whistle it, and the americanos laugh to hear their anthem, then they let us go.

Hot town, old time, toniiiiigghht!

When Paco hears of the bombardment across the river, how is he to know it should mean anything?

Manila has been under siege for months, cannon shots mixing with *campanas*, the smell of gunpowder amid the house's kalachuchi trees, the smell lingering, a discordant dish, days-old hipon with biko—the way time elevates the staleness of bagoong, melded into sweet memory by the biko, and the overall sensation (to Paco's mind) is of a disappearing-mauve gleam with hints of kastanyas—a tannish, chestnut drizzle amid plumeria—and Paco waits with patience, observing the sweat on Ambrosio's brows as he keeps stirring stirring stirring stirring the tsokolate tabléa into the pot of sticky rice—choco-la-te-*eh!*

Actually, bagoong and biko do not really mix.

But the sweat from Ambrosio's brow etches translucent pools in the sticky chocolate rice and thickens thickens thickens it.

The boy Paco watches Ambrosio's sweat pour into the biko—drip drip drip drip.

A response in his fingertips—sensation from Ambrosio's brow to little Paco's sico (elbow) and his camat (hand) down to his dudlo (fingers)—a monsoon feeling, humid, warm, electric, as of lightning—

A singe.

His feelings watching servants sweat are too much for him.

He gobbles everything up.

This new war with the allies, the kanô who have come to rescue the country from his father's other amigos, the coños, is just the detritus of mixed-up meals reheated too often, bahaw nga kan-on!—staying on and on though their time has passed.

In Paco's memory the kamia flowers have a weird waft after the war.

Bagan salitre nga nasuoyan.

Smell of saltpeter washed in the vinegar of fish paksiw.

Why should he think the sounds of gunfire in Santa Mesa, blasts like snores across the Pasig, are a novelty, since from May to December in the year 1898 the city has been in daily distracted terror?

Every day is a jumble of news—since May Day and the exciting battle at the Bay—

And the arrival of Commodore George Dewey of the norteamericanos—at first he thought the newcomers were friends—

Though his Papá calls it, our idiot ones, but no one tells the boy why.

Commodore George Dewey the kanô, or just the other coño, comes sailing in (Tay Sequil says a whole army of Filipino soldiers, costumed to the hilt, arrives with the americanos, in rayadillo blues and white drill, standing erect on the ship like toy soldiers, but Tay Sequil likes his stories with flash, says Mana Felicisima the labandera, and that's why she loves him)—on May Day Eve, of all days.

May Day is an omen of split apparitions.

It's no wonder the city erupts in sulfur sparks.

Gunfire like a celebration baptizes the new, not-Catholic, yet still somewhat clerical boulevard—formerly Cavite Road, soon to be Dewey Boulevard—but at the time his Papá and his friends are still joking at dinner about the foolishness of the foreigners.

But why?

Kay why, bakit, ¿por qué?

The boy takes another helping of escabeche.

The yanqui gringos do not know that the Spanish ships in Manila Bay are full of encantados, not soldados.

Fiend or foe?

Coño or kanô?

Which is the unlucky thing—to turn over the denuded fish or to break off the bones to get at the soft flesh under?

He contemplates the fishy endoskeleton, his appetite's remains.

In honor of the dead Abuelita, no one touches its eye.

In the kitchen, servants cross their hearts and kiss their scapulars, smelling on their fingers the last of the esteemed fish.

May Day is the day of mystics—if you look in the mirror on May Day Eve, so says Mana Felicisima the labandera, every year she tells the boy Paco, her finger to her lips—you will see—in the mirror—

Either/

Or!

Satanas—

Or your bride!

Look in the mirror ha katutnga han gab-i—you will see One—if not—the Other!

Bayâ!

In Waray, that means a warning.

But on May Day, it's only the norteamericanos who appear.

Fiend or foe?

Coño or kanô?

Satanas? Or bride?

Which is the unlucky thing?

His father Don Francisco the First snorts at the new men who come sailing in, countrymen of his faithful customers, Señor Billy Krag and Mister Ernest Jorgenson—those *estúpido* amigos who have no idea they are shelling ghosts, not soldiers.

The servants shake their heads listening to Tay Sequil, *El Excellent Cochero Exequiel!* (in his American-era taxi ads), he is all three of the annoying Wise Men, melchor gaspar AND balthazar!, with his first-hand news from all parts of the city, being a driver, and he describes the scene of the desperado Spaniards swimming to their arsenal in Cavite, splashing in the water, out of their minds.

Hesusmariosep! says Felicisima, the washerwoman from barrio San Roque—*pray for them, the coños!*

What is to become of the world when even the parish priests from the other place, España, are hiding, with their silver crosses and their candlesticks, and all the heretics are now the heroes?

And the rebelde have returned.

Mariano the mayordomo crosses himself: *Santo Niño, bendisyoni kami!*

Ave Maria! says Mana Felcisima.

Ave de rapiña, says Ambrosio the cook.

The boy stares at him in surprise.

He writes down the witty psalm.

Hah!

Tay Sequil laughs—one day the revolution will come, Aning, and you will be sorry to be such a banal man!

Do not mix up those words.

Tay Sequil, saying *banal,* means *holy,* not hard.

He's Tagalog.

So little Paco writes, and Tay Sequil laughs, ha ha ha.

Most important to Paco, school is disrupted. On top of that are the June monsoons, also a pleasure, the way storms from the bay make liquid out of stiff mosses and vegetation along the esteros, and the weather as usual transforms frogs and lily pads into flat impressions in the kasilyas, the outdoor toilet.

In short, the typhoon of these norteamericanos, the other coño, thrills the boy.

It's like when the circus comes to town, settling by the racetrack in Santa Ana, and he appreciates the diseased and ill-conceived animals, the stunted giraffes and mangy zebras and pathetic lions (the golden sound of the distressed lions, with their dried-up scabs and pitiful alopecia where their manes should be, suddenly roaring—a deep wounding sound—as he passes their cages, suffuses him with melancholy as he goes). It's the most depressing matter to the little boy Paco—the tragedy of the animals in the zoos and the circuses during Carnival. And yet he stares at them, stares at the lions, and the growling memory of their rending sounds echoes in his limbs as he returns home, the way misery eats him up, and he feels the scabs of the lion on his sico and the mange of the giraffes all about his knees—

Hayop-ha-tuhod.

This thrilling time of the americanos is like the February time of the circuses, he thinks, when the city announces the coming carnivalesque joy though all kids get is horror and yet they still pay for their tokens, with hope—though now it is weeks after the animals' arrival, and their pitiful appearance at Carnival, before the Lenten season, now bears no trace in the racetrack mud of Santa Ana.

What will it be like, he thinks as he listens to the sermons in church, to which Mariano the mayordomo still takes him every day, singing *paternosterquiesincaelis*, Mariano takes him to church come war or shine, rain or revolution—what if Noah and his ark land, stranded in the Pasig? Where would Noah and Shem and Ham and all the animals shit? Maybe out by Sapang Palay or in Abuelita's old Bulacan lands where she used to take him to count her cows—or in the swamps of San Pedro Macati. He imagines the garden of Gethsemane full of gulay—ampalaya, kangkong, okra, malunggay, kondol, patola, pechay, mongo, and sitaw. Which vegetable did Jesus hate most? Okra, he is sure. He loves best those stories during Mass when endings are not known, left to his invention (what does Delilah do with Samson's locks of hair? does she keep his curly gray hairs in a locket, about her neck near her rosary, like Mana Felicisima, Tay Sequil's holy girl? when Lot's wife turns into a pillar of salt, how long does it take her to melt? Is Lot's wife in the appetizer, his favorite, crisp and salted danggit, and if he licks the tail of danggit, will he be blessed or will he be cursed? Such transmutations distress no Catholic, and the figure he sees multiplying fish and loaves in the Blessed Sermon on the Mountain can only be—no, no, not his lazy bum Papá—but Mariano the mayordomo, of course, who makes all meals possible, now that his lola, Abuelita Nemesia, is dead—in her sleep just before the war, *r.i.p.*, and still no one will ever know where she is from).

Emotions in all directions wreck Paco—

His body is a vessel, his mind a mess.

The fear of the servants, the excitement of the servants, the scorn of the servants for the cowardice of other servants, the glee of the servants, the lust of the servants, the curiosity of the servants—he feels all of their emotions stuffed into his sensitive cavities—lungs and gums and nasal holes—during the time of the arrival of the norteamericanos—anxiety touches his skin, on chirei (kiray: eyebrow), botchen (butkon: arm), paha (paa: thigh), licud (likod: back), sico (elbow), tuhud (knee), camat (kamot: hand), dudlo (tudlo: fingers), liogh (li-ug: throat), utin (penis).

Upon his dilla (tongue).

Playing on his body like jangled piano keys of the invaders' songs. *Hot time, old town, toniiiiiight!*

In all the colors of the rainbow he hears it—the war—red orange yellow green blue *indio* violet.

Such is the state of Paco's stupor.

May to December.

So when one more rat-a-tat, gunpowder and lightning, this time across the moat, at Santa Mesa, then Pandacan, becomes news (his thrilled, tired body sleeps through it), how is he to know that his brother's empty bedroom, with its surprising, hidden paraphernalia, eyes and pyramids and suns, is collateral?, and instead of excitement Paco stares with dread, this sticky feeling, like the strings of unripe saging na saba that get caught in his throat, brownish and burning, clinging to it in a way that, for a moment, no amount of intervention, such as time, his speechless helper, can soothe.

He stares at his brother's room.

Suns atop pyramids, suns within suns, suns amid eyes. Pharaoh eyes, lion eyes, chimerical-goat-god, polyphemic eyes. And too many drawings of squares with compasses, masonic tools, the mark of a fetish.

The little boy Paco sits in his brother's abandoned room, piecing together this puzzle of sketches, scattered, fantastical pyramids of yellow suns, black suns, white stars, and dark eyes.

The empty bed, the illustrated magazines, the aparador reflecting back to little Paco only his fat, round face.

Like a bead, or the top of a pin.

The scene of abandonment: Jote's indigo room.

Stinking of smelly linen.

Paco tries to swallow the strings of saba in his throat.

He can't.

They're like a striped curse down his gut.

And when he hears the news from the servants, should he have put two and two together?

"*Haaaalt!*" say the American sentries in Santa Mesa to the two whistling boys after curfew—say the servants.

News affirms what rumors know.

"*Ha-a-alto,*" say the two Filipino boys in the night.

So the servants report.

Was it *Ho-o-ot Ni-ight?*

Or was it *H-o-o-old Time?*

Gossip is garbled.

The norteamericanos do not like being laughed at, Mariano the mayordomo intones, especially since they are the ones who have the guns.

Those Kragorgonsilyos, bah, says Tay Sequil—the anting-anting will get them.

Tay Sequil mocks Mariano—don't you worry, Aning—those bloody kanô will get theirs, and so will you! *Bayâ!* You better watch out—!

Again!, Tay Sequil says, rethinking his point—the revolution has begun *again*!

The norteamericanos shoot at the two whistling Filipino boys who do not obey their orders, say the reports in the Philippine news.

In the American news, Filipinos with guns attack the sentry, Private William Grayson, the American Hero of Santa Mesa, at Blockhouse Seven along Santol Street, while all the Filipino field officers, Urbano Lacuna, Manuel Noriel, Luciano San Miguel, are off in a meeting with their presidente, Don Emilio, in Malolos—

Private Grayson, the Coward of Santa Mesa, shoots.

The war begins on a signal from two boys—

Whistling their song in the dark.

Hot time in the old town tonight.

But why would the Filipinos begin a war in Santa Mesa—when their own field officers are in Malolos with the presidente?!?!

Tay Sequil shakes his head.

Tonto. Uwat. Gago. Nga panulay. Idiot. Padla nga istorya—what a dumb story.

Says Mariano the mayordomo, to little Paco's surprise: after all, he's a mild-mannered man of prayer.

And so the war against the Americans begins.

In Order

They're not even in order, these papers. It was not the Disaronno rearranging them, a mewling in my head that messed up time. The diarist cuts up the incident of the missed abduction of the novelist-hero in Bagumbayan (1896) with the disjunct moment a dozen years later (1908) of Jote on Moret Street *(so who is the diarist?)* walking to a tranvia stop, on the way to Padre Faura, and then somehow the war against the Americans (1899-1913) gets in the mix. In between—like shards, like splinters—are, how can I say it, notions of troops going northward, up coastal La Union against the North Philippine Sea, then inland up and down the Ilocos, but then a trip on a boat, the USAT *Liscum*, and history tells us it is back to 1901. Moving eastward by water and circular by time. And by then I know where it's going.

I know the final landscape like my palm's rhomboid lines, the slant veins on my arm, this throb.

But all I do in First Class was think of my uncle's words.

You know, ever since she was nineteen.

For how long as a child I've kept this feeling in me that a world out there, like a splinter, a shard, a keloid scar of a wound in me whose origin I do not remember, ini nga samad nga waray tikang waray tapos, has betrayed a mother's love. I cannot explain my feeling, sitting there by the airplane's window waiting for a glimpse of land. I do not know where that feeling comes from, whose words or what seeds, I have no cause or doubt to accept it, but there's a lump in me, looking out the window as glandular islands come into view—*an architectpelago! a systempsychosis!*—an imminent mass I do not wish to caress.

I have, after all, been carrying this trace, a crisscross of words through the years, I can flick at it with my Miu-Miu mules, here on the first-class Philippine Airlines carpet, its deep-navy shag against yellow suns: I can tap at it—the way I tap at this wooden box.

I am an anomalous creature with a bad sense of proportion dispensed not only by Italian bitters. I see my country from the clouds, and I don't know why, when alongside disarming beauty, the way the islands hang like droplets from some invisible eye, or semiprecious stones that are not really semi, just precious, one cat's eye, another jade, another emerald, pearl, I feel a weakness in my head, I weep. Not for it, not for the country that hangs in the ether like unsprung jewels from some divinity's long, slow fall, but because I am going home to my mother's casket, and how can one bury what one has not known.

Ave de Rapiña

The description in the journal is a terse tricolon, a run-on in Spanish, ordinary in that tongue: *I threw up, he liked the way I could recite the litany, he asked me to be his servant.*

Pages follow with a list of Latin names of the Virgin, in a school-boy's hand, as if he were writing down lessons during a blackout in Salogó, including the additions of Ambrosio the cook.

Mater Inviolata—ora pro nobis!
Virgo Fidelis—ora pro nobis!

Speculum Justitiae—ora pro nobis!
Ave Maria—
Ave de rapiña!

So the boy tacks.

The captain hears a band strike—a roundel with drums—and the captain shrugs his shoulders—

Even at West Point, he despises the ranks of them, the buglers.

As he rides the *Indiana* through Honolulu to Yokohama, he cannot put his finger to his discontent. Is it the hermetic gist, with unknown words like *bolomen* stuck in the lyrics? Is it the word *dopey*, a term that offends him, an officer and a gentleman? Yet it reminds him of the nobility of his enterprise, its rousing chorus gives him an erection, a stirring, and his loins in heat—

Underneath the starry flag
Civilize 'em with a Krag
And return us to our own beloved homes—
Huzzah.

Trained to kill Apaches and Lakota in the Dakotas and Oklahoma, his men are also prepared for such incivilities as the Pullman riots—but not for supernatural powers who do not believe they will die, terrorizing them in Santa Mesa, in Pandacan, in Baler, dressed only in holy phylactery, not even in slippers, and his superiors in Manila are senile buffoons resurrected for action after long-gone days in the Civil War, and this measly enterprise is improvised carnage left for God-fearing men like him, Waller, to redeem.

That paper-pushing agoraphobic Elwell Otis, managing the country in his bathrobe from Malacañang. Instead of being greeted as liberators, as Otis said, here they come upon their glory in this nasty war, and not the splendid one like the feats in Cuba, which Captain Waller looked forward to but missed.

He got dysentery before he could glimpse San Juan Hill and spent his days of the Spanish war vomiting out his guts in a latrine by Guantanamo Bay.

He hates the memory of Cuba. It smells of shit and Epsom salts.

And this war God got him into against shoeless men in ragged clothes gained second hand from the Spanish dead, with homemade weapons and a courage one would call devotion if not for the terror of their falling, fallen bodies—what kind of a grand victory is it to slaughter men doomed by a demonic goddess, their eerie Siren—

Kaaalaaaaya-haaan!

The fiends respond to the word like a talisman—some evil spell.

His men snatch the amulets from their necks, they divest their bodies of linen handkerchiefs and their curved swords, which turn out to be kitchen knives, and even he, against his good reason, takes a coin.

A totemic eye upon gules—blood-red against a hieroglyph.

Sometimes, feeling the eye-shaped token in his pocket, Waller feels the heat through his kersey shirt, burning up his chest. It's a sin to believe in their heathen curses, but who knows what bad luck it is to throw away their evil eye.

And so he keeps the coin, a spark by his heart.

His experience in Pandacan, when the Filipino troops rush against the Krags and mortars, yelling *kaaalaaya-haan!* (Waller looks up the sound, what was it that he had heard?), gives him this premonition, warm by his chest, of an unrewarding enterprise on this godforsaken island that, still, he will crow home about, with his souvenir enclosed.

The word is a slogan they have made up, like their country.

Kalayaan—as if the heavens had given them a password, and they run in throngs and thrones and virtues and dominations, with their machetes straight toward his bullets, and he shoulders his weapon at his moment of glory, shooting shooting shooting with his Krag, the thin blue smoke giving away his line, and the lunging, sweating, shrieking, warm body that wields a knife comes at him. *Mine eyes have seen*—really, Pandacan is not a battle but a dream, in which his enemy falls like magic, locusts raining down the trenches and ravines, running running running toward gunfire with cries and open arms, toward their hallucination, kalayaan.

His men, always on the lookout for booty, this war is not a battle but a bazaar, keep pocketing the odd objects from their bodies—paper icons wrapped in straw, the size of lozenges, embellished with drawings of suns and eyes, tied with string around their throats, and he turns away.

Anting-anting.

The newspapers thrill to the native color.

It's pathetic, this one-sided war, but still it will be nice to return home the victor with their spoils—

Damn damn damn the insurrectos.

But look at his own men—the men of Company C, straggling down the *Liscum*'s gangplank with their pup tents and meager supplies, dressed in the woolen grays of their Chinese glory, despite their time of reprieve and rest in Manila—appearing for all the world like phantoms, not soldiers.

Their damp, shriveled winter clothes are unfit for the swelter of the tropics, and the louts abandon themselves to their underwear whenever they can.

Undisciplined beasts.

Waller can predict which of these animals will go nuts, just from the heat. He'd bet on that beady-eyed boy with a wasted face, his sunken eyes and skeletal brow as broad as a gravedigger's spade, Lieutenant Edward Avery Bumpus, gun-happy alcoholic from Boston—passing right by him without a word or salute, with his own stooped, sleep-walking private, that loopy Trapp, to carry his books. Gutless Boston Brahmin. Harvard man. He won't be able to take the heat. Bumpus has the mottled, neurasthenic look of some stricken ex-Adonis, long johns peeking through his pants.

An officer and a disgrace.

But Bumpus passes him by. He, Waller, is not even a shred, not a speck in his sight.

After his last battle, amid the red-lacquered dragons of Kublai

Khan, not quite as restful as the poet of opiates describes it, a tremens during which all he can feel is a freezing of his spirit, which turns out to be malaria, soothed only by burning pipes in dark Oriental dens— Bumpus has had this odd feeling.

That the world is apocryphal.

The existence of these floating islands is a fraud that only he surmises.

It's a pleasant enough deception, he thinks, as he watches the islands drift in the moonlight while the *Liscum* leaves the bay, trailing a fantastical sunset, through which some melody runs a finger of song felt only by him, somewhere by his nape, or ringing by his amygdala, or is it the cerebellum?

What a fine state his professors will find him in when he comes back from the wars, incapable of figuring out his sphincter from a Sphinx!

He starts giggling.

The loyal chap Trapp, his henchman, grins at him as his shoulders shake.

And the glittering, ghostly cordage of the archipelago that appears then disappears in strips, like the weave of a hallucinatory noose, a drunken designer's rope, the sun blinking upon sea—captured Palawan and pacified Capiz and ill-fated Cebu and subdued Iloilo—all of it an unlikely, though artful, construction, reaching out to him its dangerous whorl; and certainly one can bear the illusion of these isles, Bumpus thinks, looking at the women who have come to greet the soldiers on the riverbank—bright-eyed in gossamer clothes, waving banners of welcome, as a brass band plays yet one more tune from home—

We're gonna have a hot time in the old town toniiiight!

It is the white man's anthem. They pander the gods with their foreign man's songs. They think the islands are real. But this conspiracy—the palm leaves, the sky, the buzz of gold-beaten dragonflies, the smell of clamshells, the sun—the reality of the Philippines is a story told by a liar, a self-deceiver, the point of which one day it will be up to him to crack—

But he must not crack first!

And at this, Bumpus brings up his hands, one to each cheek, as if to keep his face in place.

Sir, there's a tower of fire in me
Binding me with terrible strength
The whole of my mortal length
And splitting brave the skull's empery

He whimpers and whispers as he walks, cupping his freezing hands.

And Waller, looking at the familiar gesture of his hands, makes a move as if to touch him.

Sergeant Frank Breton spits as he watches Bumpus go.

If it weren't for his connections, Bumpus would be no officer, Breton thinks, but the army, the sergeant knows, is no place for democracy.

Frank Breton is hoping to see a shipment of summer cottons in this cargo hold. Plus, the troops' mail, long overdue, missing its target on the way from Tongku to Okinawa and Manila. But all the extra cargo they get is this cowering kid with a weak stomach and deep-set eyes so gray Breton thinks the stowaway might be blind as well as delinquent.

The captain, as usual, tries his Spanish on for size, even on this pint.

Sergeant Frank Breton is an efficient man with no time even for toadying. At the captain's side through dinners and walks along the *Liscum*'s deck, Breton bottles up his scorn for dumb table talk, as if these officers are buttering up some absent ladies instead of war-tested hounds who have stared at maggots crawling through crotches and shot them shot them shot them, shooting at everything they find amid the trenches, anything that looks alive. Such is the tale of

Harvard boy Bumpus, trigger-happy in Badoc, how this mama's boy lost his mind when the amigos turn out to be the opposite, enemigos, and he shoots women and children and carabaos and cows in his round of dumb glory.

Harvard boy.

In retreat from the forces of the warrior priest, that ecstatic Aglipay, so the papers call him, who go after them, what a surprise, in their northern campaign as they burn up the villages and the children and the pigs and the goats, and the women scorch under the sun, like so much tinder in a woodpile in New England—Bumpus sees woman after woman coming to get him.

Unarmed—except for their rosaries and their charms, their voices, their song, their anting-anting, and their cry.

Any veteran could have surmised the women's function.

Women warriors rising from harrowed fields in bright-colored kamisa, baskets of rice cakes on their heads, balancing their ceramic jars, hands up as if ready to dance their lantern dance, their heads held high, bearers of bad tidings and flickering light, advance toward them, the infantry companies on the war fields of Badoc, while Bumpus's men, the veterans, know that behind them are the enemigos waiting in shallow trenches amid handmade bamboo snares—ready with their knives when fools like Bumpus fall in.

No need to carry on like that.

Let the women advance—their souls' bait—until they are near enough to shoot.

Bearing his rifle like an orphan child on his shoulder, that Harvard boy, that boy-man Bumpus retreats sideways, a weeping crab of a soldier, all the while singing—

Or was it that he was howling, as the reports said, howling fit to tie up the moon—

Hot time, old time, toniiiight!

And he shoots them shoots them shoots them prematurely: the unarmed women who scatter in the Battle of Badoc.

Harvard boy Bumpus's soldiers, veterans in the lands of the Sioux, in China among the Boxers, try to catch the crab their lieutenant as he scampers sidelong, his dizzy exoskeleton, his Krag, civilizing in a blaze of muddy glory.

For Breton, it's no surprise, but even Lieutenant Colonel Foote, Bumpus's boon companion, from their days of training in New York, does not save Harvard boy from disgrace.

He spends time at San Lazaro, he loses his command.

He recovers his mind.

So his medical papers say.

Breton doubts.

But as the boat sails on, past the menacing islands of insurrection—Mindoro, Romblon, Panay—Breton's guard relaxes. Their new commander, this buffoon Waller, it turns out, is just one more straw man for McKinley—bloodthirsty like the rest.

Good.

The man learned Spanish for his useless stint in Cuba, and Waller keeps wishing aloud that this land were the other, disappointed that not too many indulge his fancy. What a pity, he says to Breton as a humped deformity of an island, which turns out to be their destination, comes into view, that the people here never learned to speak their conqueror's language, unlike the Cubans.

Breton says, Yes, sir, it is unfortunate that they have been stubborn enough to keep their own tongues.

The captain has no wit for sarcasm.

—They keep it, you know, the captain says—as if it's a weapon.

When the boy answers with the correct Castilian lisp and grade-school phrases that Waller recognizes from his own grammar lessons, the captain is pleased. When the boy calls upon the names of Mary in Latin, Waller is moved.

> *Gra-a-a-a-tia ple-e-e-e-e-naaaaa!*
> *Dominus tecum!*

And the captain responds—

Benedicta tu in mulieribus,
Et benedictus,
Benedictus fructus ventris tui…
Ave Maria!

Ave de rapiña, answers the boy.

Captain Waller has come from America to civilize the savages but, what a coincidence!, they share his medieval tongue.

—Goddamn, thinks Breton, keeping his wisdom to himself.

The populace, with its swaying marching band in slippers, that has greeted Company C is not as auspicious, and Waller lists the improvements to make.

The captain says—I need a servant.

The captain's speedy appointment in the wake of Bumpus's disaster has left Waller no time to gather all his effects.

Looking down at the trembling, Latin-singing boy, the captain declares—

—This stowaway will do.

In any case, the boy reminds him of a cat he once had in Yorktown—a gloomy but affecting runt, with a deceptive look of reproach in its sunken gray eyes that always got it more milk than it deserved.

Toward the Monsoon Glare

I never reunited with the family Rebosura. I missed them. I saw flashes of teal and hoards of taped and shuddering boxes, rumblings of my convergence with the universe from which First Class had cut my cords. The umbilicus of my homecoming was that bloodless stream of cardboard boxes, anxious addresses repeated in bold signage, at the baggage carousel at NAIA 3. I stood by the carousel waiting. But I forgot that I had brought nothing with me to convey.

I rolled my suitcase toward the monsoon glare.

Through glass doors, looking off toward the alphabetical tiers of passengers waiting under letters of their names, I realized I forgot where I was supposed to go. Tio Nemor had sent me a message. I tried to remember. My phone was locked. Who knows where it was. I hated my phone anyway. My lack of cargo also nonplussed the customs people, it was the trope of my return, but they let me go free with only one joke about Hershey's Kisses, and one boy looked at me as if in pity, did I look deported?, a balikbayan whose luckless *galabanting!* has come to a sad end? I felt his borrowed embarrassment. I was a curse upon their expectation of their countryman's fortunes, no matter how null the relation. The baggage men and taxi hucksters, too, took a step back instead of forward as I emerged from the doors. A whole swath of people falling away instead of calling out to me—for a ride, a show of generosity in a cup, a place to stay.

There is a dark, evil spell around a woman with only one suitcase, waray bagahe kawaray upay, coming home with nothing nothing nothing, early in the morning from the nonstop JFK flight at Terminal 3 of Ninoy Aquino International Airport.

Without pasalubong: a pariah.

But then I glanced at the glass portals reflecting the impression the country had of its arrivals.

I looked back at myself.

All in black.

My black long-sleeved Balenciaga (six years old from Century 21), my black Marc Jacobs faux-pajamas (bought at Owings Mills outlet store, the only tourist spot my aunt brought me to on a visit to Baltimore) that I never match with its blazer because I hate matching but still I bought the whole suit, my dark glasses with their black "handmade in Italy" weave that echoed the pattern of my snakeskin mules, my dark hat with its enormous straw brim. I looked like the witch in that wizard fantasy about returning home to the American Midwest that no Filipino bothers trying to understand. In New York I'd look trite. And in the city, actually I wear color.

At the airport, I had the aura of the recently bereaved.

There is no sign for loss in New York, no mourning armband that anyone would notice—whereas at home kin wear black bands for months, just to let strangers know, *I am grieving, touch-me-not*, we pray novenas for nine days every year for nine years, the length of time it took Odysseus to come home—and on the day I learned of my mother's death, the noise of the indifferent bars along Bleecker Street committed its ordinary cruelty.

Whereas the mongering small-time men here at NAIA 3, all of them wanting only to make their daily wages, offered me this atmospheric stage, a respectful space that I had missed elsewhere—the tardy nod to my sorrow is their invisible cordon acknowledging grief—stepping back from me in my symbolic black clothes and dark glasses, as if here, finally, it was understood.

There is a void that no amount of luxury accommodations can fill.

And I wasn't even thinking when I put on my black clothes.

At the shaded alphabetical posts, I held on to my hat's awkward brim, trying to remember Tio Nemor's instructions. Was I to stand under the initial of my first name or my last? And sure enough, once I walked beyond the security guards of the international airport, cargo men and cab drivers began saying *psst psst taxi taxi—hoy Miss! Mamser ma'am mamser*—their jumbled comprehension of gender and no sign of respect for black outfits. I was sweltering in my wrong clothing, polyester and long sleeves and too-long pants. This is why in the Philippines you do not wear black except to declare you have a burden. The lady next to me, wearing a different family reunion shirt, colored bright marigold, with the map of her pride centered this time on Kalibo, Aklan (drawn also on her fan), shared her nice breeze with me, scrupulously waving her heart-shaped fan in my direction, and I could also see Boracay's cartoonish white sand on its flipside, airing me all across my black-clad length.

"I'm sorry," she said.

"Thank you," I said, as if I understood.

Homecoming people are also really nosy.

"Funeral?" she asked.

In my family, that's the joke if you wear black.

I nodded.

"Condolence," she said, and she kept smiling and staring at me, not saying another word, vigorously fanning me all the time she waited, sharing our alphabetical initial as I imagined we did, and all the marigold Kalibo blooms got into their extra-long jeepney with its festooned Jesus and plastic water bottle of Our Lady of Lourdes (I recognized her blue sash from my childhood) dangling from its dashboard—and the entire De Leon marigold Aklanon family waved at me as if their empathy amid the joy of their return would make it all go away.

And you know, in some situations, it could.

It turns out I was under the wrong alphabet. I was under my mom's name. What was I thinking? I walked over to the right post, and there she was.

Of all people, Tio Nemor had sent his ex-wife, my aunt Doctor Tita Tita, now of Roland Park in Baltimore, to pick me up.

I was ashamed.

I had taken so long to decide to return, and here was Tita Tita—*she's only an in-law!*—come all the way from Baltimore for my mother's funeral. I vaguely recognized her driver, but my memory, I admit, was blurry, and I just nodded, bowing my head at him as he took my meager balikbayan spoils—the bag, the hat, the suitcase.

I hugged my aunt.

Doctor Tita Tita had never recovered her youthful plumpness, her glowing cheeks. Every so often, I visited her in Baltimore. Ingrid Bergman, Ingrid Bergman. Overnight her hair had turned gray. She dyed it now, but I mourned her old radiance. On the other hand, her face had angular planes that haunted you, like a Modigliani or a Klimt, its lengthened hollows and trace of pain, the trembling down-turn of her lips like a careful portrait of sorrow.

"I didn't expect you would be my ride," I said.

Her sunken eyes, whose shape you instantly forgot, taking away only your impression of abyss, a dark star, were set against her wide, high cheeks, so tightly molded against the bone that you could see it, her death-mask, beneath her cheeks' rouge.

She was still Filipino, after all—of course Tita Tita, on her journey to America, did not leave her cosmetics behind, her desire to sculpt her fate.

"Welcome home, inday—anytime, anytime, I will pick you up, I said to your uncle!"

And for a second, as she laughed and kissed me on both cheeks, genuinely happy to see me, my face wet from her lipstick, I could envision the aunt I had known as a child.

She got back into her car, and I climbed in.

The first time I visited her in Baltimore when she wrote me to see her—*even though I have left your uncle, we're still family,* she said (this was in the days of stamped mail)—what pained me most was not her different lifestyle or look (a studio in a drab block, on a secular street called Saint Paul, her self-dyed, clearly unstyled, homemade hair). What pained me was that we pretended, on top of our discomfort with the changes, that nothing had changed. My aunt, a neurosurgeon who had headed her department in Cebu, designing her opulent house of stone and marble in Danao, was a changer of bedpans for geriatric white people in a decrepit old folks' home owned by in-laws in Maryland whose nursing educations she had helped finance.

Because she could not live with a world that had killed her son.

The way brown lives prop up the diseased and dying around the globe, tender shadows in death rooms the world over and dim corridors, flattens our understanding, disables us from fathoming them, the choices they have made, and their desire. She used to have jet-black hair teased up so that the tendrils made a halo, with flips of hair framing her on both sides, like apostrophes. Ingrid Bergman, Ingrid Bergman. She had the cheekbones. She had laughed when I told her she smelled like the Hanging Gardens of Babylon of King Nebuchadnezzar. It's just *Aliage*, she had said. I remembered that gesture, how she braced me with something of her own to grasp. She still wore *Aliage*, a scent I recognized but couldn't name when she hugged me, and the last time I visited, she was proud of her new castle, her home in Roland Park.

I met the man, a robust Bawl'mor'an with the twang of his town though he had spent years away, an engineer in Brazil or Mozambique, and his time in Lusophone states that never understood him gave him, I thought, his humble yet worldly, kind of sheep-like vibe (it was his easy-to-blush pink face and his hair, I thought—his gray hair curled tightly around his broad skull like a lamb's). I liked him instantly. He had returned to his childhood home to comfort his father in his last days, and I gave Mack Richards credit that he saw in his dad's caregiver not my aunt's ghost face but a womanhood she had forgotten. On top of that, his dad, a doctor like Tita Tita, died a good death with a Filipino neurosurgeon bathing his testicles and translating for his son the slur of the father's words, including, as she fed the disordered man his mash, where in the brain such incognition comes.

But Tita Tita just called the grown engineer An Anak, the child, the son, so she introduced or named him whenever she had to name Mack Richards at all, as if they were no more to each other than a promissory note to a dead man. I'm a naïve person when it comes to my family, and in Roland Park I believed she had been given charge of the dead man's home in his will, and his son, An Anak, was around to tie up loose ends. But the way he lit up when she came into the room or told me with candor when once she went out—to water the roses or pick parsley from the front-porch pots—how much he admired her, something about her inner strength, plus she's such a good dancer! have you seen her dance? et cetera et cetera! This man's desire made me sad until I visited her again many years later, and my aunt still called him An Anak when she introduced him: he was still around, so glad to meet her relatives, long time no see.

I never understood the scandal of Doctor Tita Tita's marriage to another man in America, so secret and shameful she pretended for so long, even to me. I understood Putt-putt's sadness, and that is between his mother and him. But the response of rational grown-ups in Manila to the overseas marriage of a divorced woman made me mad. When I went home to do research for my last novel—though it turned out mainly I stayed with my mom, ill in Makati, undergoing the first of her many tests—Doctor Tita Tita called me before I left to ask if I had more kilos in my baggage: "Do you still have allowance? Do you still have allowance?" She berated me when I told her I had only a carry-on. She drove to New York to deliver a huge, arduously taped balikbayan carton—full of bathroom products, I imagined, and I lugged it to my mom's hospital bed at Makati Medical Center, where members of the family were awaiting my arrival.

Tia Pachang, matriarch of the Delgados of Salogó, ancient teacher of Spanish at F. Jhocson in Sampaloc, the family idol at the funeral of my mom's Papá, was ensconced in the room's lone visitor's chair.

She looked as wizened and shriveled and upright as she had when I first met her decades ago beside a coffin in Salogó.

Had she been born with a puckered mouth, a wrinkled bar above her upper lip as if propriety had corrugated it in the womb?

I finally understood the glory of being the carrier of a balikbayan box. I watched the fulsome gratitude of Mana Nemesia as she received the Esarora pedicure and manicure set, the smiles of the nurses who accepted their incidental, unasked-for bath towels, the grin on the face of Claudio the driver, son of Tay Lucio—my mom said, remember your Tay Lucio? that's his son!—and as he took the Marlboro carton I scrambled to remember why this gash occurred in the mind at the dim name Tay Lucio—and the joy all around for the mounds of Mounds and Butterfingers separated into family groupings for Sampaloc, Pasig Line, and Binangonan, all of her in-laws whom Doctor Tita Tita had remembered.

I raised my hands to fend off misdirected thanks.

"They're all from Tita Tita!" I said.

"Hmph," said Tia Pachang, her surprisingly sturdy teeth already clamping down on a Mounds coconut bar, her gray gums showing as her small mouth opened wide.

I watched her thin lips disappear so her jaw could engorge the goods.

I will admit that the primate look of Tia Pachang, her mandibles turning a perfectly conical shape in sideview as she bit on the bar, fascinated me because I kept thinking she reminded me of something, somewhere, someone important to me.

Her prominent, shadowed jaw mirrored her brother's, Honorable Mayor Francisco III, in his letratos in the sala, except he looked abashed.

While Tia Pachang was always the boss.

"Hmph," she said again, licking her lips and tonguing her teeth at the Mounds coconut now stuck on them, "that Teresita. She is living with a man. You know my son Paquito when he went to the States, she gave him a plane ticket to visit her, to fly from Las Vegas to Mary's Land, and he went. Hmph. That is what he said. That Teresita—she is living with a man in Mary's Land. In the land of the Virgin! Hah. Did you know that, Adina? Susmaria. *Dios la perdone.*"

And as Tia Pachang crossed herself, she twisted her lips and her tongue to dig at the dark bits stuck in her gums. Then I watched as her veined talons, skinny and weighted by her golden rings, reached out for another bite of the Mounds chocolate bar.

The crinkle of the silver wrapper echoed in the room's small space, and I wanted to tear the wrapper from her claws, put all the chocolate back into the balikbayan carton, and ship the entire shitload back to Baltimore.

"She married him so she could get a green card. She divorced Nemorino for a green card. Susmaria. She is living in sin with a man."

The sound of lips smacking on the chocolate, the timed measure of her munching, *nyam, nyam, nyam,* as she satisfied herself was obscene, but no one countered her remarks.

I looked toward my mom.

The patient lay in her raised bed, fingers pressed before her in an arc of prayer.

Her eyes were closed.

My mom did not like chocolate. At least not the kind you couldn't buy in rich, rough balls at the market and stir in a brew for breakfast.

She lived for hipon and tsokolate tabléa, and not these poisons wrapped in foil.

She was shaking her head, her eyes closed.

I didn't know how to respond.

I had just arrived.

Tia Pachang—I should call her Lola but I never have—wore the gray bun of her rigor and the righteous crease of an ancient pucker, and I was only the child of a child.

Two generations removed.

But it was not propriety that she had, I thought—it was malice.

"That's a mean thing to say," I said, though I had no idea what had gone on in Doctor Tita Tita's life, it's not as if I had ever been in my aunt's confidence—*she was only an in-law*—but I got mad. "She fell in love. She got married. She's not living in sin. She's living with a man who loves her."

Now everyone in the room, Mana Nemesia the manicurist, Claudio the son of Tay Lucio, and the three greedy children from the absent Paquito's family, all turned to look at me.

With a smile, unperturbed, Tia Pachang settled back in the lone visitor's chair, the fake leather squeaking against her bony limbs.

She kept smacking her lips, licking them clean of chocolate sweetness.

"Hmph," she said, closing her eyes, her fingers now posed before her, too, like my mom's, arced as if in prayer: her sigh replete from her mound of chocolate.

She dismissed me like that, *hmph*.

With her tiny, gray face, moribund frame, and closed eyes, she looked like an already melting, chocolate-filled corpse.

Then she spoke up from the dead.

"*Divorciada!*" Tia Pachang hissed, the word pronounced with her Spanish lisp.

We all leaned forward to hear.

"*Divorciada!*" she repeated.

And that's when I heard my mother speak.

I turned to her.

I waited for her to protest.

"Sssh," said my mom.

Her voice as the patient, the room's star, trumped her aunt's.

She put a finger to her lips.

"Ssssh, Tia Pachang. Thiyaw, thiyaw, thiyaw, thiyaw. The people—the nurses. Ssssh. They can hear."

Waller, Waller, Waller, Waller

He lists his chores and counts his master's virtues.

Everything in the book for pages goes—

Waller, Waller, Waller, Waller.

Waller takes communion at morning mass. Waller prays the novenas to the wounds of Our Lord. Waller fasts on Fridays. Waller takes offense at others' sins.

Waller, Waller, Waller, Waller.

Waller wakes the boy with a brush of his palm against his hair, he gives him extra saging na saba at breakfast, he keeps a hand on his shoulder as they walk to Sunday mass at six A.M.

It was a thrill in his body to be an object of attention—the favored son, not the killer one.

The killer of his Papá's beloved bride.

Paco makes columns and devises categories.

He alphabetizes the captain's holy acts—Latin-learning, missive-making, news-narrating, opera-orating, poem-penning, quip-quoting, rosary-reiterating.

In his tidy hand (it turns lavish and curlicued as the notebook flourishes), the boy inscribes—

The mnemonic *SALIGIA* of the friars at Calle Anda—

Superbia, avaritia, luxuria, ira, gula, invidia, acedia!

Superbia is an indigo aureole, midnight cloud of haze that follows the norteamericanos, wicked men of Waller, walking like fighting cocks around the dust plaza, shoving their kersey-clad butts at children who stare at the dirty old men's smelly behinds.

Ira to right of them, *Ira* to left of them, carbuncle-red, festering around the American camp. A glut of scarlet radiating from soldiers to villagers and back, a circular loathing soaking into the boy, wetting his mouth like clogged dregs of Giporlos tubâ, viscous and bright, glog glog glog glog into the soldiers' mouths: red *Ira* is the color of the americanos' venom (their suspicions are correct), such as the way a townsman whistles a song as he passes, *Yanqui Doodle Denggoy*, the song, though they do not understand its declensions, deserves the magenta brunt of white man's *Ira*, if he only knew.

Avaritia—brown like a santol peel left out too long, flesh color of a chico or the rotted membrane of jackfruit seeds, *an liso, an liso!*—*Avaritia* strolls down the mangroves, capturing pigs and cows, even those of the vice-mayor, meek and mild Man Dadong, whose gentle soul will soon enough stuff marmalade and melted kalamay into a norteamericano's privates, making his own kind of banana cue when the sad day comes (but Man Dadong Balais will have no memory of the event).

And *Gula*, what *Gula*, my gulay, lime-green as they come, dense and frothy as a fresh bugger, deep as the color of just-right guava. For the boy, lush green is Desire's vegetable sheen, it roams—so the norteamericanos wander the town, eating not just the gulay but also the gulaman and the gaway, plus the goats.

Then yellow *Invidia*, color of jaundice like perfect, pinched lanzones, and its twin *Acedia*, rosy hued, somewhat pink-to-fuchsia, oddly lovely, like the blush in caimito, the ombré of star apples—but as far as the boy can tell, *Invidia et Acedia* are the pastel demons that covet the bright land and jail its dark people, and all along the white men are sitting pretty, served by fools such as he.

Future senator, ambassador to the United Nations, War Reparations Commissioner!

The photographed man of the OsRox mission for independence!

Francisco Delgado y Blumfeld.

Faithful servant.

The ward of Waller.

Lolo Paco! What's going on?

The boy's young age fails to speak—*Luxuria*: inexpressible in colors or in Latin.

Pride.

Anger.

Avarice.

Gluttony.

Envy.

Sloth.

Lust.

The boy tallies the soldiers' cardinal errors, in order of iniquity and taint. He quotes the captain cursing his men who flout the rules— *no touching of the women, no gambling on the chickens, no drinking of tubâ!*—and the boy applauds his killjoy master every day.

Waller lavishes his *ira* on the soldiers, but the boy's cheeks he pats like a dog's, his warm beige-to-honey touch, the hairy heat of his *caritas*, as he passes on the way to his convent cot.

The captain has the parish priest Padre Donato's old room in the kumbento, and its stern décor adds to his pious ways.

A lone crucifix against abaca twine, nailed below the edge of stone kisame.

A view of the river.

A private, though primitive, toilet.

Frogs and lily pads in flat impressions by the kasilyas.

The boy sleeps on a cot in the hallway outside his master's door, listening to the river and the snores that sound like amphibian insomnia—the midnight rhythm of human toads.

The boy lives by concentrating his powers—

Para mantener la solidez.

He steadies himself by focusing on—

Trifles and minutiae.

Between the rumbling of Griswold and the burps of Bumpus.

Waller, Waller, Waller, Waller.

At first the boy thinks the sounds he hears are a dog's whine after being beaten. A low groaning. The diarist cannot sleep. The boy is dreaming one of his monotonous dreams about falling that mars his otherwise pleasant war journal. He gets up to check the windows, somnambulating like his abuelita Nemesia.

But all he spies are bamboo shadows and the sentry, Sergeant Adolph Gamblin or Private Gustaf Rambles, passing by, then the shuffling of someone's tsinelas.

Outside, sounds of lettuce and ismagol.

Lechuzas y chinelas.

I mean, night owls and slippers.

The boy unlocks the mystery two nights later.

Fooled by the silence in his master's room, the sleepless boy opens the door and witnesses—

Waller, Waller, Waller, Waller.

Naked.

Clutching at himself as he stands before the crucifix of Christ.

I read it over—I try other translations.

Naked.

Clutching at himself as he stands before the crucifix of Christ.

Waller grunts, flashing his fascinating implement, which looks (I think he says) like the nipple of the goat that his abuelita Nemesia the Insomniac used to milk—a squeezed, purple, and bursting organ, thrusting this way and that—the captain stifling his groaning throughout this terrible, unreadable ordeal until his face mimics the grimace of the suffering Christ on the cross above his bed—

The ripe trace of a reddening chico, his mouth, or maybe it really is the pink gape of a mortal goat, Nemesia the Insomniac's stinky, slaughtered treasure, La Cabra, under the house on Moret Street, with its sacred heart wrapped not in peppercorn and bay leaves but in a crown of thorns, the teat of his grandmother's kambing La Cabra that she pets for a year until fiesta, for there is no sin in eating your pet if it makes a good kaldereta, and finally Waller falls, holding onto it, oblivious of the crack in the door.

As he peeks, the boy sees light-filled wings—a dragonfly imprimatur in the air, the milk-eyed wisps of—but what is it—it's a midrib stalk, the gihay, striating the dark in almost invisible lightning strips—gray-lined, milky, whitening—the light-wing smoke of a lash, impending—

Waller—is whipping himself.

And in concert, reluctant, the boy feels the thin welts crisscrossing, glissando on his own spine as the whip falls on the captain's back, enflaming the man's biceps, pale as moons on the captain, and the lash burns the boy's also-pale, moon-white limbs—

From the glint of the whip—an explosion of brights!—as the boy watches by the door.

Susmariosep, Waller, Waller, Waller, Waller!

Uy uy uy.

Agi—agi!—an agi—

Agi ini nga kaagian.

The pain of this experience—

In color.

Flame blossoms, violets, maroons, firework-flares.

Impiyerno reds!

All upon the boy's body—he feels it, too.

Agi—agi!—agi ini nga kaagian—

Dios lo perdone.

The colors strike the boy on the arm (butkon), the elbow (siko), the knee (tuhod)—though all the while—he is only watching, unseen by the door.

The whips, one after the other, faster and faster, flame on his own backside (likod), a kaingin forest, a mystic flare of fire-trees all along the Malecon—a blaze.

Drops of sweat mingle with the captain's blood to trace the pathology of the captain's penance.

And the phantom drips mark the boy.

Agi ini nga kaagian.

So he feels.

(And in the darkness, yes, his finger passes over the bumps on his arm, vertical ghost keloids, a kind of shadow ravishing upon his unblemished skin.)

On the captain, jigsaw pieces of infamy all across a map of scars.

Enflamed upon the boy—the same cartographic points.

His phantom hands, following the captain's, reach for the marks of penitential lashes across the small back of his small body.

And most of all—upon his thing.

The utin.

The captain's thing is engorged, pregnant, purple.

Like a goat's swollen teat, an tete ba ni La Cabra—or a misshapen tuber.

Purple yam—color: ube.

An iya utin ube.

Hala, pasaylua, ikaw nga Lolo Paco ka.

And all he does is watch—

Peeking by the captain's door.

At first the boy thinks he is dreaming. Bangungot. Inop. Lunop. He faints. Drowns. Shadows are mocking. Sounds startle him awake. The rumbling of the river. Or are they the snores of Griswold the surgeon? Then. Grunts. Panting. The strokes of too many lashes.

Rising from his stupor, he peeks through the door.

Again.

Riveted to the captain.

He closes the door.

He falls a second time.

The captain's twin pleasures—Latin-speaking and whipping—transport the boy diarist into spasms of spying, even as daily he holds his own swollen-not-swollen penis tenderly, marveling at its mimicking ways.

The boy writes out his litany of days, repeating, *my master likes to hold it, then he whips—*

Most important—

The diarist is writing in Waray.

An iya gamit gihay.

The boy's phrase, in the tongue of my mother and the hygienic people of Tacloban and Samar and Salogó, emerges full-grown from items of housekeeping that the boy also lists.

From his mixed Spanish and Tagalog to flagrant Waray.

I hear Mana Marga's domestic speech—the whish-whish-whish of her gihay, her midrib broom—amid the boy's observations of the captain.

It's precisely this dissonance with Mana Marga's imagination that gives the boy's narration its clarity.

The evidence of the pages stares at me, smudged in some places by fungus or limatik, a bloodless leech—

The proof is grimy, with phantom blood, but it is intact.

Waray takes up this plot after the pages in Latin, Tagalog, Waray-na-Tagalog, and Spanish.

Night after night, the captain whips himself with the midribs of coconut fronds that the Waray townspeople like to strip and bunch up into brooms—long, supple fibers, thin like a king crab's antennae, the gihay—the types of brooms used for clearing yards, for unclogging sewers, for cleaning up the streets after typhoons.

Whish-whish-whish.

The fierce sound of women's gihay cleansing the city in the monsoon season that marks my experience of storms.

Waller whips himself—his lightning slashes—an agi hini nga iya kaagian—with the midrib lash of common brooms.

An iya gamit gihay, pagkastigo ha iya kalugaringon, an iya lawas baga hin Jesukristo ha atubangan han justicia ni Poncio Pilato, labi na ha iya likod (back), mga tuhod (knees), siko (elbows), paa (feet), pero labot la ha iya utin (penis).

Using the lash of the midrib he scourges himself like Jesus Christ before the judgment of Pontius Pilate, especially on his back, his knees, his elbows, his feet, but except for his utin, the phallus.

Waray is not Lolo Paco's instinctive tongue (from the journals that seems a street mix of Tagalog and Spanish—a kind of menudo with some church Latin thrown in, and choice words in antique Basque, or is it Fujian, lifted from his gray-bearded abuelita Nemesia the Insomniac, plus the mixed-up Tagalog with the Waray—of Mariano the mayordomo, Ambrosio the cook). Maybe his pure, sacrosanct Waray is the language of code—no one in the barracks can read it. Maybe Waray is the language of subversion. Maybe Waray is the language of desire: the language to speak the mutinies of the body, his New World that requires primal speech, this tongue of his unknown mother Adina Blumfeld y Catalogo, *A. B. y C.*, the tongue of the people of Giporlos.

What is clear is that the American's lurid masochism draws the servant boy to his side.

At first the boy seems unaware of his notes' erotic tension—the Freudian slips that slide off his *nota*, his *nota bene.* In the convent's private bathroom, when the troops are with the captain at reveille, the boy takes his master's stance at the open urinal and watches himself pee. Holding onto himself, he is at first surprised by the change in his body, and he tries hard not to fall into the uncleaned pit as his body stiffens into a disturbed seething, a trembling both satisfying and uncontrollable as he tries to keep his spine straight while his body shakes, so that in one moment he thinks that an earthquake has befallen him, striking him alone, and then the moment is over, he cleans up his torso, his thighs, his thing, the utin, and he gets back to his housekeeping tasks.

He concludes—*I see, Lord, agi! why you do it, it makes your body feel good.*

Nakita ako kay why, *Ginoo, agi! kaupayan man ini ha lawas.*

Maupay! Nga agi!

Open to sensations, he tries a midrib on himself.

An iya gamit gihay, ayayay.

A thing so flimsy, so sharp its sting.

He says, quote, it is like cutting ice against teeth, a feeling of pain like pleasure that makes him dizzy, unquote.

Agi, baga hin yelo ha ngipon, ul-ol ngan kalipay nga malipong gad udog.

Ha ha huh. Karasa.

I see, Lord, agi! why you do it, it makes your body feel good.

Nakita ako kay why, *Ginoo, agi! kaupayan man ini ha lawas.*

Maupay! Nga agi!

And I hear my mother praying, Lord Jesus, pardon and mercy! Through the merits of your wounds!

Oh my God, Lolo Paco, I think, crossing myself as if I still believe in my mother's God—you are going to hell!

These pages are priceless.

Where else in the military records will you find as precise a manual of masculine erotica, the anal-retentive annal—the ground upon which wars compound?

Ay sus, ginoo, Lolo Paco—my Jesus, pardon and mercy, through the merits of your wounds!

In the final weeks of Company C at Giporlos, the boy is the acolyte of the captain's scars, wiping off the captain's sweat in the morning while pretending not to notice the wounds, listening at the door to know when to enter to offer a postmortem of salabat, his ginger ablutions, also his breakfast, jealously guarding his master against the curiosity of his nasty men.

The diary becomes an expert on vascular maps—iliac arteries, capillary lines, facial rosacea, to wit—

Aguy, agi!, ha iya hita ngada ha baliatang, ada udoy!, kay baga hin may mga utod nga talinga (an kolor amo la gihap—kabusag-busagan) kay an gihay nahimo man hin mga agi nga nagsisirko, sige hin agi, agi, mga azul nga nag-aaso-aso, kumbaga, o sugad hin mga gutiyukyok nga luwag nga dinuguan ha bug-os nga kalawasan (kabusag-busagan) ha kamatuuran udog, pagkatapos ha iya braso ba (ngan ha iya nawong may daplis gihap), baga hin inagian hin kadamo nga dagum, sige hin agi, agi—may pagkaplata nga sinsilyo—pero waray—kaluoy sa diyos!—waray makaunlod ha iya, an iya mga samad, an iya kasamaran—kamakaluluoy nga nanluluya nga kapanitan, agi agi agi

Ouch, ay!, on his hip and thigh, oh boy!, marks like scissored-off ears (the colors of all are the same, the whitest of the white) that the circling

midrib slashed, ay the path, ay, so it looked, smoky blues in the air, or like teeny-tiny dippers dipped in blood about his entire body (the whitest of the white), in truth, and you know on his arms (also on his face was this phantom web) it was as if so many needles scraped by, ay the path, ay— silvery, like change (or simple, like money)—though nothing—Lord have mercy—nothing could pierce him, his wounds, his wounding—this pitiful, feeble map of flesh, oh oh oh.

Or is the phrase *agi, agi, agi* a triplicate pun?—pain, path, pen?

Oh the possibilities.

Kaupay nga agi.

And is that last term not *flesh,* kapanitan—but kapaitan?

Bitterness.

Kapaitan, kapanitan, the toss-ups of translation.

Bitterness of skinned times.

Silvery like money, simple like change.

May pagkaplata nga sinsilyo.

Agi (ouch). Agi (path). Agi (pen).

Kaagian: experience.

All in one language, too many paths to go.

This simultaneity of kaagian.

Ending in samad. Kasamaran. Samar.

Wound, wounding—a province named through the merits of— wounds.

In at least two instances, the boy hears the captain's weeping, mortifying moments of abandon.

The boy is puzzled.

Why weep when it makes your body feel good?

Kay ano nga paghiniyak, kaupayan man ito ha lawas?

And then the notebook fills with novenas.

Ora pro nobis.

The postmortems of his sins.

However, I am sorry to say this particular set of sheets is soon also filled with descriptions mostly of the boy's spirited imitations of his master's acts.

Oh my God, Lolo Paco!

Ora pro vobis.

The boy starts doing it all around the military camp, as scrupulous a chronicler of his natural feats as he is a scrubber of the mud around natural toilets. He fondles himself in loam, on talahib, in the river, on the laundry rocks, on foamy water, on grassy land.

Silvery, like change.

May pagkaplata, bagan sinsilyo.

Agi, agi, agi!

By the riverbank amid the tall talahib, in one of the twin, conical Sibley tents, where the Americans have begun jailing the men of Samar, he masturbates. He masturbates while soldiers are sending the men of Giporlos to cut up the grass then lie at night in a heap of bodies in the Sibley prisons, the men of Samar squeezed together in the hold for no reason they can fathom though the injustice they understand. He masturbates when the American soldiers are at mess, at breakfast when they are so relaxed it is the only time they do not bear guns, and the boy lies luxuriant on his master's bed—the crisp starched sheets that he will iron after he spreads his frothy streams. On those days when the captain travels without his servant to Basey to meet Colonel Morris "Coops" Foote or to Tacloban to meet General Jacob "Jakey" Smith, the boy masturbates in his great solitude on the captain's bed, spilling it with his sublime, his slime, his changeling self-possession.

May pagkaplata, bagan sinsilyo.

Now that he has discovered his body is no temple, like a meticulous anarchist he sprays his semen all over the camp of the norteamericanos in Giporlos, plus signs and autographs them in his diary, this open book.

Ay, Ambot

My mom started giggling.

We were alone. Claudio the driver, son of Tay Lucio, took everyone back home to Sampaloc, Pasig Line, and Binangonan.

"Are you okay?" I said.

"Did you see how Tia Pachang eats so much chocolate?"

My mom's eyes were shining. She was giggling in her raised bed—
ghik, ghik, ghik.

She jutted out her jaw and pretended to munch.

Nyam, nyam, nyam.

Made up and coiffed, she did not look the part of her comedy
character.

I could see she'd been imitating her aunt since she was a child.

"She eats so much chocolate," said my mom. "Like it's still World
War II, and the soldiers are giving them away and will not return."

She settled back into her matrona guise.

Nightgowned in lavender, wearing her choker of South Sea pearls.

She pressed the button to lower her bed.

As she descended, she remembered.

"When we were kids, Nemor and I used to make fun—her words
were funny. Tia Pachang and Papá would speak that language—
Nemor and I liked to mimic. *Siyawsiyaw. Thiyawthiyaw. Que the jotha
que the jotha.*"

She was giggling.

Ghik, ghik, ghik.

She was halfway down, at a precarious obtuse angle.

"Well," I said, "you also refused to learn the other one, English."

"Haha, that Mrs. Edith—she was a terror, that Parasite!"

"Ma," I said. "Why didn't you go after your Tia Pachang? It was so
wrong, what she said about Tita Tita."

But now the bed was flat, and my mom had closed her eyes.

She was silent so long I thought the painkillers had done their work.

Lingkod. Higda.

Katurog. Inop.

"Ay ambot, ikaw nga Fil-Ambot."

I could not tell if she was joking or dreaming.

"I don't know why," she murmured. "Maybe because she's—a
wakwak!"

And she started giggling again.

Ghik, ghik, ghik, ghik.

I thought her giggling would not end.

"A vampira. Did you see how she eats? She calls Teresita *diborthi-yawthiyawthiyaw*, then she eats all of Teresita's chocolates."

Her eyes are open.

I saw Adina an guapa, in her regalia, sitting straight up.

She was staring at me.

I moved to hold her. I was afraid that rising, she had broken her bones.

"Ssssssst."

It's a hiss, my mom was hissing at me.

"That woman," she said, "sssssst."

I waited for her confession, her sin of anger against the elder, Tia Pachang.

"Thiyawthiyawthiyaw," she said.

Tuyaw, tuyaw, tuyaw, I thought.

Sometimes it is insane, returning to the Philippines.

She was staring wide-awake in her steroid dreams.

And she lay back again, her shoulders shaking, ghik, ghik, ghik.

Her face was wet as she slept.

Polish

He watches as one soldier caresses his Krag rifle, polishing it at reveille, at noon, at vespers, at night. The men call Private Schermerhorn "Polish," for his obsession with his rifle. Then Polish starts to polish his face. Then he begins to polish his body—he polishes his arms below his kersey sleeve, then his pallid torso and his ghostly glutes and his illusionary abs.

Then he starts taking off his clothes, including his faded blue boxers that he had worn to fight the Boxers in the Temple of Heaven in China, and the belt buckle that he had polished into a blinding silver the day before and his dirty pants and his undershirt. He polishes his hips and his groin. Ha hita ngada ha singit. He is beginning on his utin, his most precious weapon, when the soldiers gang up on his hairy hide reeking of gunmetal and ferric oxide, and four people tie him up in his pup tent.

He's wrapped tight, like a secret missive in an abaca mat.

Claude C. Wingo, an unsung artist from Winnebago, adds the decoration of a Stars and Stripes to the moving tableau of the spangling, well-shined Polish.

So says the boy: "Ginbutangan hin bandila ni Wingo, pastilan, uday, ka mayaangyaang hini nga mga kanô—ay, huwaso—kaloka talaga, day, ang Giporlos! (exclamation point mine)."

Ay huwaso—a Waray phrase without much traffic in English, or even Tagalog. To call it an interjection of disbelief is not enough. You can imagine the people of Salogó looking at a Spaniard in Magellan's armada offering them beads of glass in exchange for their precious wine, their bahalina tubâ—*ay huwaso*. Or the stories of the Jesuit, Padre Chirino, an evangelizing gossip going on about his three-part God, a Father, a Child, and a Ghost—but it is the Ghost who gets the virgin pregnant!—a*y huwaso*. The phrase implies mockery, but also indulgence, the way to silence the fantasies of a child is to tolerate them.

A mix of sarcasm and pity cannot be divided from the mix of Tagalog and Waray in the diarist's expressions—I guess the code-switching can't be helped in a boy filled with so many tongues in a world requiring too many loyalties.

Grabe nga buyayaw man, hala ka, pastilan, talaga naman ang kanô, an iya amay nga yaik, ay kapahal—ini nga Schermerhorn, kapadla, pero labi na hi Wingo—parang iro nga gumuguliat sa buwan—

I cannot figure out his Tagalog from his Waray, even a weird Cebuano—the polyglot sounds of my own place, Leyte.

Only when Polish promises to stop polishing himself does the private get unpupped from the tent.

As soon as he is liberated, Polish starts crouching on his four limbs. Polish begins howling like a dog.

Parang iro nga gumuguliat sa buwan.

A mixed spiel.

Doggerel.

There squats the norteamericano, smeared with gun polish, blackened with paste of tin putty and ammonia, and, with his half-polished balls graffitiing the dust, he bays his heart out at the height of noon as he sits for his portrait of a person shitting in darkness. Then his friends Private Claude C. Wingo and Lieutenant Edward Avery Bumpus crowd around him, and he sees that the men are going after him once again with the pup tent and the abaca ropes—the Americans are out to get him get him get him and his gun, his gleaming Krag-Jørgensen rifle, what is an americano without his gun, with the bayonet in its forelock and a feather he had found just that morning in the plaza—a flimsy treasure from an unseen bird—a macaw or gamao or kalaw—a fighting cock—that he had bound around the muzzle of his gun—a dream escaped from a willow hoop.

And it is that wisp of a wishful flight that the boy sees as the blue explosion goes off, and it is in a puff of sky-hued smoke, in a blue phenomenal blur, that Private Schermerhorn vanishes, knocked out of his world of misery with a feather.

Schermerhorn's suicide by ornamented rifle spins the boy into another digression of pitiful novenas that oppress his spirits.

The explosion is a shock to all his senses, he feels it in his brow, a pain that goes to lungs, diaphragm, toenails, a contortionist horror, and *head, shoulder, knees, and toes, knees and toads! his rhyming lessons*—fissured and yet united in their distorted pains—his bluish-red innards, with pulses of ash and purple, explode outward and bloody, his skin, brownish-pink, scarified, then fragments, like a tissue bomb—freed in fleshy specks of rainbow shreds into the Krag's smoke, and what do you do with the scream in his knees, his bones, his cranial crevices—everything hurts and burns—

As he watches—

Asô ha tuhod.

Knees and toes! Knees and toads!

The private's body rising to the sky—he feels the charge of blue smoke right into his knees, and then north up his chest, his scaphoids, his arms: a mirror scorching, kindling in Lolo Paco's body.

He looks down at his arms, to see if he, too, has scars.

As usual—unblemished.

Waray bisan usa ka samad.

Limpyo.

Clean.

The world outside of him is a disaster while he just watches.

Doctor Tita Tita

When I saw Doctor Tita Tita at the airport, I was holding on to my stupid hat to keep it from my face. I was dying in my dumb outfit. She took me to her hotel by the water. It was she who bought me my ticket to Tacloban.

A gift, she said, a gift. She put the PAL tickets in my hand.

She was not going to the funeral.

"Can you imagine—kadako nga escandalo, inday! Imagine—with all the Delgados at the wake and the funeral. Staring at me, the ex-wife. An kontrabida. I cannot go."

"But they'd want to see you, Tita Tita. They'd be happy to see you. Honoring her by being there."

"No, they won't. They'll just want to know if I'm obese or not, or too skinny, meaning I'm poor, or my husband beats me up, or whether I'm too snobby now or what because I'm coming from estados."

She did not speak what we both understood: the *divorciada* who cannot come home.

"But I thought you came home for the funeral!"

"No," she said. "I didn't."

Doctor Tita Tita shook her head.

"But you know, inday, I do—I want to go to her funeral," she whispered. "Poor Adina."

And she started crying.

I didn't know what to do.

"Is it his anniversary?"

"No," she said through her sobs. "It's his birthday."

"So you're going to Cebu?" I asked.

She nodded.

"You're going to John-john's cemetery for his birthday. That's why you've returned home?"

"I finally got my citizenship. For so long I couldn't go home. I couldn't visit his grave."

"Maybe you didn't want to," I said.

It was the wrong thing to say.

She sobbed even more.

I counted in my mind the years she'd been married to Mack Richards.

Almost a decade more than citizenship required.

"No one understands," my aunt said. "How many times I'd be driving, out there on the highway, just going to work, and I'd stop and park, I'd be blind. From crying. One time—I almost ran over a pedestrian. I could have killed people, crying on that road. I'd just start weeping. You don't know, inday, how much it hurts. Every day. For years. Year after year. No one can understand. I couldn't go home. Because anyway if I went home, I'd only be going home—to John-john's grave."

I nodded. I held my aunt.

"So I didn't," she said in my arms.

"And now you're here," I said. "Isn't that a good sign? It's good you feel better now. That you feel well enough to be home."

"I don't," my aunt said. She pulled away and looked up at me.

"You never feel better, inday," she said.

This was the most that any grown-up in my family had ever expressed vulnerability to me.

And I could see it was because, to be honest, Doctor Tita Tita was only an in-law.

"You know, Ma would be happy if you went to her funeral," I said.

"I know. Adina had a tough life."

"People keep saying that. I mean, she had a great life," I said. "She did whatever she wanted."

"You have no idea," my aunt said.

Piensa in English

Why should they weep, when it makes the body feel good?

In the dark, the Catalogo brothers go limping to the Sibley jail, where the other men of Samar sit upon the boys' wounds because they cannot help it.

In the Sibley tents, the jailed Samarnon men have no place to stand or shit.

The boy draws.

Is it a drumstick or a bayonet?

A figure on a mat, or a torture rack?

A checkerboard in violet and red, in crimson, blue.

The next series of pages—all drawings.

So packed into the contraptions, the men smell each other's butts and breathe their wrack into each other's faces. Every morning they are let out to slash at grass, cut down coconut trees stunted from the typhoon of '97—ravage that had caught the terrible gods of the typhoon path unaware.

Surge of nightmare.

Lunop.

The ocean had howled and the waters parted just as for Moses God divided the sea, but in the instant after the howling, the waters returned, roaring upon that swath against the water—Giporlos, Balangiga, Guiuan, Lawaan, down the strait to Tacloban, Palo, Tanauan, the shoals blackened by the gods, just as for Moses—but who's their prophet, where's the exodus?—God smote the people of Egypt. After '97 for years the riverbank was barren, and the coconuts and fruit trees undone, rice fields bare. People starved. And now strangers demand they cut down the trees whose resurrection they had nurtured, had taken years—the trees that had just returned them to their ordinary lives.

Lubi lubi lubi.

The men, released from their Sibley jails every morning, hack at the lubi, their source of life.

Eighty-two men packed into the Sibleys that can hold only twenty-four. Every day the Americans count them.

One, two, three.

Uzza, dua, tolo.

The twin Bingo is as skinny as the twin Bongo, they have sunburnt, grain-colored hair—years spent on their family's rice harvests lend their locks their palay's luster. The glow on their skin is radiant in the boy, the kindling joy his body feels at the sight of Bingo and Bongo—a warmth he feels on his palms, his biceps, his buttocks. A familial love. The twins have chiseled cheekbones that add shadows to their expressions, and under the harsh noon the angles on their grave faces correct the boy's vision as he looks.

Sergeant Gamblin pinions Bingo or Bongo's arms.

Private Rambles holds Bongo or Bingo's legs.

Wolfe trusses him up.

Devore lifts the watering tube.

Griswold the surgeon, doctor of eyes, ears, noses, and throats, ensures the good working of the body's parts.

Tuhod (knees). Siko (elbow). Paa (foot). Likod (back).

On the boy, all the parts stiffen—knees, elbow, foot, back—the warmth receding as he clutches his pencil in his body's green cage, making his checkerboard of parts.

Head, shoulders, knees and toads!

The greenness of his limbs before the twin's rack.

Limbs must be in good order in order to break them.

Break, break, break, on thy cold gray stones.

O sea!

The greenness of his body's pains.

Agi, agi, agi.

Breton barks his questions.

—Who is feeding the rebels in the forest?

A blue blur on his *tuhod.*

Gambler nudges the Catalogo brother in the knee.

—Who is relaying messages to Vicente Lukban?

Teal hiss of the *siko* on the brown back.

Ramblin's elbow rams the Catalogo brother.

—We are protecting your island! You think you can beat up a soldier and get away with—*you nigger, you nigger, you nigger!*

Trample thrashes the arnis stick into the boy's *likod.*

Black—the boy feels the warmth of black.

—Who said that you can speak?

And Rambles smashes his fist upon the Catalogo brother's stuck-out tongue.

Dilla.

Dilla.

Dilla.

Tongue.

—Where are the rebels who are taking your rice? Tell us where the commander Vicente Lukban is hiding!

The Catalogo brother groans.

—*Da—Da—Da—*he says.

And Gambler gives him a whipping for syllables too sparse for use.

Every time the Catalogo brother emits the wrong sound, the two aides, Wolfe and Devore, move, and the boy's back jumps: his body tingles as he hunches, groans of pain bent over a notebook—

Slap! Crack! Whip!

Rainbow checkerboard, lace of lozenges in harlequin hues, splatter of diamonds, pain crisscrossing up and down the notebook.

His back.

Pak!

Pak!

Pak!

Pak!

Wolfe and Devore open the bound Catalogo brother's jaw with a pike. Wolfe draws a cloth over the twin farmer's mouth. Devore raises high a bamboo tube.

A purplish welt in the boy's gums, not an ube, nor a talong, his own jaw clamps down on a length of tube, violet spasm upon his open mouth, jaw raised—

Watching.

The better to pour into his eyes, ears, nose, and throat—

Griswold the surgeon observes.

The boy observes Griswold the surgeon.

To concentrate.

Para mantener la solidez.

Wolfe angles the tube of water above the Catalogo brother's surprise.

Water dribbles down Bongo, or Bingo.

Two rivers, one stream: one brother weeps at the other's flood.

And in and out and in and out, in the scribbling boy is a hole, a well, an abyss. A cratering of a corpus. What he feels—an automotive digging, deep into his body, baga hin lungon, kuno.

Samad, samad. Kasamaran.

His hand presses hard on that pencil.

He finds it hard to explain: pag-inukab hin bubon, pag-hinukay hin lungon—

Which is it?

How many orifices does a body have?

Ocular, nasal, vestibular, perpendicular—

Drilling a deep gashing flood into his gut.

And the boy is so wired to the castigation of bodies that he feels the lashes doubling upon him: the lashes felt by one twin for the other, and the lashes felt by the other for the twin.

Two-by-two of touches—

Pak!

Pak!

Pak!

Pak!

How can anyone last such a scourge?

His checkerboard of lashes, a twin laid on the ground, array of blue squares and red splashes, violet lines and black blood.

Bingo is flailing, Bongo is rigid, Bingo and Bongo are shadows of each other's moaning, the boy is a shadow of a shadow of three bodies in a well of tears.

And when finally one twin's gauzed mouth has no sound to utter, the other takes his twin in his arms, and from the diarist's waves of lines, an ocean, his drawing of one twin hanging on to the other, staggering toward the storefront of their aunt, their Nay Carmen, but which twin was which?

Ora pro vobis.

Bingo or Bongo?

Griswold the surgeon observes.

Bumpus is bored.

The sun is down, the day is done.

Bumpus whistles to the boy in the hallway at sunset, hunched, unmoving, over his cot.

"Psst!"

The boy is still.

"Hey, boy!"

The boy's head turns.

The look is blank.

"Hey, boy! And take the notebook with you!"

The boy rises, he bears his notebook, he walks toward the skeleton, Bumpus.

"*Escribe*, ha?" Bumpus says to the boy.

There is a pause.

"*Mis piensos,*" the boy replies.

"I will teach you to have piensos."

The skeleton man—calavera nga layaw!—laughs his high-pitched laugh.

"English, Francisco! Piensa in English!"

Night after night, this new pastime absorbs Bumpus, Boston Brahmin, Harvard Man.

Calavera nga layaw.

This is the witching time of year in New England.

Bumpus dictates to the boy.

The boy listens.

The boy learns.

Not just the songs.

Head, soldiers, knees, and toads—

Knees and toads!

He writes down the piensos in English of Edward Avery Bumpus.

And I can smell the orchards as the fruits are being picked.

Shall I bring the pigeons watermelons?

The moon is both a grin and a teardrop.

English unfolds from Bumpus's mouth like the rain of flowers from narra trees—yellow blossoms of random beauty with no memory in their wake.

Every day in the gloaming, after the bugler's call, the boy waits for the end of the chess games between Bumpus, Griswold, the mayor Abayan, and the priest Donato—he sits and waits for Bumpus to call.

His new hobby.

Bumpus, Bumpus, Bumpus, Bumpus.

When Bumpus is absent, he goes to look for him.

"Psst! Boy! Piensa in English!"

The boy spouts sentences, the boy's hand spills.

The English of Bumpus.

Copying, scribbling.

Escribe, ha?

The man's disjointed time.

The boy's an adept, a monastery apprentice-monk with a clean hand.

Diri kamot—agi.

Not that hand, kamot—the other hand, agi.

Ha iya agi—may agi.

Or is it—a pain?

How can I tell?

Agi, agi—

Ay!

This is the witching time of year in New England, the boy writes in a beautiful hand (an iya mahusay nga agi), *and I can smell the orchards as the fruits are being picked. I would send for a barrel of apples. I want to do a little sketching and watercolor work. At Newburyport, I came across the most delightful old house to sketch.*

The boy's pensive, thick pencil.

Kamaburut-on an iya kasurat.

A boy came out in the house where I did not think any one lived, and he came over to me and began to play with the bicycle. The boy had an old gun barrel with which he pretended to shoot the birds. The birds were in some trees welcoming the cold east wind and the beautiful day.

The boy scribbles with his fat, squat nib.

Kamabug-at han lapis.

Grandfather Bumpus used to be quartered in this old fort during the civil war. On a leave of absence I went home and spent the night in Quincy. The grounds so beautiful with the green trees and pansies and what-not. You will not know our library when you go home for vacation. I filled up my fatigue-cap full of pansies, twice, and a small bunch of violets that are too sweet to fade.

What are pansies?

The boy imagines.

Is a violet like the kamia, its beauty the size of a thumb, flowers by the river with gingered hearts and scent so pungent that even the soap from the laundrywomen's paddles does not dispel it?

The boy's pencil pauses.

Nag-aalang nga lapis.

Or is it like a gumamela, odorless and obscene as it blooms, with its pistil cocked to his face only to shrivel in an hour?

How is it that one can erase, as if that world had never happened, a life amid kalachuchi and limonsito along the Pasig with the scent of gunpowder hovering across Santa Mesa, and the hint of shrimp among trees—daplos ng hipon sa acacia—while morning has begun to smell like an arsenal, and the moss and lilies against the walls of Manila tremble from the smoke of war and the noontime echo of death's slim reverberations—

Replaced by pansies—and a bunch of violets too sweet to fade—

On the boy's lined sheets.

Ha iya agi, bag-o nga agi.

Agi!

Bumpus, Bumpus, Bumpus, Bumpus.

The notebook fills up like a fatigue-cap, twice, thrice, with violets from a distant home.

Lolo Paco writes.

I have just finished reading Mercedes of Castile *by James Fenimore Cooper. What a smoky place Chicago is but it is not as bad as Pittsburgh. My principal ambition in life is to get a good bath and a shave. This boat is a fine steamer.*

Lolo Paco scrawls.

Sige-sige it agi.

Our course so far has been west, and now we are taking a southwest course to pass north of the Hawaiian Islands and stay in as cool a climate as possible. We passed a brigantine with all sails set.

Lolo Paco's pencil muses.

Sige-sige it hunahuna han lapis.

It made me think of Washington Irving's meditations on seeing a lone ship at sea. The fog lasted all day and into the next. We have been sailing through thousands of Portuguese men-of-war, these nautiluses, these jelly-fishes, these beautifully colored things. With little pointed jelly fins on their flat, spherical bodies. Some of the waves brought the little creatures on deck, but they did not seem to have much life in them. At reveille, a man was buried. A splash, and that is all.

Lolo Paco records.

Nagsurat? O nanumdum?

I suppose I shall soon become accustomed to sudden death.

He notes.

Thackeray has a way of reminding one of early childhood—Why that is just what I thought but could not express! We expect to reach Manila. About ten days more.

Lolo Paco declares.

I went on deck. The men lined up. With mess pans in hand they took their turns and filled their stomachs. Then loafed until lunch at 2.30. The men caught three sharks, averaging ten feet. When Mr. Fish was partly out of water, a small slip noose was let down a small line, and the small mouth was noosed.

We sighted the Philippines about five o'clock.

Lolo Paco sees.

Nakit-an niya.

The sun set behind the islands, and it seemed as though the paint pot of the gods had been upset. We are coasting along to Manila, two hundred miles away.

With its shrimp smell on rocks and the streaks of eternity on its gray, metallic sheen, and the sense of an inner life always about to break, a stirring that messed with the wind, and all along the promenade, as he gazes at the Bay, he always has the sense of a spirit about to appear—ghosts of Manila galleons, or the translucent arm of a creature, half-woman, half-dolphin, about to rise out of waves—but nothing ever comes of it.

The hand shakes.

It starts a new leaf.

Bag-o nga agi, aragi-an.

I am on guard, and so I will not get to practice my small stock of Spanish on fair señoritas. I have three blankets, an old blackboard as part of a floor, a candlestick consisting of an empty (too bad!) pint bottle of zinfandel claret, my dress suit case, pail, wash basin, soap, canteen, haversack, a bolo, a native knife (relic of our Tayabas campaign), field glasses, a blanket roll—a heavy piece of canvas about seven feet square, arranged to be used as a hammock, a shelter, a bed. Then the whole thing rolls up in a good solid roll, and two heavy straps hold it tight.

An agi sige hin agi.

The marches in the country are so hard you have to carry everything with you. I march with undershirt and poncho, keeping my blue shirt in the haversack, to be used dry for warmth at night. We are always able to sleep in a native house. I remember a house, with a big roomy plan, with a kind of store on the ground floor. There were pigs beneath it, and flowers. White, the size of my thumb, with a ginger-colored heart, too sweet to fade. The living rooms were reached by a stairway on one side of the store. Stone water urns, smooth bamboo tubes for carrying water, a corral for the fighting cocks—all along the waterfront, the house's ground floor wound.

Lolo Paco continues—

A labyrinth of chickens. On the first floor, after the stairs, there were front rooms, which I appropriated; a dining room with a huge table (all of one slab, handspans thick!); then finally a kitchen, next to a balcony of thick slatted wood, floor and baluster, above the water. Mahogany was the only wood used in the building. I saw one gutter about eighteen feet long, hollowed out of a mahogany log over two feet diameter. The woods considered so valuable by us are used for the commonest purpose here. Servants disembowel cuttlefish on precious darkwood slabs. And like many things in these islands, all of these need to be brought away by us enterprising Yankees to show what is there in the rich forests.

The boy writes with a flourish.

Kahusay nga kasurat.

I have struck some hard snags since I have been in China. But I have shaken off the black mantle, which was beginning to cover my shoulders, and feel I am vindicated. And one day I will be in command again of my old company. Who could be discouraged with such a man as Father backing me up! Lieutenant-Colonel Foote and I have pleasant quarters in some Chinese trading company. They have high-quality goods. Lieutenant-Colonel Foote is always with me—he is a good friend.

The boy encrypts.

Sige hin ukab.

A hundred years is a bagatelle to the average man in China. I have been here only a short time, and I do not expect to stay much longer, as our services will be needed in the Philippines. I have become sort of callous, and as long as one can keep his health, why, duty comes easy!

Lolo Paco's script is losing shape.

Naghihikawarawara.

We had to turn out as guard of honor to General MacArthur when he left for the States on the 4th—what a tiresome affair! Judge Taft has the civil side and General Chaffee the military. The civil is still under orders from the War Department—though there is now not much trouble on the islands!

The boy's hand shakes.

There is rumor of our being sent to the south. I understand Samar has a good climate. But it is a very hard country to fight in! Guerrilla warfare has been going on under General Lukban, said to be a capable man. I do not care for that kind of warfare, for there is little glory and much hard work connected with it—Never mind! Captain Waller has got command of my company. Who knows. I have kept my stripes. He is a good fellow. This is the only privilege we soldiers have—to growl and do our duty!

The boy's upstrokes are twitchy, the loops are blots not ribbons.

I am writing this in the quarters of Aguinaldo, where I am officer for the day. Another officer and myself are taking turns staying in Aguinaldo's house in Malacañang, the street of swells. He can't be more than five feet four inches tall. At least, he has had an interesting life.

The cambers of his *Q*s, his *S*s are faint.

The black mantle is descending. The island as we near it looks like the woman's haunch in the cellars of Quincy, the dark girl we once hid in the flooring. I did not see her resurface. The wild mount heaves its oracular void, its nest of virgin hair, at me. Her eye is a boiling sun. The Liscum *turns. It is time for the tugboat* Ingalls *to give us a shove, show us the monster face.*

Et voila—*Samar.*

I wish I had bought those furs in China: I am cold.

I can no more hear love's voice, no more moves the mouth of her, birds no more sing. How quickly the dragons in gold and red lacquer are going gray, like jellyfish on the boat deck. They do not seem to have much life in them. Their drooping wings with puckered tentacles hic-cupping a yellow hiss of air, vaporous jerks, as if faded neurons are resisting. Words I speak return lonely, flowers I pick turn ghostly, fire that I burn glows pale. No more blows the wind, time tells no more truth. And what emerges from that Chinese hound, this belching chi-mera of Asia?

A little boy in a cassock with a square, straw bundle, vomiting out his guts on the captain's shoes.

Lolo Paco looks up at Bumpus from his notebook.

The boy says.

Hala! Hi ako!

That is I.

The boy writes.

I saw myself reflected—does a mirror forget? At reveille, a man was buried, a monsoon gurgling a sailor's last breath. A splash, and that is all. I shall soon be accustomed to sudden death.

It's Waller who disturbs the boy's piensa-in-English with Bumpus.

When he returns from inspection.

He stands by a crack in the door, listening to the lesson.

The bony body and flushed cheeks that the captain has mem-orized: skin prickling against his kersey cloth, staring at his lieutenant.

The captain makes a sound outside Bumpus's door.

His salabat tea—his hardboiled egg!

The boy scuttles out, and in the doorway the glow from Bumpus's pipe looks like a limb of fire, a burning finger writing homesick letters home on the thatched and yellow wall.

Bumpus does not even sit up when he sees the captain.

Nothing about Waller, his body or his hunger, registers in the fevered man.

What does that mean, the captain thinks, that in me an image is seared, lashed, but in him—not even a mark.

He slides his hand on the boy's shoulders, his breast, his flesh, his body that has ingested the words of Bumpus.

Body of words.

Amen.

Bumpus sinks back into his cot, with Algernon Charles Swinburne on his chest and his pint-bottle candlestick, empty (too bad!) of zinfandel claret.

Calista Catalogo of Giporlos

The boy watches the men corralled into the Sibleys, the easier for them to labor for his master Waller.

Waller, Waller, Waller, Waller.

Watching the men of Giporlos, the boy will bring up the secret missive—soon, I hope—tied up in his abaca mat—the undelivered message burning up a hole in the petate under his hallway cot by the captain's door.

The mission Mariano the mayordomo and Ambrosio the cook and Tay Sequil have plotted in their conspiracy to save the señorito Jote!

So I wait.

He has the message in his petate, his woven mat, to bring to his mother's home, Giporlos.

Give it to the revolutionaries, Lolo Paco—tang-ina!

But he dawdles, he scribbles, he spies on the girl in the store.

It is almost dusk, his chores are done, and he is looking for Bumpus, his next lesson, in song, in rhyme, and Bumpus is once again at the town's store.

Disloyal Bumpus.

Teaching another child.

And why would he not want to be close to her, he thinks, the dark girl in her grown-up clothes?

Her eyes' glance, her slanted gaze, his body like burnt kastanyas, it is a shame, kamakaarawod, ha iya tuhod, siko, kamot, tudlo—ha iya bug-os nga kalawasan—and she smiles at him, looking up from her scribbling, scribbling, scribbling, as if she knows his thoughts, how he wants the lesson (or is it the girl) to himself.

He runs back to Captain Waller, to the kumbento, he crosses himself for his thoughts before he lies down upon his mat, his petate.

Kamakaarawod, it iya utin, agi.

It is Frank Breton who orders the whipping of the Catalogo brother after the storefront brawl. The soldiers do not care which is the culprit—beating up an American soldier, how do they dare—is it Bongo or is it Bingo—and the diarist, to be clear, fails to record which twin was given the water cure.

His eyes move like the eyes of the men toward—

Calista Catalogo of Giporlos.

She of the slim ankles, bare and unsteady in the clear river as she stoops to lay down her bandehado, her tin basin of clothes. Then she washes herself when she has done her laundry chores. She ignores him, that sly little one who goes about Giporlos with his notebook and his gray-eyed stare, like an orphan mutt, a mute pet. She is in the cove beyond the church, by the river Balangiga, where the boy also wanders, away from the men. He seeks solitude. Like her. She sees him watching.

She smiles.

A smile that glances on the skin like the light reflected from a wing—a refracted sheen that glides along on its own orbit.

A disembodiment produced by the eye.

Rush of cochineal.

Pagpukrat ngada han daraga—madaparap nga kapulahan—

Ha iya mata, an iya siplat.

At whom?

Kan kanay?

Though he looks for her, he can barely hold it.

Her gaze.

An iya siplat.

She keeps on her patadiong and her kamisa. She lifts up her clothes. She lowers her body into the water. She gazes.

At a sight above him.

Beyond his eye.

Labaw han iya tan-aw.

And the boy witnesses, but it is beyond her gaze, on her opposite side, the appearance of the man, camouflage of green, kersey amid talahib, makaharadlok, hayop o bakulaw, the wash of the water a cool splash on his dry, distant body, a creature emerging from the trees behind her, and the woman's eyes, labaw han iya tan-aw, fail to see, she is gazing at a sight above—labaw han iya tan-aw—and so the boy waves at her, warning, he watches the incident at the river, the American soldier wading into the water, and the girl kicking, her body thrashing, the laundry clothes strewn in the stream, the water swirling as she splashes, the boy witnesses the shrieks, and the girl's face, falling into the water, splashing and muddy, and the soldier twists to see—

The captain's boy!

With his notebook.

The bruise of her welts seeping onto his clothes, the engorgement on the white man's thighs warming up the boy's legs, his torso, his thudding heart.

The soldier stands still—recognizing the captain's boy.

And at that moment she runs.

Soaked and dry, distant and engorged the boy prays—

Ave Maria, gratia plena, Ave Maria—

Ave de rapiña!

The girl vanishes.

She leaves her basin and her clothes and the scene, running to the storefront of her Nay Carmen.

It's Nay Carmen who sees the boy that vesper night, before fiesta—the captain's boy, that midget writing in his notebooks, *para mantener la solidez*, and she calls out.

"Boy! Pakadi! Boy! Espiya ka nga yaik—utot ka nga im Pating!"

To the boy, the choral laughter of the men about the yard is comforting, even neighborly.

People distrust him, the captain's boy.

For one thing, he has strange eyes.

Gray like a goat's about to be blinded for kaldereta.

The dull eyes of the soon to be disemboweled.

Baga hin kanding nga mawawarayan hin kalag.

A gray that when he looks up at the sky at the narras raining their yellow spumes creepily turns into white—as if he were destined one day to go blind (in fact, that's his nephew, the Honorable Mayor Francisco III, who dies in Salogó in 1971 riddled with cataracts and his rare breast cancer).

He speaks Waray with that stupid lisp, that katsila defect, but the townspeople indulge him.

He's just a child.

Captain's boy, you spy, you fart of the Shark, you—

Come and eat!

Pakadi! Kaon! Utot ka nga im Pating.

The boy sketches the spirits before him, along with drawings of blowpipes or snakes in Eden, and wavy lines of smoke, and shapes like drumsticks or bayonets, checkerboards of color, harlequin diamonds of wounding sparks—his scribbling, his spectating.

An iya agi, an iya kaagian.

Attention petrifies him, and he subsides in his corner, scrawling away in his journal.

Para mantener la solidez.

Agi, agi, agi!

Path, hand, ouch!

This scribbling is a familiar sight, especially to Jote.

—*Boy, pakadi! Kaon! Bisperas han patron—anyone can eat!*

—*Boy! Pakadi! Kaon! Espiya nga Utot ka nga im Pating!*

The boy looks up from his notebook.

A longed-for look.

That light-brown gaze.

A stunning blow—a perceptual vacancy in the boy.

Blankness.

And the blazing, the remembrance of his search, his yearning.

It is he.

An iya bugto.

Jote is carrying his workday's bolo knife—which the boy has just drawn on his notebook.

His wild hair tied at his neck.

Stray brown curls by his ear, on his brow.

He lays his bolo on the ground.

A curved kris, like a scimitar.

It's just a kitchen implement.

Jote, who looks both younger and more aged than his sixteen years, is staring thoughtfully at little Paco.

He shakes his head at Paco, with a finger to his lips.

His familiar gesture.

Ha iya manghod, hi Paco—

Nga Iya Irong.

Eternized.

Immobile.

Paco's body contains—

Blankness, then breath of life, he cannot breathe.

Natagan hin kaginhawaan, waray makaginhawa.

Jote puts down his knife and washes his hands with water from the tapayan and reaches for the pot of rice as Nay Carmen tells him and his companions, her visitors, the laborers imported by the town's chief of police, Tay Balê, who have come to clean up the streets of Giporlos for the norteamericanos—*Kaon! Kaon!*

—Bisperas han patron! Anyone can eat!

The two brothers stare at each other on that vesper night, so far from their home on Moret Street.

Usa, duha.

Duha nga bugto.

Two parts of one.

The one in the priest's worn cassock cut to the length of his

eleven-year-old size, the other in karsonsilyos, a laborer, a transfigura-
tion, bare-chested, curly haired, and dark-cheeked—his hair bronzed
from the sun—hair of the estranghero—face black and toughened as
the rest of them, his arms scarred and muscled, his eyes alert, with the
gray flicker no one notices as peculiar, so similar to the boy's.

Or maybe people notice, no one cares.

Everyone on their side is of a kind.

Kabugtuan.

There are more important things to think about.

When Jote, his handful of rice to his lips, glances at the boy, he
makes that sign again, familiar to Paco, prelude to their game, and in
the moonlight under the leaves of the narra tree, Jote raises his finger,
he dares the boy to speak.

The ferocity of Jote's stare would silence—lizard, pig, or brother.

The boy's pencil is stuck in his thumb.

His instinct?

To close his eyes, to raise up his nose, to figure out the scent.

An Iya Irong.

There is a stain, a gray blot, that streaks through the notebook and
shoots through its pages.

A cratering of a corpus.

A dark blot in the middle of the story—

In the pages that follow where words trace around the blot—

A moment carved.

So I unstick the pages.

I peel one sheet off from another.

They're blank.

Calmly, Jote scoops rice onto his banana leaf plate, helps himself
to pigskin, panit hin lechon, ngan lumpia, pancit ngan kaldereta, and
eats. He eats with the norteamericanos who are also wolfing down the
suckling pig (noted absence: the watermen Wolfe and Devore; Jote
keeps his eye out, but the torturers are nowhere to be found, fevered,
at the hospital in Tacloban, and thus are saved from the coming mas-
sacre intended, also, for them).

Laborers and GIs and jailed men and officers share in the feast at the storefront of Nay Carmen.

Jote spares not one more glance for Paco, an manghod, as the night wears on.

Waray na ako asiha.

Sad.

The tubâ is out, the band plays on.

Hot tiiime, old tooown—the bandurrias and the octavinas go!

Jote is done, takes his place in the rondalla.

Tocar al oído!

His fat, absurd bandurria, his medieval lute.

Come along get you ready, wear your bran, bran new gown,
For dere's gwine to be a meeting in that good, dum strange town,
Where you knowed ev'ry body, and they all knowed you,
And you've got a rabbit's foot to keep away the hoodoo;
Where you hear that the preaching does begin,
Bend down low for to drive away your sin
And when you gets religion, you want to shout and sing
There'll be a hot time in the old town toniiiight!

Paco's ears grow warm.

He knows the song.

Nanumdum, panumduman.

Makanta ako!

His eyes beam.

—*It's the americanos' national anthem. We whistle it when we pass by the sentries.*

—*What for?*

—*Ay gago! So they let us go out after curfew. To Calle Iris!*

Ave Maria, says the mayor Abayan, blessing their fiesta friends, the American soldiers of the town plaza, garrisoned at his behest (so Professor Impikoño says).

The mayor, too early in the night, is already drunk.

Ave de rapiña, winks the wise man Man Dadong, not so original.

Dominus vobiscum to you, too, says Nay Carmen Blumfeld y Catalogo, toasting the mayor.

Amen.

Amen.

Amen.

To you, says Griswold the surgeon, raising a cup to Eliseo the mananguete.

Tagay, says Eliseo the master of bahalina to his opposing confrere, Porczeng the cook.

Tagay, says Porczeng to the maglelechon Cleofe Balasbas.

To you, says Balasbas to Bumpus.

Tagay, says Bumpus to the chief of police—Tay Balê!

To you, says the chief to Breton.

But Breton says—

—Where are those women going?

Bumpus won't leave the stage.

—*The coconuts have ripened, they are like nipples to the tree!* sings Bumpus.

—Where are those women going? asks Breton, slurping the dregs of his host's wine.

—Oho, says Nay Carmen—always thinking of the women! Tagay, Señor Breton!

—*I shall kiss the coconut because it is the nipple of a woman!*

—Ohohohohoy!, says the boss mayor to Bumpus, distracting the lieutenant, here is the woman of your dreams, tenyente!, pointing out the grinning storekeeper.

Toothy and smoky Nay Carmen.

Ngipon para ha ngipon.

And Nay Carmen poses, both hands in pandanggo—one with a jar of tubâ, usa ka banga, the other a jug of tripang—munching on tripang, a seaworm, dancing and twirling before Bumpus.

Then she spits on the ground, a red splat of betel garnishing the spat-out slugs—bad trip of her tripang.

It almost hits Bumpus, in his element, on center stage.

Like a child I shall suck their milk,
I shall suck out of coconuts little white songs!

—Tagay, says his henchman Trapp, now in plainclothes kind of shrunken without his gun—to you, the good people of Giporlos!

—To you, americano mucho malo, tagay, tagay, tagay kamo dida! says Eliseo.

—Tuyo! Tuyo! Tuyo!, says Elias, his son, holding up the tail of a dried fish.

Ghik, ghik, ghik, ghik.

(Noted absence: the captain, unfraternizing and accounted for, praying in his room in the kumbento.)

Later at night, after the feast, the eighty-four laborers return to the Sibleys with no prodding from the Krags. It's late, everyone is in bed, all the cooks on their cots back from the home of Eliseo Canillas, an mananguete. The eighty-four laborers squashed up in the tents like the tripang they just ate, sea slugs tight in a banga, and the private Trapp and the sergeant Breton dream through the night of Calista Catalogo, fleeing into the mountains in her gauzy gown, her kamisa showing off her soul as she—

Frank Breton sits up in his cot, and a rush of clarity comes upon the sergeant.

—They are fleeing for their lives!

He shouts.

Then slumber takes over, and the answer crawls back into his dreams.

The sentry Adolph Gamblin? Gustaf Rambles? is dropping off at his post, full of the fiesta's moonshine, the town's midnight bait for the norteamericanos.

The boy does not sleep.

He draws out from his petate the handwritten message.

Siempre el rebelde, nunca el amigo.

Was it code?

And the other note (but how was he to know) was for his lola, an iya apoy, an nanay han iya nanay—an iya Nay Carmen.

At The Clinic

"That is how we met, you know," said my aunt Doctor Tita Tita— "that is how I met your Tio Nemor."

At the clinic in Tondo, where Doctor Tita Tita was an intern, she had met the family from Salogó: a father, a son, and a daughter paralyzed on a hospital bed.

Adina an guapa was nineteen.

We spent my first night in Manila, Doctor Tita Tita and I, on that balcony of the Manila Hilton, staring out at the Bay and the floating casinos beyond.

I asked her the questions.

Do you really want to know your mother's story? Tita Tita asked.

No, I thought.

The future is now, the past is a mirage.

She had chosen the world she perceived.

Yes, I said.

The Bay was oddly calm though a typhoon was coming—beware the storm surge, the TV newsmen kept saying via the bar's satellite connection—the high winds of the world's warming are creating a disaster yet to be recorded in time!

The newsmen's hysteria—when was a storm not impending in my country of deluge?

A supertyphoon! The oceans abnormally disturbed, climate change, global catastrophe!

A nation usually destroyed!

So much agitation, I thought, for the lash of monsoons that used to lull me to sleep.

The waters of the Bay, from our slant of sight, on our room's balcony, had the halcyon, familiar calm of monsoon reverie.

I asked Tita Tita the questions.

After all, she was only an in-law.

For her, nothing in the stories would hurt.

Tio Nemor, the brash young law clerk, was so "isputing!"—a man in a suit, with slicked-back hair, full of pomade and concern. Doctor Tita Tita was used to men and women in the hospital, residents or patients, staring first at her breasts then her face—she of the careful, hairsprayed locks and sculpted, wide cheekbones and neat, medical-student outfit. But Tio Nemor had eyes only for his sister, Adina an guapa, lying on the hospital bed. He wiped the drool off her face, he pushed back her dark hair from her cheek. The sister had the full mouth of those women in bold movies—raw like rose-flesh. Shadows played on her profile, the way in repose her somewhat asymmetrical features seemed cast in chiaroscuro—her beauty refracted, troubling and shaded and mutable, even at rest.

"What would it be like to be loved like that," thought Doctor Tita Tita as she watched the brother gazing at the sister, stroking her senseless arm.

Her first sight of Tio Nemor was this incestuous pose.

It was clear from her stillness that the sister had a kind of astasia abasia, an involuntary suspension of nervous sensation that came from the electricity, the treatment for hypomania in these private rooms at the clinic in Tondo.

What do you mean, I said—electricity?

"I don't think your uncle or your Papá ever forgave themselves for saying yes to electroshock treatment," Doctor Tita Tita said. "It was the treatment of the time. Though in my view it is not the treatment that was to blame for your mother's subsequent life."

The founder of the clinic, the formal, old-world senator with a gash on his cheek, was a common sight to the young interns. During anniversaries and Christmas parties, the *españolado*, as they called him, would give a speech in that twangy English of his antique generation, Spanish *R*s and American *T*s—*Terrreseeeda*, he would call her later when he visited in Salogó, the *T*s soft, almost an elision, an affront to her ears at first—and he'd bestow annual gifts and his honorable presence upon the staff.

That's how she had first known the man.

The founder of the clinic.

The *españolado* went in and out of the room of the family of *provincianos*—the father, the son, and the daughter.

It was only later that she understood the founder was no foreigner—he was a Filipino like her.

"Of course, your grandfather, Papá, he could not disobey his Tio Paco."

As she passed by them, their door ajar, the young intern wished to tell the family that the electrodes on the brain, the Frankenstein wires of the treatment, were scarier than the cure. The patient's amnesia and her astasia abasia, her inability to walk or remember, would be temporary, and the patient would regain control of her limbs and motion, though it was too soon to tell if the electricity would be any help.

But the sight was cruel, and as a student she had had her doubts.

It was a routine treatment at the clinic, she wished to assure the family, and if the dose titration was guessed right and the seizure threshold adequately gauged, the patient after weeks of shock treatment did find relief, or so the medical books said—she wanted to tell the man who looked so "isputing!," the sorrowing law clerk, Nemorino Delgado (she checked his name on the guest register). Sure, it would be no consolation for the sight of a sister still registering tonic-clonic spasms, side effects of the cure. But Doctor Tita Tita saw them only in passing, following her resident on his rounds, and when she saw Tio Nemor again, smoking a cigarette in the patients' garden, sitting by the fountain of nude cherubs tied up in bondage, that specialty of Guillermo Tolentino, the senator's sculptor of choice for this special mental health clinic in Tondo, endowed by him for the people, on impulse she sat next to Tio Nemor, under the bruised naked angel, to eat her lunch of danggit and rice.

It was possible, Doctor Tita Tita said, that their marriage never lived down the salt tinge of regret that began it.

The Shape of the Sword

The hallway where the boy lies in the convent facing the room of Waller, Waller, Waller, Waller is dark, and the fresh breezes of a habagat morning do not wake up little Paco: he has not slept.

He waits to hear the captain's snore—a susurrus like a crocodile's gurgle, the buaya in reverie at the old zoo that used to arrive in cages in Manila at Lent. It's the morning chain medley—all of the officers are snorers. Griswold the surgeon's is a staccato of bursts, like a blast of shells from a bay. Melancholy Bumpus's snore is a puppy dog's, nag-iininop nga tuta, in small yips, intermittent, as if even in dream his desires have no aim. Bumpus is asleep with his mail, the letters from Cambridge and Quincy tucked under his arms.

The boy hears his approach.

He has no need to look.

He sits up in the dark hallway where his improvised bed, a straw mat, has been waiting for this moment for forty-eight days.

As if he knew, in their game of *An-Iya-Irong*, that it was he who was lost, not his brother.

And it was Jote who would find him.

He lies on his mat with his notebooks beneath his head, his hard pillow.

Jote is staring at the boy.

A bolo in his grip, his costume trailing after.

—That is Nay Carmen's skirt.

And Jote stares at him, a finger to his lips.

He shakes his head at the boy.

An eternity.

That is, a second.

Jote smiles.

—I tried to find you—the boy says.

—Sssh—Jote says—I know. I heard.

He hesitates.

War has given him discipline.

He can't help it—he goes up to his brother.

An iya manghod.

He pats him on the head.

We got the message from Tio Mariano, Jote whispers in Paco's ear.

Huh? says the boy.

Ayaw kabaraka, says Jote—we have heard from Ka Mariano.

Ka? says the boy.

Sssssh! says Jote.

He puts his finger to his mouth.

It's a familiar gesture.

Don't move, Paco, until I tell you.

That's what it means.

It's their old game.

The boy hears the sounds in the captain's room—so familiar now—

Just as quietly as he appears, Jote moves toward the door.

An iya gamit gihay—

—*No!* says Paco.

An iya gamit gihay, pagkastigo ha iya kalugaringon, an iya lawas baga hin Jesukristo ha atubangan han justicia ni Poncio Pilato, labi na ha iya likod (back), mga tuhod (knees), siko (elbows), paa (feet), pero labot la ha iya utin (penis).

Little Paco rushes up to his brother, tugging at Nay Carmen's skirt.

He holds his brother back.

And that is when Jote does it.

The slash of his bolo knife that marks their brothers' bond.

It's an instinct.

He strikes at Paco with his curved weapon.

For a moment, Jote pauses.

And there it will be on the boy, the half-moon shape of a sword dripping across little Paco's face.

Baga hin luwag, ayaw pagdad-a.

Paco is too surprised to move.

His hand upon his cheek.

Jote glares at Paco, finger to his lips.

Jote opens the door to the captain's room.

And that's when the boy rushes for the weapon—

His brother's bolo—the curved tool.

—*No!*

Ayaw!

The boy grabs at the weapon, and in an awkward lunge, he slices upward.

Upon Jote's cheek.

Nasamaran.

They stare at each other—brother and brother.

Scimitars or ladles, uneven curves of half-moons.

Luwag ngan luwag.

Bugto ngan bugto.

An inutod nga bulan, nga baga hin ngisi o luha.

Manghod.

Maghurang.

Jote takes the weapon and shakes the door open.

Who is more shocked by the moment?

Jote or Waller, Waller, Waller, Waller?

The captain is stark naked before his cross.

Jote is staring, knife raised.

His Mauser, out, the gun hidden under women's clothes.

The captain, holding onto his prick in one hand, grasping in the other his silly lash, that gihay broom.

An iya gamit gihay.

Ha iya sili.

—*Jote!* says the boy.

Who is it he wants to save?

Chirei (eyebrow), *botchen* (arm), *paha* (thigh), *licud* (back), *sico* (elbow), *tuhud* (knee), *camat* (hand), *liogh* (throat), *utin* (penis).

Dilla (tongue).

All the body parts from the chronicle of Pigafetta.

Jote hacks at the officer, body part after body part, a glossary of spilled and misspelled blood, his mission in Jote's last battle, in Giporlos barrio of Balangiga, as little Paco watches, his hand upon his face, the shape of his brother's knife, his half-moon of blood.

Lolo Paco's Last Words

"She was always your Lolo Paco's favorite," Doctor Tita Tita said. "She was in college when it happened. She at first lived in Greenhills at his home for those first months in college. It's true he had wanted to adopt her when she was a child. You can imagine Adina as a baby. That's what they called her from the beginning, your Tio Nemor said to me, he told me all these stories, those days at the clinic—she was Adina an guapa from the time she was born. I told him, there there, there there. Your sister will be well, I told him. And he went on and on, telling me how women with child would come to visit the house in Salogó, to look at the gorgeous baby, like a saint, a relic. Everyone knew Adina an guapa. It was a superstition, Nemor said—from the different barrios, even from Alang-Alang, as far as Tolosa, people would come to see the baby. That's why later—But you know it was not her beauty, I think, that made your Lolo Paco want Adina an guapa. When the senator came to visit his brother—"

Jote, I said.

"Yeah, your Lolo Jote. The senator from Manila visited his brother Jote yearly in Salogó—this was before the war, of course."

Which war, I said.

"There's only one," laughed Tita Tita—"of course, the Second World War."

Ah, I said.

"So he wasn't a senator yet, now that you mention it, he was still working for Osmeña, those government missions to estados, and he was back from America. Your Tio Nemor can tell you—he knows all the historical details."

He was on the OsRox mission, I said, for independence.

Resident commissioner in Washington, DC, in 1931.

Team that negotiated the Tydings–McDuffie Act of 1934—which legislated the promise of independence in 1946.

In exchange for tariffs on the country's sugar—a law to maintain the interests of America's sugar lords.

Not to mention the agents of coconut oil, yarn, twine, cord, cordage, rope and cable, tarred or untarred, wholly or in chief value of manila (abaca) or other hard fibers.

That US law enacted Philippine independence—as long as the United States maintained dominion over foreign affairs, the constitutional convention, education, and of course, the economy, especially the agrarian exports sugar, coconut oil, and abaca.

The Tydings-MacGuffin Act, I call it, I said.

"Ah, the Tydings-MacGuffin Act!" said my aunt. "Hah. Yes, well, we were never taught that in medical school."

Makes sense. That history was being made as you were growing up, I said. I mean, Ma was born the year the Constitution was made—with the help of her Lolo Paco—1935.

"Any visit of your Lolo Paco was a big deal in Salogó, you know, with marching bands and many offerings of bibingka and suman from all the women of the town, that's what your Tio Nemor remembers."

And pasalubong of hipon and budo-bulad!

"Ha ha yes. Lolo Paco loved the salted fish. And the bagoong. He said Nay Mimang, Mana Carmen's mom, made the best bagoong. Anyway, that time he came to Salogó to visit his brother, your Papá had just had the baby."

My mom, I said.

"Yes. He was living in the house with Mamá and Nemor and the baby. How your Papá adored his uncle. He worshipped the ground his Tio Paco walked on, said Nemor. And why not? At our clinic in Tondo, he was a god—he had founded it. Your Lolo Paco sent money for your Papá's music classes, he paid for him to be *interno* at San Juan de Letran, he bought him gifts from abroad, like the music box that he got from London—"

That old gramophone?

"—and the music sheets from Germany, he sent your Papá all the books he wanted."

Those history books in the house—they were not Lolo Paco's? That book *Abraham Lincoln's World*?

"I don't know which book! Any book in English in the house would have been your Papá's."

I see.

"I mean, your Lolo Jote refused to speak English."

Or did he just refuse to speak, I said.

"Anyway, Lolo Paco saw her that day—he saw the baby of the house."

My mom, I said.

"Yes, your Tio Nemor was around eight years old or so. Now your Papá—*he* said he had named his baby Adina because of some opera, she and Nemorino were named after opera."

L'elisir d'amore, I said.

"I have no idea. Ay por bida, how Papá loved that music, it drove me crazy whenever we were in Salogó. Your Papá had all the records. He had that music box that you wind up—it's the one they keep in the sala."

The Edison Bell, I said—it still works.

"Oh my gulay. That thing drove me nuts—Papá never stopped playing that opera."

So the opera books in Salogó, I said—they are also Papá's, not Lolo Paco's? *F. B. Delgado* is Papá, not Lolo Paco?

"I don't know what you mean. They're both F. B. Delgado."

Ah.

"One is Francisco Blumfeld Delgado. Your Lolo Jote and your Lolo Paco had some, I don't know, grandfather from Austria. Or Czechoslovakia. Named Blumfeld. A musician who ran away from home in Europe. Then he ran away from Samar. When I met your Tio Nemor that was his joke—*Don't fall in love with me! We're a family of runaways!* It was, for some reason, endearing. He's funny, your Tio Nemor. He always made me laugh. The other F. B. is your Papá—Francisco Buñales Delgado."

Ah.

"Anyway, the senator—it's said Lolo Paco saw the baby, your mom, Adina an guapa, and it was like—he just fell in love. Your Lolo Paco fell in love with the beautiful baby named Adina."

Named after Lolo Paco's mom.

"Yes! Exactly! So Nemor told you this story?"

No.

"Lolo Paco held her in his arms—he thought she was named after his mother, Adina Blumfeld, the woman from Samar who died giving birth to him. But your Papá shook his head—said—no, no, he didn't. Your Papá had no idea what his grandmother's name was."

What?

"His father, your Lolo Jote, never told stories about his family. Never. That's what Nemorino said. So when your Lolo Paco saw the baby, and he heard the name, he had tears in his eyes and said, *That is a beautiful Delgado name.* It's from the opera, your Papá said proudly. And your Lolo Paco said, *It's the name of my mother.* Papá just looked confused. *You did not know?* And that's when your Lolo Paco looked at his brother Jote, so Tio Nemor tells the story, and said—*You arrre a bitterrr soul, Jote.* He spoke it in English. That's what he said to his brother. Nemor always repeats that phrase in your Lolo Paco's English, rolling the *R*s, with the pauses, like he's making a speech at the United Nations—*You. Arrrre. A bittterrr soul—Jote!*"

Tio Nemor likes to say that phrase, I nodded—but what did Lolo Paco mean?

"I don't know. It was odd," Tita Tita said, "how the senator never failed to visit his brother, and he was always sending gifts, and it was he who made sure the children went to college. And eventually—it was he who told Nemor the stories of his mother and father in Samar, how they had met and fallen in love. Nemor learned the stories when he was old enough to study in Manila. But your Lolo Jote—he just—did not speak of things."

Que se joda, I said.

"Yeah—ha ha. Que se joda que se joda. They'd sit there, talking in Spanish, because Lolo Jote refused to use English in anyone's company—though of course he knew it. He went to medical school in English! He listened to his fellow congressmen's speeches in English! But to me, inday, he spoke only in Waray—Waray was his language—his language of choice. Kinadaan nga Waray siyempre, full of Spanish. And the senator, well, his Waray was like an americano's. Kanadyan."

Ha ha, ambot, I said—Fil-ambot.

My aunt laughed.

"So they'd sit there, speaking their old childhood language. That mix of Spanish and Tagalog and Waray. Mostly Spanish. Sometimes I understood it. Mainly it would be the senator talking. His Spanish was like a schoolbook. Your Lolo Jote—it was as if—he just tolerated his brother, he let him talk, he barely spoke. I saw the senator maybe two times on his visits to Salogó, and it impressed me—how the senator whom I knew from the clinic—such a big man in Manila—the founder of our clinic in Tondo—he was, well, in Salogó—ha Salogó manghod la hiya. He was only the little brother. While your Lolo Jote, I don't know how to say it—"

He despised him.

"Yes! That is it. I couldn't really put a finger to it. He just did not think much of his brother—or of anything really. Maybe. I mean, he barely campaigned to be congressman. I have no idea how your Lolo Jote won that election. It was weird how people loved him though he never said a word."

He was the district's doctor, I said—why would people not vote for him if he ran?

"He just had this—I don't know—you know, like some mythology. But no one ever bothered to tell its source—including him. He did do a few things—like construct the wall against the river's floods."

The AWOL!

"Yeah. He built elaborate homes for his chickens, he labeled the plants in the garden—and even the insects that he framed—he labeled them with their scientific names. He made plans for flushing toilets. But it's true, yes, he was everyone's doctor. He knew everyone's pains from birth to death. That was his life. So when he ran for Congress—against his brother's party, by the way—he was not a Nacionalista, you know—well, he won."

So what happened to the baby—with my mom as a baby?

"Your Papá, of course, would not allow the adoption. This is the part of the story Adina likes to tell—the one she likes to remember. How Lolo Paco wanted *her* most of all, above all, the beautiful baby—he wanted to take her with him to Manila. Kay baug man hera—Lolo Paco and his wife could not have a child. It terrified your Papá to say no. But your Tio Nemor also said—Papá was angry. Nainsulto hin duro. Nemor was scared to hear his Papá's voice. It was like a growl—*No! No se puede!* But much later, when your mom wished to go to college in Manila, and he was a widower by that time, his wife Mamá was gone, he said yes."

And when she was in Manila Adina an guapa fell sick?

"I think your Papá always felt guilty—that he allowed her to go, then she had this breakdown, this illness, and he allowed the clinic to give her the treatment, he listened to his uncle, his Tio Paco, who was so concerned about her, you know, the senator believed that he was doing the right thing, he had given her the best clinical treatment money could buy, and who knows, really—I think it was the correct thing to do. At the time. I don't know—it was what we did at the clinic. It was how we treated. But after that—her entire life was a convalescence. No one could say no to your mom—except Tia Pachang, of course. All of them, Nemor, her Papá, even her Lolo Paco, who gave her an inheritance, he said to her before he died—"

What?

"You don't know the story? He said he would give her La Tercera."

Ah—the notebooks, I said, leaning toward my aunt.

I get it now, I said.

"What are you talking about?" said my aunt, confused. "What notebooks? I mean, the land. Your mom told me—when she visited him before she left for Los Angeles, she had to say goodbye one more time, he was already in the hospital at FEU. He died a few months later. Those were your Lolo Paco's last words to her. He said to her, ah, Adina, you're the heredera of La Tercera. She was the heiress, he said. He even noted that—in a document he gave her, your mom said to me. She had received, he said, the most valuable thing. But she never got it, your mother said—she never got La Tercera."

He Looks Up

Out the window he looks up from the notebooks and watches his good friends, the yanqui gringos, Captain Henry T. Allen, Lieutenant Harry Bandholtz, and Sergeant Frank Breton, watch Jote trot off on his way to medical school at Padre Faura that morning in June 1908. He's not surprised to see her when he looks up, but he's surprised she arrives so soon.

He sends the congratulatory telegram to Hotel Oriente when he reads of her arrival in *Renacimiento*. Every day since his return from Indiana, he reads *El Renacimiento*, as well as its Tagalog counterpart *Muling Pagsilang*, the publications that arrive at his hotel room for his perusal.

He reads about her during his year killing time in a strange place, first in high school in Compton, California, memorizing poems that always turn out to be by Alfred, Lord Tennyson, *half a league, half a league, sweet and low, on thy cold gray stones, O sea!—Break! Break! Break!* And on to the cold plains of Bloomington. *I would that my tongue could utter.* There is no recompense for the hell of solitude on those flattened plains—the four of them, he and George Bocobo and Aning de Joya and that crazy Pepe Valdez.

They will become the Four Immortals of Indiana in the Common-wealth's valedictions.

But the future is no boon to teenagers.

Books give him the comfort of familiarity—Washington Irving, William Makepeace Thackeray, James Fenimore Cooper.

Piensa! Piensa in English!

Algernon Charles Swinburne, washed down with zinfandel claret.

He's lucky to be *galabanting!*, he can hear Tay Sequil, *El Excellent Cochero Exequiel!* (in his American-era taxi ads), shouting well wishes, waving from Manila harbor as the ship slips.

Where are they now? Scattered. His father dead. (He, Paco, will feel that same carbuncle in his late years, purplish heirloom near the mole upon his breast, size of an igot.)

Tay Sequil in his straw hat and barong, smelling, he can smell it even from the distance, he thinks, of betel spit, a glob of blood, ver-milion spray upon talahib—his betel-nut blessing from Tay Sequil on Manila's pier, smiling Tay Sequil against the woolen dignitaries, the dignitaries of the Philippine Commission, and there is the floating balloon that is the governor-general, and the newly formed Constab-ulary Band—the governor loves them so much they are called *Taft's Own* (oh what a first as the Philippine Constabulary Band, and not the US Marines, lead the inaugural parade when that floating bal-loon of a governor-general becomes US president!)—in their shining khakis and ties, rounded-up rondalla players, town fiesta musicians, and one surrendered katipunero from a rebel marching band in Tanza, led by the famous artist, the great Buffalo soldier, el maestro, the Black *mago* Mr. Lieutenant Loving. The band serenades the voy-agers with a thrilling tune that he learns (in a rushed tour of New York City, finding in the Metropolitan Opera a misplaced sense of home) is the Wedding Song in *Aïda*.

But above all, he remembers Tay Sequil, Mariano, Ambrosio, and his stiff lump of a father in his wooden wheelchair—Don Francisco the First—their receding mass—moving away from him in that trick that travel has. (No one now mentions Jote, and neither does he.)

His relative sight.

An iya mga urupod.

Standing by as the world shifts.

The *Rochilla Maru!* takes the boys to Yokohama, to Honolulu. He waits for exuberance to get him on yet one more shore. Thousands of Portuguese men-of-war, nautiluses, jellyfishes, beautifully colored things. With little pointed jelly fins on their flat, spherical bodies. They do not have much life in them. *At reveille, a man was buried. A splash, and that is all.* The fish make a circle. Rippling, circling. A cut, a tear. Something is lost. He won't name it. He smells the sea. He hears his buddy, the other Francisco, coughing up in his bunk. He watches ants trace an invisible path (later he learns the path is chemical, in Biology class at Bloomington, which he aces, the way he aces so many things, his mind a trap, a mass of pheromonal mnemonic tricks he does not need to fathom). Sensations click shut. He does not bother to note. *The world is too much. Late and soon.* He is a ward of a new world, collecting knowledge.

Little we see in Nature that is ours.

Scribbling scribbling piensos in English.

Experience—if only people knew, he has a lot.

An iya kaagian.

So do the rest of his countrymen.

The wards of America.

Fish and Spoon

"It's odd," says Tita Tita, "but I understood it."

What happened?

"It began with one word."

A word?

"Yes. It began with one word. *Pish.*"

Pish?

"And then the second word. *Ispun.*"

Ispun?

"Yes. *Fish.* Then *spoon.* They were having dinner, and your Lolo Paco was there, and that girl that he had adopted, that poliomyelitic, Charity Breton, remember, she was sued by all the Delgados for taking the inheritance away. I mean, you know they won the case."

No, I said, they lost on appeal.

"Hah, yes," said Tita Tita, "so you know? But they won the case first! In the Court of First Instance!"

Oh Tita Tita—you sound like my mom.

"They went after that Charity so bad. Such a big deal, for so many years. Then they lost on appeal. Yeah. It took so long by the time that case was over, Nemor had become a lawyer! Anyway, that Charity woman was there. In your mom's medical report, Charity Breton was a witness of your mom's collapse. She came once with the senator to visit your mom. A sad sight—so young, already a cripple. She told the story to me, that Charity. Instead of saying—*please pass the fish*—one night your mom said to her Lolo Paco at dinner— the house is by Jose Abad Santos—have you been?—she said one night—*plis pass da pish.* And instead of saying, *May I please have a spoon?*—Adina an guapa said, '*May I plis hab ispun.*'"

That's it?

But that's just—talking, I said.

"She could speak English fine otherwise, you see," Doctor Tita Tita said, "like anyone else who went to school at Holy Infant."

But isn't that just about her—accent? Just a way of speaking in Salogó? What a mean woman, that Charity Breton, for conveying it as disability—I mean, Adina an guapa was always weird with words. She made words up!

"You don't understand," said Tita Tita. "It's the change that matters. First she could speak one way, then she could not. It's the loosening of associations, that's the point. The disintegration of psychic functions that arises in speech is a concern. I mean, it's not my specialty. But speech is a sign. A neural symptom. Among others, of course. Nemor said it was a mistake, the diagnosis. Her precocious madness."

That's a diagnosis?

"Dementia praecox. But Nemor believed that Adina was just nervous, anxious in Manila—without her Papá. Far from Salogó. She was homesick. It was comforting to her, he said, to speak like a person from Salogó, and not a colegiala from Manila. It was nerves, he likes to think. For him, he loved being in Manila, all the gallivanting with the boys. But for her—she was homesick, he said. You know the joke about us neurosurgeons. We operate on the brain to fix it, not to understand it. I have no idea if it was the correct diagnosis. Your Papá—he never forgave himself. It was painful to see him—to watch your Papá care for your mom at the clinic. After the electroshock treatment it was heartbreaking to see, I was just an observer—to see his daughter unable to remember who he was. She could not even remember her Papá. But she regained it, her memory. It was just a side effect of the treatment. We told him that—that she'd regain it. And she did. But he never forgave himself. For listening to the senator, for giving permission for the treatment."

All because of fish and spoon?

"It bothered your Lolo Paco. He noticed. And then of course, it was really what followed that mattered—she was unable to get up, she said to me, as if there was something eating her inside, and she believed she was made of plastic, and rotting on the inside—"

She said that?

"Yes, years later, that's how she described it. A rare moment—you know she never talks about herself. Do you notice? She does not examine herself or her past. It's her tendency. Her one memory of the past is how much her Papá and her Lolo Paco loved her. And that Lolo Paco was going to give her La Tercera, but she was cheated by that cripple, by Charity Breton."

Something was eating her up inside—those were her words?

"Something was eating her up inside, she told me, and she tore at it, her belly and her hair—it had reached her brain, Adina said, it was eating up her brain. They had to call the ambulance to the house on Abad Santos. No one could figure it out because, you know, she got well. She has a genius for self-protection, your mom. She's a survivor."

So that's why she'd disappear, I said. To the *cursillos*, to seek the bleeding tears of the Virgin of Zamboanga.

I sat there for a moment—I looked out at that twinkling Bay.

"Well, you know, why not go to the *cursillos*, and the Virgin of Zamboanga really did bleed tears. So her parish priest said! Nemor always said—just let her go."

I pointed toward the glittering lights on the water.

And the casinos? I asked.

"Well. Yes. We let her do it. But we kept tabs on her—on where she went."

Except none of you kept her from marrying my dad, I said.

I was surprised at her response—I was just poking at the wind.

Tita Tita was nodding, staring at the Bay.

"True," she said, "but you know—that's the fault of Tia Pachang."

The First Batch

In Compton, he cuts out clippings. The Anti-Imperialist League and New York's Sorosis Club and the Massachusetts Feminists do not come to Bloomington. What is *sorosis*? Gossamer their gown. Their tippet only tulle. Rush of cochineal: the iridescence of women.

They do not meet.

She has been on tour with that Massachusetts radical who was the lone white woman at the funeral of Mabini who met Ricarte in Hong Kong who reported on the burned towns of Batangas who championed her. The Filipina Rebel, companion of the white woman Helen Wilson, makes speeches in Pittsburgh, Cambridge, Chicago. She tells her story. The one he—(but he tucks the thought away, smoothed under his Brilliantina hair). When he returns to Moret Street from Samar (returned by the man who saves him—his father is grateful, the family will be forever grateful, the old man says on Moret Street to Sergeant Frank Breton, anything he needs, the old man says, if we can help, let us know, but he, Paco, prefers not to go on and on about this incident, his rescue by Breton)—by the time of his return, the country has changed.

Pacified.

A civil government rules, William Howard Taft, the governor-general, occupies Malacañang, his regime organizes the Philippine Constabulary (especially its Marching Band! *Taft's Own!*), the Philippine Scouts, the hometown boys who police America's empire—right-hand goons of peacetime.

Kamurayaw.

He's one of The Hundred, the few, the chosen few, of 1903. It's his ability to know the language, to speak English, to be his father's son that gives him an advantage. His father knows people who know people who know Taft, he aces the test, he is chosen. A prodigy, so his professors in Indiana say. In September, his professors are so proud, he will be a student of law, he's precocious.

But before his next leg, New Haven, obligations bring him home.

Traductores, not *traidores*.

No kidding.

The first batch!, they're called, like loaves, like pies, sodden in cotton camisas, wet shoes, straw hats, going two by two up Market Street, finally, in September, 1903, after twenty-eight days, how long is eternity on a boat, he and his buddy, the other Francisco, in San Francisco, warming the cockles of their white hosts' hearts to see them clothed in three-piece americanas (which his father wore to jaunts at Bagumbayan, business at the Escolta, in fact), their proud changeling guise, outfitted and housed and schooled, off to their selected tundras—Kalamazoo, Michigan; Trenton, New Jersey; Ames, Iowa.

Each place-name is an amber bubble, snow-globe of benevolence.

America is land of cows and wheat. Manhattan is in Kansas and Ithaca is not Homeric. Delfín Jaranilla of Iloilo, that skinny runt, he will be Secretary of Justice, he gets sent to Knoxville, Tennessee, where Blacks are barred from school and the pensionado is an affront to both white and black. Apolinario Baltazar of Manila (what happened to him, tokayo of the hero, anti-scion of Balagtas?) is famous for chasing a smartass white man in surveying class at Cornell with a knife. Ha ha ha. *No matter how hard you wash your hands, you cannot change your color!* Taunts, jeers, sweethearts, they make history. An anti-miscegenation bill in Indiana, spurred by that ladykiller, that handsome tango dancer Pepe Valdez. It does not pass. So many souvenirs. The hundred pensionados, *the first batch!*, are all male. The boys publish the speaking events of The Filipina Rebel (not to mention her picture) in their newsletters. What are they thinking? He and George and Aning and Pepe—the Immortal Four—they go on stage with William Jennings Bryan!, the anti-imperialist!, running for president one more time, it's his hobby—onstage in Indianapolis with that other Humpty-Dumpty, though no one is as wide as his rival, their oval ninong, balloon-shaped Governor Taft. What got into the knucklehead souls of the Immortal Four? Their guardian, the maestro Cunningham, he has his notions—*to colonize, but not by might!*—though he came to his grand idea late, after genocide. The maestro is the brains of their journey, the pensionados are his conception (at the moment, not immaculate)—the maestro Cunningham telegrams his displeasure to Paco, George, Aning, and Pepe.

But what a thrill to be on stage, Sons of Kalayaan, just like the Filipina Rebel!

Strumpet, Potenciano says, adding to his glossary of words in Chicago. New Woman, notes Silverio in Purdue. Palladian, says Carlos the pedant at Drexel. Sweet, says Ramon in Lansing. Kababayan, they admit, in Oswego, New York; Normal, Illinois; Columbus, Ohio.

When Helen Calista Wilson needs a clerk for her new offices in her stenography business on the Escolta, at the foot of the Bridge of Spain now the heart of American bustle in Manila—the better to surveil the state, my dear, the Radcliffe *interna* admits—the young woman from the famous province has the best references: the Barrettos of Zambales, the Lopezes of Balayan. But it turns out her best recommendation is her name: the two women share it. They're tokayo.

The coincidence affects Helen. She's a radical, therefore Romantic. There is, of course, Calista Catalogo's oddly Bostonian English—a familiar inflection that charms Helen Calista Wilson.

But most of all, there is the story of her war in Balangiga (that is the site they label for her trauma, though she is from Giporlos, and when the Americans burn Samar in retaliation for their forty-eight dead in Balangiga plaza, anyway they also torch Giporlos, Guiuan, Lawaan, San Roque). How quickly the refugee from Samar finds a home among the association of feminists in Manila—their names etched on the Masonic Temple: Helen Calista Wilson of Quincy, Mariquita and Ninay Lopez of Balayan, Trinidad Rizal, Teresa Solis, Maria F. viuda de Villamor, Bonifacia Delgado de Barretto of Bulacan, Bulacan. All *doñas* and *señoras* and *mayordomas* of their clans. Class drives the Philippines. Respectability has its uses. Plus beauty. Nay Carmen, her gnarly aunt, for instance, understands Calista is a draw to her sari-sari store in Giporlos, but she does not altogether get why. Why why gaway. A dark child with eerie self-possession. Nay Carmen's child, Adina, is long dead, but it is not her fault but the merciful God's. *Ave Maria, graaaatia pleeee-nah!* In her old age, her aunt Nay Carmen turns to music, those songs that burned her joy, arias of the legendary rascal—her dastardly love Blumfeld that she now tells as a musical, as if the story were not hers.

Who can blame her?

Thus neither Calista nor her aunt Nay Carmen recognizes him when he arrives—how could they? Jote is a runt when he leaves Giporlos, Calista is not yet born, and it turns out the relatives her Nay Carmen sends to Moret Street from Samar—her Tio Mariano, her Nay Felicisima, her Tay Ambrosio—are unreliable letter writers.

But from the start, the girl is riveted to the town's changes—ant trailing pheromones. First those Goliath soldiers who invade the plaza, the new guardia civil in Giporlos. Mga parahubog nga mga kapre. Alcoholic beasts. That blowpipe of a man, puydi igsumpit, hala, an naglilinakat-lakat nga kalag—Lieutenant Bumpus: he thinks he teaches her cursive that she already knows. He laughs: how quickly the girl learns. She's a quick study, a star.

And then—all the laborers that keep coming for fiesta. Her Nay Carmen gathers them as they arrive—from Guiuan, Quinapundan, and wherever forest caverns Ka Vicente Lukban lodges, making sohot sohot sohot out there in the caves. Jote's youth and his arrival surprise no one. His gaze is a trophy. The girls vie for it. They are silly. His baby encanto look, sunburned Santo Niño—*bendisyoni kami!* though the stranger has no gaze for them. Ka Vicente's men are all just boys anyway, soothes her Nay Carmen. She notices the girl's glances at the gray-eyed katipunero—labaw han iya tan-aw. Even that presidente—Aguinaldo—only thirty-two when captured. At war for nine! Agi! Mga batan-on nga parasaway—ini nga mga katipunero. Manunulay. A lifetime spent hiding and hiding. So young, the youths. But still, too bad they caught him, a prisoner in our own palace, Malacañang. Por bida. What a catastrophe to be a Filipino. Disgrasya.

Santo Niño, bendisyoni kami.

Everywhere—the dominoes surrender.

Fallen Palawan, pacified Capiz, captured Iloilo, ill-fated Cebu, subdued Masbate, massacred Batangas, battered archipelago.

Pillage, rape, rinderpest, fire.

Hunger.

Everyone is starving, reconcentrating bile. Pastilan, uday. Rebels are not found, they're made. And her town exacts vengeance that the American harrowing has stilled. Pacification is a misnomer, revolution is no dream. In Samar. Samar burns. Even before their men attack Waller and his garrison, the Catalogo women have escaped up the hills. And then their diaspora—to Matnog and Tacloban, Manila and Salogó. Launched on trading boats, the fishermen's bancas—their plans of escape in place.

Because the plan of uprising, after all, is theirs.

Rage is a good organizer.

Too bad they could not explain it to their neighbors—people

minding their own business whose towns are also burned, in the aftermath.

She arrives in Salogó with Jote, with the escaped Catalogo clan—with Bingo (not Bongo), Nay Carmen and the other Carmens, all the little ones named after the wealthy aunt.

What happened between Jote and Calista, the girl by the stream, she who becomes the Filipina Rebel while his brother Jote speaks to the trees and the insects—maya, maya, maya—bayâ!

He knows Calista left.

But why?

He seeks it in the notebooks.

La primera.

La segunda.

The chapters of his brother's life, as far as he can tell.

La donna é mobile.

Why does she leave?

He wants to know.

He has another mission, true, but it's her name that he pursues.

Paco holds on to the notebooks, evidence of the revolutionary life of his brother Jote, walking toward the tranvia stop to Padre Faura.

Paz Tilanuday.

He can see beneath the pseudonym in these notebooks.

He's no polyglot for nothing.

But who's Hua-Zhu?

He turns the page for the next chapter.

La tercera.

He wants to know.

Synesthesia

The family Rebosura was playing its reunion games at the wrong beach, Boracay. There is a banner in teal, there is a stage, there is a rondalla band. Old and young, grandmothers and nephews, all in bright marigold and wearing ismagol, play the reunion games—Discover-Discover, Going to Market, Tuktukan—Touching-the-Eggs! The apo is putting on his lola's skirt, then her bra, then her sunglasses, then her hat. Sashay sashay, Going to Market in his lola's suit. He fans his lola on the other side with his abaca fan as she gets into his clothes, she has trouble with the electrodes on her brow, and the sando is silly, she walks off, arms in the air, sashay sashay, Going to Market. It is clear they are losing, everyone is already onto a new game, the nephew claps, and now they are playing Touching-the-Eggs, a string is attached to the skirts, an egg is attached to the string, their hips shake, and the eggs on the apo go around the world. The goal is to touch the other's circling eggs. Tuktok tuktok tuktok.

There's a knock on the hotel door.

Doctor Tita Tita says, go to sleep, inday, it is three o'clock in the morning in New York! But if you're hungry—here's some food!

We were having room service, and my aunt was laughing at me.

"You fell asleep in the middle of my story!"

I remembered the image of the boy in the dream putting on his grandmother's clothes.

And I asked my aunt, Doctor Tita Tita, the neuro—is it a condition?

"What are you talking about? Go back to sleep if you want."

Is there a word for the feeling of being in someone else's clothes? To feel it when others touch something, and it seems like when someone swallows, his food is also going into your body, and pain has a color, like black for blood, and a purplish-beige tint for the lash of gihay.

"What do you mean," she said, "the lash of gihay? Kiray hin gihay?"

Doctor Tita Tita laughed.

"Gihay is for cleaning! I have no idea what you're talking about," she said. "I stopped doing neuro in 1987, inday. You know that. Have this—so good. I ordered all the merienda, every single one—puto, kutsinta, pichi-pichi, espasol, maja blanca, palitaw, biko, bibingka! Even champorado, since it was on the menu. But really, there's no bibingka like Nay Carmen's bibingka," said Doctor Tita Tita, biting into one rosebud of a cake.

Is she from Samar, Nay Carmen?

"No. From Capoocan. Daughter of Nay Mimang—Marga's aunt. But only by marriage."

So there's no word for that condition? Like seeing colors for the taste of igot?

"Ah, igot! You know, you cannot get that fruit from stores. You can only steal them from your neighbor's yard. The condition of mixing sensations is synesthesia."

I know that term, synesthesia, I said. So is that what it is?

"There's another term—for that condition of feeling others' touch or what they swallow, that has a term. I'll check. I still get papers from *Nature Reviews* and *Neuroscience*. It's all digital now! I like to keep up with my memberships. It's in my inbox."

And I watched my aunt rummage in the Coach bag (circa Owings Mills outlet mall) as if the gulf between her old and her current life were no more remarkable than finding a sawdust bunny in Discover-Discover—your change in life is some item planted for you to find, and you accept it as your prize, no matter its condition.

"Aha," she said.

She found her phone and scrolled.

I ate a pichi-pichi. I skipped the kutsinta (I hate its slimy texture, I anticipate it will always taste like plastic), and I put aside a bowl of champorado for last.

I took a tiny bite of the palitaw.

Like sawdust and plastic, just as I thought. Hotels are not the best for coconut desserts—they need to be freshly grated, just done.

"Here it is. Synesthesia occurs when normally distinct senses are blurred. Information meant to stimulate only one of your senses activates several instead. Oh, that's not what I want. Ah. Here. This is the one. People with mirror-touch synesthesia report tactile sensations on their own body when seeing another person being touched. Is that what you mean, inday?"

I was testing in my molars the soluble nature of the cake—the denser it is the more it sticks.

"It says—there is evidence that people with mirror-touch synesthesia have trouble differentiating their own body from that of others. It's also possible mirror-touch synesthetes don't just share the tactile senses of other people—they also pick up emotional cues. But—that is still under study."

So there's a name for it, I said, this condition of simultaneity.

"It's called mirror-touch synesthesia—an exciting thing!" my aunt said, scrolling through the phone, "I never studied it myself. But it's so interesting, ay sus. It is linked, inday, to that quality we have—we imitate others, even as babies! Our adaptive humanity. And we also have adaptive mechanisms to control our mirroring tendency. I've been reading about that system, ay sus, huwaso. Pero agidaw, it's scientific. The mirror neuron system mediates our tendency—cortical areas that respond when we observe the actions of others. You see? It mediates social cognition, it mediates language, it mediates empathy. A very fascinating discovery, this mirror neuron. So you see why it is called mirror-touch synesthesia?"

No, I said.

"It means that the mirror neuron system does not respond in a normal way. I mean, if you have that mirror-touch condition. Mirror touch and mirror neurons—they are linked, that's how I see it. But mirroring can be in excess, you see. So those with mirror-touch synesthesia feel others' sensations in their own body. But other people, like us—we can mediate. So."

So what?

"So there are those who have difficulty separating their self from that of others. It explains it here. You see, inday, we all have a way of representing our emotions in our own bodies. Do you get that? It's just—how it is to be human. And these representations we have of our emotions are how we engage with *other* people's feelings. People with the mirror-touch—they find it difficult to separate *their own* representations of feeling with those of others. I mean, that is not normal. It's like—they're too human. Also called the Self-Other complex. It says here."

You mean, it's like having too much empathy.

"No. The mirror neuron system activates empathy maybe. But what this science is saying is that neurons stimulate our ability to recognize the other—"

So our moral stakes are just neurology?

"Hah! That is blasphemy. Mirror-touch synesthesia is about the body's responses, inday. Morality is from God. Is it possible to have too much empathy? Is it the same as having that simultaneity, the unnecessarily multiplied somatosensory reactions to another body's feelings? Those are different things. In my view. But I'm a neurosurgeon. I *operate*, inday, I don't *know*. I mean, hah! I used to operate!"

And it hung there between us, that space in being that my aunt had traversed. Neurosurgeon to bedpan-changer, wife to *divorciada*. And it occurred to me she had the same simultaneity as the rest of us—scientific and suspicious, observant and oblivious, loving and judgmental at once. I watched this woman take the next bite of bibingka, close her eyes, dilate her tongue, and taste it, the way long ago in Salogó she and Tio Nemor nursed a critic in their gastric tracts, testing the fibrous quality of the jackfruit seeds.

An liso, an liso, inday!

The jackfruit liso was only one thing though—mealy.

Is there a cure? I asked.

"Well, I would not call it a disease," she said, munching, and I saw her mirroring my own gesture, tonguing sticky rice against her teeth. "It's a bodily condition. Like having a mole, or green eyes. Though having that mirror-touch must be hard. On the body. I've never had a patient with synesthesia. They don't go to neurosurgeons. I mean, I did spinal injuries. I guess a traumatic instance might change the cortex? Create disturbances that affect the mirror neuron system? But ay, neurology—that is not my specialty. And now—not even surgery!"

Again, we were silent.

I'm sorry, I said to my aunt, that you stopped your work in America.

"It's okay. I'm used to it now. I'm retired!"

I touched her hand and squeezed it.

"Why are you asking about this synesthesia?" she said.

It's something to do with Lolo Paco, I said. It's something I'm reading.

"Wow," said Doctor Tita Tita, taking the bowl I had set aside. She took a whole spoonful. "Isn't the food in this hotel just the best? That palitaw is excellent. And that is very high-quality tabléa in this champorado. As if it had been churned by the sweat of Margarita in Salogó."

The World's Fair

The papers say it's Helen Calista Wilson who has the idea to tour America with her namesake, Calista Catalogo, survivor of the burning of Samar. Voice of the voiceless. Rebel for a cause. She sets up a stage, in stealth appearances, at the World's Fair. In the summer of 1904 before he gets to Bloomington the boys take the steamboat to the Louisiana Purchase Exposition of the World's Fair in St. Louis, Missouri. They are celebrity ushers of the Philippine grounds. August 13 is Philippine Day—six years to the day Manila fell!—not to the troops of the presidente Aguinaldo: Spain will surrender only to America though it is the Filipinos who surround them (but that last point is not in the story)! The boys are the historical spielers at St. Louis Fair on August 13, Philippine Day, in St. Louis. *The way the storms from the bay make liquid out of stiff mosses and vegetation along the esteros* (but he tucks that thought away, like his shirt into his trousers), *and the weather as usual transforms frogs and lily pads into flat impressions in the kasilyas, the outdoor toilet.*

What the monsoon leaves America occupies.

Pieces of shit and water lilies.

So long ago, that August 13.

(He combs his hair smooth, he reaches for his face, his finger hovers, it knows where not to graze, over the dent, the scar. Sensations click shut.)

It's the job of the boy pensionados, *the first batch!*, solemn teenagers in woolen adult garb, designated spielers with shining eyes. Their job is to show curiosity seekers the curios—forty-seven acres of a miniature nation, so newly captured its treasures must be itemized to justify the expense of stealing them, A Utopia of what was Already There, *Our Islands and Their People!*, streets and plazas and fire alarms and water systems, nipa huts and gums, rosins, medicinal plants, the perfume of ylang-ylang, mountain rice and valley rice, palay de secano, palay de regadio, plus all the oils of pili, peanut, tangan-tangan, tubâ-tubâ, church tapers from beeswax, tobacco from Cagayan, piña needlework and musical instruments, gongs and gamelans, but not the rondallas with their multiple lutes (they're Castilian), kanyon and lantaka, "a Typical Manila House, with shell windows," sea corals and flaring gorgonias ex situ spreading out five feet like the bamboo flooring's dry swaddling, birds' eggs attractively displayed, carabao heads, deer and boar and a twenty-one-foot long python, and too many lizards, halô! ibid! tuko!, but only one buaya, the metonymical crocodile, stands of narra and cedar and everyone's mahogany dreams, *the woods considered so valuable by us are used for the commonest purpose here, servants disembowel cuttlefish on precious darkwood slabs, all of these need to be brought away by us enterprising Yankees to show what is there in the rich forests*, wardrobes, chiffoniers, sideboards, bedsteads, sedans—*el aparador, el comedor, la cama, la cilla*—it was only yesterday he spoke Spanish.

Lingkod. Higda.

His day is a full calendar showing aliens his familiars.

The Tonopsis Mecanica of musikero Canseco that by purely mechanical means provides melodic chords. Liquors, cigars, and in one hut, The Agricultural Pavilion, a room of hemp, molasses, rope, and rum—he extols Aladdin's strange treasures that are his father's warehouse goods. The Refraction Nephoscope of his brother Jote's professor, Padre Jose Algue, star of instruments that calculate the stars at Manila's Observatorio (out by Jote's high school haunts, near Calle Anda). A replica of the walls of Intramuros encloses the miniature Observatorio awarded prizes for its pluviographs, barometers, anemographs, psychrometers, sunshine recorders, and the universal microseismograph of the Vincentini type improved by Roman Trinidad.

A tectonic country blessed with so many instruments to measure its doom.

Above all, the Observatorio's startling relief map of the islands—a landscaped mirage, *espejismo de la nación*, Mirage of the Nation, the subjugated country sculpted in cartographic earthenwork miniature on the St. Louis lawns.

Even the river Pasig, its lilies and esteros, is faithfully contoured throughout the exposition, traversed by a model of Puente de España, a most lifelike Bridge of Spain.

The smell of pee on old wood by the kasilyas at the Pavilion of Education is also realistic.

His day is a full calendar showing aliens his familiars.

When he shows the curiosity seekers the Model School, all the children at their desks before Señorita Pilar, what is that sensation in his loins, traveling from brow to spine?

His familiar: that sensation.

His mind reaches for it.

A whiff from a hat, first golden then straw.

An emptiness in his core.

The vision of the valiant Hiloy.

An iya yaman may pagkahamot hin yamang.

He stands beneath the narra trees, and another rain, this time a cascade of yellow blossoms, catches in the ghost's earlobe, his kamisa sleeves, the man's yellow aura an illusion that Paco's body senses just because, for no good reason he can think of, he smells pee.

A perceptual vacancy.

May anyong yaman, may pagkahamot hin yamang.

Blankness pushes against his breast.

Sensation clicks shut.

It's true as the papers say—humans are in pavilions like the fishing nets, a fossil elephant, and a stuffed tamaraw, exhibited like the insects and weather instruments, the linen and tobacco. The Bagobo blacksmith shop complete in its implements includes a Bagobo, the Angat iron foundry showcases, intact, the ancient Igorot methods of crushing, panning, and smelting gold, including the Igorot, the exonym with no name, crushing and panning pale sparse flecks for the curious crowds. At the Visayan Village, a resident entertainer is "dancing like a bird," Martina the Midget she is called, in real life a cook from Iloilo (she just wants adventure, she tells him, when he sees her again).

The Model School has Señorita Pilar Zamora in western crinoline standing with model good posture before her charges—the children of the tribes. Journalists take pictures of their pets, the dogs. He sees them in their rows in this cathedral of learning (oddly, the Pavilion of Education recreates in miniature the Manila Cathedral, why why gaway). Suyoc, Bontoc, Lanao, Samal. Who knows if the tribal labels are the names the tribes claim. And the blankness surging in him is a kind of travel, his own self a receding mass, his relative sight, an iya mga urupod, as he sees himself outside of himself, and in his mind's eye (for some reason) it is the valiant Hiloy who spies on him, straw hat on his heart, as he stares at the children in the Model School. May anyong yaman, may pagkahamot hin yamang.

His tongue clicks shut.

The curiosity seekers stare at him curiously.

The designated spieler.

What has happened to his tongue?

Dila.

Dila.

Tongue.

Learner of Latin, Spanish, Tagalog, Waray, and now the Model English-speaker—blankness surges, a perceptual vacancy he does not understand.

Eso es. Maya? Bayâ. Ora pro nobis.

An iya gamit gihay, pagkastigo ha iya kalugaringon, an iya lawas baga hin Jesukristo ha atubangan han justicia ni Poncio Pilato, labi na ha iya likod (back), *mga tuhod* (knees), *siko* (elbows), *paa* (feet), *pero labot la ha iya utin* (penis).

He is staring at a lady with a chicken feather in her hat, clutching the hand of a child in a sailor suit.

Sensations click shut.

He opens his mouth.

Nothing emerges.

His buddy, the other Francisco, smiles at the crowd.

The pensionado Paco watches him speak, gesturing, the other spieler, while the Model School-Children, hair smoothly combed, ribboned and braided, the Brilliantina boys with their razor-sharp hairlines parted on the sides, so that one side of hair rises like a hump, a funny cowlick mound he, Paco, wants to tamp down, tenderly—the Model School-Children look up at him with their serious, beatific faces.

The blond child in the sailor suit, toddling up, reaches out to touch a little girl's braided hair.

Then he tugs at it.

The Model School-Girl, who has been gazing up at the other Francisco, turns toward the boy in the sailor suit, her smile still on her face as the blond boy tugs at her hair.

She slaps him.

Right in his grinning face.

The lady with a feather in her hat screams, the boy cries, there is a commotion among the curiosity seekers, and the little girl turns calmly in her seat back toward the other Francisco, tilting toward him her Model School-Girl face.

Demon, the lady in the feather hat says—*do you see how the demon savage touched my boy? How dare that nigger*—

The Model School-Girl is sitting with her hands clasped in front of her desk, with her good posture and right conduct, smiling up at the designated spieler, the other Francisco.

The Constabulary man, his stout brown face, his proud gun, is at the entrance of the Pavilion and marches up to the murmuring crowd.

Señorita Pilar is moving down a line of desks toward the girl.

The pensionado Paco finds his tongue.

Finally.

He is English-speaking!

The moon is both a grin and a teardrop.

A splash, and that is all!

The other Francisco has to take Paco away.

His body is blazing with sensations that do not click shut—the colors of his boyhood visions like sparks from stained glass converge on his body in the Model School, as the Constabulary man, the Filipino with the Colt .45, approaches, Señorita Pilar of Tayabas (capital: Baler!) yanks the Model School-Girl by the wrist, and the girl is sitting calmly in her seat, her hands clasped in front with good posture and right conduct, the Model School-Girl is dragged out by Señorita Pilar, out, out, out toward the Constabulary barracks, and the riot of colors is no rainbow as the Model School-Girl walks by—

Gambler nudges the Catalogo brother in the tuhod.

A blue hiss on the knee.

Ramblin slaps the Catalogo brother with his siko.

The teal blur of the elbow on the brown back.

Gamblin pushes an arnis stick into the Catalogo brother's—

Black—the boy feels the warm blood—

—Who said that you can speak?

And Rambles smashes a fist upon the Catalogo brother's stuck-out—

Dila.

Dila.

Tongue.

What has happened to you since we last saw you, Hiloy?

Hiloy opens his mouth.

In the gesture is a hint of—ice in his heart.

He sees how Hiloy has lost it.

His tongue.

He spends the night in the makeshift hospital next to the Constabulary barracks, speaking gibberish to a listening patient named Juan, who turns out to be the husband of Martina the Midget. Except Martina is not a midget but only an adventurous Ilongga. She arrives at the clinic after entertaining curiosity seekers the whole day in her baro't saya, "dancing like a bird."

She brings Juan his supplemental mess.

She's very proud of her plot.

She's surprised to see him, the designated spieler.

Hah, what you doing here, you pensionado boy? Intawon, intoy, what hapin hapin to you? Your face—who did that to you, toto? And she touches it, his old scar, he does not flinch. It's a pleasure to be the butt of the jokes of Martina the Midget. She was the spieler, an entertainer. Ay, pastilan, toto. And at the sound of it, her voice, jumbled cognates of his own brain come together, like a fuse, and though among his several languages only one of them is hers (and that one only in parts)—in the hospital tent he is soothed.

The medico says Juan is sick with beriberi, Martina goes on and on, I tell him he is only sick with the americano food—the rice of the americanos is not correct!

Ay, kaning iyot na americano nga bugas!

It is cereal, thinks the boy, though it's not clear what she says, he has had it for breakfast every day in Compton, saying nothing to his hosts, who are kind, he must believe, smiling at him as if proud of their feat though it is he who must eat. He wants his barol, his tahô, his budo-bulad, but it's only when Martina speaks that he understands—their cereal is not correct.

Kaning iyot na americano nga bugas.

She is proud of her plot.

She spoons into Juan's mouth the rice she has pounded herself, she has stolen extra grains from the jars at the Pavilion of Agriculture—do not tell!

Palay de secano.

The correct rice!

Ay sus, I thought it would be an adventure, says Martina the adventurer, when my cousin, he's the kapitan of my town, Juan Deloso, you know him?, no?, he's the boss, my cousin is in charge of the Visayan Pavilion!, he asks me if I want to join the trip to the Eksposisyon, I say yes, why not, but it's really just boring, being with a bunch of Ilonggos all the time. The trip to Manila was my favorite—it's a *ciudad*! We saw the teatro in Sampaloc, the band at the Luneta! A pickpocket stole my money, but that is Manila—it's a *ciudad*! They are so easy to fool, the americanos, I make up all the dances, who the hell dances like an itik-itik in Iloilo! But they pay us, you know. Fifteen centavos a day, I will get the sum when I go home, it's fun, ha ha, making up the chicken dances. Iyot, mga buang americano da. Ha ha. They are always taking my picture. Like pickpockets, but it's all right. I am famous. They take pictures of me. And the dogs. Too many pictures of the dogs! But I'm the favorite. I'd rather go back to the pickpockets in Manila—it's a *ciudad*! He has this knack, a fever brain that responds to puzzles, and he fills in her fractures with his fragments, piecing together Martina the rice thief's inconceivable Ilonggo, his body with her glee, in the nipa hut in St. Louis until he sleeps.

He wakes up to blankness outside the window, dawn's contour of shadows that is revealed to be the relief map of the archipelago on St. Louis's lawns.

Espejismo de la nación.

Martina shows him the paskinada as she scoops up the empty rice bowl, and her saya and pañuelo and her utensils, after breakfast.

She collects even the posters at the fair.

Calista Catalogo: The Filipina Rebel.

Here, she says, you go to this!

He takes the leaflet from her.

Martina says hah! That is a very educated nga birat! You go listen to her. She sets her stage at the Pavilion of War—if you can catch. Oh she has so many good stories. The Filipino Scouts, they are always on the lookout for her traveling booth, but first they listen! They never catch. Ha ha ha. I did not know that about her story of Samar—did you know, you pensionado boy?—kaning iyot—what those kanô sundalos did in Samar!

Ssssh, says Juan, ssssh.

At Food Company

It was at the parking lot in the cold shadow of Food Company that Adina an guapa, eight months pregnant, finally saw her dying father in Los Angeles in America—the Honorable Mayor Francisco Delgado III, leaning against a pale-blue Chevrolet Impala.

"Papá," she said.

The final awkward months of her pregnancy made her feel shy as she walked toward her father. She felt out of her body, unstable, unlike herself, a flower-printed balloon in high heels. She knew it would be hard for her father to know of her life in Los Angeles, amid Protestants who did not know the story of Santa Rita de Cascia, and Mexicans who shared her religion but not her spices, and no one in the world spoke her tongue, and how her husband beat her up when she said she was lonely, how he beat her up when he learned she had taken a job in a bank, the Bank of America!, how proud she was to get a job on her own, a teller at Bank of America, how he beat her up when he saw the receipts for her art classes at Burbank, she paid with her teller's money!, where did she learn about the Cubists and the Impressionists and her favorite, Piet Mondrian.

It would be hard enough for her father, Mister Honorable Mayor Francisco III, when he learned that, just as he had said, life in California, in estados, would be no escape from Salogó.

That she would always miss them—

The river and him.

Life is what you make it, her father had said, *it is not what it makes for you.*

That is what he said when she returned to Salogó three days after her disappearance in 1957, age twenty-one—and her brother

Nemorino and her uncle Guimoy and her cousin the Junior Igmenegildo and Lucio her mother's nephew who searched for Adina an
guapa for three days all around Leyte, so that by the third day of her
disappearance the entire sleepy town of Salogó knew she was gone,
captured, damaged, and shamed.

A girl taken, a woman used.

Disgrasyada.

He first took her to Ormoc, on the Cebu end of the island, and
she did not run away from him, or she could not run away from him,
Doctor Tita Tita was not sure, but Adina was ashamed to return,
Tita Tita said, and a few nights later she was on a boat, to Pasig Line
in Manila—with the homecoming boy, that US Navy shipman from
Salogó.

When she was found in Pasig Line and Tio Nemor and Tay
Guimoy took her first to her aunt's home on F. Jhocson Street, her
Tia Pachang said—Ah, Adina—you have ruined your life. You will
marry him, the scoundrel. Nemor, he must marry your sister—get the
scoundrel to marry your sister. She has ruined the name of the Delgados—*all the people know she ran away—with that scalawag!*

"Everyone spoiled your mom—except Tia Pachang," said Tita
Tita.

I don't think spoiled is the right word, I said.

Above all, Tita Tita wanted to continue her story about Tia
Pachang.

Each of us has an axe to grind.

"It was Tia Pachang who told her she had to marry your father.
You must marry him, Tia Pachang said. I don't think it was good
advice."

Why? I mean, why did she have to marry him?

"I thought Marga told you. Or your Tio Nemor."

No, they didn't, I said.

I did not say that I never asked.

"Your father thought he was special. He returned from, you
know—abroad. Your mom was engaged. To a doctor she had met in

Manila. Doctor Torres. He's still there—a surgeon at the FEU Hospital. He was a resident when I knew him. I introduced her to him. Poor Doctor Torres. She was home to arrange her wedding. But she disappeared at the party for the homecoming sailor."

What I felt from this story, even as my aunt told it, was that it was foretold. So much about my pathos for my mother had to do with glimmers of a past hinted at but not exhumed. And my capacity to keep my own counsel and refuse to ask questions was a desire to dispel it, this figment, this knowledge entombed.

An aspect of my cowardice, my indifference, my egotism and desire.

To be free, as if that could be done.

I'm sorry, I said.

"She went to a party for the homecoming sailor, a neighbor she knew as a kid, your father, and she never came back. I mean, it's an old story. You know that story by Nick Joaquin? 'May Day Eve'? It's the same. You will look in the mirror on May Day and see—your betrothed or the devil. Either/or. But what if you see both? Nemor and your Tay Guimoy were sent to look for her, I made Nemorino go look for her, and they went to your father's home, but no one could tell them where they went. Your grandfather, your father's father, your Tay Udong, he was so ashamed. Pretty soon the whole town knew Adina was gone. I mean, everyone knew her since she was a baby—she was Adina an guapa. All the way to Homonhon—people knew of Adina an guapa. Oh, the gossips, they were at it. Papá took jeepneys all over—to Carigara, Alang-Alang, Tanauan, MacArthur, Tacloban. There was no trace. The first clue we had was the sighting in the south, in Ormoc. There are ferries there you can take to Cebu from Ormoc—your dad knew what he was doing. If you don't want people to find you, going south was the way. And then finally she was found—but she was so far away—in Manila at Pasig Line."

With the criminals and assassins!

My aunt looked at me strangely.

"No. Just with your dad."

Ma said only criminals and assassins live at Pasig Line.

"Well. There are many good people in Pasig Line. But that's where she was found. With your dad. She was Adina an guapa, the most beautiful girl—everyone in the smallest barrios and river towns of Leyte knew her. Then she was taken. Disgraced."

Gindara hiya.

Disgrasyada.

The euphemism of my aunt's words.

It took a while for me to register my father's crime.

But she was the one disgraced.

Desgraciada.

An old story—May Day Eve.

Thiyawthiyaw. Siyawsiyawsiyaw.

Ghik, ghik, ghik.

The worst scoundrel among all the smugglers and killers and assassins in Pasig Line who ever hailed from Salogó!

That is what her father, Mister Honorable Mayor Francisco Delgado III, called him—the worst scoundrel.

An Akon Amay Nga Yatis.

"You know you do not have to marry him, the worst scoundrel. No matter what he did, you are your own self—you are Adina an guapa."

Adina an guapa lay on her bed back in Salogó, and her father's voice was a miserable sound, a far-away signal.

"Life is what you make it. It is not what it makes for you."

He had seen her before like this, unmoving on a bed, she looked as if she were dreaming, or dead.

He clutched her hand. He whispered.

"It is you who will make your life, Adina."

She remembered.

Papá took her limp body in his arms, he kissed her brow, he whispered.

"It does not matter what people say," her father whispered to her, as if it would soothe, "everyone knows—you are Adina an guapa."

It would be hard enough for her father to know, as Adina an guapa walked toward him—a miracle vision, a man leaning against a pale-blue Chevrolet Impala, in the cold shadow of Food Company in east Los Angeles in California—it would be hard enough for him to know—

That he was correct.

Life in America was no escape from Salogó.

Her surrender to her disappearance—

Of what she had done to her name.

All the people know!

But it was not she who had done it, I told my aunt—it was my father who—took her.

"This sorrow has happened to many women," her Papá had said, as if he understood his daughter's silence. "You are not the only one. Life is what you make it, inday, Adina. You will make it. I am with you. You will heal. You do not have to marry him. The worst scoundrel!"

It would be hard enough for her father to know, as she walked toward him in the parking lot at Food Company in east Los Angeles, and he looked quizzically at her as he leaned against the pale-blue Chevrolet Impala—

But it would be harder for her, Adina an guapa, to tell him—

That he was correct.

She could see, even at a distance in the parking lot, that it was not she, but it was her Papá, a grieving man in the sun, who needed her protection.

I am with you.

A premonition.

She knew that fact as she walked toward him.

That the Honorable Mayor Francisco Delgado III was dying.

As she walked toward the pale-blue Chevrolet Impala, toward her father looking at her against the concrete sun, the blazing steel-gray tremor of sky one with the trembling corpuscles of heat in the parking lot (it was May, and I was almost done with first grade) and the occult gray of her father's cataract eyes, so that skyscape merged with landscape merged with love, a shimmering loss of perspective, she knew she would never tell him what life in America was like—this place her husband had taken her, east Los Angeles, where she had succumbed to the promise of a life elsewhere, with its ex-boxers who threw refrigerators instead of their wives onto lawns (so the neighbor, an otherwise kindly pugilist, Dick Remorse, explained his violent ways with his home appliances—an Irishman, my mother explained him to me, and she liked him because sometimes he went to church, plus he liked adobo). Where drunken women danced naked on broken porches (what a strange place it is, she thought, this America), how she wished to make her own home with her own chosen discount furniture and faux-Tiffany lamps and framed pictures of geometric paint drops, instead of the boring, fully furnished rooms of the naval compound in Long Beach, she liked to redesign her environment, how she made drip paintings on the naval apartment's screen door, just like the painter in the book from her class at Burbank, and she would have finished her modern art, too, if her husband had not arrived home early, wasted from his job, and he beat her up when he saw the paint on the apartment that was not their own.

Stupid ignorant bitch, he told her, *you think you can do anything you want, just like you did in your uncle's home? The one who was going to give you your millions—your La Tercera? Where's your La Tercera now, hah! You think you can do whatever you want.*

Well, this is America, he told her. *You do what I want.*

She would never tell the Honorable Mayor Francisco Delgado III how, when she bought odd materials, like canvas cloth and gold glitter and pieces of wood and Elmer's glue, her husband would say he should not have married her, he could have any woman he wanted, he, a US Navy shipman come home the hero from estados in their town in Salogó, and she, a small-town woman with a history of crazy, beginning with her demented grandfather, Cong. J. B. Delgado Street, the madman assassinated not by the Japanese but by his fellow Filipinos, her Lolo Jote, a bandit and assassin in the times before the Japanese!, and everyone in Salogó knows the story of her mental breakdown in Greenhills at the age of nineteen, how the electric shock to her brain was no cure, it was a disaster, a lifelong hole in her crazy brain, the electroshock treatment watched over by the famous senator who had ordered the cure.

Her beloved.

Her Lolo Paco.

His cure that did no one any good.

You act like the princess of Greenhills, he said—you're just a Delgado with bad-luck blood.

That is what he said, her husband.

Everyone knows you're a sick woman, he said, no one has any secrets in Salogó.

And she is a bitch who likes to put on airs when it's only air that props her up, all of her stories, her fairy tales about the senator who ordered the doctors to electrify her, put wires in the brain of his silly ward—that's what you get for being a rich man's ward, don't you know—that it is your Lolo Paco—he, your God of Greenhills, he threw you into the loony bin!

Do you think he loved you that much, if he loved you so much—Don't you see it's your Lolo Paco who messed up your brain? And do you know why?

He was ashamed of you, you bitch, your Lolo Paco was ashamed—

That is when she hit him.

He kept saying his name.

Lolo Paco. Lolo Paco. Lolo Paco.

His name in her husband's dirty mouth.

She fought back, she slapped him.

He would have killed the baby in her womb, torn up her insides, if she had not blacked out.

He beat her up only to keep her sane, her husband explained to the authorities who were called to their home by the pugilist, the Irish neighbor of Catholic heritage, Dick Remorse.

He beat her up for buying new curtains in her favorite color, tangerine, he beat her up for buying her daughter a brand-new doll that fascinated only her, not her daughter, the segmented figure with a Japanese face, a moveable doll of the future, he beat her up for buying art materials, wasting his money on air, just air, do you know what it is like to work for money in America, he said to her, and you waste it on canvas and dumb fake gold and stupid glue and ugly, orange, crazy-woman crap, this useless useless art?

Still Adina an guapa was beaming, a beatific pregnant woman, as she walked toward the pale-blue Chevrolet Impala toward her quizzical father in the cold shadow of Food Company, and as the car moved toward her, the driver of the Impala said it was not his fault, she kept walking, her arms lifted in welcome, to that skyscape merged with landscape merged with love, a shimmering loss of perspective, and when the driver hit her, Adina an guapa murmured, but the driver of the Impala did not get it—

Yes it is true, Papá—

Life is what you make it.

Her husband, the telegram in his hand, was mystified by her telepathy.

He received the telegram from his brother-in-law Nemorino, about the Honorable Mayor Francisco III's illness (the family's genetic cancer, a rare tubular carcinoma in the old mayor's breast, but slow-moving and medullary, though still ineluctably fatal, decades later in my mother's breast).

How strange that my father received the telegram that day Adina an guapa, after her car accident, after her bout at the mental clinic in Anaheim, after her crying for her phantom Papá, after her days of nightmare in that haunted old asylum near Disneyland—that day after she gave birth too soon, in aftershock, at the naval hospital in Long Beach.

Clutching the telegram, my father had a premonition of his wife's witchcraft, the curse of the bad-luck Delgados upon him.

So narrated my aunt Doctor Tita Tita the day before I left for my mom's funeral.

"And that is why your father would never go back to his hometown

Salogó!" said Tita Tita. "He became superstitious after the telegram. Though it was only a coincidence, he got scared!"

She laughed.

An akon amay nga yawa.

"Hah," said my aunt. "Don't say bad words. He's your father."

All unaware that her father lay dying, Adina an guapa had wished to name her baby Francisco the Fourth—

Against the objections of her husband.

The baby's name: a compromise.

Adino, sweet Adino, born premature in the naval hospital at Long Beach.

At the hospital, when she learned of her father's death in Salogó, Adina an guapa did not do what she wanted.

She wished to pull out her tubes, she wished to slap her face and hands and belly until her body bore no feeling, no sensation at all, she wished to lie down sobbing on the cold, unswept tiled floors, a garish checkerboard of dirt, a harlequin inlay of grief, at that naval hospital in Long Beach.

She wished to die.

It was a terrible howl, dark as a ball of molasses, a dense kalamay of boiling hurt, a tumor in her womb—her grief—

And then she saw it—the cone of light.

Projecting from the hospital window, placed high where patients could not reach, the light pierced through a sky of glass straight to mother and child, like the image on her scapular saint, Santa Rita de Cascia, but in Long Beach, the light of the Holy Ghost was upon her—Adina.

A hospital Piéta.

She heard the voice.

She looked down at her baby, at Adino, sweet Adino, and Adina an guapa repeated its words to him—*life is what you make it.*

She left America and her husband, with her two live baggages, six and zero.

Her husband let her go, frightened by her telepathy.

For her father's funeral.

She never went back.

Labaw han Iya Tan-aw

She of the slim ankles, bare and unsteady in the clear river as she stoops to lay down her bandehado, her tin basin of clothes. Then she washes herself when she has done her laundry chores. She ignores him, that sly little one who goes about Giporlos with his notebook and his gray-eyed stare, like an orphan cat, a dull pet. She is in the cove beyond the church where the boy also wanders, away from the men. He seeks solitude. Like her. She sees him watching her.

She smiles.

Though he looks for her, he can barely hold it.

Her gaze.

The way her beauty blinds.

In Samar, she keeps on her patadiong and her kamisa. She lifts up her skirt to her knees. She lowers her body into the water. She gazes.

At a sight above him.

Labaw han iya tan-aw.

Beyond his eye.

At the Fair, he tries to catch it, her eye.

The Four Seasons

"That's it," Doctor Tita Tita said, "your luggage? Oh, you, inday, you travel too light."

We were going down the elevator to the lobby to have breakfast before catching our flights.

I walked around the lobby: I checked the banks of elevators to see if I would still find them on the walls—*The Four Seasons.*

I remembered where I had found them last—by the grand piano.

No trace.

"They used to have her art here—on this wall."

"I know," Tita Tita said, following behind. "She was always borrowing money from me to make them. Then she never paid! She'd say, I have to roll the money over, roll the money over for my next order. Promise, I'll pay you back with the next one. Promise, promise."

My aunt laughed.

"That's the way it always went. Nemor said—let it be. If we can help, let it be."

She lived in the future, the present has no consequence, the past is a fantasy.

"Hm," nodded my aunt, "that's a way to put it."

Oh by the way, I said, speaking of the past. Do you know anything about these?

We chose to sit by the patio side, looking again at last night's view, now brilliant and azure, sunlight raking the water.

This was a good way to be home: staring at this ancient Bay.

I opened my handbag.

My aunt shook her head.

"What is it?" she said.

I found it a long time ago, in one of those huge cabinets in Salogó, I said.

She leaned over to examine it.

"Oh my God," said Doctor Tita Tita, lighting up. "It's the box! Hah. Your Tio Nemor has been looking for a box. He turned the house in Danao upside down, he said, looking for a box. He asked me if I had stored it. But the house in Danao has long been empty."

Oops, I said. I took it with me before I left for New York. A long time ago. He's been looking for it since? I should have told him. I stole it from my mom.

"No, just a few days ago, he was looking for it—something about legacy, some papers."

You mean there's profit in it, I said.

"Oh you, maldita. He thought maybe I had stored it in Cebu. He said some historians—they're interested. I told him to ask you—you're the one interested in history. Maybe you know."

I checked my PMs because I knew I'd see new messages.

Let's meet @ Hotel Sirena Mano Nemor tells me its you who must have it I have an offer you cannot refuse!

Still chasing me across the seas.

So someone finally wants to publish Lolo Jote's story, I said.

"Hm, no, no, he did not mention your Lolo Jote. He said it's a book by a woman. A woman from Samar—Paz something something. A weird last name. Never heard. That's what the historians were asking him about. But I said to him—I don't get it—why should your mom own this woman's papers?"

The Filipina Rebel

Her first impulse is to snatch the notebooks from his grasp. She guesses the stranger is the brother. Not that Jote ever spoke his name. An manghod. He was just the younger brother. The young man's face is in profile against the capiz shutters' dark mahogany. She's alert to everything when she comes in: dusty floorboards, grand piano still covered by lace runners at mid-morning, lampaso she almost trips on as she enters. Telltale signs. Negligence. It's clear this place is no longer run by Tio Mariano. Tay Sequil, *El Cochero Exequiel!*—he now plies his horse-drawn taxi at the Escolta. Funny, she took a ride with him once—a gallant man, Excellent!, as his ads say. A man of memory. She appreciates that. She's written them down—stories of Jote's times with the rebels, the original gangsters under this house on Moret (the valiant Hiloy, the crippled Marcelo, and the surprising appearance of the great man himself—Macario Sakay, the Terror of Luzon). She knows she's already been seen from the high windows, the house has a panoptic view from its corner, with its garden and the old duyan in the back—and the narra and the limonsito and the kamia—the rose bushes out front, hedging the chickens, and in her first days in Manila, when she had been welcome on Moret Street, missives in her petate, from Salogó, from Nay Carmen, the niece, after all, of Mariano the mayordomo, with whom she deposited her Nay Carmen's letters—she gave him lamano, finally she met her Tio Mariano, who was glad, everyone was glad to see someone alive from Samar—she used to sit at that window at dusk.

Those are mine, she thinks, when she sees Paco with the notebooks. And suddenly she understands it. Her error.

And Jote's guile.

Siempre el rebelde, nunca el amigo.

The message in the petate was simply to say: help is coming—

Keep the faith.

Jote did.

At Impresa Mondejar in Tacloban she had the notebooks bound, chosen the gold etching herself. She understands, seeing them in the somber, suited man's hands—it's she, Calista, who was the fool, not Jote.

Her project was to record as much as he could remember. It was important to draw out his words. Out there in their refuge, hiding and hiding—after their escape from the battle in Giporlos. To fill history's blank pages. It was dumb. But he had the wit of the hunted. He would not speak. He gave no evidence. But surely we need to remember, she said. To extract his words. *La primera.* The day at the Luneta when the hero Rizal dies? I had glazed banana. And the hero? He wore a hat. And Ka Vicente—what was he like? Fat. The Battle of Manila? There was a song. And? He whistles a tune she cannot name: it's familiar. His trip up north to join the troops of the presidente, he and Marcelo and the valiant Hiloy—*los tres mosqueteros!* Did you see the presidente in Malolos? The wily fox is always a town away, *siempre siempre siempre,* he'll never be caught, *nunca nunca nunca.* The burial of the bastard from Ateneo, the comedy nerd of Calle Anda, happens in a ditch in San Juan. Betel spit marks it. What were your ways of rest? His gray eyes go dark. He says, Do you know there were playwrights in the jungle? Also barbers. His syllables mock. And the great Isabelo Abaya—was he so loved as people said? A duyan. In Abra. And the great General Juan Villamor—did you meet him? A woman makes fresh bibingka *cada día cada día* in the town of Vigan. Maupay maupay! Knock knock knock. Who's der aber? Badoc Badoc Badoc, full of manok. And locusts. Were his words jokes or traps? Gently gently with his solemn eyes. At first she thought it was a good disguise, the fugitive rebel's obsession with his manok, petting the chickens who saved them on the waters of Himanglos, while the americanos and their spies hunt all around Leyte for him and his kind.

In Salogó, he becomes a bum at the merkado, he and Bingo like to comb the coxcombs of Ka Tinong's pets, admiring their jester caps, priming their golden hackles.

Birds are a comfort: fowl and words don't mix.

All those days before the uprising she is riveted to him, one of the laborers come for the cleansing, but in Salogó, at rest in his refuge, she realizes—it's his silence that gives him power. The rumors of his exploits: he was only a child against the men of Otis in Santa Mesa, or was it Pandacan?, barely a teen escaping the torches of the butcher of Batangas, the demon Bell burning burning burning the barrios of Batangas, Laguna, Tayabas, a youth, a hardened youth running from pincer troops of Arthur MacArthur up in Candon, he seeks the Brigada Tinio, the troops of El Bandido, follows their path through Pozorubio, Lubuagan, misses them at Tangadan, luck, luck, luck is all he has, he meets up with the Bishop of Badoc (Aglipay fights to his own tune, scalawag!, says *La Independencia*)—

The gaps in his past have glory.

What are not told, she fills.

Anyway, is it possible to be in so many places at once?

Rumor is the secret weapon of revolution—the people are nosy, everyone's an analyst, like chess fans or better, bettors of jai alai, hugador!—cobbling messages of war from *Independencia* and from the nameless amigos passing by the store.

Of course she has long heard of Jote, son of Adina Blumfeld y Catalogo.

A. B. y C.

His legendary birth.

Is that why he becomes the right hand boy of the Chief, of Tay Balê—

Why he's assigned the plum?

Or is it that he has a look in his eye, the boy of no nerve, with his look that kills?

Siempre. El rebelde, nunca el amigo.

In any case, he has the prime job on the day of attack on the garrison at Balangiga.

With Tay Balê, to go after the leader of the invaders in the priest's own kumbento—to behead the head—

Waller Waller Waller Waller.

One more notch in the boy Jote's epic of no words.

Her heart when she sees him come up to the townspeople's fast in the hills, his return with the chief and his men, they all look crazed, bewildered, glorious, so much blood, so much blood on their clothes, bolos, cheeks, hair, lofting their captured Krags, stolen cooking implements, stereo cards, the americanos' scattered letters, bayonets, thuds so hard she thinks bones will crack against her chest, stop her breathing, tear her lungs. She will remember all her life the joy in her body that she thinks will kill her when the men come back from battle. Even now, there's a bruise in her breast at the memory of her war. It's what keeps her alive. Scarred, scathed, traumatized, brutal, triumphant, victory encased in his exulting body, his bright eyes. The wonder of their action. That they have survived. She touches his cheek: glob of blood, betel-red, in her fist. It's only later that she perceives—

Something has shattered.

When the rebels and the women leave Samar, according to plan because, Nay Carmen says, *God watches!*—*Santo Niño, bendisyoni kami!*—with the norteamericanos dead at their bloodied garrison, at the town plaza that the people take back from the kanô (tricked and hacked, hacked hacked hacked at breakfast, the Americans' cereal undone, oatmeal on the wounds of her tutor Man Dadong and her godfather Tay Balê, who scatter, too, to the winds, the last nguya of saging na saba smeared on her countrymen's knives), after the tumult of their crossing, on their midnight launch toward Cabalawan wrapped tight in each other's arms on Nay Carmen's bancas, the abaca trading vessels whose pilots row across the strait by dark, by skill, by stars, their landing under cover of night, and by sled, foot, kalesa trudging through the groves, lubi lubi lubi lubi, how long is eternity across the coconuts of Leyte, to reach Florentino Peñaranda's beach, Ka Tinong's barakasyunan by Himanglos—with Bingo (not Bongo) and Nay Carmen and all the young Carmens of Giporlos.

In the jefatura of comandante Peñaranda, the last officer of the katipuneros yet roaming the hills of Baybay, pursued into peacetime, kamurayaw, by the Krag rifles of Jakey Smith's men, the Samarnon sought rest.

Surely she and Jote have the right to rest.

The samadnon—the wounded.

Paco looks up.

At the moment, for a moment, her heart lurches.

He looks so much like Jote.

Thin mouth, sharp cheek.

Solemn, glaucous eye.

But this man is no—

Calista, says Paco. I mean, Miss Catalogo. So glad to meet you. Finally. I've heard so much about you.

He doesn't move from the shadows.

He sits by the windowsill.

He takes in her figure, the long-skirted, Western suit, the gray pearls at her throat.

Heredera of Nay Carmen.

Boy! Pakadi! Boy! Espiya ni Utot ka nga im Pating!

The choral laughter of the men about the yard is comforting, even neighborly.

She, too, stays where she is.

At the entresuelo, about to step up.

Her skirts trailing on dissolute rags and lampaso.

She nods her head.

From whom have you heard, she says.

It's not him, she thinks—it's just an manghod. An Irong. My Little Brother, the Nose. Jote tells only one story about him—a day at the Luneta. But the brothers Jote and Paco are legends in the life of her Nay Carmen, mother of Adina Blumfeld y Catalogo.

She has a small, round face, smooth like a metal bead or the top of a pin. A smile like sunshine.

She has sausage curls: coiling about her cheeks in the style of the foreign.

Style is her poor mother Carmen Catalogo's second rebellion.

Nay Carmen's stature in town long defeats her old vanity, and her indifference to appearances is a mark of her power. Calista becomes her little store helper, happy to fish out the isda-isda cookies from Nay Carmen's pretty glass jars, measure out the fresh purple hipon— usa ka takos, duha ka takos. Nay Carmen adopts her brother's sons the twins, a common arrangement, Bingo and Bongo, so many poor nephews in Lawaan, not to mention all the little Carmens in her wealth's wake. The boys lay palay on the mats to dry, they haul the lubi for the kilns, they guard the drying copra. Calista counts out the budo-bulad, usa, duha, tulo, leafy packets of betel, smooth hard globules of kalamay, she pours out suoy and patis into reused jars with faded takop that customers bring, she ladles with such precision they tease—*ay agi, pasobrahi gad ako, pastilan, uday, ikaw nga bata ka! Carmen, komersiyante gayud ini nga imo daraga, uy!* Nay Carmen dresses the girl, an daragahay, in the art of her first profession—bright sinamay, jusi cloth, piña treasure—the art of her weaving. The child loves equally the brilliant silks and the soft pastels, but most of all she likes hearing the customers' voices, their stories. When she's sent to school—first at the kumbento, with the tall priest who scares her, Padre Donato, then with her private tutor, meek and mild Man Dadong, an bise-kapitan nga taga-Letran—she's eager to know, her hunger remarkable, Man Dadong says—*ah, hala, adi na an guti nga maestra!* But even as a child she understands her honor is borrowed from her apoy, her Nay Carmen. The old woman's past—the romantic drama with musikero Blumfeld—*ay ta waray kay hudeo ngay-an, susmaria!* (the townspeople add local color, extra beads of bigotry, crossing themselves)—the loss of Nay Carmen's only child Adina, the absence of her grandchildren—*what is an old woman without her apo, kairo!*—stave off the town's envy of Nay Carmen's luck with land, her savvy as a trader.

After the typhoon of '97, which devours the coast—lunop, lunop, aguy, hagi, hagi, grabe nga kasugad, kairo han kalibutan—from Lawaan to Tacloban, devastating the saging, the rice, and the coconuts, the coconuts—Carmen Blumfeld y Catalogo weathers the storm. Kalooy sa diyos. Everyone is in her debt, and whatever trouble there is in Manila has no currency for Nay Carmen. Her warehouses there, of rice and abaca and copra, are blessings: the store of goods sent off to Don Francisco, the father of her apo.

Until the americanos arrive.

But Nay Carmen is smart—she offers the kapre and the bearded 'paches her tubâ and lambanog, free samplings, she reserves bahalina, the freshest wine, for ini nga mga parahubog nga mga mananap, *these alcoholic pests!*, she glows with pride when the young lieutenant who looks like a *calavera*, nga iya kalag, Bumpus, teaches his words to the girl, who repeats them with her perfect pitch, an daragahay, whose talent is learning—at twilight, when the day is done and he and Tay Balê, the chief of police, sip wine and play chess.

So when a wild man kapre, not the Apache Denton, Nay Carmen's friend, or Bumpus, the kalag, but a blondie who smells of ferrous oxide, Trapp? Crapp?, nga mananap, touches her niece, an daragahay, while she is at the store pouring tubâ and suoy into the jars, to reveal the modest kamisa beneath her shawl, he touches her body, like she is a pig or a mango, and when Nay Carmen complains, they arrest her nephews instead! the Catalogo twins! for beating up the kapre, siyempre someone beat up that Crapp, he touched an daragahay!, and the foreign men torture Bingo (or Bongo), though it is she who has complained, and the americanos confiscate Nay Carmen's produce when she goes up to Captain Waller herself.

And the day Calista returns from the river—her brilliant silks, her pañuelo, her face muddy and bruised—*it's all right, it's all right,* Calista says, *I ran away, I am not hurt*—who knows who knows, the townspeople say, the nasty details are on their tongues, the townspeople's round-robin of malice and pity, and when Tay Balê, the chief of police, spits out the dumb reasoning of that tonto kapitan, that Captain Waller—*it's the fault of your women, their clothes are so flimsy, the outfits of harlots!*—her storefront is a meeting place, no one bothers to know exactly how or when the seed of revolt grows, it's just there, like the lubi—it ripens.

What did he do to you what did he do, *demonio demonio* nga yawa nga americano kamo dida?

Americano mucho malo.

Her body is soothed and soaked in guava leaves and luy-a, her aunt's warm hands and her whispering love cleanse the girl's bruises on her face and her breasts and her thighs, she asks the girl—does it hurt here, does it hurt—the girl weeps—and in the end, as if in wonder—if it weren't for the boy, she says—

What boy?

There was a boy—when that man Trapp, or was it Crapp—when the soldier saw the boy—I got away—

It's all right, it's all right, an akon daragahay.

It imo kinabuhi, ikaw an magbubuot—diri iba.

I'm well, Calista Catalogo says to him. Thank you for your note. But there was no need for all the florid congratulations. All I've done is return home.

He recognizes.

His memory of her in Samar has no meaning to her.

She has no memory of him—the captain's boy in Giporlos.

But your speaking engagements in the States, reminding the

Americans of our war for independence. Congratulations on your success, he says.

Easy for you to say, says Calista—you reap the benefits of our defeat.

I reap the benefits for our future, he says—there are other ways to work for—

He thinks—he will not be brought down by her eyes.

She thinks—she has no stake in this unnecessary meeting.

For—our kalayaan, he says.

The word falls like a cement slab on a foot. He's embarrassed. He sounds like one of those orators he hates, the peacetime mouthpieces, slick heirs of kamurayaw.

Our kalayaan? Her eyes have a way of closing: a slit of a sneer.

Yes. I, too, wish for it. But I work another way.

Keep your fantasies to yourself, she says.

How can she hurt him if she does not know him?

Boy! Pakadi! Boy! Espiya ni Utot ka nga im Pating!

The choral laughter of the men about the yard is comforting, even neigh-borly.

So where is he? she asks.

Jote? he says.

He wishes to see me.

She holds out the note she had received at the Hotel Oriente.

You know, Paco says, gesturing toward the notebooks—he never mentions you.

Cruelty, she thinks, is a little brother's smile.

Did he give you permission to read them?

Why do you think, he asks, after all that time you spent together, he never mentions you at all?

So who told you about us?

He didn't speak.

Tio Mariano?

He does not answer.

So, she says, so what?

You know I told him I saw you at the St. Louis Fair, he attempts.

Really? That was a long time ago.

August 13, 1904, he says.

He sees her back arch. An error: only spies or lovers are so precise.

It was Philippine Day, he says, that's why I remember.

That's what I mean, she says—it was a long time ago.

I tried to come up to you after your talk—but your bodyguards—they were clever. I wished to talk to you. Because—it was my mother's hometown.

I know.

Yes, of course. Of course, you know. It's odd Jote never mentions you—in his notebooks.

A man of few words, your brother.

Well, actually—there's a lot of information here.

She's silent.

You were gone from your booth before any of us even understood your talk at the Fair was finished. You just—disappeared.

Anarchists are good organizers, she says.

You weren't scared about coming home?

I thought the governor-general's men would arrest me, she says—right when I got off the ship. Yesterday. I was waiting. But I got an invitation to Malacañang Palace instead. Hah. Great policy, this benevolence.

It's smart, he says. Assimilation.

Cooptation. It's certainly worked for others.

He's silent.

He taps his finger on a newspaper.

Did you see the results of the elections—in *Renacimiento*? Justo Lukban, he's the brother of Ka Vicente, remember him?

She stares at him.

Of course you remember Vicente Lukban—the Terror of Samar! His brother Justo just won a seat in the Municipal Board. Pretty soon, people like Lukban will be ruling Manila. They say his brother Ka Vicente will run for governor of Tayabas. Imagine that. The

Terror of Samar will be governor of Tayabas—and he's not even from there!

What about Ka Vicente, what was he like? Fat.

Paco points to another story: And see, the presidente's aide-de-camp—Aguinaldo's doctor—Doctor Villa—

Did you see the presidente in Malolos? The wily fox is always always a town away—siempre siempre siempre.

You mean Simeon Villa? she asks—captured with the presidente at Palanan?

The same. Villa won a seat, too—in Manila.

How the Americans *love* that story, she sneers, her eyes narrowing—it's so thrilling to them, dios ko—the story of the Filipino presidente and his men betrayed in Palanan—by the Macabebes—by his own people! *A tragic irony!* Kamakalilipay para ha era. We're bandits with no cause—or traitors of our cause. Either. Or. Agi. They need to make up their minds. But even the Macabebes—whom I do not absolve, by the way, they are betrayers—but as I try to explain—well, you heard me—you went to my speech. They are agents of their own will, too. We must imagine. Each with his own reasons. Which the enemy will not bother to know. And please—if I may repeat. They retail the story of Aguinaldo's capture by that infernal Funston— they talk about Funston's victory—as if it is about the rebelde and not about the imperialist. I mean, who profits from the perversion of the traitor Macabebes? What exactly do you think is the range of motion of our desire, subject to the invader's will? Which they pursued, by the way, across the ocean, at gunpoint. That's surely relevant. All their Colts and Remingtons and Krags—

She stops.

He looks out toward the window, toward his friends.

Allen and Bandholtz and Breton.

She's speaking too fast.

She knows she does this when she's mad, the way her heart beats faster, a bruise in her breast, and she imagines her friend Helen in the audience, her hands gesturing—*slow down, Calista, slow down!*

He turns his eyes back toward her.

While their enemies, he quotes, *were barefoot, carrying garden knives. An honorable war those americanos waged.*

Yes, she says, that is what I said in St. Louis.

I remember, he says.

Her time as an orator in America attunes her to gaps between her words and her public. She understands that the simpler her concepts, the more power they convey. To enrage and shame, to arouse and enflame. But her purpose, she thinks sometimes on those stages, in Quaker churches, in socialist halls, in women's clubs, is pitched toward a target she's not fully able to conceive—not toward the conqueror in bustle and crepe, the women in the assemblies who are riveted to the dark figure in her voluminous clothes, her starched lace shawl, the butterfly gauze, her peacock skirt with the serpentine tail, her elaborate hair and its jeweled comb, their Muse of Liberty from across the Pacific, speaking to them of insurrection. When once she wears a peplum jacket and petticoated dress in the style of her audience, Helen tells her—it does not have the same effect. And in fact she is more comfortable in her own clothes, she prefers her Nay Carmen's piña, its scratched sense of home, but her concern remains—

About their unintended effect: to keep her in her place, an exhibit.

And it is this contradiction, precisely, that occurs to her one night, at an event before the cooperative movement in Connecticut, she remembers, on stage with the writer of the hour, James Marie Hopper. The man's on stage to make a name—"the Joseph Conrad of America," the critics proclaim, except his book *Caybigan* is not set in the Congo but in Caloocan. They, feminist and artist, come at the invitation of the Danish journalist, an amiable man, a "prisoner of war," so he calls himself, who wrote a sensational diary of his time, *Ten Months a Captive in the Philippines!* (her love Jote would have been one of his prison guards, out in Vigan, but she never tells her host that), and as she ascends the stage, she sees her image in a mirror (the meeting is in an old theater, with props for a matinee in the wings)—and she understands as she comes face to face with herself, in her Nay Carmen's jewels, the embroidery and rage that is her inheritance—

That her speeches are also for herself.

In that moment in Connecticut she understands all of the glass shards are hers, the victor, the victim, the rebel, the woman, the reader, the leaver, the survivor, the translator. The traitor. The one who abandons, the one who loves. To conjure them all, simultaneity and mess, that is her calling.

But the problem history poses, she thinks, facing her audience in Connecticut, is insoluble on the stage.

She sighs. She takes a breath.

She speaks more gently, in a hush, to his little brother, an manghod, this smug Paco.

It's better, you know, she says to Paco, to see any series of events as, well, umm, a set of multiple, umm, even contradictory—incidents—the strands of which—at best—

He leans forward to get her gist. He's not sure if it's her beauty that confuses him.

The strands of which, she says, only an accurate, materialist sense of history explains—a sense that history is in motion, in process—not just an object on paper, or a thing in the mind—

Ay, she thinks. She has lost him.

Paco thinks, Calista's life with radicals has obscured her intelligence.

She has a smile on her face, her shoulders are shaking, and he sees—

The Filipina Rebel is giggling.

Ghik ghik ghik.

Ay, she thinks. I have lost him.

But she's never looked for him, this man Paco. It's Jote she has lost. She understood too late. Jote's guile. *Siempre el rebelde, nunca el amigo.*

Paco reaches for a word, he grasps at his point.

He puts his finger on the nouveau publication, the English-language *Manila Times.*

Yes. See here—this is what I mean. Simeon Villa won a seat on Manila's Board along with the brother of the Terror of Samar, Justo Lukban. I mean, Villa speaks only in rabid Spanish lampoons, not even bothering to learn English! But he now has a stake in this government. The Federalistas are challenging the results, of course. And their partners, the Americans, denounce Villa's election. We'll see if their protests prosper. But the point is—he ran for office! And look at this—also—what has happened to Manuel Tinio, the revolution's great general? His valiant war in the Ilocos? The papers called him El Bandido. Leader of the great Brigada. Even my father's American friends admired Tinio—slipping away, week after week, from the pincer forces of Arthur MacArthur. Hiding and hiding—tago ng tago—never catching. Anyway, El Bandido—well—he was just elected governor of Nueva Ecija!

Tinio's from there, she says—that's his fiefdom. The people of Nueva Ecija are his paisanos. Of course he won.

Is that not obvious, she thinks. The revolutionary was also their overlord.

And Aguinaldo's general in Luzon, the great friend of my brother's hero, Ka Andres—Mariano Alvarez. He ran for office in Cavite. He won.

Of course, she says.

This boy is an idiot, her shoulders say—her shrug is a performance.

He's their great katipunero, she points out—why would they not vote for him? The people of Cavite worship General Alvarez, as they should.

Just read the news in *Renacimiento*, the *Times*, he continues. How all the heroes have changed their tune! Juan Villamor—the bandit of Bangued. What an operation it was to get him to surrender—he spurned even his sisters. Did you see him at St. Louis? One of the big shots awarding prizes at the Philippine Exposition. There is a circular going about to educate the general's children in the United States. And his cousin Blas, right-hand man of Tinio—he's the first governor of the American-made Mountain Province! The right-hand man of Worcester—hah! He's now the aide of those you called *ave de rapiña*!

Ah, she says, I see. You're not talking about the people—about their choices—the fact that they prefer the men of their revolution. Many of whom also happen to own the land they till. It's a cunning gambit of the Americans, I admit—to keep the surrendered leaders of the people in their place, running for office. But you're not talking about the people's choices. You're condemning *the individual choices of the heroes.* I get it.

I'm not condemning, he says. I'm just pointing out. They went to war against the Americans, now they're running for office under American rule. I mean, don't you think it's sad?

Survival is a whore, she says. Peace is a bastard.

I mean, why curse people like *me* out when *they* are doing the same thing?

I never cursed you, she said. I just want to know where your brother is—he said in his note he would be home.

I mean, where's their idealism, their honor?

Well, where's yours?

He opens his mouth—but he stands silent.

Come on, Paco, she says—this can't be the first time you've grasped how shiny objects—

He shifts. He stares at the capiz windows.

She continues—

How our shiny objects are also signs of loss.

And the way he turns again, toward her, his odd gray eyes now clarified by a slant of light, brings back an image in her recall.

For one thing, the boy has strange eyes.

I don't know what you mean, he says.

Your beautiful diploma from Indiana, your entry into the *colegio de derecho* of Yale. Shiny shiny objects. Don't look surprised. I've followed the exploits of the brothers Delgado. I read the news in the papers, too.

You judge me, he says, for my success.

I don't think of you, she says.

I really do not think of you.

I miss Jote, she wishes to say.

But Jote's silence, on the other hand, was also not livable.

It's so tiring she could weep.

She has spoken to so many boys in americana suits in colleges parsing the motives of the heroes, failing to mention their own.

The bloodshed, she thinks.

So much blood, so much blood on their clothes, bolos, cheeks, hair, lofting their captured Krags. The memory of the joy of their return—it's what keeps her alive. Scarred, scathed, traumatized, brutal, triumphant, victory encased in his body, his bright eyes. The wonder of their action. That they have survived.

I've only come, she finally says, to see Jote. But I see that my wish to see him—

And here she falters—

Is a trap, she ends.

A splash, and that is all.

He means nothing to her, he thinks—she has no memory.

And it's a relief.

His past in Samar is released from him.

Released from her spell, and he sees her in the flesh, not in illusion.

It was so long ago anyhow.

Seven years, almost to the month.

It comes out as a gasp, the way the thought emerges from his body. She mistakes it.

She says: I'm sorry. I don't mean to be rude.

Her look softens, the way she's learned from her times on stage when she's been harsh, and she shifts her strategy. She touches her shawl.

I only bring it up, she says, because it is also possible the heroes throwing their hats in the elections can be signs—

Of the violence wrought by the conqueror, he finishes.

She stabs her finger in the air, like a teacher.

She smiles.

Very good memory, Paco!—*sobresaliente!* You have a good recall, she says. That was a long time ago, that speech—in 1904. Yes—and she warms up to her old topic—even now, she says, you cannot imagine, I cannot imagine—how any rebel can be at peace: the surveillance alone, the policing—an entire imperial apparatus, Constabulary, Scouts, schools, bridges, roads, voting, elections—where even our ways of self-creation are a form of policing, our desires produced from their measures of counterinsurgency—certainly in some matters there is benefit, but consider, for instance when the towns of Asia Minor—

—made a tribute to Rome, and Rome bought commodities from them, at a price too dear, and in this way the provincials of Asia got back from their conquerors a portion of their tribute, and yet for all that—the provincials remained the ones who had been cheated!

Yes! she says, her eyes now widening, smiling—correct! You have a good memory!

That's my talent, he says.

Sobresaliente—and the conclusion?

—the capitalist class as a whole cannot defraud itself!

She clapped at his good reply.

Yes!, she says—you are a good student. The goods of the conquered of Asia Minor were still paid for *by their own money*! And for us—our goods have been paid for by our own blood.

And she continues—

And your education, too, your grand education is the sign of an enormous violence upon you.

But she has gone too far.

You are, he says—and his voice catches—a bitter soul, Calista!

It's a relief and a release to understand, he thinks, that he is nothing, nothing at all to her.

A splash, and that is all.

But it is also a weapon, she says, she extends her point—it's also a bludgeon, your education. It's a weapon that is yours to wield against them, the colonizer, no matter their intentions for you.

His thin mouth is pursed, he speaks his words carefully, in English.
His *R*s roll, his *T*s slide.

You are, he begins—

A disgrace to womanhood, he continues slowly, carefully—and
your own *trrrabajo*—you think it is—without blemish? Funded by—
by the Sapphists!

She brings her hand to her mouth, the gesture of the Filipino
maiden.

She's giggling again.

Ghik ghik ghik.

And she steps up into the sala, she moves the lampaso and the
rags to the side and lifts up her saya, she takes the notebooks from his
hands before he has the chance to move.

She's laughing as she swipes the journal, holds the bound books
against her chest, and he has stood up as if to take them from her, but
he remains where he is.

In that moment, as he turns, she sees.

He has turned his other cheek toward her, and the shape of the
scar is blazoned by the keen tropical morning light.

A swath across his left cheek that seems a shadow of a scimitar, an
orange peel, or the dark side of a half moon.

The sun makes the cloven skin glimmer, undulate in the silver
trench of his scar.

Her hand moves back up to her mouth.

She almost drops the journal, but she catches it, she holds it tight.

He, too, has a scar, admits Paco.

I know, she says.

An iya samad.

The story?, he asks.

She stares at him.

Eternized by her desire to know.

No, she says—I don't know the story.

If you give me back the notebooks, he says, I'll tell you.

PART FOUR
THE TYPHOON PATH

✳ ✳ ✳

The Funeral

The house in Salogó will soon be dismantled. Tio Nemor has declared the opposite. But the bustle of the maids emptying out bedrooms and cabinets betrays him. The funeral for my mother was the affair it should have been in a house like ours. Congested, gluttonous, with too many pigs, and people in various modes of mourning, including celebration, gambling, tsismis, and a pallbearer's gross and accusatory weeping (this from Paquito, formerly of Nevada, son of Tia Pachang who's conceived a hatred for me, I had no clue, after rumors of an old hospital incident at which he was absent: he says I called his own recently dead mom a puta to her face, bravery I wish I had, and his loud and embarrassing weeping told everyone I'm an *ingrata* daughter who never went home except to bury my mom—criticism no harsher than mine).

There was no tango. Corroy Montejo, Tacloban's giantess of choreography, had to make do with towering above us, in her gorgeous sequined balintawak, eating lechon along with everyone else.

Instead, the usual busy kitchen with so many bodies, and this vague undercurrent, only on the cusp of being destabilizing, that suffuses intergenerational family gatherings, and this weird yet abiding vocal and ritual affection founded on nothing but knowledge that somehow everyone was related to our moms pervaded the entire affair. Tay Lucio was there with his apo, who looked exactly like his dad, the driver Claudio, Doctor Tita Tita's all-around man in Manila (I finally remembered who he was: it was Claudio the driver who had met me at NAIA 3). Three generations of carpentering, wiry men, including the apo, Francisco, nicknamed Kikoy, whose faces, I thought for a moment, were my tether to this land, and one day, yes, ruthless as my memory is, I will forget who they are.

Tay Lucio looked at me, and his eyes were red. They were red for my mom. He had worked with her since 1971. In his habitual dignity—he spoke with his eloquent hands, after all, the way he so carefully crafted her art's frames according to her instructions—he nodded at me, about to say something, then he looked away and did not speak. No one has much in Salogó, and he hesitated the day before to take Doctor Tita Tita's gift (in her wisdom, my aunt in Manila had insisted I carry home a balikbayan box)—a carton of Camel cigarettes, which I thought was gross and vulgar to give to the grieving, but Mana Marga made me do it—and it's his pause, the way at first he shook his head, that I will remember.

As if the day of my mother's funeral was not a day for his profit, but I was glad to see him later, by the AWOL, enjoying a cigarette out by Himanglos.

The Widow Ebangheline, with her now adult daughters, protecting the pigs' heads from abduction by in-laws, was doubly widowed after all these years, but this time of a horrid natural cause—easily treatable tuberculosis. The mourning ladies, now paid by Venmo, looked chosen for their physical approximations to their graveyard calling. It wasn't just me. Everywhere, it seemed, was ambient grief. The FrankenPresley combo had long disbanded, "Frank" to construct things in Qatar (and fall off a scaffolding, from good-luck job to bad-luck job, so the funeral drinkers who were happy to survive him by staying home shook their heads), the other, "Presley," actually named Oscar, moving appropriately to Las Vegas (near his old buddy, the Junior Igmenegildo). Instead, we listened to my mom's cousin Bronson, on her maternal side, not a Delgado, said Mana Marga—he was from Pasig Line—who wept as he sang "Always on My Mind," a terrible excuse for Elvis, a cadaverous man with a pinched face and big ears, drowning in his clothing, trembling through the lyrics—*maybe I-I-I-ay-ay-ay—maybe I-I-I-ay-ay-ay*—and he was so tearful I gave him extra money that Mana Marga told me was unnecessary—he was not weeping for my mom but for his brother, she said, a different cousin named Brando, also from Pasig Line, who had just been killed by the goons of a man whose mistress the disappeared Brando had been hired to stab to death.

Oh my God.

What a terrible, convoluted story, I exclaimed to Mana Marga.

His brother Bronson has not stopped crying since Brando disappeared, she said sadly—look, see how Bronson is wasting away.

A little girl in the kitchen rushed to me after the song—she ran as if she knew me.

"Carmen! Carmen!" The Widow Ebangheline came out, laughing, "That's your ninang, Carmen! Bless, bless!"

And that is the apo ha tuhod of Nay Carmen, Mana Marga said—remember my aunt who sold bibingka? Of course, I do, I said, and the child took my hand.

At that moment, I wished I had brought some balikbayan doll to give her.

And I tried one last time to know.

Mana Marga, was your aunt Nay Carmen from Samar?

"She was from Capoocan," said Mana Marga, "near Carigara."

Oh, I said.

"But her uncle, her dad's brother—you know, apoy Bingo, the one who constructed the house by the barakasyunan? Father of Tay Guimoy? My apoy Bingo—he was from Giporlos."

And Nay Carmen's father, the brother of Bingo—was he named Bongo?

Mana Marga shrugged.

"She never talked about him. I never knew his name. Her father—magkaruha adto hera—he died in Samar, in Giporlos, before they arrived in Capoocan."

What does magkaruha mean? I asked.

Mana Marga raised two fingers, entwined them.

"Twins," Mana Marga said, "kun baga sering pa man—magkaduha hera. They were doubles. Two by two. Her dad and apoy Bingo were twins."

Usa.

Duha.

Tulo.

"And your lolo, Jote, it's like he was the third twin—he could never be separated from Apoy Bingo."

And she raised her two fingers again, entwined them. "Bagan hera an magkaruha."

I saw my classmates from Divine Word Missionary School. I saw Elvis Oras, the fashion prodigy, but we used to call him Child Laborer, for his after-school job that he loved, sewing sequins at his aunt Mrs. Young's mestiza-dress shop. Now he was the heredero of Young's Fashionne House (but he still liked to do the beading himself)— an extremely well-groomed kid who used to compete with Winston Querer to be Number Four in the front-row seats of our hierarchical education. He was now a beautiful, exuberant, ironic man. I always loved Elvis because early in life he had wisely chosen his faithful god—fabric. He inspected the lace of my outfit, made me turn around to check the tag, an old splurge, a Vivienne Westwood, and most of all he approved of the lining—he touched it with reverence. The mark of luxury, said Elvis Oras, feeling the cloth with the solemnity of his lifelong experience, is in what cannot be seen. Lorelei, who had gone to school with me at the state university (in high school she was always Number Three, and even in college she focused on her biology labs and avoided us, Trina and me, when we tried to get her to join the marches), was back home from Geneva. She was home to attend the launch of her parents' new business, at corner Burgos and Juan Luna, The Hotel Sirena, she explained, named (in my mind) after their daughter who had financed the enterprise. Lorelei was a climate scientist at the United Nations, and she hugged me as if I had defended her from Trina Trono ever since we were children— which I never had. Winston Querer, whom we called without mercy but with love (or so we believed) our Flamboyant Gay (as opposed to Elvis Oras, our tailored gay, who dressed in white linen shirts and chinos), was absent. By high school Winston wore cosmetics and danced like John Travolta to "More Than a Woman" in a fringe disco skirt. He became a plastic surgeon in Cebu only to die of a stroke, his arrhythmia undetected. Elvis Oras crossed himself at the memory as he gave me the info on his best friend. Queen Sirikit, who had turned Praise-the-Lord, a.k.a. the charismatics, whose congregation at random moments become vessels of the Holy Spirit, had seven children and a business selling electric fans and kitchen appliances by Magsaysay Boulevard. Queen Refrigerator, as Elvis Oras called her, became charismatic after her doctor-husband four-timed her with as many nurses. Margot (rhymes with igot) Abella was Tacloban's best dermatologist, and she observed my mom in her coffin with a professional nod. William McKinley Maceda was in his collared shirt and high-waisted pants, still a salesman for Electrolux vacuums, but at least, so whispered Elvis, he was not asking people to become a Mormon. Teeny-tiny Benito Lupak, former ice-candy dealer, was unrecognizable—a brawny man in a barong. He leapt from the van in Ray-Ban sunglasses, and Elvis Oras remarked, "Ay, udoy, Sikyo, pasaway, ano ka, stuntman from *The Bodyguard*?" Benito was a City Fiscal, in the same office as Tio Nemor, and his teeny-tiny weapon, a Tokarev, visible at his hip, explained his new nickname: Sikyo—Security. Ferdinand Enage Dumpit was an actual guard, at the provincial jail, near the place once named Camp Bumpus, the old American garrison, now a luxury resort owned by the Trinidads. I blessed the hand of our old principal, my aunt Tita Patchy, her triplicate moles as hairy as ever, privileged sign of her being a Delgado, sitting half-blind—also a Delgado trait—in her wheelchair. All of them arrived in the air-conditioned van from Tacloban paid for by Sirit, who could not come. Sirit and her family, including her husband the mayor, an avid biker, were in Europe, on Sirit's annual tour of her Marian saints while the mayor biked around France.

Mayor Tour-de-France, Elvis muttered, touring-touring while a supertyphoon is coming.

The consul Charity Breton Delgado never arrived, of course.

Not even a wreath from Greenhills for her cousin Adina an guapa.

Leche. That Gotas de Leche.

By the afternoon, there were so many mourners we had chairs along the AWOL, where the pechay garden used to be. People from Santa Rin and as far as Alang-Alang teared up to see me, kissed my face, called me Chicharita. I had no idea who they were. Weeping for my mom. I felt something distending in me. My shame, or my alienation. People with memories in which I had no share though I was her only daughter. There were so many mourners arriving into Salogó the jeepneys were now heading straight from Cong. J. B. Delgado to her wake, the Widow Ebangheline said. She was proud. How everyone loved Adina an guapa. She was so good. See. Your mom helped that man with his wedding—he wanted to elope, but she said, no, it must be in church. She helped that woman with her daughter's schooling—she is now in Hong Kong, she built a house for her mother, it is made of jalousies and cement, oh wow! And Adina an guapa, she laid her hands over that man's son, hala, his leg got well, he grew up to go to Saudi! She was so good, Adina an guapa.

And once again the Widow Ebangheline cried.

A woman in black sidled up to me, she had been waiting her turn. She held my hand to her stomach: she was pregnant. Bless me, she said, Mana Adina had blessed my first child, he is so healthy, look. I looked at the morose kid clutching her black hem, wearing clothes too big for him, like Benito Lupak in second grade. She kept my hand on her belly. She pressed my palm on her fervid body, and I thought I felt it, her child coming alive at my touch, I said, oh my God, and she beamed—you can be the ninang, please give me your address in estados.

Adino, sweet Adino, my brother. It was he, most of all, who looked like my mom. I have long felt cursed for looking like my dad—I inherited none of Adina an guapa's grace. But my brother had the fulsome mouth, the delicate features, the heart-breaking face. I could not look at him without seeing my mother, dressed all in black, cradling him in her arms from Los Angeles (along with the Sacred Heart of Jesus). He was suited in his role, a dark-browed mourner with stooped shoulders, and when he lifted our mother's coffin, his glance was intolerable precisely because it was familiar. His baby face. He had long lost an ability to attach with wholeness to the world. Sometimes I think I'm a stranger to Adino, sweet Adino, who had fallen ill in America, a precocious madness. *Dementia praecox.* After a stint in government service in California, he returned home believing, for some reason that his EEO case must have laid out if only I had read it, that white people were out to get him, and my arrival from the States was no boon. When he came back to Salogó, I was in New York and had already published my third novel, and he was a Certified Public Accountant who won a case for racial harassment from the Department of Agriculture in California. After that, my mom would not leave his side in Salogó, and he would not leave his chickens. I mean roosters—*gallos* are male. He created an entire galyera for them, against the AWOL of Himanglos, and he has gained peace from importing them from around the world (except Texas)—his Gold Laced Wyandotte, his Spangled Orpington, his Black Australorp, his pair of Russian Orloffs. They're so fancy their provenances have embossed cards. He is a serious researcher of our family names, and his pets are Nemesio, Mariano, Bonifacio, Francisco, Jorge—all male. Mixing genders destabilizes his coop. He gave me a chart when I told him about my own discoveries—it's a print download of an elaborate, private family tree that he has registered on ancestry.com. I thought at first it was the genealogy of the chickens. He shared the tree with me with the look he had as a baby when he allowed us to carry him aloft in our Santacruzan parades, his infant look of faith, our king Constantino, trusting the world of his childhood, of Salogó.

Putt-putt arrived from Cebu, where he had a heart-to-heart with his mom at his brother's grave.

It was Mick-mick who met me at the airport in Tacloban with Tio Nemor.

I had no coin but my relationship to them, but Mick-mick bore a package, he had a treasure that he wished me to see. Mickmick was clearly treasured himself—middle-aged and smiling and overfed the way some families believe food is compensation for any turn of fate.

He was carrying it at the airport, giggling even from far-off, at the gate, at the prospect of my remembrance.

A carved empty box with the initials *F. B.* in oyster filigree.

As if it were only yesterday, Mick-mick greeted me—"Do you remember, do you remember, the box we found in the aparador in Salogó. I kept it for you."

Mick-mick also collected Pepsi-Cola tansans, McDonald's toys, Coke movie trailer giveaways, and now Major League Baseball trinkets from cousins around the United States, a new hobby begotten by a gift from his mother in Baltimore—a hoard of signifiers of his allegiance to moments he, in turn, will not forget.

Tio Nemor hugged me.

I never did lamano to Tio Nemor.

With people you love you hugged, you kissed them on the cheek, you never forgot and you always forgave. It was when I saw Tio Nemor that I broke down, I had no defenses for my memory, I knew how much he loved my mother, I knew he would protect her until he died. I hated his politics, and I knew that he could sell his soul on a dime, and his loyalty to me would remain intact, and he beat up John-john all those times, and like Doctor Tita Tita, no more will he bring back that light.

A light in Tio Nemor is done.

He was wearing his Ray-Ban sunglasses, the City Fiscal look, barong and takong, his pants sagging behind him, and there was, in the way he carried himself, his enduring self-worth. In my eyes, it was earned. He waved a hand at the kargador, in that irritated voice he had, come on, come on, but he didn't have to signal twice, a quick man in slippers, cigarette in hand, took up Doctor Tita Tita's awkward cardboard box of pasalubong, the kargador was a boss of his trade who waved for us to follow him, but I kept my luggage to myself, I let no one take it, and Tio Nemor took me onto his jeep, with him and Mick-mick, and only toward the end, as we reached the bend into town (I was surprised at the journey—instead of a day it seemed barely an hour, down the cleared, novel, cement roads through Palo, through Alang-Alang to Salogó)—only when we reached Cong. J. B. Delgado Street did he ask me about them, the notebooks.

I said yes, they're mine. I have them.

And, of course, last but not least, my dreaded appearance before Mana Marga.

She who had cared for my mother from their days in elementary school, when she was the adept, the Model School-Girl of English Language and Vocabulary with Mrs. Edith Taffie, she was the scholar of *catechetical instruction!*, but my mom was the princess, and the way caste works in a class-driven world interlaces love with inequity and devotion with boundaries, and I never had the ability to see Mana Marga whole the way Mana Marga saw my mom, while my mom, who had no qualms about her hierarchical position, our status quo, was loved by all, and I, who was never comfortable, I hated the world where the station you were born in was no measure of your worth, I was the interloper, an outsider, and I couldn't love Mana Marga in the way she and my mother survived, faithful, each bound to the other in her own way.

Only this late did I understand that their bonds were also their own to measure.

Instead, I could only feel guilt, the most useless of emotions.

And I obeyed Mana Marga throughout the funeral affair.

She met me in Salogó as I got off Tio Nemor's jeep, walking toward us with that gait and poise, her shoulders erect and mouth proud, as if it was she, and no one but she, who had engineered our reunion.

In her high heels and cosmetics, she mirrored my mom, but in her tight bun and googoo oils and gawgaw—she was all her own.

She kissed me on both cheeks and said, pastilan, uday—you're thin.

Mana Marga was busy, she was everywhere at once, the mistress of an elaborate festivity, and the entire event was presided over by the prospect of her lechon paksiw.

She kept appearing and reappearing at my place by the window now that everyone was gone.

Her signature bun formed the apex of a pyramid atop her head, with her sharp ears as the cone's geometrical ends. Her hair shone. Her pungent fumes—googoo oils and gawgaw mixed with *Aliage*, her gift from Tita Tita's balikbayan box—suffused my solitude. Mana Marga still liked to use the ancient iron, with its jagged and burning coals that gave it the look of a glowing monster, a scarifying totem with fiery jaws, wielded with care by the maids who long ago had folded and pleated my uniforms. Even though electricity has arrived in Salogó, Mana Marga still lays banana leaves beneath the ironing board's cloth, and a moist, sweet spume casts sorcery over her chore. Mana Marga's stiff-katsa polka-dot outfits smelled of steaming leaves and cornstarch and the hissing lumps of coconut shells hacked from trees right outside our windows.

I did not need to look up to know when Mana Marga was about.

Every time she came near me, the smells of my childhood malingered.

She kept offering me roscas and bibingka (but the bibingka was stiff, in sad rigor mortis, far cry from Nay Carmen's old magical cakes)—as if to distract me from her secret obligations around the house—and the whiff of her oils hovered over the empty shell of my work, this domed box.

Agapito Pedrigal, a.k.a. Padrax, the lapida maker, has not even finished carving out the words on my mother's tombstone—one of the last on my list of the chores left to the living.

But from the bustle around me, I knew the memory of my mother would soon be erased.

I had already given the Catholic hospital her wheelchair. The oxygen tanks went to the cancer society in Tacloban, as she wished. The funeral flowers were in the garden, by the AWOL, mulching the guava trees.

The house in Salogó returned to itself after death's invasion.

I tried to make myself useful in those last days, but my place was long taken. My mom's troops, cousins and nephews and nieces, were practiced—platoons of servants and relations in her deathbed progress from Makati Medical Center to Tacloban to Salogó, massaging her limbs, combing her hair, manicuring her nails, changing her bedpan, pushing the trolley of her morphine drip.

My mom was treated like a baby and a boss.

Everyone liked to repeat to me how her face never gave in to disease—

Kaguapa la gihapon ni Adina an guapa.

Kahusay.

They underlined every detail of her end.

They said—I could only imagine.

Lying at Makati Medical, she had the skin tone of the newlywed in her old passport photo taken before she left for California in America—a smooth flushed face in a pixie, unsmiling, startled by the flash, my young mother in her Roman-Holiday, Audrey Hepburn bob.

The oncologist told her that the flush on her cheek came from steroids, but my mom contradicted him, crowed Mana Marga.

"Doctor, it is because of my inventions!"

Even as she lay dying, first thing in the morning she lathered herself with her concocted potage.

Look closely, inday!

The way as a kid I watched her with her Pond's Cold Cream, cucumbers and papaya and grapefruit peels—*pipino papaya and pomelo everlasting!*—on her cheeks and chin while Mana Marga boiled a pot of water.

She looked like a fruit salad.

She sat up before Mana Marga's basin of steaming water and placed her face, *her fruitened plain!*, its creamed skin against the heat, and she closed her eyes above the steam while Mana Marga hovered—my mom's lovely face in meditating profile, like a bodhisattva, a Cleopatra in steaming milk. And her peaceful profile as she bent over the milky pot and breathed in the fumes of her cosmetic invention, her face haloed in a boiling kaldero would have the gauzy, hallowed, and citrusy permanence that remains in my memory.

In that cosmetic pose, she also looked like Mary, Queen of Scots, holding her neck out for her beheading.

Mana Marga would return the basin to the floor then gently pat my mother's upturned face.

You could only be Cleopatra if you had a slave.

Look closely, inday!

No matter how much I stared at my mother in her coffin, I recognized, like too many daughters, that I will never know who my mother was.

A mother is someone who is hard to know.

But as I looked at Adina an guapa, I thought—

Life is what she made it.

It imo kinabuhi, ikaw an magbubuot—diri iba.

I did not say goodbye to my mother as they lowered her into her grave.

It was Mana Marga who knew where the pain lay, which touch soothed which hurt.

It was Mana Marga, I finally understood, who had been summoned to the house in Salogó when Adina an guapa returned, *¡desgraciada!*, as her Tia Pachang announced—after her abduction by *the worst scoundrel*—a *scalawag*—it was Mana Marga who had kept the neighboring ladies and the drinking men out out out of the house in Salogó when Adina an guapa returned from Pasig Line—it was Mana Marga who had mixed the arroz caldo, with the bitter ginger my mom disliked, she had made her sit up and drink the salabát, and pretty soon the tabléa, and she spooned into her mouth the hipon, my mom's favorite, she fried the budo-bulad, she pushed rice into her patient's mouth with her fingers, her thumb tipping the softened grains in. She soothed and soaked my mother's body in balm and leaves and luy-a. She cleansed the body. *Does it hurt here, does it hurt?* It was Mana Marga who had heard the words of my young mother in her delirium, the words now sealed in Mana Marga's lips.

I know this because, when I asked about the incident, Mana Marga looked at me with a face meant for haunting.

She looked with anger.

Memory was a taint, the past was a soil, and my tardy question was my shame.

I could see in Mana Marga's eyes, when I asked the question—

That it was I who was the *desgraciada*.

"Ayaw paglabti an diri angay labtan. Kay ano yana ka la napakiana?"

Her eagle eyes—*don't touch what you should not.*

And why ask only now?

"Why not ask about her exhibit," Mana Marga accused. "It was at the Cultural Center!"

What exhibit? I said.

"The Inventors' Society of the Philippines! They gave her an award a few months before her last illness."

For what?

And my heart lurched as I thought of her art—*The Four Seasons.*

"For her lotion, of course—for *Adina EVERLASTING PANTY-LESS STOCKINGS!™* But they also gave her space for all her inventions, her frames, her lotions, her *Three Ps Everlasting Cosmetics!* Just this year. It was in an exhibit at the Bulwagang Juan Luna! At the Cultural Center. I went to the opening! Only *I* went to the opening! Everyone else was busy. Busy, busy, busy. Too busy to see the exhibit of their sister, their aunt! Nemorino, Putt-putt—no one went."

Tears welled up in her eyes, and Mana Marga wiped them away.

"Oh how Adina cried. Because no one else came but me."

And the look in Mana Marga's eyes killed.

There was something in me that died.

I remembered those times when I lay sleeping, and I heard the sound of her snoring, an unearthly awakening, that startled me.

I thought it was her heart against my ribs.

But the heart was mine, beating to the sound of my mother's breathing.

And I would be happy when I woke up, to hear her heart beating. To know Adina an guapa was alive.

She died in her sleep, in her own bed, as I slept in America.

"Your friend Sirit, asawa ni mayor, she saw the exhibit," Mana Marga added, "at least. She helped your mom select some of the frames."

Even on her worst days, when people reported how she had lost her bearings, and she had sold the last of her beachfront property in San Jose, and she had offered up to Mana Marga, for her life of faithful service (so the cousins reproved), a few square feet of ancient beach land by Palo, and she had practically given away her grand-father Jote's abaca lands in Basey to some teenage stranger (whom gossips said looked like John-john, though Mana Marga would have none of that), and even her clothes had been offered to her favorite beggar, the aristocratic Mrs. Kierulf, jewel-toned election gowns from mothballed aparadors—now a sight wandering Tacloban, who knows—the sequined gowns hanging from the clavicles of the ageless beggar Mrs. Kierulf—

Still, Adina an guapa had kept the house in Salogó intact, over her dying body.

But strangers were now coming to appraise the old house's wood.

John-john and Putt-putt and I used to waltz around the house on the coconut husks that the servants used for waxing floors, and we danced with the shaggy lampaso against our instep. Rocking around the clock tonight, our hips doing the twist as the mahogany floors grew shinier, mirror-like, with each swish of our hips and pass of the lampaso, each swipe producing a fine, horizontal glaze.

Instant gratification.

We'd sweep the mahogany staircase, the narra floor planks with the rich, reddish sheen of YCO floor-waxing, a century of upkeep thick with a century's crust, up to the dining room table with the capacity to seat an entire municipal council plus a marching band of musicians—that massive table, one of a kind, a continuous block of molave.

The History Matronas

The table was the first thing that greeted me when I entered the house. I came back to its decrepit welcome—the uneven wood of that ancient, implacable table, with its jagged punctures from our childhood games. As far as I could tell, it was hewn from the rotted, pig-blood ground, straight from the soil like some moss-grown Odyssean bed. Agents of house-designing, retro-loving expats were opening and closing the creaking komedor in the dining hall and the broken aparador in the bedrooms. Some greedy, riverine bulletin must circulate among hardwood scavengers in the islands to prompt this descent of vultures—seedy men with measuring sticks and furtive gazes, knocking on wood.

The laws against logging ancient hardwood are redundant, after all—the old narra and molave forests have long disappeared.

These prospectors love rotting homes like ours. They denude them of mahogany like meticulous fire ants scraping out the carapace of a twitching roach.

The official mourners, all women, have left the house—the toothless itinerants in their faithful veils who go from one bereaved home to the next singing their novenas to the dead.

Ora pro nobis.

Mana Marga went off to the kitchen, supervising the making of the lechon paksiw—the ritual stewing of the leftover pig's meat and cartilage and bones once funeral guests are gone.

What is left to salvage, apart from dregs of pigs' heads in the kitchen, their snouts in the air saluting their own demise, was in the balikbayan boxes scattered about the sala.

My mother's cousins were gone, bequeathing us the mess of their cardboard luggage. Tay Guimoy's grandchildren, prophetic owners of a corporation of Filipino caregivers tending geriatric Americans in Baltimore, have carried off the University of the Philippines diploma of Lolo Jote, framed, *circa* 1912. He was not even their grandfather—relatives of Mamá, not Papá—but no one bothered with the disappearance. I could not blame them. The Junior Igmenegildo, the family's celebrity swindler, fortunately incompetent, has law-abiding children in Nevada plying that other therapeutic calling, casino dealing. They couldn't care less about what is left in the house—rotting chairs of abaca twine, the scarred molave table. The old pictures on the walls are now packed somewhere in the recycled boxes, except for the one still in the abandoned house of Doctor Tita Tita in Cebu, who knows— the life-size double portrait of Lolo Jote and Mama Bia. A long time ago, when he had stopped coming to Salogó, and his private law practice post-rebellion kept him in mint, and he still imagined their marriage would survive, Tio Nemor had taken that portrait with him, ostensibly to clean it, or maybe as talisman for a hoped-for future, a reorganized life.

But she did not return, and I have not seen the portrait since.

A space in the sala was cleared for my work on these diaries—the last refuge of memory in the house.

With the mourning chores all done and guests all gone, I had no idea what to do with my freedom before I returned to New York.

The storm bulletins kept telling me—I should make sure I make my flight.

A storm was coming, and Tacloban, as always, was in the typhoon's path—the eastern brunt of the archipelago, its vulnerable spine against the Pacific. In my experience, it's a brunt that goes from Tanauan through Tacloban, and up through Samar along Leyte Gulf: Guiuan, Giporlos, Balangiga. Our coast directly faces the Pacific, and every year we're the eye of storms.

The landfall of catastrophe—from Magellan through MacArthur—has been ours.

The news anchors were already in town, positioned for the phenomenal event.

A supertyphoon, it was called, but as far as I could tell, in Leyte, every typhoon is a supertyphoon.

We just wash it away with gihay.

But even in Salogó, westward of the winds, people were battening the hatches.

I kept reading.

I threw the letters into the trash, the ones Tio Nemor kept showing me.

They've been at it, he said, since Adina died.

Tio Nemor told me at first he was bewildered—what did he have to do with Paz Tilanuday, the woman the antique collectors in Manila bugged him about?

The stuff and moldering books he found in the cabinets that he ransacked anyway, just in case, were all his Papá's, he said, not even his grandfather Jote's—the old mayor's *Reader's Digest*s, scratched records, old suits, damaged opera books, broken octavinas. What collection of papers were they talking about?

He pried open the wooden drawers of the massive, wind-up Victrola, and all he found were musical scores, songs from his own opera-namesake, *L'elisir d'amore*. He checked the cloth sleeve of the Edison Bell gramophone.

He got a pillbox filled with random sticks of fallen needles.

Even the history books had his Papá's name on them—*F. B. Delgado*.

Francisco Buñales Delgado.

What were these collectors going on about?

The hoarders of history wanted to pay money for his grandfathers' papers, but he had never paid attention to the house and had no idea where to look.

The history matronas—collectors of Ming vases from village graveyards and revolutionary waste from people's attics—were insistent.

The messages kept coming.

Not to mention their rivals, aging men of mystery, smelling of brilliantine and starch—history's Pomade Brigade.

The *Inquirer*'s obituary, one of those triumphs of pomposity useless to the dead and embarrassing to the living, trotted out the court case that Adina Delgado had pursued. The newspaper odes on her Lolo Paco's legacy included the following embroidery: that the history of the country is locked in a box among my mother's effects.

It's a preposterous bag that's out, and I can only guess who's leaking these dumb embellishments, to promote their value for her own sinister reasons, and the history matrons have been writing my uncle every week, he said, out to get the notebooks.

Adding to the mystery is the twist—how my mom, unknown to history, has long owned original papers in the pseudonymous hand of a rebel during the Filipino-American war, the anarchist Paz Tilanuday—her version of the war against the Americans.

I kept getting these handwritten notes now, from her hotel in Tacloban, delivered by jeepney to the house in Salogó, not too subtle about being the advance guard of the matronas' greed.

She had just arrived she said—business kept her from the funeral. Apologies.

The last time I saw Trina Trono in full glory was at Malacañang Palace, when she harangued the pockmarked minion of Benigno Maria Espasol—that gun-toting Rudy Da Moody.

And now that Rudy Da Moody, to no one's surprise but my chagrin, has become the boss of Danao, Doctor Tita Tita's hometown—the gun-loving, motorbike-riding Boss Mayor, paltik politician, who turned his back on Manila to save his province's ass from drugs and crime, so he says. It's people like Rudy Da Moody who rise while the leaning boy against the Manansala mural—Andro Leonardo in his contrapposto pose, his cigarette aloft, like the Filipino-rebel version of Michelangelo's *David*—it's he who's dead, gunned down.

I noticed the online posts and reposts, where the mayor of Danao in a polished video declares—*I hab my rice sacks ready, to send to my sister cities in Leyte por de supertypoon!*, to the cheering of his Facebook minions. Rudy Da Moody has cast off his Lacoste shirts, his preppie style. As he's gained power, he's shed his dependency on his uncle's Yellow Brigade—that former Assistant Secretary to the Secretary of the President: ASSP for short, who now, in a twist of fate, was his nephew's sick appendage.

"This is damning," Trina Trono had said at Maharlika Hall, "you know every single piece of material in these boxes should be catalogued and filed, not burned and wasted. Even the receipts of shoes and piles of lipsticked tissue should be sorted: our history is in the details. We demand that you hire a Palace historian to deal with all this—junk!"

"Don't give up," one of her handwritten notes said, addressed to me on the brand-new stationery of Hotel Sirena, corner Juan Luna and Burgos.

"Who else will keep the flame, if not you—a writer and their grandchild?"

Your clichés are not convincing, I replied.

I sent her notes written on the back of her own missives, just to let her know I was not keeping any of her garbage—and I gave them to the driver of the next jeepney, to send on to Trina Trono.

Anyway, the nation is all just—apo ha tuhod.

So many generations removed.

And, I added, given the caste system of this country—the stories of some are exhumed, sure, but the stories of the best are lost.

I thought of Bongo, or was it Bingo, any number of lost names.

Not even their children know their story.

Their plot drowned in Himanglos.

On one hand, it was true: the folders and the notebooks are perhaps the only extant manuscripts of this unwritten war not in the hands of the US military or the National Archives or stolen by history's bibliokleptomaniacs.

No diary by a Filipino revolutionary in the war against the Americans survives.

At least in print.

There is an unpublished text, the *inédita crónica* of Juan Villamor, stashed somewhere in an Australian university, of which two of three parts are intact.

Part One, *The War against Spain.*

Part Three, *The Postwar Period.*

Part Two is unwritten.

Juan Villamor, the Ilocano revolutionary who became the American-era governor of Abra, never wrote Part Two: *The War against the Americans.*

And the diary of Simeon Villa—father of poet José Garcia Villa, whose former apartment I pass whenever I walk toward D'Agostino's on Bethune—a manuscript captured at Palanan by Arthur MacArthur's forces under Colonel "Fighting Fred" Funston, is in the Philippine Revolutionary Records (formerly the Philippine Insurgent Records when it was in the U.S. Library of Congress), tranquil in the National Archives.

Villa's diary also exists in mimeographed typescript, translated into English, in the New York Public Library.

But the fact is, like my mom, most Filipinos prefer to keep history in the dark or, in these days, sold to the highest bidder.

Who can blame them.

It's kind of painful to remember.

I told Trina—don't bother. These notebooks are a mess.

And I don't just mean the physical disorder of the papers.

Sure, their fragility adds to their value—even if the history matronas will not be able to read them, they will kill to own them, and they'd be right.

There are no papers like them.

What I mean is—the effects.

Sometimes I think I understand the sensations, and the chronological order begins to make sense. But then a word circles back to a fragment in another, and a detail in the middle has the sense of being repeated in converse order, so that the story inches back to the start, and every time I read it, the shifting sense of a reader's place, the various removes in time, or is it the uncertain merits of authorship, as of a ghost writer in the text—who is speaking to whom? (I hear my piano teacher Miss Custodia in her basso profundo, in presto, in agonized prestissimo: *for whom* do *the bells toll?*)—and in the end the entire arrangement has this miraculous yet unstable quality of any act of reading, in which your vantage rewrites the page.

Bullshit, replied Trina Trono.

The text is not about the reader, or even the author—Trina wrote—the text is the actual words on the page that can be authenticated by an appraiser!

The Instar

On the day his brother holds in his hands his death warrant, the evidence of his war, Jote walks amid the circle of narra trees in the vast garden of the house on Moret Street. In the season of the narra's yellow flowers and the smell of kalamansi, which the servants call limonsito, the season of the kamia falling on his hammock, upon his palm: petals, ginger-colored, the size of his thumb—

He sits up in the hammock amid the narra trees, the faint-hearted flowers.

The birds sing.

Maya, maya, maya.

Or did they sing baya—leave it alone?

Or bayâ—in the other language—a warning.

You better do it or else!

Jote sees a boy's face, transposing into a garden creature—a green-gray bug, a locust or cicada—a flash of a thorax and a hairy flutter of a leg, a blur of a wing briefly obscuring the boy's expression as the huge bug face settles away to contemplate a patch of grass toward which to fly.

His body has already ingested itself, releasing enzymes to dissolve its old slime, organizing its imaginal discs (discs for his hair, his thorax, his eyes), his imago of wings tucked inside his body (though only Marcelo Badel y Zorilla can tell), and he wriggles out finally from his pupal orb. Is revolt only a stage of molting, the instar before maturity happens, or is it the entire process of dissolution, still to come?

He grows up translating his world into glimmering, correct spelling on the page: his chrysalis of action, words transformed, from one meaning to another, while sounding the same. He takes in his world, which has no need for explaining. It is. And everywhere he goes during the war, there are others. The slightest shifts in consonants produce inconsonant worlds. What codifies vision. The red spume from the old servant that almost hits him on his cheek but falls instead on the path. A glob of blood. The days in the trenches of Malabon, the rice fields of Baler, grasslands of Tanauan—every time he sees squirts of red, vermilion spray upon talahib and dirt and hillocks, ruby ground that buries them, his companions (Hilario Sayo, slain in Badoc, Valentin Lagasca, shot with Abaya in Candon, Igue Resurreccion, fallen in Malolos)—he thinks of that betel-nut blessing from Tay Sequil. The dark red blobs of Tay Sequil's betel-nut spray that fall right next to him in Bagumbayan.

On the day his brother holds in his hands his death warrant (but how is Jote to know?)—the sheaves that spell out his war—Jote remembers how he used to sit with Tay Sequil, *El Excellent Cochero Exequiel!*, and the other servants in the driveway of the house on Moret Street, surrounded by spreading, thoughtful spit, the wet betel-nut flowering that looked like scattered gumamela petals and smelled of guts.

As he walks toward the tranvia for Padre Faura.

It's Jote she has lost. She understands too late. Jote's guile. *Siempre el rebelde, nunca el amigo.* Her project had been to record as much as he could remember. It was important to draw out his words, she said. Out there in their refuge, hiding and hiding—after their escape from the battle in Giporlos. To fill history's blank pages, she said. It was dumb. He would not speak. He gave no evidence. It was only later— she understands his guile too late. She keeps the moment under wraps in her memory. When it comes to mind it is like scraping a cut.

She asks her questions—what about Isabelo Abaya, Manuel

Tinio, Ka Vicente Lukban, she dredges the names from the news. She asks—what about Macario Sakay? And it is at the name (she thinks it was that name)—Macario Sakay—there came the flash in his eye. The look that kills.

His raised finger. To his lips. His typical gesture. *Basta na.* It is a tumbling of words she regrets. *Do you know Macario Sakay—God bless the man wherever he is hiding—he only wants to do art—he's a playwright!—and thank God he's still alive, hiding and hiding, don't you want him to live?—do you know there was one Juan who loved opera—he wished to play the Barber of Seville—to play the fool, that's what he wanted!—and Valentin Lagasca—with what care he chose the fresh silot—you do not know—no one understands the way Lagasca could be happy, punyeta, with just one-half of a husk of silot—and Marcelo Badel, a terrible pharmacist he would have made, so distractible, he drove me nuts—all he wished to do was—kadamo na an namatay—it amon la gusto—mabuhi. None of us—none of us wished—*

For death.

Including—

And here Jote stops. He falters.

We only wished to live.

He takes her in his arms when she cries, he pats her head as if she were his little brother, he holds on to her, tight.

But after that moment, there could be no more words between them. She left.

Like scraping a cut, her memory.

An iya samad.

Who is to tell our part, Calista Catalogo says to The Nose, the sniffer, if he cannot?

Leave it, she says, leave his story to him.

You mean, he says, for us to do our part?

Call them off, Calista says—you know you can—your yanqui gringo amigos, who, as anyone can see right now, outside the window, wait for your evidence, surveilling the story, that book in your hands, that will give them the right to pounce—on your own bugto—and I'll tell you my part in this journal, how I transcribed it, *William McKinley's World.*

Prenda, Prenda

From the sala's capiz windows, I watched her rise from the limousine like a movie star, in jeans and sunglasses, with baby Chona May at her hip wearing a ribbon on her head that matched Mana Marga's Disneyland polka-dot skirt. Mother and child emerged like the lost family of Tom Cruise waiting for the paparazzi, but all they got were these sweet gawkers in slippers, the nosy children of Salogó. Her figure, even from afar, gave off that purposeful uncertainty of age offered only by the best plastic surgeons. Her hair, predictably, has turned gold.

If I did not know how old I was, I'd peg her at twenty-two.

After her, about to step out next was Trina Trono, in newfangled buzz cut and safari suit.

It's been a while since our days playing jackstones, our legs creating triangles by Saint Paul's Creek.

Trina Trono emerged from the limousine.

As far as I could tell, she emerged with her Napoleonic complex intact.

She wore a stupid beret and sunglasses, as if that would make her incognito instead of conspicuous in Salogó.

She does look a bit like a half-pint soldier, maybe Manuel Noriega-cum-Daniel Ortega, a Sandinista *and* right-wing thug, I mix them up, when once upon a time she used to be a Thumbelina-sized Mahatma Gandhi. She walked up the broad, creaking steps like some refugee from political insurgencies of the eighties whose style remained unchanged though her politics has evolved. If Daniel Ortega became a born-again Christian, it was no surprise that Trina Trono, whose best days are behind her, was now a schemer for the Trinidads.

I had known that any moment Trina Trono would find her way to Salogó.

Her stubbornness was admirable.

Let them come in, I said to Mana Marga.

I guess I've been expecting them, Trina and Sirit, since I got the messages out on the roof deck in New York.

I could see the ravage and rot of our home in Salogó in the eyes of my old classmate Divina May Trinidad, née Kiring, the Bahrain Beauty, as she ascended the ancient stairs defensively and awkwardly holding her baby—the windows' unrepaired capiz, the gaps in the nipa on the roof, the decay that welcomed you as you climbed. A history of cross-purposes in the stubborn cobwebs around the house. Sirit's wide eyes encompassed them in an instant. The deadwood of the broad, nineteenth-century floorboards with missing puncheons that showed up the packed soil beneath, where the pigs and goats and all of us—John-john, Putt-putt, Mick-mick and baby Adino—used to play. I could smell the mold, the termite dust, and Baygon pesticide and YCO Floor Wax and Salogó dirt—the centuries' old mud of monsoon homes in Leyte.

I imagined the funerary specks of insects on the walls and windowsills, despite all of the maids' cleaning—the daily return of dung beetles and mayflies, and the steady invisible line of their tender pallbearers, the ants. Hidden as the rot had been by the bunting of the funeral, the house now looked, too, like the family's shell, a blasted cocoon.

The black fumes from the Petromax lamps on the lintel posts, the maps of candlewax tracing the progress of darkness from the molave table to the kitchen sink to the balcony's balustrade, from which tallow dripped into hardened inlet shards toward the river—I saw my world in others' eyes.

Her lacquered figure appeared by the niche of the Sacred Heart.

From where I sat, with the papers and bereft walls and empty bookshelves, across from the bedroom where my mother had been born—I noted where dusty candlewax hung from the shelf of that scarred statue transported from LA to Salogó to Tacloban and now—back again.

I saw this map of degradation about the house as Sirit stood by the entresuelo.

My useless consolation was that I had the papers, secreted in their wooden box.

"Such a charming home. So antique, so—authentic."

"Nice to see you, Sirit."

"Oh, Chicharita."

And she began sobbing as she rushed to hug me.

I let her.

"Oh, I'm so sorry, I'm so sorry I could not get to the funeral."

I stood back and watched her cry, I watched her dab at her tears, they barely touched her mascara.

It was Mana Marga who came forward to hug Sirit.

She folded Sirit in her arms, then she took the baby, Chona May.

Then she and the yayas went off to the kitchen.

Relieved of her burden, Sirit began her spiel.

"We were at our annual pilgrimage, you know, to Our Lady of Fatima this time. In Portugal! I missed your mother at Makati Medical, I missed her wake. Oh, I'm so sorry, I'm so sorry. We were on our way to Our Lady of Medjugorje, but—the mayor— you know, my husband—Manny—he was called back. Because of the storm. Too bad, I have been looking forward to Yugoslavia! But because of this supertyphoon, they made him come home. He has to be with the people. So we cut off our trip—for the people! And I thought—oh, now I can see Mana Adina. I can go to her grave in Salogó! Oh, you know, I heard so much from your mom about your life in New York. My eldest daughter, Bernadette May—she said she saw you."

"Bling-bling?"

"She said you met."

"Yes, I saw her."

"I told her to buy your books and get signed copies. Mana Adina was so proud of your books, I want to read them—"

"Oh, don't bother. You know you'll never read them, but yes, you should buy them. At least. Would you like some roscas? And tabléa tsokolate? Before you return home? The chocolate is pure cacao. Thick as the mud in the river. Yes, it is nice to see you again. Maybe the baby Kringle-kringle wants some cookies?"

"Chona May is the baby," corrected Trina. "Kringle May is the grandmother."

"Oh, yeah. My best regards to your mom. Vice-mayor now, isn't she? Your husband's right-hand woman. All in the family. Mana Marga, our guests would like some merienda?"

The click-click of Mana Marga's emergence from the kitchen punctuated the atmosphere, and no one spoke.

But then Sirit piped up.

"It's such an adventure to finally get here. To Salogó. Wow. What a—landscape. So lush. Your mom used to describe it—in my mind it is the center of the universe, the way your mom talked about Salogó!"

"Yes, that is true. My mom did talk about Salogó as if the world begins and ends here, which for her, I guess, it did."

"And for so long she was the center of *our* world, in Tacloban. We so miss Mana Adina. My mother and I. No woman is like her."

"She was a character," nods Trina.

"Yes! She had strength, such zhouai de vivray. She always made everyone happy when she was around. She had a knack for joy. And to think of her sorrows, her past—"

"I know her past," I interrupted. "I'm her daughter."

"I hate to say," said Sirit, munching on the cookie, holding a hand against her chin to catch the roscas crumbs, "I hate to say—"

One is meant to eat roscas with a trough against the jaw—it crumbles at the touch. And sipping the tabléa tsokolate, Sirit's red lips were turning black, which was the secret pleasure of watching people drink tabléa—they looked for a second like ghouls, a gratifying sight.

"I hate to say, please don't get me wrong," Sirit said.

"Then don't say it," I said.

But she went on.

"I don't know if you know—you have been gone. Away—abroad all these years. Oh, the pain in her life. Oh, the tragedy and the sorrow. That she covered up with—"

"What?"

"With generosity toward us, toward my mom and me, toward the rest of the world!"

"I know what she did, Sirit. I know she gave your mom her land as collateral. That's long been your mom's business. We all know that. Prenda. Prenda. No need to go into dramatics. We know. I know my mom took money from your mom. Who knows. She needed money, let me guess, to bankroll an exhibit? To help pay for someone's wedding? You know she had an exhibit at the Cultural Center? She borrowed money from your mom. Let me guess. In exchange for prenda. And I guess my mom never gave the money back. But when your mother Kringle May claimed the last of my mom's lands, my mother was ill, you know. She was dying of cancer."

"We call the subdivision we bought from your mom—we call it La Tercera—in honor of your mother."

"What did you call it—what did you buy?"

"La Tercera. We know the whole story—her long court case with the consul Charity Breton—"

"And you are calling it La Tercera? You mean to humiliate my mom, even in death?"

"Oh, no, no. You misunderstand. No. No. We wish—we wish to honor her at the museum we are going to set up. The papers of her great-uncle, Senator Francisco Delgado y Blumfeld, will be the gem of our collection. Isn't that right, Trina? Trina will be in charge of our museum. The only extant memoir of the American war! Imagine. And our museum will own it. Not even the National Library has anything of the kind. Pinggoy Gomez, the director of the National Archives, tells us there is no set of diaries like it."

"Pinggoy Gomez? He has not seen the diaries."

"Don't worry. Professor Impikoño has given him a detailed commentary."

"That shit. That Impikoño! That blabbermouth ABD graduate student. Who told him he could tell?"

"Pardon? And Father Edgar Allan Pe, you know, our dear, old Father Vice-President from high school—the one who married—he tells me—"

"That asshole of an adulterer, that ex-monsignor!"

"I am sorry? Even Miss Custodia Balasbas, she was our piano teacher, remember? She was raving about the papers. She's a great scholar, did you know? Remember Miss Balasbas? From Samar? The one with giant legs like cabinets—we used to feel so sorry for her. Elephant Katol. Very pitiful. But her legs were really gigantic, like a monster. It is a virus. Remember her? She's so excited about the papers—and she should know. She's from Balangiga!"

"Goddamned traitors these elephantiasis scholars! Every god-damned traitor is just ready to make a buck. How much are you paying them, huh, Sirit?"

"They are my advisors on the museum project. Volunteers. Unpaid."

"Figures. It's disgraceful, the way you use people's desires for—for your goddamned stolen lands, for your vanity projects. You should be ashamed of yourself, Sirit. I expect more from you, if not from your criminal in-laws."

"It is not a vanity project. It is not stolen. Oh, Chicharita. Is it really criminal?"

And Sirit had that look on her face, from our childhood, of not knowing what was going on.

"It is for the good of the people," she wailed. "And they are profes-sors, scholars, and it is not right—just because you are sad over your—"

"I am not sad. I have no such minor feelings. I am angry. How dare they give away the story of the papers—without my permission. It is I who hold the diaries—and they are not going anywhere. I am sorry, Trina. Sirit. Baby Chona May. I need to go. I'm packing. I have to leave. I need to get back to work. Mana Marga, can you give them a Tupperware of the cookies? My mother says they are the best cookies in Leyte, the roscas of Salogó."

May Kiriring

So they all went back down, bodyguards and Bahrain Beauty and baby Chona May, but Trina Trono stayed behind.

"I just want to say I'm glad you're figuring out a way to deal with— your mother's loss. It's a good thing. To keep occupied with your grandfather's papers. It's tough for you, I imagine."

"Thanks. But I'm just reading," I said. "I've just finished reading all the pages."

"So where are they? Hey, wow, this table is all mahogany."

"Molave."

"One whole, solid block. No kidding, this house is old. Have you ever had—this whole building—appraised? So where are they?"

I pointed to the box under the molave table.

"Hmm," said Trina, going off to inspect it. "Who's *F. B.*?"

"I don't know," I said. "At one point, I thought it was an American sergeant, named Frank Breton."

"Related to Charity, the orphan, the ward?"

Trina always did her homework.

"I have no clue," I said. "But you're right—it's a good question. Why are there so many wards in this story? That theme of the ward still confuses me. And we remember the wrong people. The proper heroes—no one bothers to tell a thing about them. I mean, their relatives do not even know their actual names."

"Can I touch?"

"And the story was not finished, as far as I can tell—but there are no more pages. The rest are blank. There are all of these blank, stuck pages. You end up guessing what came after—how, after all the years of secrecy and surveillance, they were preserved. I mean, they were just stashed in an aparador, moldering with the ants. My mom never even opened her Lolo Jote's papers. Just kept in the dark. Pastilan, uday. Huwaso."

"So is it okay? Can I open?" said Trina.

I could see Trina had not heard a word I said.

"Sure."

Trina bent toward the box with that demonic grin she had.

"It's empty," she shouted from the dining room.

There was no way she was going to get them.

She brought the box over to me.

She tapped on the empty shell of Mick-mick's box of oyster fili-gree.

"You are not getting the papers, Trina," I said.

"Even for a million pesos? Two million?"

"You're crazy."

"They're willing to pay you half the amount, right now."

"Who's they?"

She nodded toward the limousine outside the capiz windows. The outrageous car was running its wasteful gas. Salogó's teenagers and children were gathered outside as if at any moment a marching band might come out the doors for their amusement.

"I hope you don't mind. She wanted to come. She insisted. She remembers you fondly."

"You don't know how sorry I am about that marriage."

"To a maniac who cut her hair in public when she once escaped their home."

"Oh my God," I said. "I forgot about that."

"Well, he's the mayor now. Don't worry. She will have all the protection she needs."

"Except the protection she needs is from him."

"It's a mess, what happened to Sirit," said Trina. "It's her mother, you know, who wants the papers. Sirit is only the messenger. It's not her fault."

"Kringle May Kiring? The vice-mayor? Very diligent secretary that Vice-Mayor Kringle May has. She keeps sending letters to Tio Nemor."

"Yes, Kringle May is the guardian of history in our day and age. Good friend of your mom, you know. She wishes to set up a museum of the city of Tacloban, right there on her new property, sorry, I mean—well, they took it, that property—you can see it from the airplane before you land—in San Jose, at La Tercera Manor Homes and Beach Resort."

"That property is not La Tercera."

"Well, when your mother sold the property, that's what she called it."

"My mom was ill. I mean, no one should ever take my mom at face value. There were always two sides. My mom sold nothing."

"What do you mean?"

"Do you think they ever got the original deed of land?"

"You mean—she tricked the Trinidads?"

"Well, she was dying. What did it mean to her if she lied? She gave me an envelope. I have it. I received it in New York. The original deed of that land."

Trina was grinning.

She clapped her hands.

She gave me a high five.

"The envelope with her last will?" she said.

"And testimonies. Given to me by Bling-bling Trinidad herself."

The look of admiration in Trina's eyes was gratifying.

"Hah—your mom was something else," said Trina. "And she was no liar."

"No?"

"She was an inventor."

I smiled.

"Thanks," I said.

"Sirit was always a faithful friend—your mom trusted Sirit."

"Sirit is just—clueless. She'll do whatever she's told," I said. "My mom told her to send me her Last Will and Testimonies, on her deathbed, just imagine how dramatic my mom was, and of course Sirit did. My mom knew Sirit, just as she knew me."

"That over your dead body you would never sell La Tercera."

I shook my head.

"That is not La Tercera," I said. "What my mom knew was that unlike Tio Nemor, I would never goddamned sell a thing to the Trin-idads."

"I'm sorry about your mother," said Trina.

"So am I."

"She was in a class of her own."

"Yes, she was."

"Sirit loved your mom."

"I know."

"She brought her child with her. So she could see her godmother's ancestral home in Salogó. Your mother's godchild, Chona May."

"My God—is every single child her godchild? Chona May Kiring! Chona-with-a-ringing-in-her-brain. *May kiriring, kiriring, kiriring!*"

Trina was laughing.

"Yeah, I know, it's a wacko family, starting with their names," Trina said. "You know the joke in Tacloban."

"No."

"Hello, hello. Knock, knock," said Trina.

"Who's there?" I said.

"Chona!"

"Chona who?"

"Tsuna Mi Trinidad!" said Trina.

"That's just dumb, Trina—you're nuts."

"Yeah. First you are a Kiring, then you become a Trinidad. What a fate."

"Monstrous," I said. "It could have been avoided."

"Touché," said Trina. "But you know they are offering good money."

"No one is getting the papers. No vampira nor bakulaw."

In our first year of high school, Sirit and I shared the same path to the Divine Word Missionary School.

In my mom's world, this unrecorded history of families that mattered and families that did not, lodged only in her head—the better to keep it pure, scornful, and unrevised—was the sole version of the universe she tolerated. Families in the gray shade, like the Kirings, lived in the useful sphere that money sustained. But in my mind, I keep remembering that pun in the name—*Kringle-with-a screw-loose! Kringle with-a-mad-rattling-in-her-brain!*—the onomatopoeia of madness—kiriring, the ring-ring-ringing in your brain—

And it's greed, to me, that is most insane.

When we were young, and we had just moved to Juan Luna Street, Sirit had a uniformed servant who crossed the street with her, holding up an umbrella. A complete affectation, good sumsuman for merienda gossip. Not quite pulutan, maybe aperitif. Another maid carried her striped, green-and-white rolling schoolbag. We happened to be crossing the street to school, and Sirit stood beside me, her pair of maids at her heels, sacristans bearing the incense.

I was sleepy in the morning, and being also judgmental I was not fond of kids at school. Apart from Trina Trono, I wanted no friends.

I was messy—disorganized and forgetful—and my mom was never interested in my prospects. She took it for granted I'd do well, but I saw she also didn't care if I didn't. She had other concerns. For her, school was as useful as raising chickens, less significant than knowing how to churn tabléa tsokolate to a fine boil or folding a cloth napkin into neat, flower-like shapes, just so, at each placemat, and I grew up with my books and my prejudices intact.

I had no discipline, the principal kept telling me. Tita Patchy would punish me for not wearing my necktie and send me to the library for not carrying a handkerchief or forgetting my ID or failing to cut my fingernails when after the Flag Ceremony she inspected us for our hygiene. My punishment was the library, Tita Patchy's hellscape for delinquents and derelicts. So I finished *The Bible Story: Complete Ten-Volume Set*, and the classical myths of Greece and Rome, and the entire collection of *Old Mother West Wind Tales* by Thornton W. Burgess, about bog creatures in some place so foreign to me, Cape Cod, that its weatherscape and fauna were like Narnia—I especially liked Ol' Mistah Buzzard, a wise, ugly figure who spoke in nature riddles, and Little Joe Otter, a slimy swimmer with a good heart. Trina Trono, on the other hand, got punished for writing slogans—in the girls'

Comfort Rooms—that she copied from her dad's resistance journals, *We Forum*, *Malaya*, and *The Washington Post*.

The library had that lousy whiff of forgotten times, when shiploads of Midwesterners came to teach the tales of Hiawatha and poems by Longfellow and Kipling and too many by Alfred, Lord Tennyson, and songs about kookaburras and the girl from the Red River Valley, with her bright eyes and sweet smile, and that song, way down upon the Swanee River—

> *far, far away!*
> *There where my heart is burning ever,*
> *far from the folks at home!*

A jumble of transported antebellum crap sung by us in Tacloban with gusto. Also, Old Black Joe—*I'm coming, I'm coming, for my head is bending lo-ow*—*I hear those gentle voices calling Old Black Joe.* Correction: not just the mold of antebellum. I have the Jim Crow world—instead of that country's luminous glory, Reconstruction, which should be its honor's fulcrum if it had any sense—rote in my bones. I was cursed with photographic memory. I could keep in my head the exact page in the section on Flowers in the *World Book Encyclopedia* where the pansy or the fringed gentian appeared, at bottom left, westerly, though it was, so said the text, easterly, of eastern USA and Canada, and not where we were in eastern Philippines—the geography I learned was upside down. The gentian was a delicate purple scarf of a flower that looked to me like the shawl of a flamenco dancer. Later, pansies were sewn lovingly onto velvet slippers for good old Mister Laurence by the gentle, dying Beth in *Little Women*. Violet, a genus of spring flowering plants from the family Violaceae, native to the temperate Northern Hemisphere, looked to me slightly like the kamia, except bruised. The flowers I knew, the kalachuchi, the sampaguita, the gumamela, were not on the list offered to me. Like enchanted beings, they were incognito—plumeria, jasmine, hibiscus—found through language's abracadabra. This puzzling, these transpositions of worlds, became my pleasure. I'd find myself in odd ways. Though I don't think I've ever lost it—my center. This translation, it was just another way to be. In high school I moved on to books I can still remember in my sleep, with silky bookmarks and gilt trim—volumes by Kierkegaard, Kurt Vonnegut, and Kafka—and those were just the names with *K*s. The books were donations that did not fit our spiritual educations, so the school trashed them in a heap, out by a broken electric fan and some forgotten rugs. I spent my high school years wearing the wrong necktie and not trimming my nails, dusting and reading those discarded books.

That day on the way to school, Sirit and I kept in step.

Then she spoke.

"You know I'm so shy to be walking with you to school."

I had no idea what she was talking about.

I looked at Sirit, with her baby-doll cheeks, who was blushing as if she were gathering the courage to speak.

"You're always reading those books, you know," she said, "in the library."

I stared at her.

"You're so smart," she said.

"You know it's punishment, don't you?"

"What?"

"Reading in the library is the tenth circle of hell, says Mrs. Empanada."

Then I ran away from her before she could become my friend.

I said to Trina Trono—"No dice. Those papers are mine, I am taking them with me to New York, and you can tell your Vice-Mayor Kringle May Kiriring—Buzz. Off!"

Trina was staring at me, her hands crossed, laughing.

She fell to the floor, the empty box in her hands.

I brought over the plate of roscas, sitting before Trina.

"What?"

"Buzz off! Kiriring-kiriring! Buzz buzz, who's there?"

"Haloooo!"

"Ibid!"

We sat there together on the floor, the empty filigreed box between us, sitting the way we used to do, at recess, our legs in the crossed angles of our games.

Trina reached for a roscas and, expertly cradling the crumbs, began finishing it off.

"Why are you doing what you're doing, Trina," I said. "It's not like you."

"You mean—why I want a museum? Why I want the city to own the papers? Why I want a place for original scholarship and research in Tacloban? Why I want to be the one to publish the notebooks?"

"No. I mean—working for the Trinidads."

"I work for no one," said Trina. "I just get what I want from the people who can do it. That's all. It's the way to get things done."

I shook my head.

"Fairness never wins," said Trina. "You'll be fucked over. Neither justice nor peace. The world has no capacity for it—not for justice or peace."

"You mean—the country?"

"No—I mean the world. You know, like the one you're going back to. Especially the one you're going back to. Your America. But keep on writing, go ahead—keep writing as if it matters. Yours might be a better illusion than Sirit's."

"Thanks," I said.

"Don't let that go to your liver—ayaw pagdako hin atay!"

"Hah," I said.

"I said it *might* be a better illusion. But me—I'm done! With people power, protests, with depending on the moral reductionisms of others. Fantasies and illusion. Yeah sure—fuck the oligarchy. Don't get me wrong. That *is* what I do. I fuck them over for my own purposes. I want a good museum. So I get things done. That's it."

I didn't believe her.

"It's a heavy tradeoff for working with murderers, with the country's age-old thieves," I said. "It's just—depressing. I don't see how that's a viable way of living."

"It isn't," Trina said. "It's never been."

Trina took the last bit of roscas.

"Anyway," she said.

For a moment there, she looked as she used to, a Thumbelina-sized Mahatma Gandhi.

"If you really think you're getting those papers to New York," she said, shaking off the crumbs from her hands, washing her hands of me, "then—"

"What," I said.

"Then you better get going because a supertyphoon is coming. No plane will leave after the storm surge comes."

At the Hotel Sirena

Tio Nemor dropped me off in Tacloban at the Hotel Sirena, my layover, as he called it, before the airport.

I had said my goodbyes to Adino, sweet Adino, in Salogó.

He was tending his chickens.

Do you see that guy, Adino said, pointing at a resplendent bird—Nemesio, the Golden Laced Wyandotte.

Golden Nemesio was sitting pretty under a gumamela bush.

That's not where he sleeps, Adino said. Something's going on with Nemesio. His hut is over there.

Adino was very careful not to speak a word of English to me, using words like didto an iya ginkakaturugan, instead of *hut*.

He pointed to Mariano, a stunning speckled figure, pecking under an eave.

That guy, Adino said—that guy's back is to the river. But usually he likes to run on the AWOL.

—It iya ayon pagdinalagan hito nga—pader.

He would not say AWOL.

Hmm, he said—something's going on. No one is in his right place.

—May nananabo. Waray usa nga aada ha lugar.

And this one, Adino said—

—Ini hi Francisco—paragmulay hiya ngada han usa. Ito hiya! Mahilig magmulay! Baga ba han hadto ha aton—an kuwan nga mulay ba—*Pamiling-Pamiling!*

This one, this Francisco, he likes to play a game with that one—that one! He loves to play! Like when we were little, you know.

And Adino refused to say the name of our childhood game—*Discover-Discover.*

Kuwan, he said—*an kuwan nga mulay ba*—he hesitated—he grasped for a translation.

Because he knew it—at the tip of his tongue he had the actual English word.

But Francisco, as both Adino and I could see, was heaped underneath a pile of swept-up leaves, with the other Russian Orloff—Jote.

—Agi—nga mga parayaw, I said.

Adino grinned at my Waray.

—Maupay ito nga bantog ha era, he said fondly—mga parayaw!

That's a good word for them, he said—

And now I have no translation for my term.

Like so many words that exist without another's measure—pastilan, huwaso.

Mga parayaw.

They lay there, a pair of *gallos,* each with an elaborate ruff, their parayaw feathers—a preening set, one collar more russet than the other, but the other with a spangle of imbricating spots, so that when it ruffled its feathers, the carefully mottled array disarranged into a blur, claret and gold, only to flutter back into its gorgeous, oculate design—their yellow chicken legs reaching out occasionally to scratch at the leaves.

There's something going on, Adino reflected, reaching out to pet the feathery collar, check Jote's walnut comb—mga parayaw ini hera—they like to strut about, playing and catching each other. But something is happening.

He stood up, and he raised his chin as if to scan the river with it, sniffing the air, his single mole, by his lip, marking the moment.

I stood there next to him, only up to his shoulders, he was now so tall, my brother, an akon bugto—and I stood there with my suitcase and handbag and absurdly wide straw hat.

He was silent, taking in the river's breeze.

Well, I have to get going, I said. The jeepney's here. You sure you don't want to come with me to Tacloban?

He shook his head.

He smiled at his chickens.

—Adi la kami, he said.

I tiptoed to kiss him on both cheeks.

—Pagbuotan, I said.

—Ikaw gihap.

But you're going up to Tio Nemor's?, I said—when the storm comes. Their place up in the hills, in Santa Elena—it will be safer.

He nodded.

I'm sorry about the house, I said, that they want to sell it. I hope they don't. I think they're wrong.

—Ayos, he said.

Then his eyes widened, he was grinning.

He looked so much like Adina an guapa—having multiple instincts at once.

—Waray makakadara kun diri ako upod!

No one can take it without me.

Ha ha, he said, no one's taking this house without me.

I waved goodbye from the jeep.

—An bagyo ito!

His eyes were wide—a revelation—

It's the typhoon, he said.

He stood there in the yard, with his labyrinth of chickens, and the jeep revved up but stalled, waiting for him to elaborate.

Adino, sweet Adino, raised his finger up toward the heavens, the Pope amid his fowl.

They know the storm is coming, he said, and all of these guys—

—Hala! he said—

And he swept his hand over them, the spectacular creatures in their scattered places—Nemesio, Mariano, Bonifacio, Ambrosio, Francisco, Jote—his male brood—

—Ini hera: waray sarabutan ano it era bubuhaton.

Hala! he said—they have no idea what to do.

At Hotel Sirena, Man' Pete and Mana Floria themselves were at the welcome desk, registering their guests. At first I did not recognize Man' Pete because he was dressed, and I used to know him in his sando and drawstring shorts, taking a shower with his pig to whom we gave our kitchen slop so we could help eat it at fiesta. Man' Pete was now isputing, and he smiled as he wrote down my name, welcome, welcome, long time no see—and he whispered to me—"it's on us, ayaw kabaraka, and you can also eat everything you want—see, we have—an all-you-can-eat buffet!"

Mana Floria had a huge smile, looking so pleased to see me.

"Did you see the chandelier? Lorelei shipped it. It's from abroad. Europa."

She still looked like the ravishing, tanned mother of Emperor Nero—with her aquiline profile of an ancient Roman queen.

"And look what we have on the walls."

She showed me her quartet of them.

The Four Seasons.

I couldn't speak. I stared at them—the golden flourishes and the leaves.

Man' Pete was smiling, staring at me then looking back down, stamping dates on his logbook.

Tears welled up in Mana Floria's eyes as she saw mine.

"It was the least we could do, to buy her frames, inday, we knew it would help—when she needed—"

"Sssh," said Man' Pete. "Man' Adina is at rest now. She's resting in peace."

"We are sorry we could not be there—at the funeral—we were so busy with the opening—"

"I saw your wreaths," I said. "They were gorgeous. Mahusay hin duro."

"I told Lorelei to get the orange bouquet, the Mirinda style, the Mountain Dew or the Lem-O-Lime—you know your mom loved the bright ones, the soft-drink colors."

"They were beautiful," I said, "so thoughtful. The same as your hotel—it's—it's the best place I have seen in Tacloban!"

Mana Floria's smile was so wide, then she flicked her shoulder, in that gesture of warding off the bad luck of others' good wishes, and Man' Pete knocked on the counter's mahogany top—puwera buyag!—*afuera, afuera*—out out!—so many ways to cast out the demons in others' words—knock on wood.

"Man' Adina had a good idea!" said Mana Floria.

"Yes, yes, she advised—she helped us buy the land—you know, life is what you make it!" said Man' Pete. "She helped us buy when Mana Talia died."

"But I think Mana Talia will be happy with what we have done to her home," said Mana Floria humbly.

Man' Pete looked glad at my surprise.

"Ah, you don't remember—this is the old home of the Quintanas! We bought!"

Mana Floria looked even prouder at the thought.

"You should see the memorial we have, inday—go show it, Pete—our little museum—to the memory of her love, Congressman Quintana."

And I checked out the exhibit dedicated to the man who "rebealed," the former ambassador whose scandal during the 1971 Constitutional Convention as "Con-Con" delegate for the first district of Leyte disturbed the nation. He had been chosen for the convention, called out from retirement by the dictator himself. Still, he revealed. I read about him all over again—about the envelopes—*enbelops!*—adding up to eleven thousand pesos, which Eduardo Quintana, Jr., received from his cousin, whom he called Meldy. A caption mentioned the title of his unfinished memoir—*Returned to Sender.* There were pictures of his postwar ambassadorial time, and later his trips to Lourdes and Fatima with his prim-looking wife, Natalia Pariña viuda de Quintana, decorous and formal in her jacquard suits and Hanes pantyhose. I read the articles I had already read, when *We Forum* republished exposés of dictatorship after the dictator fled. There were preserved lace handkerchiefs with Mana Talia's initials, *N. Q. y P.*, and glass cabinets of her ternos but only one of his barongs. I wanted to check if the gowns had the tags of Elvis Oras's shop, Young's Fashionne House. There was a picture of the congressman's gravesite, at his mother's mausoleum in Salogó. *Requiescat*, Congressman Quintana, Mana Talia's love—1900-1985. His memory is also enshrined, the newspaper articles reported, in the resistance heroes' memorial, Bantayog ng mga Bayani. Born in a world of revolution, died at a time of revolt. I was proud of this exhibit put together by Man' Pete and Mana Floria, who were only his neighbors—this evidence of pride and protest in a city that has no honor, electing year after year the same scum. Maybe one day, I thought, Congressman Quintana's act of revelation will have its due, and someone will publish his account, *Returned to Sender.*

The four-poster bed Lorelei's parents gave me overlooked the corner where I could see our old place on Juan Luna Street. I thought I saw a sliver of the wide-open patio, or so I imagined, with hanging orchids and red-waxed, waterlogged floors. I looked out at the city's layers and roofs, the same middle-class ruin against impoverished decay, and the storm walls of debtors and their usurers and gamblers and their goons, and mangrove-hacking lumber shops against the stalls of mat and binagol sellers, and chicken coops and sidewalks that doubled as sewers where as kids we played, after the typhoons.

I could see, in my mind's eye, women with long skirts wrapped about their legs in businesslike knots.

An era gamit gihay.

And the whish-whish-whish of streetcleaning brooms—that

fierce sound of women cleaning up the city after the monsoons that clarified my childhood on Juan Luna Street.

Charcoal smoke from caramel desserts steaming from the corner plywood stall—I dreamed of Mana Belen's kamote cue and banana cue sizzling in their glut of sugar: the bubbling kalamay like boiling suns. The burnt sugar smell of merienda—I felt it, a tangerine waft over me, in this mirror touch synesthesia country, as I dreamed.

Higda.

Inop.

In my dream, I heard the howling.

I never dream except for innocuous things, like finding a key. Or dreaming that I dreamed.

I was tucked into the sheets, under that gauzy mosquito netting, the moskitero that the screened, airconditioned room did not need, and yet I appreciated it, I appreciated the antique design touches of Lorelei's Hotel Sirena. I heard the wind's growling, this steady, slow whistling—a rumbling at first in the distance, by Cancabato Bay, the waters of Panalaron, over Leyte Gulf, rumbling from the Pacific, whooshing, whooping, whirring toward the fishermen's boats by the airport, and soon the howling.

The sound of an unspeakable, swooping, remorseless keening.

Powered by ocean, wail by sea.

The ground underneath me was stirring, as if for a moment that spot of earth was its aim, and the swelling of the waters and the towering of the waves and the destruction of the city was upon us, and all I wished to do—all I did—was reach for it—

The box.

I leapt out of bed, but the box was already open, its domed lid to the winds—it was not in my hands to save them—the leaves and the pages and the news clippings and the notes and the witness of history—the words—whirling in the wind.

They were gone.

I clutched at air.

I grasped at wetness vanishing as the howling became a wilderness became a growling that emerged from out of its ages. The sound of a scream was of a million voices buried in the mud and the slime and the ancient sodden sweeping—the black waters of the ocean that the world's surge unearthed.

I held nothing, nothing in my hands.

A splash, and that is all.

The screaming did not end.

Epilogue

Lunop.

Inop.

The English term in the news stories—storm surge—had tricked the people of Tacloban.

Lunop it ngaran nga makaharadlok.

That is the word they understood, the age-old totem, the terror in speech. Lunop would have warned them.

I saw the destruction from the roof deck in Manhattan. I was still groggy from jetlag and the last elements of comfort from the First Class cabin of Philippine Airlines. I had dragged home my suitcase and my bag and straw hat—I was back in New York with the same baggage. I wound through JFK, and this time on the Airtrain, on the subway to Penn Station, on the taxi ride to my apartment, I held tightly to the box, I kept it on my lap, checking the lid to make sure the papers were there, in their faded, silken plaid lining, with all the bugs intact, groggy with jetlag I thought of my dream, and I felt the urgency of my return with my mother's papers—the three bound journals, and Lolo Paco's entries, the unrequited version of Paz Tilanuday y Hua-Zhu, this work that I had before me to somehow order the world I knew.

On the roof deck the day I heard the news, I was reading the last draft of my novel on my computer, and I realized with surprise—my book was done.

It sometimes felt like a memoir, I thought, but that could not be helped.

I could send it to my agent now if I wished.

And I opened up my mail and saw it.

The destruction of my city.

I saw it unfold online.

Two days and a half after my flight.

Tacloban's devastation.

The ocean raked itself, it scraped its own depths, it bore its force and age and elements upon its coast, the black mud of an ocean that is not bottomless for its bottom has swept away our dead.

A howling with speed and force and fury unknown in history's recorded time.

So the news reports said.

Climate change, global warming, and a too-long history of human regret.

No one answered my calls.

My one thought—Adino, sweet Adino.

I opened up Messenger, WhatsApp, Viber.

I got no answer.

I spent the first days on Facebook.

I scanned any news videos I could find.

I stared at streets I absolutely could not recognize.

Nothing I know mirrored what I could see except perhaps the pictures of the dead in a war I have been writing about that no one remembers.

The city was not a city.

It was a wasteland of a wasteland.

Of bodies and mud and the limitations of terror—of the sights we are unable to believe.

It's another aspect of horror to learn from news reports because no CNN news anchor says the actual names of streets, no one bothers to note whether the wrecked building is on Burgos, corner Veteranos, or Real, by Diorico's Bakery, or Zamora by the Kierulf Building, corner Salazar, once known as Bonanza Theater, that was already a wreck before the typhoon.

The specifics that map my reality do not occur to strangers, and no news report, no foreign video actually informs.

The generalities I kept gathering were another form of injury.

I could get no phone connection to Mana Marga, to my uncle, to Adino—who anyway refused to own a phone.

In the first shocking hours, the city was silent—turned back to the old times of blackout nights in Salogó, unanchored like another planet, the unreached abyss. No electricity, no signal, no message.

But even when connection came, there was no word.

I went back to scanning Facebook, that blighted Filipino forum, for all it could offer, the wash of refuse by Santo Niño church, I followed where a camera would go, if it would go by Juan Luna, the homes of childhood we have lost. Tens of thousands of people dead. I thought I heard the *campana*, the sound of the bells, by Santo Niño church, on one video, and I followed the stranger's unsteady camera, I recognized a gate, made of stone, maybe the corner of Sirit's old house, so it was not my street, and I recognized the fake-Georgian posts—it was Gomez, not Juan Luna. I saw the lines of people on Maharlika Highway, a path of zombies looking for their dead, an intolerable dirge, the long funeral procession of a city of weeping.

Eight thousand dead in twenty minutes.

Lunop.

Inop.

Bodies washed up by the area in San Jose, where fishermen and their children were not saved because the office of the mayor, acting stupidly and too late, evacuated them to a schoolroom, also by the ocean. The mayor's brand-new resort, across from the island Dio, La Tercera Manor Homes and Beach Resort, was underwater, an easily reconstructed impunity, I could see, and the cyclist brandished his heroic sorrow, Mayor Tour-de-France clutching a fallen shingle, to show the world how he, too, was one with the people he had not thought to save.

MacArthur's statue in Palo on Red Beach remained, waiting for its final bombing.

My old teacher in New York, to whom I had given my first novel so long ago, when at the height of a rebellion I had read his essay about teaching, in *Harper's*, emailed me out of the blue—"Shocked by the dreadful news from the Philippines and hoping at least that you & yours are safe. I remember that Tacloban is your city."

It was a twist in the heart to hear someone from so long ago and who remembered.

"May your muse still be singing," he said. I quote him verbatim: "It's been difficult, of course, to read about Tacloban and other eastern towns and to see the camera reports. The situation is horrific, beyond words, but only words can help us see what we need to comprehend."

It was the sweetest thing to say because I knew, at the time, his words were also at an end. His wife wrote me a separate letter—he was folding up a life.

I tried to write her, his wife, to explain what it was like—that when I think of any name from my childhood whom I wish to ask about, after this typhoon—

I need to dig up all the names.

Elvis Oras, Lorelei, Mana Floria, Man' Pete, Queen Sirikit, Margot, William McKinley Maceda, Benito Lupak, the museum to the memory of Mana Talia's love, Congressman Quintana.

Tio Nemor, Putt-putt, Mick-mick, Mana Marga.

They survived.

Up at Santa Elena.

They were high enough for the storm not to reach them.

We found Adino, sweet Adino.

Of course, he never left Salogó.

He refused to leave with Mana Marga, and he lied that he would follow.

He did only what he wanted.

He would not leave his chickens, and so the chickens saved him.

The storm bypassed Salogó: the town is inland, west of coastal winds, and the house by Himanglos stands. Nasamaran. Waray kaguba.

Delgado Clan of Moret Street
Sampaloc, Manila

BONIFACIO DELGADO
(m. La abuelita Nemesia)

FRANCISCO DELGADO — *m.* — ADINA BLUMFELD
THE FIRST   Y CATALOGO

FRANCISCO NEMESIO
BONIFACIO DELGADO
Y BLUMFELD
(m. Mercedes "Chedeng" Barretto)

JORGE MARIANO
CARMEN DELGADO
Y BLUMFELD
(m. Maria "Mama Bia" Buñales)

ROSARIO "CHARITY"
BRETON-DELGADO

BONIFACIA "PACHANG"
DELGADO

HON. MAYOR
FRANCISCO BUÑALES
DELGADO III
(m. Virginia Tarcela Cubilla)

FRANCISCO "PAQUITO"
OF LAS VEGAS

NEMORINO
(m. Doctor Tita Tita)

ADINA AN GUAPA
(m. "the worst scalawag")

Laberinto de Gallos*
(A labyrinth of chickens)

Catalogo Clan of Giporlos
Samar

✴

JORGE MARIANO CATALOGO
(m. Carmen Balais)

MARIANO CATALOGO II

CARMEN CATALOGO
(m. No-Name Blumfeld)

JORGE CATALOGO

MARIANO
THE MAYORDOMO

JORGE CATALOGO II

ADINA BLUMFELD
Y CATALOGO
*(m. Francisco Delgado
the First)*

FRANCISCO
"BONGO"
CATALOGO
(d. 1901)

JORGE "BINGO"
CATALOGO

CARMEN "MIMANG"
CATALOGO BUÑALES
*(great-aunt-in-law
of Mana Marga
née Buñales)*

JORGE MARIANO
CARMEN DELGADO
Y BLUMFELD

FRANCISCO
NEMESIO
BONIFACIO
DELGADO
Y BLUMFELD

NAY CARMEN

BONIFACIA
"TIA PACHANG"

CATALOGO COUSINS:
BUNCH OF LITTLE
CARMENS AND
CALISTA CATALOGO

HON. MAYOR
FRANCISCO BUÑALES
DELGADO III

NEMORINO
(m. Doctor Tita Tita)

ADINA AN GUAPA
(m. "the worst scalawag")

TAY GUIMOY OF THE
BARAKASYUNAN

*Grandchildren are four
ex-nurses who own
retirement homes in
Baltimore, Maryland*

ROSARIO

ADINO,
SWEET ADINO

(based on a computer printout submitted to ancestry.com by Adino, sweet Adino)

Selected Sources for Readers

"Affairs in the Philippine Islands, Hearings before the Committee . . . [Jan. 31-June 28, 1902] APRL 10, 1902. Ordered Printed as a Document - Google Play." Google Play Books. Google. Accessed September 20, 2022. https://play.google.com/books/reader?id=hnZKAAAAYAAJ&pg=GBS.PA842&printsec=frontcover.

Alejandrino, José. *The Price of Freedom (La Senda Del Sacrificio): Episodes and Anecdotes of Our Struggles for Freedom*. Metro Manila, Philippines: Solar Pub. Corp., 1987.

"Alice in Asia: The 1905 Taft Mission to Asia." Smithsonian's National Museum of Asian Art, March 25, 2020. https://asia.si.edu/essays/alice-in-asia/.

Alunan, Merlie M., Mercurio Phil Harold Lacaba, Voltaire Q. Qyzon, Janis Claire Salvacion, Firie Jill Ramos, Michael Carlo Villas, and Aivee C. Badulid. *Tinalunay Hinugpong Nga Panurat Nga Winaray*. Diliman, Quezon City: University of the Philippines Press, 2017.

"American women in the Philippines." The Philippines and the University of Michigan, 1870-1935. Philippines. Accessed September 20, 2022. https://philippines.michiganintheworld.history.lsa.umich.edu/s/exhibit/page/american-women-in-the-philippines.

"Asociacion Feminista Filipina Historical Marker." Historical Marker, February 12, 2022. https://www.hmdb.org/m.asp?m=25095.

Balce, Nerissa. *Body Parts of Empire: Visual Abjection, Filipino Images, and the American Archive*. Manila, Philippines: Ateneo de Manila University Press, 2017.

Borges, Jorge Luis. "The Shape of the Sword." In *Labyrinths: Selected Stories & and Other Writings*. New York: New Directions, 1964.

Borrinaga, Rolando O. *The Balangiga Conflict Revisited*. Quezon City: New Day Publishers, 2004.

Bumpus, E. C. "For the Love I Bear My Dead and as a Testimony to the Courage and Devotion of the Comrades Who, with Him, Gave Their Lives to Their Country." HathiTrust. Accessed September 20, 2022. https://babel.hathitrust.org/cgi/pt?id=loc.ark%3A%2F13960%2Ft1sf3n53c&view=1up&seq=25.

Cullinane, Michael. "The Duranos of Cebu." In *An Anarchy of Families: State and Family in the Philippines*. Ed. Alfred McCoy. Quezon City: Ateneo de Manila University Press, 2017.

"Delgado, Francisco A." US House of Representatives: History, Art & Archives. Accessed September 20, 2022. https://history.house.gov/People/Detail/12104.

"Dictionary English - Waray (Philippines)." Glosbe. Accessed September 20, 2022. https://glosbe.com/en/war.

"Eduardo Quintero (Diplomat)." Wikipedia. Wikimedia Foundation, May 28, 2022. https://en.wikipedia.org/wiki/Eduardo_Quintero_(diplomat).

Eyot, Canning. *Story of the Lopez Family: A Page from the History of the War in the Philippines*. Nabu Press, 2010.

Foster, Genevieve. *Abraham Lincoln's World*. New York: Charles-Scribner's Sons, 1944.

Freeman, James M., and Frederick Funston. *True Story of the Capture of Emilio Aguinaldo, Self-Styled "George Washington of the Philippines": With Tabloid History of Spanish-American War: To Which Is Appended the Speech of Congressman J.M. Robsion of Kentucky*. Knoxville, TN: Trent Printing Company, 1927.

Hallock, Jennifer. "Lt. Col. Walter Loving and the Philippine Constabulary Band." Jennifer Hallock, March 28, 2021. http://www.jenniferhallock.com/2020/09/13/walter-loving/.

Historic Images. "Historic Images Outlet-Original Vintage News Photo Prints. 1960 PRESS PHOTO UNITED NATIONS FRANCISCO A DELGADO, SOVIET NIKITA KHRUSHCHEV." Historic Images. Accessed September 21, 2022. https://outlet.historicimages.com/.

Hollie, Pamela G. "Marcos Son-in-Law Issues an Apology." *The New York Times. The New York Times*, February 10, 1982. https://www.nytimes.com/1982/02/10/world/marcos-son-in-law-issues-an-apology.html.

Hopper, James. *Caybigan*. New York: McClure, Phillips, 1906.

Ingles, Raul Rafael. *1908, The Way It Really Was: Historical Journal for the U.P. Centennial, 1908-2008*. Diliman: Univ. of the Philippines Press, 2008.

Kafka, Franz, David Musgrave, Tania Stern, and James Stern. *Blumfeld, an Elderly Bachelor*. London: Four Corners Books, 2009.

Lollobrigida, Gina, and Carmen Guerrero Nakpil. *The Philippines*. Liechtenstein: Sarima, 1976.

Lunop: Haiyan Voices and Images. Tacloban City, Leyte, Philippines: Leyte-Samar Heritage Society, Inc., 2015.

"Macario Sakay." Wikipedia. Wikimedia Foundation, June 26, 2022. https://en.wikipedia.org/wiki/Macario_Sakay#cite_note-antonio_abad-5.

Marx, Karl, Ben Fowkes, and David Fernbach. *Capital: A Critique of Political Economy; V.1*. London New York, N.Y: Penguin Books in association with New Left Review, 1990.

McCoy, Alfred W. *Policing America's Empire: The United States, the Philippines, and the Rise of the Surveillance State*. Quezon City: Ateneo de Manila University Press, 2011.

"The Nameless." ALEJANDRO, Leandro L. | The Nameless. Accessed September 21, 2022. http://www.nameless.org.ph/alejandro.

Ochosa, Orlino A. *The Tinio Brigade: Anti-American Resistance in the Ilocos Provinces 1899-1901*. Quezon City: New Day Publishers, 1998.

Pigafetta, Antonio, and James Alexander Robertson. *Magellan's Voyage around the World*. Cleveland: Clark, 1906.

Polotan, Kerima. *Imelda Romualdez Marcos; a Biography of the First Lady of the Philippines*. World Publishing Company, 1969.

Report of the Philippine Exposition Board to the Louisiana Purchase Exposition and Official List of Awards Granted by the Philippine International Jury at the Philippine Government Exposition, World's Fair, St. Louis, MO. United States: n.p., 1904.

Richardson, Jim. *The Light of Liberty: Documents and Studies on the Katipunan, 1892-1897*. Quezon City, Philippines: Ateneo de Manila University Press, 2013.

Sadowsky, Jonathan. "Electroconvulsive Therapy: A History of Controversy, but Also of Help." Scientific American. Scientific American, January 13, 2017. https://www.scientificamerican.com/article/electroconvulsive-therapy-a-history-of-controversy-but-also-of-help/.

Salinas, Joel. *Mirror Touch: A Memoir of Synesthesia and the Secret Life of the Brain*. New York, NY: HarperOne, an imprint of HarperCollins Publishers, 2018.

"Savage Acts: Wars, Fairs, and Empire 1898-1904: Ashp/CML." Savage Acts: Wars, Fairs, and Empire 1898-1904 | ASHP/CML. Accessed September 20, 2022. https://ashp.cuny.edu/savage-acts-wars-fairs-and-empire-1898-1904.

Scott, William Henry. *Ilocano Responses to American Aggression 1900-1901*. Quezon City: New Day Publishers, 1989.

Sonnichsen, Albert. *Ten Months a Captive among Filipinos; Being a Narrative of Adventure and Observation during Imprisonment on the Island of Luzon, P.I.* New York: C. Scribner's Sons, 1901.

Sutherland, W A. *Not by Might: The Epic of the Philippines*. Topeka, KS: Southwest Publishing Co., 1953.

Taft, Helen Herron. *Recollections of Full Years*. New York: Dodd, Mead, 1914.

Villa, José García, and John Edwin Cowen. *Doveglion: Collected Poems*. New York: Penguin Books, 2008.

Villa, Simeon. Ms. *Translation of Simeon A. Villa Diary*. Translated by J.C. Hixon. New York Public Library, Manuscript and Archives Division, n.d.

Villamor, Juan. *Inedita Cronica De La Guerra Americano-Filipino En El Norte De Luzon, 1899-1901 = Unpublished Chronicle of the American-Filipino War in Northern Luzon, 1899-1901*. Manila: Imp. J. Fajardo, 1924.

Acknowledgments

My thanks to Jessica Hagedorn, who told me I should write a memory of my mother "straight, without embellishment." I kept her words in mind though I disobeyed and wrote a novel. Thanks also to Viet Thanh Nguyen, whose remark once about a story I told him in Manila about my mother opened up another way to remember. My gratitude to Oscar Campomanes, whose tips on the lives of revolutionaries after the war against Americans included the story of the Lopez sisters of Balayan by one "Canning Eyot." There's a section of Maximo Kalaw's The Filipino Rebel that I've always wanted to revisit: so I did. Thanks to Kiko Benitez for pointing me to that novel. Thanks to Nerissa Balce for her tip on the Bostonian turn-of-the-century activist Helen Calista Wilson. Thanks again to Rolando Borrinaga for his works on Samar. I'm also indebted to the work of Reynaldo Imperial on the revolutionary war in Leyte against the Americans. I'm grateful to the poet Merlie Alunan, who gave permission to use her Makabenta translation for this book: the gentle but radical humor of Makabenta's Waray was a guide for this novel, but thanks to Merlie for her own work as a poet and scholar of our languages and literature.

I am grateful to the above scholars and writers: but the fictions are all mine, including my mix-ups and errors.

This book mixes up at least six languages in common use in the Philippines (though we do have 150 or so languages, that's true). At last count, given the novel's mélange of speeches, I've checked fourteen languages at play in La Tercera. If I may say so here: I'm grateful for the rich culture of survival that marks the Filipino—the mark of our survival that lies, in more ways than one, in our tongues.

Dila.

Dila.

Tongue.

Taking on a book is always a leap of faith. When a book is done, I marvel at how so many have taken that leap. As always, my thanks to my agent Kirby Kim and everyone at Janklow Nesbit. My huge gratitude once again to Soho Press: to Mark Doten, for his fabulous reading of this text that only Mark, with his consummate artist's eye, could have read with such exactitude and grace, to Rachel Kowal, for her patience and care with my late revisions as the book went to press, to Paul Oliver and to the entire team at Soho who continue to inspire me with their dedication to their art, and to all at Penguin Random House who join in helping to get art out.

In advance, I thank my family who have yet to read this book—the Delgados of Leyte, especially my siblings, whom I hope will read it in the spirit of its writing: with memory and love, which cannot be divided from honesty and respect. My gratitude also for their good humor: thanks to my cousin Dennis Delgado for a tsunami joke I stole from him.

This book is for mothers. In memoriam I dedicate it also to Ken's mom, Rose Byrne of Aclare, County Sligo, Ireland, who died the year I finished La Tercera. I thought of her life, too, as I wrote about mothers.

My love as always to Ken and Nastasia: without whom no book would be complete.

This book is for my mother, Virginia Delgado (1935-1999), with all my love.